I0770533

High Tide

Paige Marie

For Cheeb.
There's no Seaview without you.

Author's note

See the back of the book for a content warning.

One

Delia

I have a very specific routine.

My alarm wakes me up at five-thirty. I climb out of bed, slip on leggings and sneakers, and head on a two-and-a-half mile run around the park by my apartment. On the way back, I stop at my favorite coffee shop for an oat milk latte and spinach egg wrap. I eat quickly and then stretch, hydrate, and shower.

At eight, I settle in the plush desk chair in my home office and boot up my laptop. The day mostly consists of emails and phone calls and brainstorming ideas for my latest brand campaign. On Fridays, I log off at five on the dot. I change into a blouse (preferably black) and a pair of heels (preferably Jimmy Choos) and take an Uber to a bar on Boston's North End to grab a drink (preferably chardonnay) with my two best friends.

My schedule might sound militant, but each step in my routine is designed to help me maximize the day. My morning run eliminates sluggishness, and my latte and spinach egg wrap serve as the perfect post-workout pick-me-up.

After a long and productive day of work, I put on an outfit that makes me feel confident and join my friends at the bar, where I enjoy several glasses of wine without fear of a hangover (thanks to the hydrating I did earlier).

Many people believe the key to living your best life is living in the moment. My theory? Happiness is the result of extensive planning. If you sit around waiting for good things to come to you, you'll be met with disappointment. The only way to guarantee happiness is by arranging it yourself. Mapping out every moment. Creating to-do lists and alarms and calendar reminders. If you plan for happiness, it has no choice but to find you.

It's that very thought that spurs me to silence my buzzing cell phone as I push through Bar Westbrook's saloon-style doors. I have a strict no-phone rule when I'm out with friends. Checking your messages even once during a night out immediately ruins your fun. There's no reason to look at a text from your boss or a notification that your ex-boyfriend posted on social media when you're with friends. My messages will still be there when I get into my Uber later tonight.

Dropping my phone in my purse, I scan the bar for Mariah and Kali. Bar Westbrook has a fantastic wine selection and the best beer cheese in the city, so naturally, it's packed on a Friday night. Luckily, my friends have already secured us a corner booth. I snake through the throngs of tables, eventually reaching theirs.

I sigh as I slip into the booth. "I need a drink."

Mariah laughs. "Bad day?"

"Long," I clarify, dropping my purse on the shiny wooden tabletop. I work in digital marketing, and my office is fully remote. "I had a four-thirty meeting with a client." The woman emailed me this morning asking if I had time in the afternoon for a quick virtual meeting.

Of course! I wrote back. *My schedule is open till five.*

Unsurprisingly, the client picked four-thirty. Serves me right for expecting her to abide by the unspoken rules of corporate America.

Mariah arches a pale brow. "Why?"

"The client asked for a meeting. I couldn't say no."

"You absolutely could," Kali says, shaking her head disapprovingly. "It's marketing, Del. It's not life or death." Kali works for a different marketing firm, and Mariah is a communications manager for a local hospital. The three of us met in a pilates class two years ago. We hit it off right away, bonding over our love for hikes and shopping trips.

"It was a newish client," I explain. "I don't know her well enough to ignore her emails." My client's family owns a small beachwear chain in Cape Cod. They hired my firm to help them enhance their digital presence. Unfortunately, the client's overbearing eighty-six-year-old father insists on being part of all our meetings, despite having no knowledge of technology or digital marketing. "The client's father founded this beachwear company, like, forty years ago. He's a real set-in-his-ways type."

Kali gives me a knowing look. "How's the company's website?"

"Prehistoric." A lot of small business owners struggling on the digital front swear their website isn't the problem. *It's a great website! My nephew designed it himself! No one's ever had an issue with it.* The trickiest part of my job is telling clients they're wrong without pissing them off so much they no longer want to work with me. "I showed him the sites of some of his competitors. I think I convinced him that he needs an upgrade, but getting him there was long and painful."

"Hopefully, you won't be dealing with those kinds of clients for much longer," Mariah says. "You should be getting that promotion any day now, right?"

I shrug. "There are no guarantees."

Kali rolls her eyes. "C'mon, Delia. That job is yours, and you know it." She's right. My boss, Nina, is retiring at the end of August. She's been dropping not-so-subtle hints over the last several months that she wants me to replace her as our firm's marketing manager. I haven't been offered the job officially, but I know it's coming soon.

I should be ecstatic. The position comes with a hefty salary increase *and* the chance to work with some of our firm's most prestigious clients. Others would kill for that kind of opportunity. The thing is, I'm not excited in the slightest. I nearly threw up the first time Nina suggested the idea of me taking over for her.

At first, I thought it was just nerves. I've seen what Nina does on a daily basis. I know I could handle it. But the more I pictured myself becoming a marketing manager, the more I realized it wasn't imposter syndrome getting the best of me.

I genuinely do *not* want this job. I like my work. I'm good at it. But I like a lot of other things more. Going out with friends. Running in the park. Visiting local wineries. A higher-ranking position means more responsibility. More hours spent in front of my laptop instead of doing things I actually want to be doing.

I have a nice work-life balance in my current role. I'm terrified I'll lose that if I get promoted. I haven't told anyone about my fears, especially not Kali or Mariah. They both work a billion hours a week, and they love every second. They wouldn't understand my concerns.

"We'll see," I say.

A server appears to take our drink orders before Mariah and Kali get a chance to say anything else about the promotion. We ask for a bottle of chardonnay for the table. The server scribbles something in his notepad and says he'll be right back with our wine.

In the meantime, my friends and I start our Friday ritual: filling each other in on everything that happened to us in the past week. Mariah wrapped up a big project, so she's in good spirits. Kali, on the other hand, went on the worst first date of her life on Tuesday. Her date spent the entire dinner complaining about his ex, then he left Kali with the check. Kali swears she's quitting dating apps forever. I don't believe her. She's been saying the same thing since I met her.

At some point during Kali's story, the server returns with our chardonnay. He pours each of us a glass. Mariah raises hers, calling for a toast.

"To Kali," she says. "May her future dates keep the ex talk to a minimum."

"And not stick her with the bill," I add.

Kali flips us off as she inhales her wine.

I'm about half a glass deep when it's my turn to share. I'm feeling relaxed, buzzed, as I tell Mariah and Kali about the amazing new takeout place I tried. Halfway through my story about the best chicken marsala I've ever tasted, I notice Mariah glancing back and forth between me and the bar area.

"What is it?" I ask.

"There's a guy looking at you," Mariah replies, her voice hushed as if she's relaying top secret intel. "Left end of the bar. Dark hair. Glasses."

Casually, I set my wine glass on the table, shifting my attention to the bar. Patrons swarm the area like bees on honey. Some have their eyes glued to the Red Sox game on the massive flatscreen. Others shout drink orders at the frazzled-looking bartender behind the counter.

Through the commotion, I manage to spot my apparent admirer. He's got a strong chin, and he's wearing a light-blue button-up with the top two buttons undone. He catches me looking and smiles, lifting his beer glass in greeting. Instantly, I tear my eyes away.

"He's cute," Mariah says, giving me an encouraging smile.

Kali's lips twist in disapproval. "He looks like an investment banker."

Mariah gives her a baffled look. "So?"

"Guys in finance never shut up about finance," Kali says. "Delia should steer clear of that guy, unless she wants to spend the night hearing about his job at JPMorgan."

"That's not true. Jared works in finance. He barely talks about work."

"Mariah, your husband is an anomaly. You've been in a relationship too long. You've forgotten what single men are really like." Mariah looks as though she wants to argue, but she's got nothing to go on. She met her husband, Jared, at college orientation. They've been together ever since. Unlike me and Kali, she's never faced the abject misery of dating in your twenties.

"Maybe so," Mariah admits. "But I'm not suggesting Delia marry the guy. He could be good rebound material." She keeps her tone light, but she isn't fooling me. Mariah has been trying to convince me to go home with a different guy at the bar every Friday for the past two months.

"Delia, you're awfully silent," Kali says, pinning me with her dark eyes. "Care to weigh in before Mariah asks a random stranger to do you in the parking lot?"

I smile at Mariah, then I let her down easy. "I'm not dating right now." Or ever again, probably. But I don't share that detail. Mariah thinks I'm still hung up on my ex-boyfriend, Austin. Declaring myself permanently single would only aid her misguided theory.

Sympathy washes over Mariah's face. "It's hard starting over. I get it. But don't give up dating altogether just because Austin sucked."

"I'm not." I met Austin at a different bar a few blocks from here. He told me I had pretty eyes and asked if he could buy me a drink. Normally, I would've declined, but he had a nice smile and a good sense of humor. He was new to the city, and we got along well, especially when he asked if I knew any good trails in Boston. Our mutual love for running and expensive wine blossomed into a relationship.

Being with Austin was easy. We went on morning runs and took trips to the farmers market and had double dates at fancy steakhouses with

Mariah and Jared. We never had an incredible emotional connection, but I was comfortable. I thought Austin felt the same. So it came as a total shock when he ended our relationship three months ago. He told me we didn't have substance. He wasn't wrong. I just didn't know it was a problem.

Relationships don't have to be complicated. If two people share common interests and have a mutual sense of respect, they can build a beautiful life together. It doesn't need to be messy and chaotic and passionate. Unfortunately, Austin didn't see it that way.

After the breakup, I decided I was better off avoiding relationships altogether. They only lead to complications, and those are the last things I want in my life.

"Mariah, I promise you'll be the first to know when I'm ready to start dating again," I say. She means well, despite her pushiness. "Now, can we please talk about something other than finance guys I have no interest in?"

The conversation shifts to summer plans. Kali wants us to take a girls' trip this year. She's thinking Vegas. She tells us about this new place on the Strip that serves chocolate chip pancakes the size of a person's head.

"They're forty-five bucks a stack, so we may have to split an order," she says, swishing her wine around her glass. "Unless I become an expert at counting cards in the next two months. In that case, I'll treat all of us to a stack."

Kali scoffs. "Forty-five dollars? For pancakes?"

"They're gourmet."

"I don't care if they're made of gold," Kali says. "I'm not paying forty-five dollars for something I can make at home with a ninety-nine cent box."

"Are you *sure* they're forty-five dollars?" I ask, having a hard time believing anyone in a solid mental state would pay such a steep price for breakfast food.

Mariah nods. "I'm positive. Look it up for yourself."

Still skeptical, I reach for my purse and grab my phone. I press the button on the side, and the screen lights up. Shock barrels through me as I see three missed calls and seven texts from my sister, Izzy. I read the first message.

Call me. ASAP.

Two

Delia

The thing is, Izzy is prone to exaggeration.

She's always had a flair for the dramatic. When Izzy was in elementary school, she used to treat her mild shellfish allergy like a life-threatening condition. She refused to walk down the frozen food section at the grocery store for fear of inadvertently coming into contact with shrimp. She even accused me of trying to poison her one night when I asked our parents if we could have lobster rolls for dinner.

Given Izzy's history, I'm a bit skeptical when I read her seemingly urgent messages. Is this really an emergency, or is it an innocuous situation that Izzy has blown out of proportion? Is she in the hospital with a broken leg, or did she burn her finger on the stove? I won't know until I talk to her, so I tell Mariah and Kali I need to step outside for a minute, then hightail out of the bar and hit call on my phone.

"Finally," Izzy says with an exaggerated sigh when she picks up seconds later. "I've been trying to get a hold of you forever." I roll my eyes at her theatrical tone as I stand on the narrow sidewalk in front of Bar Westbrook. If Izzy is calm enough

to have an attitude with me, then clearly, this isn't an emergency.

"What's going on, Iz? I'm out with Mariah and Kali." There's no reason not to cut straight to the chase. I'm not looking to have a thirty-minute phone call outside of a busy downtown bar. The sooner I get off the phone, the sooner I can head back inside and finish my glass of chardonnay.

"Have you checked your email?" she asks.

Check my email? On a *Friday* night? I would rather pull out my fingernails with tweezers. "No. Why?"

"Just do it."

Reluctantly, I lower my cell phone from my ear and put it on speaker. It only takes a few seconds for me to log in to my email. I glance over several junk emails before landing on an unread message from an unknown sender with the subject line *Response Requested*.

Confused, I open the message.

Dear Ms. Forrest,

I would like to offer my sincerest condolences on the passing of your grandmother. Aggie was a wonderful woman. She will be missed. I am the executor of Aggie's estate. I am reaching out to notify you that she left her house to you and your sisters. Please contact me at your earliest convenience so we can go over the details. My number is below.

Sincerely, Eleanor Teigen, Esq.

I read it a second time. Then a third. "Is this a joke?"

"So you got it, too," Izzy says. "Morgan and I figured as much."

"You and Morgan got the same email?"

"We sure did. We've been on the phone, trying to figure out what the hell is going on for the last half hour. She's on the other line. Hang on a second. I'm gonna merge the calls." The line goes silent for a moment, then Izzy returns. "Delia? Morgan? You both here?"

"I'm here," my youngest sister, Morgan, chirps in her soft voice. "Hey, Del."

"Hi, Morgan," I say, removing the phone from speaker mode and bringing it back up to my ear. I wedge the device between my ear and shoulder and cover my other ear with my palm in an attempt to block out the sounds of the bustling city. "Any idea what's going on?"

"Not really," she replies. "I looked up Eleanor Teigen. She's an estate planning attorney who works in Seaview. The email address on her website matches the one that messaged us. It seems legitimate." Morgan sounds clear-headed, rational. She's always been the most logical of the three of us. It's probably why she's getting her master's degree in data science. "I think Grandma Aggie really left us her house."

"Maybe her attorney mixed us up with someone else," I say.

"Who? We were her only grandchildren."

"Are we? We barely knew the woman. Who's to say she didn't have a second family somewhere?" I know I'm being ridiculous. Obviously, Grandma Aggie's attorney didn't contact the wrong sisters. Still, nothing about this feels right. I'm looking for any way—rational or irrational—to make sense of it.

My current theory? I fell and hit my head on the way out of Bar Westbrook, and this conversation is a hallucination brought on by a traumatic brain injury. These thoughts, however illogical, are easier to digest than the idea of my estranged grandmother giving her longtime home to me and my sisters.

Grandma Aggie died four days ago. She had a stroke in a supermarket parking lot. Her heart stopped before the ambulance made it to the hospital.

I found out almost a full twenty-four hours after she passed. A friend of my late grandmother called Mom to ask about funeral arrangements. When Mom called me to break the news, I didn't know how to feel. I *still* don't know, even after days of sitting with it.

The sudden death of a family member *should* be a gut-wrenching shock, but that wasn't the case with Grandma Aggie. Because she might have been a blood relative, but she wasn't my grandmother. Not in the ways that matter.

Years ago, she and my dad had a massive falling out. I was in first-grade, so I wasn't privy to the details. All I know is that from then on Grandma Aggie cut my family out of her life completely. She lived a couple of hours away, so we didn't see her often, but we used to spend a week at her place every summer. Grandma Aggie let me and my sisters drink chocolate milk out of teacups and took us for ice cream almost every night. Staying with her was the highlight of my childhood summers. So, naturally, I was devastated when she disappeared from our lives.

For a long time, I assumed Dad told Grandma Aggie she couldn't see us anymore, and I resented him for it. Why should me, Izzy, and Morgan be deprived of a relationship with our grandmother because of issues that didn't involve us? It wasn't until I got older that Dad admitted he never made any sort of declaration. He wanted us to have a relationship with Grandma Aggie. *She* was the one who decided to stop seeing us.

Learning the truth stung, but I'm glad it happened. It helped me see the ugly reality of my grandmother. She punished my sisters and me for her problems with Dad when we were only kids. We didn't know anything. Anyone who would stoop low enough to penalize children for adult problems must have deep-seated issues.

As if to add insult to injury, Grandma Aggie didn't bother reaching out when Dad died six years ago. She didn't call or send flowers or even attend the funeral. Needless to say, I'm not particularly broken up about her passing. I wasn't rooting for her demise, but I didn't have a vested interest in her well-being. It was like hearing about something terrible happening to an acquaintance or a long-lost friend. Sad, of course, but it didn't really affect me. Which is why it's all the more confusing that she seemingly gave us her house.

"Maybe it's a scam," Izzy suggests.

"How? The lawyer is trying to *give* us a house," Morgan says.

"I don't know. It's just a theory," Izzy says defensively. "It's better than Delia's theory that the lawyer fucked up and emailed the wrong people."

"That *wasn't* a theory. I'm thinking out loud. Trying to find sense here."

Izzy lets out a harsh laugh. "Good luck with that. Nothing about this makes sense. Who leaves a house to people they hate?"

"Grandma Aggie didn't hate us," Morgan says.

"Really? Then what would you call the lack of communication over the last two decades? A misunderstanding? I hate to burst your bubble, Morgan, but I don't think Grandma Aggie's birthday cards have been getting lost in the mail all this time."

"We shouldn't argue about this," I say. We can't turn on each other. Bickering will get us nowhere. "Let's call Mom. Maybe she'll know what to do." To my knowledge, Mom hasn't spoken to Grandma Aggie in years, but she knows more about my grandmother than any of us.

I pull up my mom's contact and press call. She answers the phone in a groggy voice. "Delia?" It isn't very late, but Mom prefers to be in bed before nine. I don't want to disturb her, but this isn't the sort of thing that can wait till tomorrow morning.

"Hey, Mom," I say. "Sorry to bother you. I need to talk to you about something important. Izzy and Morgan are on the line, too."

"Hi, girls," she replies, sounding slightly worried. "What's going on? Is something wrong?"

"Nothing's wrong," I tell her. "We just got some…unexpected news." We explain everything about the email from Grandma Aggie's estate lawyer.

"She left you the *house*?" Mom's voice takes on a shrill note that has me cringing and moving the phone away from my ear.

"Mom, Grandma Aggie never contacted you over the years, did she?" I ask. At this point, my only reasonable thought is that Grandma Aggie tried to get in touch with us years ago, and Mom never told us.

"I haven't heard from Aggie in twenty years." There goes that theory.

"Any idea why she would do this?"

"Honestly, I never knew what to think when it came to Aggie," Mom says. "Your dad's mother was prideful, stubborn. Incapable of letting things go. Aggie lived in that house for a long time. Probably sixty years. She loved that place. She wouldn't have left it to the three of you unless she really wanted to." But why? What motive could explain this? I'm disappointed that Mom doesn't have an answer. What's even more disappointing is the fact that I'll probably never get one. The only person who knows the truth is no longer on this planet.

"What are we supposed to do with it?" Izzy asks. "It's a house, not an old tea set. That's a lot of responsibility. Besides, none of us live in Seaview." She makes a solid point. Izzy lives in New York City, where she works as a graphic designer. Morgan is a grad student at Finlay University in Boston. Our lives are very different. Separate.

"That's something you'll have to decide amongst yourselves," Mom says. "Sell it. Keep it. The decision is entirely up to you."

The three of us spend the next several minutes trying to convince Mom to make a decision for us, but she doesn't budge. She insists that we need to be the ones to do it since Grandma Aggie left *us* the house. Personally, I think Mom is using it as an excuse because she doesn't know what to do, but it ultimately doesn't matter. Mom gets off the call soon after, leaving me and my sisters just as lost and confused as before.

The line is silent for a moment before Izzy says, "Well, that was pointless."

"What are we gonna do?" Morgan asks, her tone fraught with panic. I picture her features crumpled with worry as she paces the length of her small studio apartment. "I have finals in a few weeks. I don't have time for this."

"We don't have to do anything," Izzy replies. "We could tell the estate lawyer that we're not interested."

"But it's Dad's childhood home."

"So? You said it yourself—you don't have time for this. Besides, Dad hasn't stepped foot in that place in a long time. I don't think he'd care."

"He grew up there, Izzy," Morgan says. "Abandoning it would be wrong."

Silence follows. I can tell that Izzy and Morgan are waiting for me to voice my opinion, but I'm struggling to form it. I see both points. On one hand, I have zero interest in owning a place that once belonged to Grandma Aggie. She treated my family like garbage. I don't want anything associated with her. On the other hand, my dad grew up in that house. The thought of letting his childhood home fall to pieces leaves a bitter taste in my mouth. I don't know if I could stomach it.

I need more time to weigh my options. "We don't have to figure this out right now," I say. "We should sleep on it. Give ourselves the night to think things through. We can talk again in the morning when we have clearer heads."

"That's fine with me," Izzy says.

"Me, too," Morgan agrees. "But we really do need to figure this out tomorrow."

"We will," I say, sounding more confident than I feel.

We end the call with a promise to reconnect in the morning, but I don't know if things will be any clearer by then.

Three

Delia

I don't stay at the bar.

After I get off the phone with my sisters, I run back inside to pay my share of the tab and say goodbye to Kali and Mariah. My friends seem disappointed by my abrupt departure. They ask if something's wrong, and I lie and say I'm not feeling well. I'm not in the mood to rehash the details of the phone call yet. I want to be alone for a while. I'll fill Mariah and Kali in on everything another time.

By some miracle, I'm able to catch an Uber fairly quickly. Within twenty minutes, I'm back at my apartment. I fish the key out of my purse and unlock the door. Stepping inside, I make quick work of removing my heels before heading to the kitchen. I flip on a light switch, bathing the room in bright light, then snag a glass out of the tall cabinet. I use the fridge dispenser to fill the glass with water and take a long drink.

My head throbs. It feels like my brain just went through a meat grinder. I need Tylenol, stat. I head to the medicine cabinet in the bathroom and grab a bottle of Tylenol. I drop a pill in my mouth, chasing it down with a gulp of water. Then I pause, gazing at my reflection in the mirror.

I look as lost as I feel. My eyes are tired, and my skin is clammy and sallow. I turn the faucet on the sink, splashing a handful of cool water on my face. It does nothing to erase the uncertainty sloshing around inside me.

A house. My sisters and I are responsible for a *house*. And not just any house—the one that belonged to our grandmother. The one where our father grew up. Earlier tonight, Izzy said we should just forget about it. Tell Grandma Aggie's attorney we're not interested. Morgan argued that we can't abandon Dad's childhood home. That means it's up to me to make the decision.

In my mind, I create a pros and cons list. Taking ownership of the house would ensure Dad's childhood home doesn't fall apart. And if my sisters and I sell it, that could mean easy money for the three of us.

Then again, home ownership is a big responsibility. We don't know what state Grandma Aggie's house is in. What if it requires a lot of repairs? Besides, I'm not sure I want to step foot in my grandmother's old place. Or be surrounded by her things. Grandma Aggie has been a source of ire for me for many years. I don't like to think about her. The last thing I want is to comb through her belongings.

My skin smells like beer and greasy food, so I decide to take a shower. Uncertainty grips my thoughts as I peel off my clothes and step inside the small plastic tub. I picture Grandma Aggie's old house as hot water rains down on my face. I haven't been there since I was a child, but I can still see the quaint two-story house with light blue shutters and a square-shaped lawn in my mind's eye.

I don't have many memories of the house, but there's one that sticks out. Sitting on the front porch steps with Grandma Aggie one evening as she told stories about Dad as a child. When he was four or five, Dad had a habit of sneaking out of bed at night to steal cookies from the jar in the kitchen. He got away with it for a while. But then Grandma Aggie began to notice how quickly the cookies were disappearing. She heard Dad's footsteps on the stairs one night and realized what he was up to.

The next night, she replaced the cookies with apples and waited downstairs until Dad came down. Grandma Aggie said the look on his face when he realized he'd been caught was priceless.

I frown at the memory. The love between Dad and Grandma Aggie faded a long time ago, but it's hard to think about innocent stories like this one and not be reminded of the fact that they used to have a good relationship. Dad always spoke fondly about his childhood. He wouldn't have traded it for anything. He wouldn't blame me and my sisters for wanting nothing to do with Grandma Aggie's place, but I think it would've disappointed him to know that his former home might fall into disarray.

I imagine Grandma Aggie's house slowly deteriorating. Paint peeling off the sides. Shutters falling off windows. Weeds sprouting through the cracks in the wooden porch. Sadness swirls in the pit of my stomach. It feels like letting the memory of my dad crumble.

I can't let that happen. I won't.

When I finish my shower a few minutes later, I slip on a robe and start toward my home office. Flipping on the lamp by my desk, I settle in my chair and grab a pen and a fresh sheet of paper. I stay up most of the night doing what I do best.

I plan.

***

"We're selling the house," I declare to my sisters on a FaceTime call the next morning. I thought a video call would be best for this conversation, so I could gauge Izzy's and Morgan's reactions. So much gets lost over the phone.

Morgan's eyebrows shoot up. "What?"

"It's the solution that makes the most sense," I reply, taking a sip of my coffee. Thanks to my late-night planning session, I didn't get much sleep. I'm relying on caffeine to get me through this conversation, then I'm taking a much-needed nap.

Izzy looks less than impressed. Even on a blurry video call, I can tell she's narrowing her pale blue eyes at me. "Did you miss the part last night when Mom said the three of us should make this decision *together*?"

I bite the inside of my cheek to hide my disappointment. Neither of my sisters seems convinced. That's okay. I didn't expect them to jump on board immediately. It's going to require some persuasion. I'm up for the challenge.

"I heard everything Mom said," I tell her. "And I spent all of last night thinking about this. I think selling is our best option. Our only option. I know you don't want anything to do with Grandma

22

Aggie's place, Izzy, and I get it. Neither do I. But we owe it to Dad to do something. If we sell, we can get the property off our hands without leaving it to rot."

Izzy sighs. "That's still a lot of work, Del," she says. "We'd have to go to Seaview. Check out the place. Probably clean it up. Then we'd have to find a realtor. Who knows how long that would take?" I've already thought about these questions, and I'm prepared to answer them. But I'm cut off by a harsh grinding sound before I get a chance to plead my case. It sounds like a rock getting caught in a gear. It's coming from Izzy's end of the call.

"What is that?" Morgan asks, frowning.

Izzy blows a strand of curly hair out of her face, then rolls her eyes. "My dishwasher." With a huff, she hops off her bed and heads to the tiny kitchen in her apartment. "It's been making this noise for months, but it works fine. It just needs a little…support." She sets the phone on the counter. I watch in disbelief as my five-foot-two sister throws her entire body against the dishwasher like a battering ram.

"Don't you think you should call your landlord about that?"

Izzy laughs as she continues to slam herself against the machine. "Why? He's not gonna do anything about it. We've had a busted window and a non-functioning air conditioning unit for months." She hits the dishwasher again, and it finally stops making that ear-piercing sound. "Besides, it's still functional."

"Functional?" Morgan repeats. "It sounds like it's about to explode."

"It cleans really well. It even gets out those annoying red sauce stains on Tupperware."

Sensing that this conversation is about to veer off course, I bring my sisters back to the issue at hand. "We've got a lot of important stuff to talk about," I remind them. "Izzy, are you good, or do you need to go beat your dryer with a hammer?"

Izzy laughs. "You think I can afford a place with *in-unit laundry*?"

Ignoring her smarminess, I say, "Putting the house up for sale would take some work, yes, but the payoff would be worth it. I spent some time last night researching properties in Seaview. A lot of places, even small ones, are going for five or six hundred thousand dollars."

Morgan's eyes nearly budge out of her head. "You seriously think we could sell Grandma Aggie's house for six hundred thousand dollars?"

I bob my head. "Seaview is a beach town. Grandma Aggie's house is only a mile from the ocean. People are willing to pay a lot for that kind of real estate."

"But we don't know what the house looks like," Izzy points out. "Grandma Aggie was almost ninety. She probably hadn't upgraded anything in years."

Luckily, I thought about that, too. "We might have to make some updates, but we'll get our money back after the sale," I say with confidence.

"But how are we going to pay for those updates?" Morgan asks. "Don't get me wrong— I'm all for selling. But I'm also a grad student. I don't have the money for a bunch of home repairs."

"I know my dishwasher is top-notch," Izzy says, "but neither do I."

"I can front the money." I've always been financially responsible, so I've built a decent-sized savings account over the years. I don't mind bearing the costs up front when I know I'm in a better financial position than my sisters.

Hesitation crosses Morgan's face. "That shouldn't fall on you, Delia."

"It's not a big deal," I say. "I have the money, and I want to do this. Besides, the payout from the house would be good for all of us. Morgan, you could pay off your student loans, and Izzy might be able to afford an apartment with appliances that aren't trying to kill her."

"I'm not opposed to selling," Izzy says, pinning me with a glare. "Obviously, that kind of money would be life-changing. But I'm swamped at work right now, and Morgan's in the middle of the spring semester. God knows when the three of us would find the time to take a trip to Seaview to deal with this stuff."

"The only thing that needs to happen in the immediate future is getting the deed transferred to us," I reply. "I can handle that. Seaview's only a couple of hours from Boston. I'll set up a meeting with Grandma Aggie's estate lawyer and drive down there. I'll scope out the place while I'm in town. Get a sense of what we're dealing with."

"Are you sure?" Morgan asks hesitantly. "It seems unfair for you to get stuck with everything, Delia. Especially if you're already covering the renovation costs."

"I'm with Morgan," Izzy says. "Grandma Aggie left the house to all of us. It's not only your responsibility, Delia."

I take a slow sip of coffee. "I'm offering the solution that makes the most sense. I live closest to Seaview, and I work from home. It's easy for me to take a trip there. Plus, I really think selling is the right move. We can't leave Dad's childhood home to waste. Selling will allow a new family to make a home there. That's what Dad would've wanted, and you know it."

I watch my sisters' faces, patiently awaiting their replies. I'm fairly confident I've convinced them. Morgan was already on board with selling, and Izzy won't be able to say no now that I've forced her to think about what Dad would've wanted in this situation.

Morgan relents first. "I'll agree to this, but only if you agree to take a bigger cut of the profit, Delia. You're fronting the money *and* doing more of the work. It's only fair." The money isn't a major concern for me. As long as I get back everything I put into the renovations, I'll be fine. Saying yes to Morgan's term is a no-brainer.

"And I'll only agree to this if you promise to share the work, not do it all on your own," Izzy adds. "I mean it, Delia. If we're doing this, we're *all* doing this. It's not just your project. Got it?" Her condition is more than reasonable. I have no problem agreeing.

"Those terms are fine with me," I reply, feeling triumphant.

My plan worked. Good.

Now, I can only hope I haven't promised more than I can deliver.

Four

Delia

"I've heard a lot of excuses over the years, Delia," my boss, Nina, says over the speakers in my car as I drive along the sun-soaked freeway. "I've never had an employee call off work because they inherited a house."

"Believe me," I tell her. "I'm still trying to wrap my head around it."

I messaged Nina early this morning to let her know I needed to take a personal day. I'm making the two-hour drive from Boston to Grandma Aggie's hometown, Seaview. I left my place at six-thirty. I'm not scheduled to meet with Grandma Aggie's estate attorney until nine, but I wanted to build in extra time in case I got lost.

Nina called me about an hour into my drive. She wanted to make sure everything was all right. I rarely take personal days, but when I do, I plan them weeks in advance. Nina had to know something was up when I abruptly asked for time off.

"How are you holding up?" she asks. "It seems like a lot to process at once." Her tone holds genuine concern. I've worked for Nina for four years. She hired me right out of college. She's become somewhat of a mentor to me. I always know I can go to her for advice, career or personal. Which is why I told her everything that unfolded Friday night, beginning with the email from Grandma Aggie's estate attorney.

"I'm hanging in there," I say. "I wasn't expecting to become a homeowner overnight, but it is what it is."

"Plans change, honey. That's the beauty of life."

"If by beauty, you mean stress and panic, then sure."

Nina chuckles. "Don't be so cynical. This could be a good thing. Maybe you'll get out there and love the house." The house where my miserable grandmother chose to live out her days? Doubtful. But I keep my pessimism to myself.

"I'm only meeting with the attorney and picking up the keys today," I say. "I should be back to work tomorrow."

"Don't even worry about that," she replies. "Take all the time you need. If that means a few more days, then so be it."

"Thanks, Nina."

"Of course," she says. "Anyway, I should let you go. But I mean it, Delia. However much time you need. You have to take care of yourself before you can take care of anything else."

"I'll keep that in mind."

"You should. It's good advice, especially for a future marketing manager."

I hate the way my stomach clenches when she says that. It's a reflex. The dread that fills me any time someone mentions my impending promotion. My mind whizzes with thoughts of stress and deadlines and new responsibilities. My grip on the steering wheel tightens as panic builds in my chest.

"Right. Well, thanks again," I tell her before quickly ending the call.

I cross the border into Seaview around eight-thirty. The morning sky is light and foggy. The streets are quiet and lined with seafood joints and bathing suit shops and surfboard rentals. Driving down the road feels a lot like looking at an old photograph. It makes me think of childhood summers. Of flip flops and ice cream sundaes and adventure.

I have time to kill before my meeting with the attorney, so I decide to grab a cup of coffee. I notice a sign for a place called Ralph's Diner and veer into the tiny parking lot. I cut the engine, then climb out of my car and stretch my legs for a few minutes before heading toward the door.

The bell above the door chimes as I step inside. It feels like I've taken a time machine to the 1950s. Shiny black-and-white tiles cover the length of the floor. A long L-shaped counter lined with cherry-red barstools dominates the corner closest to the entrance. Framed pictures of retro Corvettes and electric guitars and long-dead celebrities hang on the walls. I expect to see a tacky neon sign displayed somewhere, but there's none to be found.

An old woman with curly white hair and purple cat-eye glasses smiles at me from behind the counter. "Welcome to Ralph's," she says cheerily as she wipes down an empty section of the counter with a rag. "Take a seat wherever you like. I'll be with you shortly."

"Thanks," I reply, scanning the place for an open seat. Most of the booths are occupied, so I opt for an empty barstool at the end of the counter. Beside me, an older man munches on a pile of scrambled eggs while he reads a newspaper. What's next? Is someone going to ask me for a nickel so they can play Johnny Cash on the jukebox?

The waitress approaches, handing me a large laminated menu. She wears a name tag that says Annabella.

"Can I get you started with something to drink?" she asks.

"Coffee, please. Black." I stifle a yawn in between words. Exhaustion weighs on my eyelids. I had to forgo my morning run today so I could get an early start, and I'm feeling out of sorts.

"Sure thing," she replies. "I'll be right back."

As I wait for my coffee, I pull my phone out of my pocket. I've got texts from Mariah and Kali asking me how the drive went. I met up with my friends last night so I could fill them in on everything with Grandma Aggie's house. Both of them offered to come to Seaview with me, but I turned them down. I told them I could handle it on my own.

Truthfully? I didn't want them to see me panic. A mix of nerves, grief, and frustration has been swirling around in my stomach since I decided to come here. I don't know which emotion is going to take control when I walk inside Grandma Aggie's. I'm like a time bomb. And I'd rather Mariah and Kali not be there if I turn into a weeping mess or start smashing my grandmother's old furniture.

I also have a message from Morgan in our sisters' group chat. *Let us know how everything goes.*

I just got here, I write back. *I'll keep you updated.*

Izzy's response appears seconds later. *Be sure to check the place for booby traps.*

I roll my eyes. *The only thing that needs to be checked is you.*

Annabella returns with a steaming cup of coffee. The smell of fresh brew makes my nose tingle. "Here you go," she says, sliding the ceramic mug across the counter.

"Thank you," I reply, wrapping my hands around the warm mug.

"That's a lovely bag." She gestures to my gingerbread Kate Spade tote.

I smile, appreciating the compliment. "Thanks. I got it during a Black Friday sale last year. Thirty percent off. It was still expensive, but it's much easier to justify it to yourself when you think you're getting a deal."

"Don't I know it. My husband and I bought a pool last summer. We thought it would be great for the grandkids, and the store offered us free delivery. We didn't consider the fact that the only thing they want to do when they come to visit is go to the beach."

"That's the power of a discount. It makes you abandon all logic."

Annabella chuckles. "Can I get anything else for you?"

"I'm good for right now. Is there any chance this place has WiFi?"

She nods. "We sure do. But I can never remember the dang password. Let me check with my husband to see if he knows." She turns on her heels and walks up to the rectangular window that connects the dining area to the kitchen. "Ralph!"

A small man with pink-stained cheeks appears at the window. He looks roughly the same age as Annabella. "What is it?" he asks.

"What's the password for the WiFi? I've got a young woman here who would like to use the internet," she explains, motioning toward me.

Ralph gives me a once-over. "Try RalphsDiner."

I type the password, but get a message saying it's incorrect. "It didn't work."

"Did you capitalize any letters?"

"The R and D."

"Try it all lowercase."

I enter the revised password, to no avail. "That didn't work either."

Ralph strokes his chin and shares an uncertain look with his wife. "I could've sworn I told Alexander to make the password Ralph's Diner."

Annabella shakes her head. "Alexander didn't set up the internet. He couldn't figure out how to do it, remember? We had to hire that kid from the computer store."

Ralph snaps his fingers. "That's right. What was that kid's name? Eli? Joseph?"

"No, I think it started with a C."

"Christopher, maybe?"

Recognition flashes in Annabella's eyes. "That's it!"

None of this information has anything to do with getting me connected to the diner's WiFi.

Annabella and Ralph triumph in their victory for a few seconds before they realize they haven't actually solved the problem.

"Shoot," Annabella mumbles.

Ralph glances at me again. "Try TheRalphsDiner."

Playing password roulette is not on my agenda today. I decide to put the old couple out of their misery. "Yep. That worked. Thanks."

After I finish my coffee, I pay my bill and head out. The attorney's office is less than a mile away, so I don't see any point in driving there.

Opening the Maps app on my phone, I begin walking down the street. It's a warm morning, the sun bright and the air crisp and salty. A sign with a large arrow pointing to public beach access sits several yards ahead. I'm tempted to follow it, but I don't have the time. Besides, I doubt my suede pumps would hold up in the sand.

The meeting with the estate attorney goes smoothly. Eleanor Tiegen is a ballbuster in a sleek pantsuit. She informs me that Grandma Aggie put her assets into a trust, which means they pass automatically to me, Morgan, and Izzy. We don't have to go through the headaches of probate court, which is a small mercy.

Grandma Aggie left us everything. Her car. Her bank account. Her belongings. I'm relieved to learn that she paid off her mortgage a long time ago. The only expenses my sisters and I need to worry about are property taxes and utilities, which we should be able to cover with the few thousand dollars in Grandma Aggie's savings account.

After Eleanor finishes going over the details, she hands me the house keys and sends me on my way. I walk back to my car and plug Grandma Aggie's address into my GPS. My heart races as I start up the engine and begin the drive. I pass a number of beautiful beach homes, but I can't focus on them enough to appreciate the views.

My mind whirls with fuzzy memories of my last trip to Grandma Aggie's. I remember eating lobster tails on the back porch and sliding down the stairs with a couch cushion. I wonder how much the house has changed over time. Will it look the way it does in my memory, or will it be totally unrecognizable?

A few turns later, I reach my destination. I park on the side of the road and climb out of the car. Cupping a hand over my forehead to block out the sun, I take a long look at the house in front of me. Blue shutters. White siding. A dark-wood door. A stone path leads to the front steps, and several rickety Adirondack chairs occupy the porch.

A lump builds in the back of my throat. This place feels familiar and unfamiliar. It makes me think of Dad. His kind smile and his hearty laugh. The way he always had an answer to everything. Grief threatens to knock me off my feet, but I push it down. I need to do this. For myself and Izzy and Morgan.

I grab my bag off the passenger seat and start toward the front door.

I have no clue what's waiting for me inside.

Five

Delia

"It's a fucking disaster."

Morgan's brown eyes go wide and doe-like on my phone screen. "What do you mean?" she asks, her voice taking on a note of concern.

My eyes flicker around the small, cluttered living room. Cardboard boxes jammed with shoes and wine glasses and tax documents and children's toys cover nearly every square inch of the pale carpet. I barely made it to the couch without breaking my neck.

"I mean, Grandma Aggie kept every single thing she ever owned," I explain. "I found a bag of grocery receipts from 2006 in one of her kitchen cupboards."

I did a full sweep of Grandma Aggie's place when I arrived this morning. I figured there would be some mess—my grandmother lived here for sixty years, after all—but I never expected the total shitshow I found.

Grandma Aggie's home looks like a giant garage sale. Every room, including the upstairs bedrooms and attic, is packed with stuff. I spent most of the morning and afternoon cleaning the kitchen, throwing out expired food, organizing piles of dishes and utensils to donate, and scrubbing down the sink and floor. By six, I was wiped. I ordered a pizza and FaceTimed Izzy and Morgan, figuring it was time to break the bad news.

"Are you kidding?" Morgan asks.

I shake my head. No point in sugarcoating it. "I just sent you and Izzy a few photos."

Seconds later, Izzy's horrified gasp floods my ears. "Oh my god, Del. It looks like a tornado ran through a landfill."

"I know." I lean back against the couch. "It took me five hours to clean the kitchen." Who knows how long it will take to finish the rest of the house? I only planned on staying here one night, but the thought of leaving such a disaster behind feels wrong.

"At least things are starting to make sense now," Izzy says. "Clearly, Grandma Aggie left us the house to torture us. She's probably laughing from hell as we speak."

"Izzy," Morgan says in a reprimanding tone.

"What? She didn't speak to her own son for the last fourteen years of his life. Maybe this was her plan for revenge all along."

"That can't be true," I say. "Grandma Aggie's lawyer told me she created the trust only four years ago. If she was doing it to get revenge on Dad, why would she leave us the house *after* he died?"

Even after meeting with the lawyer, I still have no idea why Grandma Aggie decided to give everything to us. She didn't contact me or my sisters in the last four years. I wonder what changed. Did she suddenly feel guilty about ignoring us for years? Or did she realize she had no one else to leave her things to?

"Who knows? But she definitely succeeded," Izzy says.

"How does the rest of the house look?" Morgan asks. "Aside from the mess, I mean. Does it need a lot of repairs?"

"It definitely needs work," I admit. "The carpet in the bedrooms is pretty dated. So are some of the light fixtures. And basically every wall could use a fresh coat of paint." I don't have to be an expert in real estate to know that houses with antiquated floors and dingy walls sell for less than modern ones. We'll lose out on serious money if we don't put in some work.

"Well, this sucks," Morgan says.

"Are you really going to stay there tonight, Delia?" Izzy asks.

"Yeah." I don't want to spend the night here, but I'm too exhausted to drive to a hotel. Plus, there's a lot of cleaning left to do. "I think I might stay for a few days, actually."

"What? Why?"

"To make some progress on this place."

"But we agreed to do this together," Izzy reminds me.

"That was before we found out the place was a disaster," I argue. "We have to clean everything out before we can paint the walls or put in new floors. I'm already here. I might as well make some progress so we aren't totally screwed…"

I trail off mid-sentence as my ears pick up a strange noise that seems to be coming from the backyard. It sounds like…rummaging. I listen closely. The noise grows louder. Panic erupts in my chest. *Oh, god.* What is that? Is a local kid stealing from Grandma Aggie? Is a rabid raccoon living in the backyard? Nothing would surprise me at this point. Nothing.

"Delia, are you okay?" Morgan asks.

"Hang on a second," I tell her in a hushed voice.

Pulling myself off the couch, I scramble across the living room and into the kitchen. I peek into the backyard from the window above the sink. The yard is empty, but the shed door is wide open. It was shut when I went out there earlier, so I know someone or something must have opened it. Was it the wind? Or is one of my theories correct?

I get an answer a second later when a tall guy emerges from the shed. A tall, *shirtless* guy. He's wearing a dark baseball cap, so I can't get a good look at his face. His body, on the other hand…holy shit. He looks like an out-of-place male model. He has tan skin and well-defined arms and lean muscles running down his abdomen. My face heats as I take in the jeans hanging low on the stranger's hips. He pushes a lawn mower out of the shed and shuts the door behind him.

"What is happening right now?" I whisper in a mix of shock and admiration.

"What is it? What's going on?"

"A shirtless guy is mowing my lawn."

"I can't remember the last time a guy did that for me," Izzy mutters.

"No, I mean literally." I lift my phone to the window so Morgan and Izzy can see for themselves. My eyes stay glued to the man as he starts up the lawn mower. The machine roars to life, then the guy begins to push the mower across the yard.

"I'm not hallucinating this, right?" I wonder aloud.

"Definitely not," Izzy confirms. "He's hot."

"Thanks. Be sure to tell the police that after he murders me."

"What kind of murderer would mow your lawn before he kills you?"

"I don't know, Iz. What kind of person randomly mows someone else's lawn?"

"Why don't you go out there and ask him?"

Has she lost her mind? "No way."

"Then don't do anything about it. Take it as a gift from the universe. It's not like you wanted to mow the lawn, anyway," Izzy says.

"Uh, you should probably say something," Morgan says. "Grandma Aggie might've hired this guy to take care of her yard. If he doesn't know she died, he'll probably come to the door expecting to be paid."

"Shit," I whisper. Morgan's right, and I don't have cash on me. Besides, if Grandma Aggie was paying this guy to mow her yard, then she might have been paying him to do other work around the property. I can't have a random stranger showing up and scaring the life out of me at various points in the day. "I'm going out there," I say. "If neither of you hears from me in five minutes, call 911."

"Don't be such a pessimist, Del," Izzy says. "Get his number."

"If you want it so bad, come get it yourself."

"Don't tempt me. Can you put the phone in front of the window again?"

I make a point to roll my eyes at the camera. "Goodbye," I say in a flat tone before ending the call.

Still clutching my phone, I take one last look out the window, then head to the back door. I pull back the sliding glass door and step onto the porch. The old wooden boards creak beneath my feet.

I expect the guy to look up as soon as I come outside, but he keeps pushing the mower across the yard, seemingly oblivious to my presence. It gives me no choice but to follow the steps down to the backyard.

"Excuse me!" I exclaim over the roar of the lawn mower, waving my arms to get his attention. The stranger's eyes flash my way. I wait for him to turn off the mower. Instead, he redirects his focus to the patch of grass in front of him. He continues on as though he didn't see me, which is ridiculous because I *know* he did.

Anger rolls like a tidal wave through my blood. What the hell? Who deliberately ignores someone after making eye contact with them? Doesn't that violate the laws of common decency?

Grandma Aggie's disaster of a house has pushed me to my capacity for bullshit today. I'm not going to let some asshole trespassing on my property push me around.

Fists curled at my sides, I stalk over to him, stopping directly in the lawn mower's path. The guy pauses. He's tall. Six-two or six-three, if I had to guess. He has broad shoulders and a strong jaw. His navy baseball cap shadows most of his features, but his body language makes it clear he's irritated with me.

"Can you turn that off?" I ask, motioning to the buzzing lawn mower. The stranger says nothing as he releases the lever to shut down the machine. Silence falls over the yard, tense and pervasive. I'm debating whether to demand he leave or ask what he's doing here when he interrupts my thoughts with a question.

"What do you want?" His tone is flippant, dismissive. My rage surges. Who does this guy think he is?

"I want you to leave," I tell him. "You're trespassing."

He leans his hip against the lawn mower's metal handlebar. "Is that so?" he asks, his words laced with condescension. I grit my teeth to hold back a slew of curse words. Clearly, this man wants to irritate me. Laying into him would only give him satisfaction.

"Yeah. It's this crazy new law that prohibits someone from coming onto another person's property without permission," I fire back.

The stranger laughs. "I figured I had your permission, since you spent the last five minutes watching from the window."

Heat blooms across my face. I can't believe he saw me. The humiliation is so strong I want to die. Nevertheless, I fold my arms over my chest, pretending to be unaffected. "I thought you might be the town lunatic," I say. "Now, I can see my suspicions were correct. I already called the police. I suggest you get out of here while you still can."

He laughs again, to my annoyance and surprise. Though I haven't actually called the police, I assumed the threat would be enough to scare this guy off. Apparently not.

I turn on my heels, planning to go back in the house and contact local authorities for real, but then the stranger shouts, "You must be one of Aggie's granddaughters."

I snap my head back. "You knew Aggie?"

He nods. "I live back there," he says, gesturing to the small white house on the other side of Grandma Aggie's fence. So he was her neighbor. There are both pros and cons to this development. On one hand, this guy is probably not an ax murderer. On the other hand, he lives a few hundred feet away. I can't decide which is worse.

"I've been cutting Aggie's grass for a while," he says.

"Well, your services are no longer needed."

He gives me an assessing look. It makes my skin prickle. Suddenly, I wish I had the foresight to throw on different clothes before I came outside. I changed when I got to the house, since I expected to spend the rest of the day inside cleaning. I'm dressed in a flimsy cotton tank top and a *very* short pair of athletic shorts.

"I can see that," the guy says. He releases his grip on the lawn mower and starts walking toward his own yard. "Good luck." There's a gate in the fence dividing our properties. He lifts the latch and pushes it open, disappearing behind the fence.

So much for a small town welcome.

"Asshole," I mutter as I grab the lawn mower and wheel it back to the shed.

Six

Tanner

I finish the frothy dregs of my beer, then drop the empty glass on the bar top. Jacob, who's nursing a glass of IPA, arches a brow from the stool next to me.

"You all right, man?" he asks. He sounds concerned. I don't blame him. I'm not a heavy drinker, especially not on weeknights. I haven't finished a beer that quickly since college. But I needed to take the edge off tonight.

I flash Jacob a sarcastic smile. "Fan-fucking-tastic." I lock eyes with the bartender, motioning toward my now-empty glass. She's dealing with another customer at the other end of the bar, but she gives me a small nod, signaling she'll be with me shortly.

"You sure about that?" Jacob's expression tells me my attempt at humor didn't fool him in the slightest. I'm not surprised. He's my oldest friend.

Our moms have been best friends since they were teenagers. Jacob and I knew each other before we even knew how to talk. When we were kids, people assumed we were only friends because of our moms. We seemed like polar opposites. I was the kid who played in the mud,

43

while Jacob preferred having his head in a book. But we share a sense of humor and a lot of the same interests. He's the closest thing I have to a brother. Which means he has no trouble seeing through my bullshit.

"Tough day is all," I say, rolling my sore neck back and forth. I worked for twelve hours. I started the morning in the office, slogging through paperwork before I headed to a job site to help my crew start on our latest build: a three-thousand-square-foot oceanfront rehab.

Normally, I'd leave the heavy lifting to my crew, but I want to be involved with this project every step of the way. It's the largest undertaking in the history of Ryan & Son Construction. The first real chance I've had to prove myself since I became president three years ago. And the client owns several dilapidated properties in town she's looking to fix up. If we do well with this one, she might hire us for the rest, which would be a big boost for Ryan & Son.

I need everything to go smoothly. It's *my* family name on the line. My dad's legacy. I can't afford to make any mistakes.

"It seems like all your days are tough days, doesn't it?" Jacob observes. He probably figured something was up with me when I texted an hour ago, asking if he wanted to grab a drink tonight at Seaview Tavern. It's a popular hangout spot on the weekend, but it's a ghost town the rest of the week. Jacob likes to joke that the only people who come here on weekdays are the sad and pathetic. I guess it's fair to put me in that category.

I've been working nonstop since I took over the company. Dad always warned me that the first few years would be brutal. Still, I didn't expect to be pulling twelve-hour days on a regular basis. It's draining, physically and mentally. I've been meaning to hire some extra help around the office for a while, but that involves job postings and interviews and other shit I don't have time for.

I invited Jacob out because I needed to blow off steam. I don't want to talk or think about work right now. It's making me miserable.

But there's another reason for my dark mood. A prissy brunette one.

"I met Aggie Forrest's granddaughter today," I say. "She's a real piece of work."

"Aggie Forrest," Jacob repeats, brow furrowed in thought. "That's the old lady who lives behind you, right? The one whose grass you cut?"

"The one who *lived* behind me," I clarify. "She, uh, died recently."

Aggie Forrest was my neighbor for years. I didn't know her well, but about six months ago, she came by my house and asked if I could start mowing her lawn for her. *It's getting too tough on my knees*, she said. Aggie offered to pay me, but I wouldn't accept her money. Her yard isn't very big. It wasn't much of a hassle.

I heard about Aggie's passing a few days ago. A guy on my crew happened to be at the grocery store when she collapsed in the parking lot. He thought it was a stroke, but no one really knows for certain. Aggie's family didn't have a memorial service. There hasn't been an obituary in the local newspaper either.

I always got the impression that Aggie wasn't close to her family. She told me she had grandchildren, but I never saw her family visit, and she didn't leave the house often. She tried making small talk whenever I stopped by to mow. I figured she was lonely.

"That's too bad," Jacob says. "You liked her, didn't you?"

"She was nice enough."

"So, what happened with the granddaughter? Did she leave her jump rope in your yard or something?" he asks.

I shake my head. "She's not a kid." Definitely not. The woman looked to be in her mid-twenties. She had golden-brown hair, plump lips, and big brown eyes framed by thick lashes. She wore a tank top and a tiny pair of athletic shorts that put her strong, lean legs on display. She's probably the most beautiful woman I've ever laid eyes on.

Too bad she's also terrible.

I mow the grass on Mondays. Even though Aggie died, I decided to cut hers today. I figured no one else was getting around to it anytime soon. There was no sense in letting the grass get out of control. Five minutes in, I noticed a woman staring at me from Aggie's kitchen window. I planned to ignore her, but then she came outside, making that impossible.

Jacob's eyes narrow behind his glasses. "Did you sleep with her?"

"Fuck, no." I'll admit, the woman's attractiveness caught me off guard, but when I realized she must be Aggie's granddaughter, my interest disappeared faster than a flash of lightning.

I watched Aggie spend the last years of her life alone in that house. Not one family member came to see her. But a week after Aggie's death, her

granddaughter starts poking around the house?
Yeah, fuck that. I'm not getting involved with a
woman who couldn't be bothered to visit her
elderly relative's place until after she was gone.

I decided to piss off Aggie's granddaughter. It
was childish, but watching her pretty face flood
with rage when she realized I was ignoring her
was the highlight of my day.

"That woman is not my type," I say.

"Why? Afraid she'd want to see you for more
than two minutes at a time?" I shoot Jacob an
unimpressed look, but he isn't wrong. I don't have
time for dating. Running the company keeps me
too busy for it. I haven't gotten laid in almost a
year. I've never been a big relationship guy, but I
miss sex. And I'm feeling more on edge than ever,
thanks to my encounter with Aggie Forrest's hot
granddaughter.

"I don't see a line of women waiting at your
door," I fire back. Jacob's views on relationships
are a lot different than mine. He's looking for
long-term commitment. Marriage. Children. A
white picket fence. I'm not opposed to any of
those things, but it's hard for me to imagine a life
where I have time for them.

"So, is that the whole story?" Jacob asks. "You
met your neighbor's granddaughter, and you
didn't like her?"

"Pretty much. We argued for a minute. I
irritated her a bit, but that's all."

"Don't you think that's a bad idea? What if she
becomes your new neighbor?"

I laugh at the idea. "No way she's keeping that
place." I'd bet anything she's planning to put that
house on the market. Aggie's house seems small

and dated, but places in Seaview sell fast, thanks to the proximity to the beach. "She's gonna sell, then use the money to buy herself a fancy elliptical or a white leather couch."

Jacob clicks his tongue. "Be careful, Tanner," he warns me. "Making those kinds of assumptions is the swiftest way to get knocked on your ass."

His words have no effect on me. "I know her type." It didn't take long to figure out Aggie Forrest's granddaughter. Entitled. Stuck up. Feisty. "She'll be out of Seaview in a day or two. I'll probably never see her again."

Jacob shakes his head in disapproval. "Famous last words."

Seven

Delia

It's almost midnight by the time I decide to quit cleaning for the night.

Every muscle in my body feels like it's on fire. Exhausted, I find a pile of spare blankets in the hall closet and spread them across the living room couch in an attempt to get comfortable. There's a guest room upstairs, but I haven't had a chance to sort through it yet. The bed is covered in cardboard boxes and god-knows-how-many dust mites.

Given how tired I am, I expect myself to crash the minute my head hits the pillow, but being alone in my grandmother's place at night feels like being inside a haunted house.

My nerves shoot up every time a floorboard creaks or a shutter rattles in the wind. It's impossible to close my eyes, so I stare at the darkened ceiling. My mind races a million miles per minute, conjuring up images of ghosts and killers and demons that prey on foolish young women who stay by themselves overnight in unfamiliar places. A gust of wind slams against the side of the house. Goosebumps spread across my skin.

I slip the pillow out from beneath my head and smack myself in the face with it. I'm twenty-six freaking years old. Ghosts stopped scaring me a long time ago. One creepy night cannot turn me into a paranoid conspiracy theorist.

After an hour of tossing back and forth, I give up on the idea of sleep. I sit up and turn on the lamp on the small end table by the side of the couch.

As I rub my tired eyes, I blame my sudden paranoia on the stress of the day. I came here to look around the property and note anything that needs to be repaired. I never expected to find this place in a total state of disaster.

Mom told me Grandma Aggie loved the house. If it mattered so much to her, why did she let it fall apart? Getting this place market-ready is going to take a lot of time and effort. Weeks, probably. Maybe months.

I promised Izzy and Morgan I would wait for them so we could work on it together, but I can't leave our grandmother's house looking like this. *I'm* the one who pushed for us to sell. I insisted it would be difficult but doable. Therefore, I owe it to my sisters to accomplish something while I'm here. At the very least, I should clean a bit and find a contractor for the renovation work. I need to get some estimates on the repairs.

But before I can do anything related to the house, I need to head back to Boston. I planned for this to be a one-night trip. I didn't bring enough clothes, food, or other essentials to stay here for any substantial length of time.

The next morning, I get up early and email Nina, letting her know I'm going to need another personal day. I take a hot shower in the upstairs bathroom, which contains the ugliest aqua tile known to humanity (another thing that needs fixed). Then, I put on a black tank top and a pair of high-waisted jeans. Grabbing my bag, I head out the door. I'm craving a cup of coffee, so before I start my drive to the city, I pull up to Ralph's Diner.

As I enter the retro-inspired eatery, I lock eyes with the older waitress who complimented my purse yesterday. Annabella. She gives me a warm smile.

"Back again already?" she asks in a surprised but pleased tone. I assumed she wouldn't remember me—the diner was packed yesterday morning. But, then again, this is a small town. She probably doesn't see a lot of new faces around here.

I sit on an empty stool at the long counter. "What can I say? I like good coffee."

"Coffee. Got it. Is there anything else I can get you?" My gaze automatically travels to the large glass display case on the opposite end of the counter, filled with bread and bagels and sticky pastries. A wave of hunger rips through my stomach.

"I'll take a blueberry muffin, too," I say.

Annabella looks pleased by my decision. "Wise choice," she says. "My husband makes them from scratch."

"Do you two own this place?" I ask.

She nods with pride in her eyes. "Been in business for forty years."

"Wow. That's impressive." I like my job, but I can't imagine working a day past retirement age.

Nevertheless, I can respect someone who has found passion in their work. Doing anything for that long requires serious commitment.

"It pays the bills," Annabella says with a shrug. She turns, grabbing the coffee pot off the burner behind her. She fills a ceramic mug with the steaming hot liquid, then slides it in front of me. I wrap my hands around the warm mug, blowing on the coffee before I take a small but satisfying sip.

Annabella saunters down the counter to fetch a muffin from the display case. "So, what brings you to Seaview?" she asks.

Unease washes over me. Oh, how a seemingly harmless question can have such an uncomfortable answer. "I'm here to clean out my grandmother's house," I say, curling my twitching fingers around the mug. "She passed away recently."

Annabella takes a long look at me. "Are you one of the Forrest girls?"

Surprise hits me like a semi-truck. "Yeah. I'm the oldest. Delia."

"I'm sorry about Aggie."

"Did you know her well?" I don't feel comfortable accepting her condolences, so I figure it's best to deflect to something else.

"Only in passing," she says. "Aggie used to come in for breakfast a lot. She told me she had three granddaughters. You look a lot like her." I've only seen a few photos of my grandmother, so I don't know how much (or little) of a resemblance we share, but I smile and nod, anyway.

"She left her house to me and my sisters," I say. "We're fixing it up so we can sell it."

Annabella uses a tiny pair of tongs to snatch a blueberry muffin roughly the size of my palm out of the display. She places it on a dish. "Aggie owned that place for a long time, didn't she?"

"She did. It's a nice house, but it's been a long time since my grandmother did any work to it. My sisters and I need to do some repairs before we can put it up for sale. Is there any chance you know a good contractor around here?" I wasn't planning to ask that question, but I figure I might as well. It can't hurt to get a local's perspective, right?

"Ralph and I always use Ryan & Son when we need something done," Annabella says. "Their prices are fair, and they do excellent work."

"Thanks. I'll check them out." I type the company name into the Notes app on my phone, so I remember to look it up later. When I glance back up, Annabella drops the muffin in front of me. I quickly peel off the paper wrapper and take my first bite. *Oh, my god.* Sweetness explodes on my tongue. It tastes fresh and light and heavenly.

I barely finish swallowing before I say, "This is, like, the greatest thing I've ever had."

Annabella laughs. "Forty years is a long time. You figure out what works, eventually."

"Can I get a couple of these to go?"

Minutes later, I leave the diner with a full stomach and a bag of blueberry muffins. I make the long drive to Boston to collect my things.

It's a little after two o'clock when I get back to Seaview. I stop at a grocery store in town, where I pick up bagged salads, deli meat and cheese for sandwiches, and several meals from the heat-and-eat section. I'm a lousy cook. At home, I rely mostly on meal delivery services. I figure it's for the best if I stick with pre-made meals while I'm here. That way, there's less of a chance of me accidentally burning down Grandma Aggie's. I also buy some cleaning supplies. I know I'm going to need them.

It isn't until I'm shoving the groceries in the backseat of my car that I remember Grandma Aggie's stroke happened in a supermarket parking lot. The thought gives me pause. My eyes circle around the near-vacant lot.

Is this where Grandma Aggie was standing when she died? Was she putting groceries in her car? Thinking about what to make for dinner? A chill runs up my spine. Did she realize something was wrong? What was going through her head in those final moments?

I shake off the morbid thoughts, throwing the rest of my groceries in the car and pulling out of the lot as quickly as possible. I make a mental note to shop somewhere else for the rest of my time in Seaview.

When I finally get back to the house, I put away my groceries and then go upstairs, armed with my new cleaning supplies. I'm going to need somewhere to sleep that isn't the couch, and it's not going to be Grandma Aggie's room. I pop open the door to the guest bedroom, taking in the piles of boxes and general state of disarray.

Let's get this over with, I think to myself as I head inside.

Eight

Delia

I'm almost finished with the guest room.

Well, *finished* might be a stretch.

I've almost made the bedroom livable. I threw open the windows to air out the dusty smell and doused the room with a bottle of lavender air freshener. I removed all the boxes from the bed and tossed the tacky floral quilt in the washing machine. Finally, I wiped down the streaky mirror on the wooden dresser. The drawers were filled with men's dress shirts. They must have belonged to my grandfather, who died nearly thirty years ago. I shoved the clothes into a large trash bag, which I'm planning to take to a thrift store later.

When I finish cleaning for the day, I find a phone number online for Ryan & Son Construction. I spend a few minutes on the phone with an employee, explaining the work I want done. I schedule an appointment for someone to come to the house tomorrow to take a look around and give me an estimate.

I get off the call around six, feeling tired but productive. There's still a lot of work ahead of me, but I made substantial progress today. That's something to celebrate.

I warm up a chicken dinner I bought at the grocery store, pour myself a glass of wine, and then head outside to the back porch. It's a warm, breezy night. I sit and eat at the small picnic table. I text Mariah and Kali to let them know I'm going to be in Seaview for the foreseeable future. They're disappointed I won't be back in the city for Friday drinks, but they understand, especially after I send them pictures of Grandma Aggie's place.

I finish eating, but I still have half a glass of wine left, so I stay outside for a while, enjoying the stillness and the fresh air. My apartment in Boston has a small balcony, but I don't sit out there often. I live in a loud, busy neighborhood. The sounds of horns honking and patrons shouting at the bar across the street don't make for a relaxing outdoor atmosphere. Most of the time, I don't mind the noise, but the quietness is a nice change of pace. It would probably get exhausting over time, though. Being out here by yourself.

I wonder how many nights Grandma Aggie sat out here, surrounded by nothing but her own thoughts. A kernel of sympathy pops in my chest, but I remind myself that any loneliness she felt was self-inflicted. Grandma Aggie could've had her grandchildren here with her. She cut us out of her life. Deliberately. The consequences of her actions were her own damn fault.

Shaking off my pity, I stand up and carry my wine glass back inside.

The next day, I prioritize work. Being off for two days means there's a lot for me to catch up on, so I set up at the kitchen table early in the morning and boot up my laptop. I spend most of the morning cleaning out my overstuffed inbox and working on my campaign for the beachwear company in Cape Cod. I take short breaks here and there to sort through boxes of Grandma Aggie's belongings as I wait for the contractor to arrive.

The doorbell rings around one in the afternoon. Finishing off the email I'm writing, I hit send and then climb out of my chair, heading to the front door. I yank it open without looking to see who's on the other side.

Big mistake.

Grandma Aggie's asshole neighbor/lawn mower stands on the porch.

He's wearing a shirt this time, but he's not wearing a baseball cap, so I'm able to get a better look at his face.

He must be in his late twenties or early thirties. His eyes are pale green, almost gray. He has a strong nose, hard-set jaw, and a pair of thick, straight brows. His bone structure is something sculptors would envy. You could sharpen knives on those cheekbones. They give him a sort of prettiness that you wouldn't expect to see on someone like him. His stained blue jeans and faded T-shirt contrast with the elegance of his face, but even old clothes can't detract from his undeniable attractiveness.

Why does he have to be hot? That beauty is wasted on someone so rude and arrogant. Of course, his appearance shouldn't matter to me. I'm not dating right now, especially not small-town jerks. This guy isn't welcome here. Not after the way he talked to me in my own backyard. I'm going to make that *very* clear.

"What do you want?" I ask, throwing the first words he said to me right back in his face. It feels good for all of two seconds. Then he smirks, and the satisfaction in my chest turns into uncertainty.

"I think that's a better question to ask yourself," he replies. "You called me."

"I did not…" The words die on my tongue as I notice the emblem stitched in the top left corner of his black shirt. Fuck. Me. "You work for Ryan & Son Construction?"

He practically looks giddy as he says, "Tanner Ryan. President of Ryan & Son Construction." He offers me a handshake, but it feels like an insult, so I don't take it. Instead, I do the best I can to maintain a cool expression as panic alarms sound in my head.

What are the odds that Grandma Aggie's jerk neighbor happens to own the construction company I called? Is this being filmed for a prank show? Are there TV cameras somewhere taping my reaction?

"You must be Delia Forrest," the guy, Tanner, says. His smugness is palpable. "I have to say, you seemed a lot nicer on the phone." Oh, my god. That was him? He must've been losing his mind yesterday when I called about getting an estimate.

"My mistake. I didn't realize who I was talking to."

He smirks again. I hate him. "Can I come in and take a look around?" he asks, nodding toward the house. Is he serious? I assumed he came here to make me feel ridiculous for calling his company, not to actually give me a quote. I have no intention of hiring him or Ryan & Son to fix up Grandma Aggie's.

"No," I answer immediately. "I don't need your help anymore."

"Really?" His voice is colored with doubt.

I nod. "I already chose a different contractor." Maybe it's petty to write off an entire company because of one person, but that person is the owner. Besides, Tanner has been nothing but petty to me since we met. It's only fair I return the favor. "Sorry for the inconvenience," I add as I start to shut the door. "Thanks for coming out, anyway."

"Wait." He puts his hand on the wooden door frame. "Who did you hire?"

No one. But I'd rather have no contractor than you. "I don't think that's any of your business," I tell him, folding my arms across my chest.

"You should at least let me give you a quote," Tanner insists. "I'm here. It'll only take a few minutes. It's best to keep your options open. Plus, a lot of places will try to highball you if they think you know nothing about construction." I don't know anything about construction, but I'm annoyed by his insinuation, nonetheless.

"Who says I don't know anything about construction?"

"Appearances lead to assumptions, don't they?" Tanner scans my high-neck blouse and paperbag pants with a knowing look in his eye. I'll admit, my clothes scream "corporate" more than "construction site," but I still don't like him making assumptions about me. He doesn't know me at all.

I take the jab in stride. "My worn-out jeans are in the wash." I deliberately rake my eyes over his clothes before returning them to his face.

"I'm just saying, you shouldn't take the word of one contractor."

I tilt my head. "Says the contractor?"

Tanner shrugs. "Can't hurt to get a second or third opinion. Look, I live in this neighborhood. I know the value of homes in the area. Let me check out the place, and then I'll be out of your hair." His expression turns serious.

I weigh my options. Kicking Tanner off the property seems like the most satisfying choice, but I need a contractor, and the waitress at the diner said Ryan & Son is the best in town. Would it really be in my best interest to tell him to screw off? It wouldn't get me any closer to getting Grandma Aggie's place on the market. I might as well get an estimate, even if Tanner is insufferable.

Reluctantly, I open the door for him. "Fine. Come in."

Wordlessly, Tanner steps inside. His large frame looks oversized in the small tiled foyer. He takes a sweeping look around the space, his gaze landing on the large stack of cardboard boxes piled in the corner.

"I love what you've done with the place," he says.

I roll my eyes. I can't remember the last time someone irritated me so much. It was probably Izzy. She had a tendency to borrow my clothes without permission when we were teenagers. We fought about it constantly.

"You can thank Aggie for the mess. Clutter was her style, apparently."

"You're planning to sell, right? That's what you said on the phone."

I nod. "My grandmother left the house to me and my sisters. One lives out of state, and the other is a grad student. There's no sense in us keeping it."

"What about you?"

"What about me?"

He lifts a brow. "You've got no interest in living here?"

"As welcoming as the neighbors have been, my life is in Boston," I say in a tone so artificial it might give me a cavity.

"Figures you're from the city," Tanner mutters.

Neither of us says a word as we reach the upstairs landing. I give Tanner a brief tour of the bathroom, then Grandma Aggie's room, pointing out the features in need of updating. When we stop in the guest room, Tanner takes a long look at the dingy carpet. It's the color of dishwater. I'm pretty sure it was white at one point.

"How long do you think this carpet's been here?" he asks.

"Considering how much dust I found when I first came in? A long time."

"I bet the wood floors are in decent shape. You could remove the carpet. Restore the wood." I glance around the room, liking the idea of hardwood floors a lot more than I'm willing to let on. Tanner must pick up on my reluctance to agree with him. "It won't kill you to admit I had a good idea, you know."

"Oh, I think it might."

He laughs quietly. "You'll probably want to switch out these light fixtures." He reaches up to grab the pull chain on the antique-looking ceiling fan with brown paneling and gold accents. "They look pretty dated."

"They're like that in the kitchen and living room, too."

Tanner bobs his head as if making a mental note. "Floors. Lights. Is there anything else you're thinking about doing?"

"I'd like to get a quote for redoing the back porch." I noticed several rotted planks when I was outside eating dinner last night.

"What about the front? Because that's not in great shape either."

I give him an annoyed look. "I'm aware. Thanks."

"Buyers will be more concerned about the front porch than the back."

"Not if they actually want to live here," I argue. "The back porch is massive and secluded. It's a huge selling point."

"I don't disagree with you. But if you can't get people in the door, what good does it do?"

"Fine. I'd like a quote for the front porch, too."

We head back downstairs. It only takes a couple of minutes to show Tanner the rest of the small house. We finish the brief tour in the kitchen. Tanner pulls a small notebook and a pen out of his back pocket.

"When were you looking to have this work done?" he asks.

"As soon as possible. We're hoping to sell the house by June."

Tanner looks less than enthused. "Seems ambitious." His attention shifts to the cluttered living room, doubt swirling in his eyes. I get it. If I didn't know myself, I would probably have my own suspicions about my ability to clean up this place in such a short amount of time, but I'm highly motivated. Getting this house ready to sell is the only thing standing between me and returning to my normal life.

"Obviously, there's a lot of cleaning left to do," I admit. "My grandmother didn't take very good care of the place."

"Can you blame her? Wasn't she, like, ninety?"

"Yeah. But it wouldn't have killed her to throw something out every now and then." I'm not holding a grudge against Grandma Aggie for living the way she wanted to in her own home. I'm annoyed that she left me and my sisters to pick up the mess. She didn't need to keep every scrap of paper she ever owned, did she?

"And it wouldn't have killed you to visit her every now and then."

I freeze, taken aback. Did he just— "*Excuse me*?"

Tanner offers a dismissive shrug. "I'm just saying, Aggie lived here by herself for a long time. I'm sure she would have liked to see her family every once in a while."

I open my mouth, but no words come out, shock and anger rendering me speechless. I've dealt with Tanner's unwarranted judgment up until this point without losing my head, but *that* comment has finally pushed me to the edge. Who does he think he is inserting himself into my family drama? I'm not going to stand here and let him insult me. And I'm certainly not going to pay him to do it.

"My relationship with my grandmother is none of your business," I say in a voice laced with fury.

His eyes widen. As if he's suddenly realizing he put his foot in his mouth. "I wasn't—"

"No." I hold up a palm to silence him. "I don't care how long you knew Aggie—you don't know me *or* my family. You have zero right to judge us based on something you know nothing about. And I have no interest in working with someone who thinks it's appropriate to treat customers like this." I hit him with a stern glare as I motion toward the front door. "Get out. And do us both a favor and don't come back here again."

Nine

Tanner

I'm a dick.

I've always known it, but it's never been more apparent than after Delia Forrest threw me out of her grandmother's house. I shouldn't have gone there. I could've sent anyone from my team to give her a quote, but I chose to do it myself. I wanted to see the shock on her face when she opened the door and saw me standing on her porch.

Never in a million years did I expect to hear her voice when I picked up the phone at Ryan & Son two nights ago. I recognized it immediately. When she asked to schedule an appointment, I couldn't help but see it as an opportunity to mess with her.

Pissing her off is fun. Her cheeks turn pink and her eyes narrow and she crosses her arms in a way that calls attention to her phenomenal rack. She'd probably curse me out if she heard that last thought. I picture her pursed lips and furrowed brow and smile to myself. Then I remember the anger in her voice when she kicked me out. My amusement morphs into embarrassment and regret.

I didn't mean to be so brutal about her not visiting Aggie. The words slipped out as an afterthought, and I don't blame Delia for getting mad. Hell, I would've been furious if a stranger gave me their unsolicited opinion about my relationship with a member of my family.

I don't know what kind of relationship Delia had with Aggie, but she *just* lost her grandmother. The last thing she needed was my judgment. Especially when she's got that shitstorm of a house to handle.

Before yesterday, I'd never stepped foot in Aggie's house. I had no idea it was such a disaster. I wonder if Delia had any sense of the mess she was walking into or if it was an unwelcome surprise. Either way, my cruelty didn't help things. I wanted to irritate Delia, not upset her. I went too far, and I know it.

Why am I such an ass?

"We're moving along pretty well, don't you think?" Marvin, my foreman, asks, pulling me out of my self-loathing thoughts.

I nod. "Everything looks good so far."

We're standing in front of the site of the new oceanfront project. An old house used to sit on the property, but the windows were broken, and the water damage inside made the place unsalvageeable. We bulldozed the house to give ourselves a clean slate. The land has been cleared and leveled, and the crew is busy fixing up the old foundation.

Everything seems to be chugging along smoothly. That knowledge should help me relax, but it does little to ease the knot in my chest. I've stressed the importance of this build to my crew, but I don't think anyone understands how much it really matters to me. No one except Marvin.

He's been with Ryan & Son for ages. Over the years, he's become a pseudo-uncle to me, so he reads me fairly well. Unfortunately, he's planning to retire soon. He hasn't said the words yet, but I know they're coming, and I'm dreading the moment they do. Losing Marvin will be a huge blow.

Marvin pats me on the shoulder. "Everything's gonna work out just fine," he says. He smiles and runs a hand through his salt-and-pepper beard. It's thick enough to lose coins in. "You've got a good team. Trust your people to do their jobs."

I wish I could make myself believe him. My crew is phenomenal. I have no reason to doubt the people who work for me, but it's hard not to worry when one project can alter the trajectory of the company.

This project is my first chance to show off my capabilities as the company president. We've had steady work since I took the reins, but it's mostly been single-family builds or home renovations. The same things we've always been doing. Oceanfront is a new territory for us. If we pull this off, it will prove that I can take the company in a positive direction. It's the type of validation I desperately need.

I've held various roles at Ryan & Son over the years, most recently as vice president. I've known since I was a kid that the company would be mine someday, but I always expected to have my father alongside me. I thought I could count on him for advice or to tell me when I'm doing things wrong.

Becoming president without him there to guide me has made for a shaky transition. It left plenty of room for questions and self-doubt. I'm worried I'll never be half the leader my father was. That's why I need this project to go well.

It's these thoughts that have my mind turning back to Delia. I shouldn't have been so cruel to her, especially when I know what it's like to be in over your head. She's got a lot of work to do at Aggie's place. My upsetting her probably didn't help the situation.

The more I think about it, the more one thing becomes clear.

I owe Delia Forrest an apology.

***

Delia

Music blasts through my headphones as I sprint along the beach. It's almost sundown, and the sky has turned a beautiful shade of pinkish orange. Sweat beads across my forehead as I pump my legs across the uneven sand. I'm exhausted, but I have too much anger whizzing through me to slow down.

I'm still fuming about what happened with Tanner this afternoon. I can't believe he had the nerve to call me out for not visiting Grandma Aggie. His condescending words reverberate in my head like an echo. *I'm sure she would have liked to see her family every once in a while.* He's wrong. Grandma Aggie didn't want me to visit. She didn't want a relationship with me, period. Tanner has no idea what he's talking about.

I don't know why he feels comfortable enough to make sweeping generalizations about me, but a bad granddaughter wouldn't have come to Seaview. And she certainly wouldn't have put her life on hold to clean her grandmother's landfill of a house. *I'm* the one who got blindsided here. I'm doing the best I can. I don't have to justify my decisions to anyone, let alone a stranger. Still, that's a lot easier said than done.

I've never been good at accepting criticism. In school, I was the kid who argued with teachers if I didn't get the grade I felt I deserved. I've always felt the need to prove myself to anyone who criticizes me. Make them see they're wrong. But I get the feeling Tanner made up his mind about me and my family before I even stepped foot in Grandma Aggie's house. Nothing I say to the jerk will make him change his mind. I need to let it go.

Who cares about Tanner's worthless opinion?

That's what I tell myself as I continue my run. I need to focus on what really matters. The things I can control. My top priority should be finding a new contractor. I'll do some research when I get back to the house. I'm sure it won't be hard to find someone who will take my business without insulting me to my face.

Twenty minutes later, I've run to the point of exhaustion. I slow my pace to a walk and then turn around, starting back the way I came. Eventually, I reach the wooden stairs leading to the public beach access parking lot. Grandma Aggie's place is only a mile from the beach, so I walked instead of taking my car. It's a decision I'm regretting at the moment.

As I follow the sand-covered sidewalks back to town, I pull out my phone and type in Mom's number. We've texted a few times since I arrived in Seaview, but we haven't talked on the phone, and she's been bugging me to call her.

She picks up on the first ring. "Hi, sweetheart," she says. "I'm glad you called—I was just thinking about you. How's it going?"

I wipe the sweat from my forehead as I debate how much I want to share with her. Mom has a tendency to overreact when she thinks me or my sisters are in trouble. Saying the wrong thing could send her into a panic. "It's...okay," I say. "The house is a mess, but I'm making progress."

"Morgan sent me the photos you took," Mom says. "I can't believe it. Aggie used to take great care of her place."

"Well, she hasn't in a long time." Judging by the size of the dust bunnies I found in her closet, I'd reckon Grandma Aggie hasn't touched a broom in decades.

"Is it safe for you to be staying there, Delia? I don't like you being there by yourself." Mom's voice takes on a note of concern, and I know I need to be delicate with my response. If I'm not careful, she'll get in her car and drive to Seaview right now.

"Totally safe," I insist. "The house itself isn't in bad shape. It's just cluttered."

"How much longer do you think you'll be there?"

"I don't know. There's a lot of cleaning to do. Plus, I'm trying to find a contractor to make some improvements since things need to be updated before we can sell. I'm guessing I'll be here for at least a couple of weeks."

"*Weeks*?"

"I'm fine. I promise."

"That's a long time to be in that house by yourself," she says, sounding worried. "Why don't I drive down for a few days and help you out? I have plenty of PTO. It should be no trouble getting off work."

"That's really not necessary." Mom had surgery on her hip last fall. She shouldn't be moving heavy boxes in a cluttered house. "I'm doing fine on my own. Besides, I'm working from the house. Having you there would only serve as a distraction."

Mom huffs. "I think I could stay out of your way, Delia."

"I know you're only trying to help, Mom, but I'm all right," I say. "If it gets to be too much, I'll go back to Boston and wait for Izzy and Morgan. In the meantime, I want to get as much done as I can. Okay?"

Mom relents. "Fine. But that doesn't mean I like this."

"I wouldn't expect you to. But thank you." My mother is smart enough to realize she won't be able to change my mind on this. I'm relieved she isn't trying to fight me.

"So, how's Seaview been treating you?" she asks.

"It's quiet. Pretty." Having just convinced her not to drop everything and come to Seaview, I figure it's best not to mention Tanner. Mom would freak out if she knew the things he said to me. "I had the most incredible blueberry muffins at this little place on Main Street. Maybe you've heard of it. It's called Ralph's Diner."

"Hmm. That sounds familiar. I might've eaten there with your dad."

"I met the owner. She said she knew Grandma Aggie."

"I bet most people in town did. Aggie didn't travel much. The first time she left Seaview in years was to attend your dad's college graduation."

"Seriously? Years?" I repeat, shocked by the revelation. I knew Grandma Aggie loved Seaview, but staying in one place for years at a time seems like overkill. I love Boston, but I wouldn't confine myself to the city for the rest of my life. "Was Grandma Aggie unfamiliar with the concept of a vacation?"

"Your dad said she was a homebody," Mom says. "I think it got worse after your grandfather died. Aggie wanted everything she loved to be in one place. She was furious with your father when we didn't move to Seaview after we got married."

"Why would she expect that?" Mom grew up in Boston, and Dad moved there shortly after college. It makes sense that they planted roots in the city.

"She thought it was what your dad wanted. That he would spend a few years in Boston before coming back to his hometown to settle down. Aggie was outraged when your dad told her we were going to buy a place in Boston. I think she saw it as him abandoning her. It took some time for her to get over it, but it was always a source of contention in their relationship. Aggie knew how to hold a grudge."

"Does this have anything to do with why they stopped talking?" I never really had interest in learning the details of my dad's complicated relationship with his mom. It doesn't change the fact that she didn't want me and my sisters in her life. But after spending several days in Seaview, my curiosity has been piqued.

I want to understand what led to the breakdown of their relationship. What could've been awful enough to make my grandmother ignore her family for the rest of her life?

"As Aggie got older, your dad started worrying about her living in that house by herself," Mom explains. "He wanted her to come live with us. She refused. A few years later, Aggie suffered a pretty scary fall in her driveway. She slipped on a patch of ice and fractured her tailbone. Couldn't get up by herself. She shouted for help for almost an hour before a neighbor heard and called an ambulance. Anyway, the whole thing spooked your dad. He brought up the possibility of her moving to Boston again. It didn't go over well. They fought, and then they just stopped talking."

That's it? A disagreement over living arrangements? I expected a huge family secret or a horrible insult to be the source of their conflict. Something big and dramatic and impossible to ignore. I can't believe their long-stemming feud started over something as insignificant as where Grandma Aggie lived.

"That seems like a massive overreaction," I say.

"I don't think either of them thought it would last forever," Mom admits. "If you ask me, the real thing that kept them apart all those years was stubbornness. They could've gotten past it if one of them had been big enough to reach out. The more time went by, the harder it got to pick up the phone."

I'm still thinking about Mom's words after we get off the call. I don't know how someone could throw away their relationship with their family over something so trivial.

Didn't Grandma Aggie realize Dad wanted her to move in with us because he cared about her? How was staying in Seaview more important to her than her own safety? And was it worth losing me and my sisters over it? Apparently so. I already knew my grandmother was a selfish person, but now I'm starting to wonder if she was worse than I ever thought.

Finally, I make it back to Grandma Aggie's neighborhood. The driveway comes into view, and I realize someone's standing on the front porch. The sound of my footsteps on the pavement alerts the visitor to my presence, and he turns to face me. A ball of dread forms in my stomach. It's Tanner. Again. He's hovering by the doorbell. I bet he just rang. If only I'd taken another five minutes on the beach. I could've avoided this interaction entirely.

What is he doing here? I specifically told Tanner to stay away. Does he not realize he's unwelcome, or is he looking for a fight? I'm tempted to yell or fling something at him (a shoe, maybe?), but I decided the best approach is not to engage. That's what they teach you in grade school, isn't it? If you ignore someone, they will go away.

Slipping my key out of the pocket of my running shorts, I climb the steps to the porch, dutifully ignoring Tanner.

"Delia, hang on a second," he says.

I slide the key in the lock, pretending not to hear him.

"I need to talk to you," he adds.

Nothing, Delia. Give him nothing. I need to talk to Tanner like I need a hole in the head. I turn the key and unlock the door, opening it just wide enough for me to slip inside.

I'm about to step through when Tanner says, "I'm here to apologize." The words catch me by surprise. I tell myself there's no sense in arguing with him, but that doesn't stop a harsh laugh from escaping from my lips.

I glance over my shoulder, giving him my most unimpressed look. "*You* want to apologize to *me*?" I don't know what he's playing at here. A person doesn't go from insulting a stranger to their face to saying sorry in such a short span of time. I'm not interested in listening to his excuses. "I think I'll pass. Go find someone else to terrorize."

"I'm serious," he says, eyes wide and palms lifted in surrender. "What I said to you was out of line. Your relationship with Aggie is none of my business. I'm sorry." He sounds sincere. I wish he didn't. It would be easier to shut the door in his face if his apology came across as disingenuous.

Maybe Tanner honestly regrets how he acted. Or maybe he's trying to save face for the sake of his construction company. I don't know him well enough to tell whether this is an earnest gesture or a calculated business move. Fortunately, it doesn't matter. Tanner might be my temporary neighbor, but he's not the only contractor in Seaview. I don't have to interpret his apologies or hear his excuses.

Without a word, I step inside the house, slamming the door behind me.

Ten

Delia

The next few days pass in a blur of cleaning spray and cardboard boxes. When I'm not working, I spend nearly every moment going through Grandma Aggie's belongings. I've gotten through most of the junk in the living room, making small piles of things to keep and large piles to donate. Each box I open chips away at a piece of my sanity. I don't know why Grandma Aggie felt compelled to save every busted appliance, refrigerator magnet, or woven basket she ever owned, but she did. And now it's my problem to deal with.

On the rare occasions I'm not sorting through boxes of my grandmother's belongings, I'm calling construction companies. Since Tanner's visit, I've had two other contractors walk through the house. The first one gave me a quote that was almost double my expectations. The second told me they wouldn't be able to start working until September. I'm waiting on call backs from a few other places, but I'm not optimistic. I'm either going to have to adjust my expectations for getting the house on the market or drop the idea of renovations altogether.

Later that week, I'm sipping coffee in a corner booth at Ralph's Diner, trying not to think about my disappointment. I've taken to coming to the diner after my morning runs. The coffee is good, and the muffins are even better.

It's around seven, and the morning rush is in full swing. Annabella flits around the crowded restaurant, slinging platters of pancakes and sausage to hungry customers. I'm ready to pay my tab and head back to the house, but Annabella's so busy she hasn't made it back to my table in a while. I'm tracking her movements around the restaurant, waiting for the opportune moment to call her over.

I'm so preoccupied watching Annabella that I don't hear the footsteps coming my direction until they stop directly in front of me. Looking up, I'm shocked and annoyed to see Tanner standing by my table.

He's wearing a pair of frayed jeans and a red baseball cap that brings out the green in his eyes. A thin layer of light-brown stubble coats his chiseled jaw. I search his appearance for an imperfection, but I can't find one. He still has the same flawless features. Maybe he was a saint in a past life. I can't think of another reason someone as miserable as Tanner would be blessed with such good looks.

"What are you doing here?" I ask, making no secret of my displeasure. I haven't seen Tanner since I slammed the door in his face the other night. I hoped it would be the last of him. Obviously, that was wishful thinking.

"This is the only place in town that serves decent coffee," he says.

"Well, you should find a table," I tell him, motioning toward a vacant table on the opposite side of the diner. "Looks like they're filling up fast." A fresh wave of customers enters the restaurant, filling the air with loud chatter, but Tanner makes no attempt to move. He stares at me expectantly, as if he thinks I'm going to invite him to join me. Averting my gaze, I take a sip of my coffee.

"Delia?"

"Yes?" My tone is clipped.

"Can I please sit down?"

"Why?"

"I'd like a chance to apologize. Properly."

I study his eyes for any trace of humor, his lips for the semblance of a smile. Nothing. Tanner looks earnest. Something about that puts me on guard. Tanner has done everything to make me feel like an entitled brat since the moment we met. I find it hard to believe he's had a change of heart.

What does he gain from apologizing to me? The only thing I can think is that he must be worried about how this could affect his company. Tanner insulted me, a potential customer, to my face. He's probably afraid I'm going to leave a scathing review for Ryan & Son. He's not wrong to be concerned. I'd be lying if I said I hadn't thought about pouring my frustrations into a nasty Yelp review.

"If this is about the renovations, you can forget it," I reply dismissively. "I wouldn't hire you if you were the only contractor in the state of Massachusetts."

Sighing, Tanner runs a hand over his face. "That's not what this is about," he says. "Can I sit? Please? Give me two minutes to explain myself."

I'm about to tell him no, but something stops me. Confusion. Curiosity. Who knows? I'm suddenly interested in hearing how Tanner plans to justify his behavior. I can't think of a single good reason for someone to act the way he did. What could his strategy possibly be here?

"Two minutes," I tell him sternly.

Tanner nods, then slides into the vinyl booth across from me. He folds his large, calloused hands on the edge of the plastic table. "I lived behind Aggie for several years," he says. "I didn't know her very well, but she seemed like a decent person. A few months ago, she asked me if I could start mowing her lawn. She said she was having knee problems and couldn't do it herself anymore. I said yes.

"Aggie always came outside on the days I mowed. Sometimes she'd bring me cookies or iced tea. Other times she'd just talk. At first, I thought she was doing it to thank me for helping with the grass. I realized after a couple of weeks she was just lonely. She mentioned she had family in Boston, but I never saw anyone visit her. So when I saw you here for the first time after she died, it sort of pissed me off. Still, it wasn't fair of me to say anything. Nor was it my place to make judgments. I hardly knew Aggie. I don't know anything about your relationship with her. I shouldn't have said a word to you. I'm sorry."

I trace a fingertip around the rim of my coffee as I slowly digest Tanner's words. Have I lost my mind, or does that explanation actually make sense? If I had an elderly neighbor who seemed lonely, I probably wouldn't take too kindly to her family, especially if I saw them for the first time after she passed away. Tanner shouldn't have inserted himself into my family business, but I can at least see why he felt the way he did.

"I didn't know Aggie either," I say, surprising myself with my confession. I don't owe him an explanation, but the words pour out of me, anyway. "She didn't talk to me or my sisters. She didn't get along with my dad, so she never had a relationship with us. I didn't expect her to leave us anything, let alone her house."

"You don't have to explain anything," he insists. "It doesn't matter if you had a relationship with her or not—I never should've gotten involved."

That was…unexpectedly mature of him. I didn't think Tanner had it in him to offer a genuine apology. Maybe we can settle this situation like adults. I don't particularly like the guy, but that doesn't mean we have to be hostile toward each other. I'm going to be in Seaview for some time. Tanner lives behind me. I don't want to be afraid of bumping into him every time I leave the house. It's good we aired everything out. Now, we won't have to dance around each other.

With a slow nod, I say, "I appreciate the apology."

Tanner reaches a palm behind his head, scratching the back of his neck. "Listen, about the house…" Irritation surges through me, hot and fast. He's bringing up the renovations? Seriously? Was all of that just a sales pitch?

"Are you joking?" I ask, throwing my hands up in disbelief. "The house? Did you seriously apologize so you could get me to—"

"I'm not asking you to hire me, Delia," he says, cutting me off. "I'm offering to do the renovations for you. I won't charge you for labor."

My jaw must be on the floor. "What?"

"You'll have to pay the cost of materials," Tanner says. "I'm not actively trying to lose money here. And I'll probably have to do most of the work in the evenings, so it doesn't conflict with my other jobs. But I can get started as soon as you'd like. Based on what I saw the other day, I don't think it'd take more than a few weeks."

I'm hearing him, but I'm also not hearing him. It feels like I'm listening to an infomercial. Tanner is the aggressive voiceover guy, trying to sell me an idea I know is too good to be true. "And you're *not* gonna charge me for labor?" I ask.

"No."

"But that's hours of work. Thousands of dollars."

Tanner raises his brows. "I know. I sort of own a construction company."

I won't let him distract me with his attempt at humor. Not when it feels like I'm being duped. "This doesn't make any sense." What's his angle? How would he benefit? "Why would you do all that work for free? What would you be getting out of it?"

He smirks. "A new neighbor."

I want to throw my coffee in his face. "Funny." So he's not being serious about this. Figures. I need to get out of here before I actually commit a crime. I whip my head around, searching the diner for Annabella. Where is she?

"I didn't know Aggie well," Tanner says, his expression growing serious. "But I know her house meant a lot to her. I want to make sure the place gets fixed up properly. Besides, there's some incentive for me, too. I live nearby. Whatever you sell the place for will affect the value of my property. I don't want my home value to tank because you hired a crappy contractor."

"That's what you're worried about? Your home value?"

"It's mainly the Aggie thing," Tanner says with a shrug. "But, yeah, I'd be lying if I said that thought hadn't crossed my mind."

"And what? You just decided over the last few days that you wanted to do this?"

"Actually, I was planning to offer before you kicked me out."

"You mean before you acted like an ass and got yourself kicked out?"

Tanner ignores the slight. "If you don't want me to do it, that's fine," he says. "You can hire a different contractor, but it's going to cost you a lot of money, and they might not start on the work for months. I'm offering you a simple solution here." It pains me to admit, but he makes a good point. I've been struggling to find another contractor. Tanner's offering me a perfect solution. Nothing beats free and immediate.

Still, there's a nagging voice in the back of my head that's telling me to be careful. A verbal agreement is only as good as the word of the people who make it. I don't know enough about Tanner to trust that he'll stick to his promise. I don't want to make the mistake of trusting him when I shouldn't.

"Would you be willing to put this in writing?" I ask.

Tanner doesn't hesitate. "I'll sign whatever you want."

"Any chance you have a pen and paper?"

"No," he says, "but Annabella does." He waves to the curly-haired waitress as she passes by our table. Annabella stops, greeting us with a smile.

"Hi, Tanner," she says. "I didn't see you come in. What can I get for you?"

"Nothing for me right now, Annabella," he tells her. "But could we borrow some paper and a pen?"

"Of course." Annabella tears a sheet of paper out of her tiny server's notepad and then grabs a spare pen out of the pocket of her apron. She sets the items on the table. "Holler if there's anything else I can do for you."

As she turns to walk away, Tanner asks her to hang on for a second. His green eyes flash to me. "Did you wanna order something?" he asks.

I stare at him for a moment, confused. "What?"

"You were looking around when I came in," he explains. "I assume you were trying to get Annabella's attention."

"Oh." I'm surprised he noticed that. I turn to face Annabella. "Can I please get my check and a blueberry muffin to go?"

Annabella nods. "I'll have that for you in a moment."

Once she's gone, I take the paper and pen and write the terms of a very simple contract.

Tanner Ryan agrees to complete the necessary renovation work at Aggie Forrest's house without charging Delia Forrest for labor. Delia Forrest agrees to bear all material-related costs.

I slide the paper to Tanner, who skims it. "Give me the pen."

Our fingers brush for the briefest second as I hand him the pen. It isn't much contact, but it makes my skin tingle. I quickly draw my hand back, hiding it beneath the table beside my thigh. *Shit.* It's only been three months since I swore off men for eternity. I'm in for a long and miserable forever if all it takes to get me going is a slight touch.

Fortunately, it doesn't seem to affect Tanner. If it does, he doesn't show it. He signs his name at the bottom of the contract, then gives the pen back to me so I can do the same. I add my signature next to his, making it official.

We've got ourselves a deal.

Eleven

Delia

"So, you actually hired the guy?" Morgan asks.

With my cell phone wedged between my shoulder and ear, I step on the small stool in Grandma Aggie's closet, grabbing a dusty shoebox off the top shelf. "I had no choice," I say. "He's going to save us thousands of dollars."

It's the night after I made my deal with Tanner, and I called my sisters to update them on everything that's happened over the last few days. Neither of them could believe what Tanner said to me about not visiting Grandma Aggie, but they were even more surprised that he volunteered to renovate without charging us for labor.

"Personally, I'm loving this development," Izzy says. "It sounds like Hot Lawn Mower Guy is doing us a solid. Why question it?"

"Because it seems fishy," Morgan argues. "Why would someone offer to do all that work for free?" Her suspicion doesn't surprise me. In the last twenty-four hours, I've cycled through my own feelings of doubt and distrust.

It's hard to understand how anyone could go from being a massive dick to doing me the biggest favor of my life, but I've told myself to stop questioning it. When you're stranded in the middle of the ocean and a rescue boat shows up, you don't ask the captain to show you his boating license—you climb on. Not having to pay a contractor is an enormous burden off my shoulders. Tanner is obnoxious, but I'll suffer through his presence if it means saving myself thousands.

"Who knows? But he signed a contract." I've got the sheet of paper tucked in a drawer in the kitchen for safekeeping.

"Is that binding, though?"

"I think so. Any contract is technically binding as long as both parties agree to it."

"Both of you are thinking about this too much," Izzy says. "Hot Lawn Mower Guy agreed to this because he obviously wants to sleep with Delia." It's a typical Izzy response. I shake my head, despite the fact that she can't see me. If only she heard the way Tanner tore into me the other day. Then she wouldn't harbor any ideas about him being interested in me.

"Trust me," I reply, "he doesn't. I've only spoken to the guy, like, three times, but he's made it abundantly clear he doesn't think very highly of me."

"Hating you and wanting to sleep with you aren't mutually exclusive," Izzy argues.

"You see, that's the sort of thinking that needs to be dissected in a therapist's office," I say as I step down from the stool. A wave of dust flies off the top of the shoebox, making my eyes water. I move the box to one arm, using the other to wave away the dust cloud. "We're not in second grade, Iz. He's not pulling my hair to get my attention."

"Del, that's *exactly* what he's doing. You can judge me all you want, but it's the truth. No one in their right mind would volunteer to do hours of unpaid labor for a stranger unless they were attracted to them."

"Maybe Tanner's not in his right mind," Morgan suggests. "Delia found him mowing Grandma Aggie's lawn, remember?"

"Who cares? He's hot, and he's interested in Delia. That sounds like the perfect hookup to me."

"You saw him for ten seconds on a blurry FaceTime call," I remind her. "You don't know that he's hot." He is. Obnoxiously so. But Izzy doesn't need to know that when she's already advocating for me to sleep with him.

"Google is a thing, you know. I searched for Ryan & Son Construction while you were talking. Found a picture of him on the company website. He's gorgeous. So is his dad, by the way. Are you looking for an older guy? Because I'd totally be supportive of that, too." I'm not dignifying the last comment with a response.

Without a word, I exit Grandma Aggie's bedroom and take the stairs down to the main level of the house, my grandmother's old shoebox hanging loosely at my side. I walk into the kitchen and set the box on the counter.

"Don't listen to anything Izzy just said," Morgan tells me. "Tanner sounds like a jerk. Plus, he's working for you now. It would be messy."

Izzy lets out an annoyed huff. "You're a buzzkill, Morgan."

"I'm looking out for Delia's best interests."

"No, if you were looking out for Delia's best interests, you would tell her to call Hot Lawn Mower guy right now and offer to ride his—"

"Oh my god," I interject. "Please do not finish that sentence."

"What? I was going to say lawn mower. You're the one having dirty thoughts."

"I'm not having any thoughts about this. I'm not hooking up with Tanner."

"Not with that attitude."

"I'm not interested in him," I insist, cocking my hip against the counter. "I'm not interested in anyone. Between work and the house, I've got enough going on right now." Hooking up with Tanner would only add to my already elevated stress levels. I don't want to make my life more complicated.

"Well, then I've got some good news for you," Izzy says. "You won't be alone for much longer. I just booked a flight to Boston. I'll be there next week."

"Seriously? I thought you were too swamped at work."

"I explained the situation to my boss. He agreed to let me work remotely for a few weeks so I could help you deal with the house."

A smile lifts the corners of my lips. Being alone at Grandma Aggie's place over the last few days has been strange and isolating. Having even one of my sisters there will make things infinitely better.

Morgan sighs disappointedly. "I wish I could be there, too. I've still got three weeks left in the semester."

I dismiss her concern. "Don't worry about it. Having Izzy here will be a big help. Focus on your classes. There will be plenty of work left for you when the semester ends."

"Yeah, Morg," Izzy agrees. "There will be plenty of Grandma Aggie's shit left for you to move."

We talk for a few minutes about the details of Izzy's flight. When I look at the clock on the stove and see it's almost six, I tell my sisters I have to go. "Tanner's supposed to be here any minute to take measurements."

"Give him a warm greeting for me," Izzy says.

"Goodbye," I say flatly before ending the call.

Alone with my thoughts, I slip my phone into my back pocket and direct my focus to the box from Grandma Aggie's closet. I spent the last hour pulling jackets and dresses off hangers and shoeboxes off the top shelf. Figuring it would be more efficient to sort everything at once, I brought the items down to the kitchen. Long dresses that reek like mothballs and bright blazers with shoulder pads have turned the table into an exhibit for the worst fashion trends of the last century. Boxes cover most of the counter.

I've got my work cut out for me. The only consolation is that I'm standing next to the garbage can. At least I won't have to move far to throw Grandma Aggie's junk away.

I open the first box, expecting to find dusty shoes or old vinyl records tucked inside. Instead, the small package is stuffed with trophies. Confusion swarms my thoughts. I don't recall any stories about my grandmother's athletic pursuits. Am I missing a piece of her history? Was

Grandma Aggie a world-class shuffleboard player?

I grab a tarnished gold trophy shaped like a cup off the top of the pile and read the inscription at the base. *Second Place. Keith Forrest. Seaview High School.* My stomach twists. Quickly, I take the remaining trophies out of the box, checking the inscriptions as I go. I'm shocked beyond words when I realize all of them belonged to my father.

I knew Dad ran track in high school. He took fourth place in the state tournament his senior year in the boys' one-hundred meter sprint. Mom has the trophy on display in her basement. It doesn't surprise me that Dad won other races. What I can't understand is why Grandma Aggie kept these trophies.

I assumed she scrubbed the place of my dad's existence. I haven't seen any photos of him displayed anywhere, and I know there used to be a framed picture of Dad and my grandfather hanging over the fireplace in the living room. When I was little, Grandma Aggie told me it was her favorite photo. If she was willing to take *that* down, why would she keep Dad's trophies?

I'm still staring at the trophies when a thud comes from the back porch, startling me enough that I drop the trophy in my hand. It hits the side of the counter in its descent and then clatters against the tile floor.

"Shit," I whisper, clutching my chest. My heart booms like a freight train. I scurry over to the sliding glass door to look for the source of the commotion. Annoyance replaces my nerves when Tanner appears in my line of sight. He's standing on the porch with his broad shoulders facing me, holding a long yellow tape measure.

I shove the sliding glass door open and step outside. "What are you doing?" I exclaim, my voice filled with every ounce of frustration I feel.

Tanner turns, shooting me a confused look. "Taking measurements." He checks the watch on his wrist. "This is the time I said I'd be here, isn't it?"

"Well, yes. But I expected you to use the front door. Like a normal person."

"I didn't know you wanted to see me that badly. My apologies."

God, is he capable of saying anything that doesn't make me want to punch him in the face? "There's a doorbell for a reason. You scared the shit out of me!"

"I didn't realize you scared so easily."

There's the answer to my question. "Are you actually trying to argue that I'm in the wrong for telling you how to come and go from my property?"

Tanner shakes his head. "Of course not. You can make any rules you'd like, darling." Something murderous takes over me when he calls me that. It's like he wants his head on a serving platter.

"Do *not* call me that."

He appears undeterred as he slides the tape measure into the pocket of his gray cargo shorts. "You can always find something to call me," he says. "Even the scales."

"Oh, there are a lot of things I'd like to call you. But I think they'd be considered employee harassment now that you technically work for me."

Tanner tucks his arms into his chest and lifts his chin in challenge. "I can take it. Give me your worst, *darling*."

I almost do. A barrage of insults instantly forms on my tongue. But then, Izzy's words echo in my brain, a brutal but necessary reminder. *Hating you and wanting to sleep with you aren't mutually exclusive.*

Is that what Tanner thinks this is? Is verbal sparring his idea of foreplay? I told Izzy and Morgan I had no interest in hooking up with him, and I meant it. But I don't know what's going on in his mind. Maybe Izzy's right, and Tanner expects this bickering to lead him to my bed. If that's the case, I need to make myself clear. Under no circumstances will I be sleeping with him.

I clear my throat and straighten my shoulders, putting on the most professional front I can manage. "I've got a lot to do tonight," I say. "Do you want to come inside and take measurements or not?"

Tanner frowns. "Of course. Wouldn't want to waste any of your time." He sidesteps me and enters the house. A wave of woodsy aftershave hits my nostrils as he passes. I trail him into the kitchen, shutting the door behind me.

As Tanner heads toward the stairs, I ask, "Do you need help with anything?"

He studies me over his shoulder. "I think I can manage," he replies as he rounds the corner to the staircase.

I start combing through Grandma Aggie's belongings again the second I hear Tanner's footsteps upstairs. I repack Dad's trophies and write "keep" on the side of the box in thick black letters. I'll bring these over to Mom's place next time I visit. She'll be thrilled.

Once I take care of the trophies, I sort through my grandmother's clothes. Most items end up in a box to be donated, but I save a couple of neutral cardigans for Morgan and a floral sundress for Izzy. Nothing from Grandma Aggie's wardrobe fits my personal taste, but I think my sisters would like a few things.

I'm still going through clothes when Tanner returns. He steps into the kitchen as I drop a pale pink dress with puffy sleeves in the donation box.

"I got everything I needed for now," he says. "You gonna be here tomorrow night?"

"Yeah. I'll be here all day."

"I'll be back tomorrow with a friend of mine. He's gonna help me move the furniture so I can take out the carpets. Which bedroom are you sleeping in?"

"The guest room."

"I'll start with Aggie's room then. You'll have to find somewhere else to sleep when it comes time for me to work in the guest room. I can't have a bunch of stuff lying around when I'm tearing out carpet and staining wood."

"That's fine." Although it won't be pleasant, I'll survive a few nights of sleeping in Grandma Aggie's old bedroom. "Should we figure out a schedule for when you'll be coming by? I know you said it would probably be in the evenings, but it would help me to have some sort of idea of when to expect you." I'd rather not have Tanner

scare the shit out of me by showing up on the back
porch on random nights of the week.

"I'm not sure I can do that," he says. "I don't
work set hours. It all depends on what's going on.
We'll have to take it day-by-day. See when I'm
available." Day-by-day might be the single worst
phrase in the English language. I don't do things
day-by-day. I like to have them planned,
organized. The thought of waiting on the whims
of Tanner is enough to make my eye twitch. My
displeasure must be obvious.

"Is that a problem?" he asks.

I shake my head. "No, of course not." I'm not
in a position to argue—he's doing all of this work
for free. Still, that doesn't erase the growing
sickness in my stomach. "I just…like to plan
things. But it'll be fine."

The assessing look he gives me makes me
squirm. "Right. Well, I'll try to keep you posted.
Wouldn't want to disturb you and your plans." His
voice drips of condescension—it makes me want
to scream.

"Thanks. Your consideration means a lot," I
mutter dryly.

Tanner chuckles to himself. "I'll get out of
your hair for now."

"Hang on." Skirting around the kitchen island,
I snatch a slip of paper from beneath a magnet on
the fridge and then hand it to Tanner. "It's a copy
of our contract," I explain as he studies the paper.
"I thought it was only fair you have one."

His brow arches. "Because I need some way to
keep track of this very official business
arrangement?"

"You know, you don't have to act like a jackass at every given moment."

"I'll keep it somewhere safe." He folds the sheet of paper once, then slides it into his pocket. His green eyes shift toward the front door. "I'll grab measurements on the front porch on my way out. If that's all right with you."

"Yeah, that's fine."

"Good. I wouldn't want to scare you again. Now that I know how delicate you can be." He grins at my annoyed expression and then starts toward the door.

"Have a good night, Delia," he shouts as he lets himself out.

Twelve

Tanner

I'm sitting on my front porch steps when Jacob's gray sedan pulls up the driveway. I see his puzzled look through the dark windshield. He cuts the engine and climbs out of the car, hands stuffed in his pockets as he makes his way toward the porch.

"You're greeting me on the porch now? I'm touched. Though I'm not sure what I've done to deserve the honor," he says.

I rise to my feet, dusting my palms on the legs of my jeans. "It's not what you've done," I tell him, "but what you're gonna do. I need your help moving furniture for a client."

He raises a brow. "So we're not watching the game?"

Earlier this afternoon, I texted Jacob, inviting him to watch the Red Sox game at my place, but that wasn't the real reason I asked him to come over. I need his help getting furniture out of Aggie Forrest's old bedroom.

I didn't need to lie. Jacob's a loyal friend. Always has been. He once spent a weekend helping me tile a client's kitchen after I realized I had forgotten to assign the job, and no one on my crew was available. Jacob would've shown up tonight, no matter what.

The problem is, I haven't told him I offered to renovate the house for Delia. The last he heard, I couldn't stand Aggie's snobby granddaughter. He's going to have a field day when he finds out I volunteered to fix up her grandmother's place for free. I lied because I wanted to stave off his curiosity for as long as possible. It seems my time has run out.

"It's only a few pieces of furniture," I reply. "We'll put on the game after we're finished. It shouldn't take more than fifteen minutes."

Jacob nods, though he looks skeptical. He's probably wondering why I didn't ask someone from work to help me move the furniture. "All right," he says. "Should we take your truck, or do you want me to drive?"

"Neither. The house is right over there." I motion vaguely toward my backyard, hoping Jacob won't make the connection, but his eyes narrow, then widen like dinner plates.

"Isn't that Aggie Forrest's old place?" he asks.

"Yup."

"You're working for Aggie Forrest's granddaughter?"

"Yup."

"You said you couldn't stand her."

I shrug, hoping my dismissive attitude will diminish his interest. "She hired Ryan & Son to do a few renovations. I wasn't gonna turn down work just because she's a pain in the ass."

Jacob cocks his head to the side, seemingly unconvinced. "So why didn't you have someone else do it?" he asks. "It's your company, Tanner.

You don't have to be involved with every project."

I grit my teeth to hide my irritation. I was hoping he wouldn't ask that. Now I have no choice but to come clean. "I have to do this one myself."

"Why?"

"Because I'm not charging her any labor costs."

My friend laughs. "You can't be serious."

"It's a long story."

"You're renovating a stranger's house for *free*," Jacob says, shaking his head in disapproval. "I don't think there's any story that can make sense of that."

"Not free. Delia's paying for the supplies." It's a weak argument, and it doesn't change the fact that I've agreed to a job that's going to be nothing but an unnecessary headache. I barely have time to keep up with my *paid* work. The last thing I need to take on is an unpaid renovation project. But I had to do something to make things right with Delia. Fixing up her grandmother's place was the first idea that came to mind.

When I saw her later at Ralph's Diner, I made my move. Looking back, it probably would've been wiser to offer to do the renovation work for half the cost. At least I would've made something off it. But it's hard for me to keep my mouth shut when I'm around Delia. It's like the filter between my brain and my mouth switches off, and every half-baked thought pours out of me.

It's how I got myself into this mess in the first place. I don't know what causes it, but I need to put a stop to it before it lands me in even more trouble. Nevertheless, I'm a man of my word. I agreed to the terms of Delia's deal. I'm going to follow through with them.

"It isn't that much work," I insist to an unimpressed-looking Jacob. "It won't take more than a few weeks. Besides, Delia isn't gonna sell the place until it's renovated. The sooner it's done, the sooner she's gone." I need Delia Forrest out of Seaview for my own sake. I can't have a woman who makes the most ill-conceived shit come out of my mouth live by me. Who knows what I'll say next? I'll probably insult her, then offer to build her a new house.

Jacob folds his arms against his chest. "That's what you expect me to believe? That you're doing this so you can get rid of her?"

"I don't care what you believe. It's the truth."

A grin tips up his lips. "Is she pretty, Tanner?"

I flip him off as I start down the driveway. "Fuck off."

Jacob laughs all the way to Aggie Forrest's house.

Delia promptly answers the door after I ring the bell. She's wearing a cropped tank top that hugs her chest like a second skin and a pair of black leggings. She has on some kind of lip gloss that makes her pink lips look soft and shiny.

I try my hardest not to stare. Delia's hot. There's no denying it. But getting involved with her would be a disaster of epic proportions. I might've judged her too harshly the first time we met, but she's still a pain in the ass. Plus, I don't have time for women. As much as my body wants to get inside those skin-tight leggings, my head knows it's a bad idea.

Still, that doesn't stop me from messing with her.

"Your trained monkey has arrived," I say, shooting her a cocky grin. Delia looks like she wants to throttle me, and I haven't even stepped through the door yet.

"You used the door this time," she observes. "Good to know you're capable of following basic instructions."

"They're pretty hard to miss when you're shouting them in that shrill voice of yours."

Her eyes narrow. "My voice isn't shrill." She's right, but I'm more interested in annoying her than being honest. She's pretty when she's flustered.

"My bad. Must've been a bird squawking in the backyard then." I can practically see the smoke coming out of Delia's ears.

"You probably know all about bird sounds. When was the last time you interacted with something that didn't fly or walk on four legs?"

A laugh slices through the air, but it doesn't belong to me or Delia. I glance over my shoulder to find Jacob fighting back a smile.

"Sorry," he says, pressing a hand to his mouth.

I ignore him, turning my attention back to Delia. "This is my friend, Jacob Howell," I explain, gesturing to the laughing dipshit behind me. "Jacob, this is Aggie's granddaughter, Delia Forrest." I move slightly so Jacob can step up to the door.

Delia gives him a friendly smile. "It's nice to meet you."

Jacob smiles back. "Likewise."

"Thanks for coming to help. I appreciate it."

Because I'm an asshole, I say, "So *that's* what you sound like when you're being polite."

She doesn't react to my words. "Do you want to come inside?" she asks, looking directly at Jacob. She steps out of the doorway, making room for us to walk inside.

The first thing I notice when I enter the house is that the foyer is a lot cleaner than it was the other day. Gone are the saggy cardboard boxes that littered the floor and the old mothball smell that stunk up the air. I'm impressed. Delia wasn't kidding when she said she wanted to get this done quickly.

I shift my eyes toward the narrow staircase that leads to the second floor. Getting furniture down those stairs is a pain I'd like to avoid. "Is it all right if we leave the furniture on the upstairs landing?" I ask. "We'll make sure it doesn't block any doorways."

"Fine by me," Delia replies. "I cleaned out my grandmother's room. The furniture is all that's left."

I lock eyes with Jacob, then gesture toward the stairs. "Great. We'll be back down in a few minutes."

"Wait," Delia calls out. "Do you need another set of hands?"

Surprise filters over me. Is she offering to help us? "Why? You got a friend here or something?" That comment puts me on the receiving end of a well-deserved death glare.

"I meant me," she clarifies.

"You want to help us move furniture?"

"Yeah. Why not?"

It's not that I don't think she's capable. Delia seems strong, competent. But based on her smooth hands and shiny fingernails, she also seems like the type to avoid hard labor. I didn't expect her to offer up her help. "No reason."

"Help would be great, Delia," Jacob interjects. I glower at him, but he pretends not to notice. "I'm assuming you don't work in construction."

"No, I'm in marketing."

"Well, I'm an actuary," Jacob says. "Together, we might form one competent mover."

Delia laughs. It's a soft, ringing sound that makes me think of the wind chimes in my mom's backyard. "I hope so," she says. "Otherwise, I think the vein in your friend's forehead might pop."

Jacob scoffs at the idea. "That thing's been looking like that for years. We've got nothing to worry about." They share a laugh at my expense. My fists curl into balls at my sides. I can't tell if I'm more annoyed with Delia for teasing me or Jacob for making her laugh.

"You finished?" Their laughter quiets as we head upstairs. We follow the short hallway to Aggie's bedroom, which is empty aside from the bed and dresser. The emptiness draws attention to the dirty walls and the dingy carpet that appears to be covered in some kind of animal fur.

"Did Aggie have a cat?" I ask.

"A long time ago, I think," Delia says. "It died before I was born." That must've been the last time Aggie ran a vacuum in here. Although she seemed like a nice woman, I can admit she treated her place like a dumpster.

"Let's start with the mattress," I say, maneuvering around the bed frame. Taking one side of the mattress, I instruct Jacob and Delia to each take a corner of the other. I count to three and then we lift the mattress off the bed frame. It's not heavy. We tip the mattress on its side so we can slide it through the doorway, then lean it against the wall on the landing.

Afterward, we head back to the bedroom and make quick work of the metal bed frame. That leaves the dresser. It won't be as easy to move. It's bulky and wooden. Probably weighs a couple hundred pounds. It's also a piece of junk. Several drawers are missing handles, and there's a notable crack in the surface.

I turn to Delia. "You wanna keep this thing?"

She gives me a funny look. "Yeah. I'm not buying new furniture for this place."

"You sure? It'd probably make for decent scrap wood."

"I'm not getting rid of it."

"I'm just saying it's not—"

"You'll have to excuse Tanner," Jacob says. He hits me with a look that screams *Can you please stop being an asshole for five seconds*? He smiles at Delia. "Making furniture has given him a superiority complex. He's been telling me to get rid of my coffee table for years."

"That's because your coffee table is a piece of shit," I mutter.

"See?" Jacob says. "He just can't help himself."

Curiosity fills Delia's brown eyes. "You make furniture?"

"Woodworking," I say crisply, hoping my one-word answer makes it obvious that I'm not interested in talking about my hobbies. Fortunately, Delia takes the hint.

Jacob eyes the dresser. "Any idea how to go about this, Tanner?"

"We can slide it instead of lifting. Jacob, you and I will push from the back. Delia, you'll take the front end."

She blinks. "You want me to walk backwards?"

"Sure do. I'll try to make sure you don't hit a wall."

"Gee. Thanks."

We gather around the dresser, with Delia on the end by the door and me and Jacob taking the end closest to the window. Then, we start pushing the dresser across the carpet. It's a lot heavier than the mattress, so it takes more effort to move, even a short distance.

As we push the dresser into the hall, Jacob and Delia voice their displeasure.

"Can we stop for a second?" Jacob asks in a strained voice.

"Yes, please," Delia agrees.

"We've only got a few more feet," I tell them.

Delia glares at me. "Do you want to do this by yourself?"

"There's that shrillness I was talking about earlier."

She releases her side of the dresser immediately. Luckily, I'm expecting it. We pause for several seconds so Delia and Jacob can collect themselves, then we finally lug the dresser into an open space on the landing. When we're finished, we head back downstairs.

Delia stands by the front door, wringing her hands. "Thanks again for your help."

Jacob nods. "Of course. Happy to do it."

"Do either of you want to stay for a beer?" she asks, shocking me with the invitation. From the uncertain look on her face, it seems like she shocked herself, too.

"I wish I could, but I've got plans tonight," Jacob says, despite his "plans" consisting of watching baseball at my place. "But I'm sure Tanner would love to. He's got nothing going on tonight."

Delia's attention zips to me. I'm at a loss for words. I planned on turning her down. Helping with the house is one thing, but spending time with a woman I find attractive when I've already decided she's off limits seems like a terrible idea. Thanks to Jacob's prying, I don't know how I can reject her offer without coming across like a prick.

"What kind of beer do you have? It's not some weird fancy shit, is it?"

"It's normal beer from the grocery store, Tanner."

It's the way she says my name that gets me. I haven't heard her say it before. I like the sound too much. It's why I have no control over the next words that come out of my mouth.

"Why not?"

She bobs her head. "Great. I'll grab a couple of beers from the fridge. We can drink them on the porch." She leaves the room, and I'm prepared to rip into Jacob, but he's already halfway out the door.

"You're welcome," he says, laughing to himself as he leaves.

Thirteen

Delia

What have I gotten myself into?

That's the question swimming in my head as I step onto the back porch with two cold beer bottles dripping in my hands. I find Tanner sitting atop the picnic table, his worn-out boots resting on the bench. He glances over his shoulder as I shut the sliding glass door behind me. I walk toward him, handing him a beer as I take a seat beside him on the table.

We drink for several minutes without saying a word. The sounds of chirping birds and rustling leaves spare us from total silence.

Oh my god.

What have I gotten myself into?

I don't know why I asked Tanner and Jacob to stay for a drink. It was a mistake. A temporary lapse in judgment. After we finished lugging the furniture out of Grandma Aggie's room, it occurred to me that these guys had given up part of their night to help a virtual stranger. I wanted to thank them. Offering them beer seemed like the best way to go. I didn't know if they would actually say yes, but I expected them to come to a decision *together*. I never thought the night would end with me and Tanner drinking alone.

What are we supposed to say to each other? We're always bickering. We can't make small talk. I wish I would've thought this through. Who knows how long it'll take Tanner to finish his drink? We could be here for twenty or thirty minutes. I don't think I can handle the awkward silence for that long.

Pull it together, I tell myself. This was my idea. I need to say something. Taking a swig of my beer, I rack my brain for conversation starters. *C'mon, Delia. Think.*

Tanner beats me to the punch.

"So, marketing," he says.

I pause mid-sip. "What?"

"That's what you do, isn't it? It's what you said earlier."

"Oh, yeah." For a second, I forgot Jacob asked me what I do for a living. "I work in digital marketing. I mostly deal with small businesses that want to enhance their online presence. You'd be surprised how many companies haven't updated their websites since the turn of the millennium." A couple of months ago, I worked on a campaign for an engineering firm that had a landing page that said "Coming Soon—Fall 2003."

Tanner frowns. "How often does a company's website need to change?"

"To keep it modern? At least every few years. But it's also important to update a website when there are major changes within a company. Leadership adjustments. New services. That kind of thing."

"Well, there's another thing I need to look into," he mutters, sipping his beer.

"You haven't updated your website in a while?"

"Haven't been on it in ages," he says. "Our business is mostly local. We've been in the community for a long time. People know us."

"Your website's not too bad," I tell him. "That's how I got the company phone number."

Tanner chuckles. "You're probably the first customer to find us online."

"Technically, I didn't find you online. Annabella at Ralph's Diner recommended you."

"So *that's* who I have to thank for this."

I roll my eyes, unaffected by the insult. "You should be happy she recommended your business. How else are you gonna find new customers if you don't update your website? Advertise on the back of milk cartons? Hand out flyers in the town square?"

"I'm not sure you're the type of customer we're looking for, darling," he says. "You're not exactly paying us."

"I was going to pay you. You offered to do the work for free. Don't blame me for your poor business acumen."

Tanner shakes his head. "So, did you have to take off work to deal with the house?"

"No, I work remotely." Still, Grandma Aggie's house threw a wrench—no, an entire tool box— into my life. I can't imagine what I would have done if I couldn't work from home. I probably would've had to take a leave of absence.

Curiosity flickers in Tanner's eyes. "You said Aggie left the house to you and your sisters. Why are you the only one here?"

"My sisters' schedules aren't as flexible as mine," I explain. "I offered to take care of things myself."

"Seems like a lot for one person."

I rest the beer bottle on my knee. "It is what it is. Someone had to do something."

"And that someone happened to be you?"

"I'm the oldest. Plus, I'm a planner. It made the most sense."

Tanner smirks over the lip of his beer. "That doesn't surprise me."

"What? Me being the oldest?"

"No, you being a planner," he clarifies. "I bet you keep color-coded binders or some shit."

"There's nothing wrong with being organized," I argue, hating that his assumption isn't far off base. "Besides, I don't have to justify myself to you. You're a judgmental ass."

"I'm not denying that. But I wasn't judging you."

"You're joking, right? You've been judging me since I got here. My clothes. My ability to move furniture. My beer selection."

"In my defense, I'm a prick, and you're easy to rile up."

"*That's* your defense?"

Amusement washes over Tanner's features. He says nothing, but I can hear his thoughts loud and clear. *Yeah, and you're kind of proving it right now.*

Shoving aside my annoyance, I decide to change the subject. "What about you?" I ask. "How long have you been working in construction?"

"Pretty much my whole life," Tanner replies. "My dad founded the company twenty-five years ago. I started coming to job sites with him when I was a teenager." Is that legal? A construction site doesn't seem like a suitable environment for a teenager. I shudder at the mental image of a prepubescent Tanner hammering on a rooftop.

"So you always knew what you wanted to do."

Tanner nods. "Got my degree in construction management and then took over Ryan & Son about three years ago."

"And you make furniture in your spare time." It surprised me when Jacob said that Tanner builds his own furniture. I can't imagine many guys in their early thirties would say their hobby is woodworking.

"Jacob doesn't know how to keep his mouth shut," Tanner grumbles.

"He seems nice," I say. "How long have you known each other?"

"Since we were kids. We basically grew up together."

I let out a small laugh. "That explains it." Seeing the confusion on Tanner's face, I elaborate. "I wondered why a seemingly nice person would be friends with you. Childhood obligation makes sense."

Tanner narrows his eyes. "A friend is someone who likes spending time with you."

"I'm familiar with the concept."

"I wasn't sure," he says. "You act like you hate me, then you invite me for a beer. Seems like you might be desperate for companionship."

I meet his challenging gaze with my own. "It's not an act, and you were desperate enough to accept the invitation."

"How could I not? Our conversations are always so stimulating."

Without a word, I lift my beer to my mouth, taking a long drink. Silence sweeps over us once again, but it feels comfortable this time instead of awkward.

A couple of minutes later, Tanner polishes off his beer. He steps down from the picnic table, the empty bottle dangling at his side.

He raises a brow. "You gonna be around tomorrow?" he asks.

I nod. Tomorrow's Saturday. Although I won't be working, I've got plenty of cleaning to do. My weekend will probably consist of emptying cardboard boxes and eating takeout by myself. It's a very depressing mental image. I take a bit of comfort in the knowledge that Izzy will be here next week.

"I've got nothing going on in the morning," Tanner says. "How about I come over around eleven to start working on that carpet?"

"Actually, I'm painting the bedroom tomorrow." I'm planning to hit the hardware store first thing in the morning. Grandma Aggie's dingy walls desperately need a fresh coat of paint. I've never painted a room before, but I watched a few tutorials online last night. It seems pretty straightforward.

"You're doing that by yourself?" Tanner sounds skeptical, and it's hard to hide my annoyance. I know he doesn't have the greatest opinion of me, but does he seriously think I'm incapable of putting paint on a few walls?

"I am," I say. "And you can keep whatever joke you're about to make about me being incompetent to yourself."

To my surprise, he doesn't return my hostile tone. "What time were you gonna get started?"

"I'm going to the hardware store for supplies when it opens in the morning. I'm planning to start as soon as I get back."

He taps his chin. "How does ten sound?"

What? "You want to help me paint?"

"It'll be quicker with two people, won't it?"

I'm baffled, truly. What is this guy's deal? One minute he insults me, the next he volunteers to do me exceedingly generous favors. "You don't have to do that." Tanner and I are not friends. We're not even friendly. I don't understand his motivations, and I'm starting to feel guilty about his continued niceness. What's he getting out of this? It seems like he's deliberately putting himself on the bad side of a deal. "I'll be fine on my own."

Tanner sighs as if I'm being ridiculous. "I'm not doing it for you," he says. "I don't want to be stuck looking at your crappy paint job for the next few days."

So much for him being nice.

"Ten works for me," I tell him.

"Good. Then I'll see you tomorrow." Tanner throws his beer bottle in the recycling bin on the porch, then lobs a grin at me. "Pleasure, as always." He heads down the steps toward his yard, leaving me no choice but to watch as he disappears from my line of sight.

Fourteen

Delia

The next morning, I wake up early and go for a sunrise run on the beach. When I get back to the house an hour later, I take a quick shower and put on fresh clothes. By the time I finish drying my hair, it's around seven. Perfect. Seaview Hardware just opened. Grabbing my keys, I head out the door, climb into my car, and put on directions for the hardware store.

After a few minutes of coasting along the town's sleepy roads, I reach a quaint blue building with a sparsely-filled parking lot and a sign that says "Seaview Hardware" in bold script. My phone chimes right as I park. I fish through the loose change and tubes of lipstick at the bottom of my bag until I get my hands around the phone. A text from Mariah awaits.

Mariah: I hate that you're not here this weekend.

I smile to myself. Kali, Mariah, and I have texted here and there over the last few days, but we haven't spoken much.

Delia: Me too. But the house is a mess. I don't think I'll be home any time soon.

Mariah: You're kidding.

Mariah: We need you back for Friday night drinks.

Sadness tugs at my gut. Last night was the first Friday I didn't spend with my friends in as long as I can remember. I miss them, and I hate that I don't know when I'll see them next.

Delia: I'll be back as soon as I can.

Mariah: You better. Call me when you have time. I miss you!!!!!

I slip the phone back in my purse, batting away the feelings of homesickness before they have a chance to take root, and step out of the car. The hardware store's automatic doors slide open as I approach.

I walk inside. The air feels cold and smells like wood. Large fluorescent lights run the length of the high ceiling. I scan the signs hanging above the end caps of each aisle. Hardware. Electrical. Bath. Finally, paint.

As I head down the paint aisle, I see shelves filled with swatches of every color of the rainbow. I gravitate toward the neutrals. I'm scouring the paint samples when someone with a soft voice says, "Excuse me," and gently taps me on the shoulder. It's a small, non-threatening touch, but it still startles me. My heartbeat jumps, and the sample in my hand slips out of my grasp, fluttering to the concrete floor.

An old woman stands beside me. She has chin-length hair and wears bright red lipstick on her thin lips. She gives me an apologetic smile. "I'm sorry," she says. "I didn't mean to disturb you."

"Don't worry about it," I tell her. Swooping to my knees, I snatch the paint sample off the ground and return it to its place on the shelf. "Is there something I can help you with?"

"Are you by chance related to Aggie Forrest?" she asks.

"Um, yes. I'm her granddaughter."

The woman claps her hands with enthusiasm. "That's what I thought!" she exclaims. "You look just like her." This is the second time someone has told me that. How much of a resemblance could there really be?

The woman thrusts out a hand. "My name is Nancy Orson," she says. "I'm an old friend of Aggie's. We were on the board of the Seaview Historical Society together for twenty years before Aggie stepped down last fall." I had no idea Grandma Aggie was part of the town's historical society, but it makes sense, given everything I know about her. She loved Seaview. Naturally, she'd want to preserve and document its history.

Feeling slightly dazed, I shake hands with Nancy and introduce myself. "It's nice to meet you. I'm Delia."

"I'm sorry about Aggie's passing."

I don't know how to respond to her condolences. *You knew her better than I did* feels like the wrong approach. "Thank you."

"Are you in town to deal with her belongings?"

I nod. "Aggie left her house to me and my sisters. We're planning to sell, but there's a lot of stuff to pack up before we can get to that point."

Nancy laughs wistfully. "That's Aggie for you. She had a hard time letting go of things."

Everything but her family, I think darkly.

"Anyway, I'm glad we bumped into each other. I'm putting together a book on Seaview's history.

I was going through some pictures from past historical society events, and I found a few of your grandmother. I'd love to show them to you if you ever have time."

I'm speechless for a moment. Obviously, I want to say no. I meant nothing to Grandma Aggie. I don't want to waste time looking at photos of her and hearing stories about her life, the one she chose to live without her family. But I can't tell Nancy that. She called herself an old friend of Grandma Aggie's. I would look pretty heartless if I said I had no interest in learning about my grandmother's past.

So I lie through my teeth. "That sounds great."

Nancy looks delighted. "Wonderful." She reaches into her purse, pulling out a laminated business card that she then hands to me. *Nancy Orson, president, Seaview Historical Society.* "That has my number on it. Call anytime, and we can arrange a day for you to come by the historical society."

I drop the business card into my bag with no plans of using it. "Sounds like a plan."

Nancy places a delicate hand on my forearm. "Aggie would be so happy to see her granddaughter there," she says. "She talked about you girls all the time."

I try not to let the surprise show on my face. Grandma Aggie didn't have a relationship with anyone from my family. Did she tell people she did? Why would she lie about that? My best guess is that Grandma Aggie didn't want her friends to know the truth. Maybe that's why she left me, Morgan, and Izzy the house. She wanted to keep up appearances, even in death.

It's a sobering thought.
Grandma Aggie manages to disappoint me, even when she's gone.

Fifteen

Delia

A knock at the door comes sometime midmorning. Crossing through the kitchen, I open the front door and find Tanner waiting on the porch. He steps inside, giving me a strange look as he crosses the threshold.

"What?" I say defensively, my skin warming under the heat of his gaze. Is there something on my face? I shoveled down a bagel with cream cheese for breakfast. Have I been walking around with breadcrumbs on my lips?

He shakes his head. "Nothing," he says. "I'm just surprised you own anything you're comfortable getting paint on. Figured you'd have on one of those plastic ponchos that people wear at amusement parks when it rains."

I give my outfit a quick assessment. I didn't think too much of it this morning, throwing on a pair of black leggings and a baggy Boston Marathon T-shirt that I knotted at my waist with a ponytail holder. It seemed like the perfect thing to wear for a day of painting. Leave it to Tanner to find something wrong.

"The store was out of ponchos," I reply. "I thought about asking you if I could borrow something, since there's obviously nothing in your closet that can't get paint on it, but I managed to find something myself."

My eyes wander over Tanner. He's dressed in blue jeans and an olive green crew neck that outlines his strong arms. The color complements the light-green shade of his eyes. He decided to forgo his usual ball cap today. His dark hair appears slightly damp at the ends, loose strands curling over his forehead.

It should be illegal for a guy as insufferable as Tanner to look so good all the time. It's absolutely unfair.

He smirks. "If you want to wear my clothes, all you have to do is ask."

My heart picks up speed, and my breath catches in my throat. My brain—the traitor—chooses that moment to make me aware of how good Tanner smells, a heady mix of soap and pine and something else I can't quite place. His suggestive words, combined with that intoxicating scent, make my brain spiral for a second. I wonder what it would be like to have that scent surrounding me. His skin pressed against my own, and his warm breath on my neck.

Horror slashes through my thoughts like a knife. I can't believe I actually imagined what it would be like to have sex with *Tanner*. Sure, we had a pleasant conversation over beers last night, but that doesn't change the fact that I don't like him. This is Izzy's fault. The idea never would have entered my mind if it weren't for her insisting that Tanner wants to sleep with me. I'm going to kill her. Slowly and brutally.

Clearing the deranged thoughts out of my mind, I say, "I'd rather drop dead."

His smirk widens, as if my hypothetical death is the most amusing concept in the world.

"So," he says, eyes flashing to my T-shirt. "You're a runner."

I resist the urge to tug at my shirt collar by locking my hands behind my back. "Yep."

"When did you run in the Boston Marathon?"

"Oh, this isn't mine," I quickly reply. "It's my ex's."

There. Nothing like the mention of an ex-boyfriend to diffuse the tension in a room. It sucks the ease out of the conversation like a vacuum.

I didn't mean to bring up Austin. It's not like I kept his shirt because I miss him. I found it at the bottom of my laundry hamper a few weeks after our breakup. Wanting to avoid an awkward meetup with my ex, I decided not to give it back. I only wear it because it's comfortable, and I don't own a lot of loungewear.

I stopped associating the shirt with Austin a long time ago. I'm about to clarify that to Tanner when something stops me. What am I doing? I don't need to explain my feelings to Tanner. Nothing is going on between us. Insisting that I'm not hung up on my ex-boyfriend might give Tanner the impression that I'm interested in him. Why else would I clear things up?

Maybe it's for the best if Tanner thinks someone else is in the picture. I don't want him or anyone else (*cough* *cough* Izzy) misconstruing our banter for flirting. Letting Tanner believe I haven't gotten over my ex might be the easiest way to prevent that from happening, even if it hurts my pride.

Tanner clears his throat, his face showing no emotion. "You should check out the trail by Main Street," he says. "It's about three miles. Has great views of the water."

"You run, too?" Tanner's undeniably fit, but I got the sense that his physique came from manual labor, not running or spending time at the gym.

"Occasionally," he says with a shrug. "I haven't run the Boston Marathon, but I can keep up." The jab at Austin's expense doesn't go unnoticed. What's funny is that Austin never ran the marathon. He bought the shirt last year when we watched Mariah in the half-marathon. But mentioning that to Tanner feels like handing him a win, so I keep my mouth shut.

I pull my phone out of the waistband of my leggings, checking the time. "We should be good to start painting," I say. "The directions on the primer said it would take forty-five minutes to dry. It's been about an hour."

"You already put up the primer?"

"I told you I was going to the hardware store this morning."

"I know. I thought—"

"What? That I was incapable of doing it on my own?"

Tanner laughs. "That you would be smart enough to save yourself the hassle. You've still got all this cleaning to do by yourself, darling." He motions aimlessly around the house. "Take the help where you can get it."

"You should be thanking me," I tell him. "We'd be spending a lot more time together if I hadn't done the primer myself."

He looks confident when he says, "I'm sure we would've found a way to pass the time."

Without responding, I head upstairs. Tanner follows. We make our way across the cramped landing, then enter Grandma Aggie's bedroom. It smells strongly of primer. A pile of unopened paint cans sits in the middle of the carpet. Beside the pile rests a small work table covered in paint brushes, rollers, and plastic trays. There's a ladder set up in the back corner.

"Looks like you've got everything we need," Tanner observes.

"What can I say? I'm a regular handyman."

He walks to the center of the room, crouching to pick up a paint can. His brow furrows as he scans the label. "What the fuck is Misty Morning Sky?"

"Blue," I explain. "Gray-blue." My plan to paint the bedroom white or beige went out the window when I found the prettiest shade of blue at the hardware store. It's a subtle color, and it has a beachy sort of vibe that fits perfectly for a house in Seaview.

"Why didn't they just call it that?" Tanner asks. "This flowery bullshit doesn't actually tell you anything about the color."

"It's a description of a color," I point out. "Besides, the paint company makes, like, four different shades of gray-blue. They can't give all of them the same name."

"Gray-Blue One, Gray-Blue Two, Gray-Blue Three…" Tanner lifts his fingers one by one as he lists his absurdly simplistic paint names.

"Maybe they expected their customers to have a little imagination."

He lifts a brow. "They wanted their customers to imagine their house looking like a misty morning sky?"

I groan in frustration. "I don't know. Ask the paint company, not me."

Once Tanner lets go of the paint thing, we grab our rollers and get to work. We start with the back wall. I focus on the lower half while Tanner uses the ladder to reach the spots closer to the ceiling. He shows me a technique that involves painting in the shape of a W and then going back to fill in the empty spaces. It's supposed to help the paint go on evenly.

It doesn't take long for us to fall into a rhythm. As annoying as Tanner can be, he doesn't seem to mess around with work. We paint in silence for a while, the only sound coming from the tiny radio I found in the back of Grandma Aggie's closet. The sound quality isn't very good. It's static mixed with the occasional garbled song.

We finish the first coat around noon, but we need to wait at least four hours before applying the next one, so Tanner heads home for a bit. I fix myself a turkey sandwich and then stuff a bunch of Grandma Aggie's clothes in a garbage bag that I tie up and stick in the trunk of my car. I'm planning to drop the items off at the nearest thrift store tomorrow.

Around four-thirty, Tanner wanders back over, and we resume our painting. We're about halfway through the second coat when my arm starts getting sore. Rather than suffer quietly, I distract myself with conversation. Peeking over my shoulder, I see Tanner painting on the ladder in the left corner of the room.

"So, as a contractor, do you take on any kind of work or do you stick to specific areas?" I ask. "Like, would someone call you if they wanted to put a new roof on their house or increase the size of their kitchen?"

Tanner looks wary. "I hope you're not thinking about either of those things," he says. "My generosity has its limits, darling."

"God, no." I'm not trying to extend my stay in Seaview by adding an unnecessary project. "I'm just trying to understand the scope of what you do." He seems surprised by my interest, but he doesn't question it.

"It depends on the client," he says. "We specialize in home construction and renovation. We do a lot of kitchen and bath remodels, additions, those kinds of things. But we're expanding on the construction side. We recently started on our first oceanfront build."

"Oceanfront? You mean, like, a beach house?"

Tanner nods. "It's our biggest project to date." Wow. I can't believe he's constructing a freaking beach house.

"That seems like a big deal," I say.

"It's a lot of planning and managing. My crew's doing all the real work. I'm in charge of making sure we stay on track and keeping the client happy."

"That sounds a bit like my job. At least the keeping-the-client-happy part. They sure love to give their opinions, even when they don't know what they're talking about."

"I once had a guy ask if he could get a discount on a floor restoration because the floor was already there."

I give a small laugh. "You did not."

"Sure did. I told him he was more than welcome to do it himself."

I laugh again, louder this time. "No offense, but it's hard for me to picture you interacting with a client. You don't exactly strike me as a people person."

"Since when were you worried about offending me? Have the paint fumes gone to your head?" Tanner asks as he climbs down from the ladder.

"Sorry. I forgot you don't understand manners."

Tanner heads toward the work table and then drops his roller on the paint tray, coating it in a fresh layer of gray-blue. "Dealing with people is kind of inevitable in my job," he says.

I wonder what it's like to own a company. To have employees and make decisions that affect people's livelihoods. It must be stressful. Does Tanner enjoy it? Is it a lot of pressure? I'm about to ask when he suddenly reaches for the dial on the radio, turning up the volume.

I take it to mean he's done talking about work.

Forty minutes later, we're done with the second coat of paint. I step back for a moment to admire our handiwork. The walls look clean, refreshed. I'm ready for a hot bath and a large glass of wine, but I've got brushes and rollers and empty paint cans to deal with first.

I stop Tanner as he starts to clean up.

"You can go home," I tell him. "I can take care of the mess myself."

He looks over at me, lifting a finger up to the side of his face. "You've got a little paint right there," he says, rubbing his fingertip over his left cheek.

Reflexively, I scratch the same spot on my own face, but I don't feel any dried paint. When I glance back at Tanner, his eyes shine with amusement. Bastard. I can't believe I fell for that.

"You suck," I say.

He only grins as he gathers up the supplies.

Sixteen

Delia

I spend the next two days working through the boxes in the dining room.

Izzy's scheduled to fly in Friday afternoon, and I want to finish as much work as possible before she gets to town. I love my sister, and I'll be happy to have her here, but she's not the most organized person. I've been making a lot of progress over the past week. I don't want Izzy's arrival to slow me down.

Lucky for me, the dining room doesn't take long to clean. Though the space is cluttered, the boxes mostly contain dishes, glasses, and utensils. I manage to pack everything in bubble wrap, load it in the backseat of my car, and drive it to the thrift store in only a few hours. Then I vacuum the carpet and wipe down the dusty wooden table. The furnishings appear a bit dated, but the room looks much better now. Sunlight pools in from the tall windows, and a metal chandelier hangs over the massive table that dominates the room. It looks like the perfect space for intimate dinner parties and holiday gatherings. Surely, potential buyers will see that.

On Tuesday, I'm catching up on work emails when my phone rings. Seeing my boss's name flash across the screen, I grab it off the table and answer right away. "Hi, Nina."

"Delia, hi. How are you?" she asks in her heavy Boston accent. "Everything going okay at your grandmother's place?" My eyes travel around the kitchen. The house is still a disaster, and my contractor makes me want to tear my eyes out, so okay might be a stretch, but I'm not bogging down Nina with my problems.

"It's coming together. Slowly but surely."

"I'm glad to hear it," Nina says. "Listen, I wanted to give you a heads-up that I just got off a call with the vice president of digital marketing. With my retirement coming up, she wanted to know if I had any recommendations for my replacement. I gave her your name."

My chest feels hollow as I say, "Wow. That's so kind of you, Nina. Thank you."

"Of course. You've been an enormous help to me these last several years, Delia. There's no one better suited for the position. Obviously, you'll have to interview, and the job will be posted online for other candidates to apply, but I made it clear that choosing you would be in the firm's best interest. Don't be surprised if someone contacts you in the next few weeks to schedule an interview."

An interview. For a job I don't want. Sickness spreads through my stomach. I ignore the feeling of dread and thank Nina for the opportunity.

When we end the call a minute later, I set down the phone and begin massaging my temples with my fingers. *This is good. The job is good,* I remind myself. I'm qualified to take on this position. Nina wouldn't have recommended me if I wasn't. It's probably self-doubt dredging up these feelings. Everything will be fine.

I get back to work, but I'm interrupted again a few minutes later by a text.

Unknown number: You home tonight? Jacob and I can get going on the floors.

Surprise and confusion wash over me. Tanner and I never exchanged numbers.

Delia: How did you get this number?

Unknown number: You gave it when you called Ryan & Son.

Unknown number: Is that a yes?

The second message appears only seconds after the first. I roll my eyes at his impatience. If he weren't doing me a massive favor with the renovations, I might wait twenty minutes to respond just to mess with him.

Delia: I'll be here.

Tanner hasn't come by since we painted the bedroom on Saturday. I've caught glimpses of him in his backyard (I'm not stalking him—he lives *right there*), but we haven't spoken since. I'm still surprised by how well we worked together. Part of me expected us to bicker so much that we wouldn't get any painting done, but we finished the work, and the room looks good. It makes me wonder if my first impression of Tanner might've been off-base.

Maybe he's not a total asshole. He's rough around the edges, but he can also be generous. After all, he's helping with the house, and he used to mow Grandma Aggie's lawn for her. If Tanner were really a prick, he wouldn't have done either of those things.

It's around six when Tanner and Jacob show up. I say hello and let them inside, expecting them to head upstairs immediately. But Tanner pauses at the bottom of the stairs, a question in his eyes. "You wanna help? I'm gonna take out the carpet myself, but Jacob's starting on the tile in the bathroom. I'm sure he could use a hand."

"Really?" I ask, surprise evident in my voice. I didn't think Tanner would want my help, let alone ask for it.

He nods. "It's pretty simple—I can show you how to do it. Unless you've got other things to do. In that case, don't worry about it."

"I've got nothing going on tonight." I planned on FaceTiming Izzy and Morgan while Tanner and Jacob worked, but my sisters can wait. "Give me, like, five minutes to change and then I'll be ready."

Running upstairs to the guest bedroom, I swap my blouse and linen shorts for leggings and Austin's old Boston Marathon T-shirt. I throw my dark hair in a ponytail and then walk out of the bedroom and shout for the guys to come upstairs.

Tanner reaches the top of the steps first. He glances briefly at my shirt and then heads inside the small bathroom, Jacob following him. It's a tight fit for the three of us, so I swing myself up on the counter to make space, my legs dangling against the cabinets.

Tanner sets his toolbox on the other side of the counter. Opening the box, he pulls out three pairs of clear plastic goggles. He gives a set to me and Jacob before putting on his own.

I toy with the goggles in my lap for a moment. Tanner stares at me expectantly.

"What?" I ask.

"Your goggles," he says. "Put them on."

"But we haven't even started."

He leans against the wall, arms folded over his chest. "I can't show you how to do this if you aren't wearing the proper safety equipment." He's being ridiculous. I'm sitting a solid three-and-a-half feet off the ground. Tanner would need to hit the tile with the force of a boxer if he wanted debris to get anywhere in my vicinity.

"I wouldn't fight him on this, Delia," Jacob interjects from the opposite side of the bathroom. He's perched on the edge of the bathtub, looking too tall and gangly for the small area. His goggles are already on. "Tanner's a stickler for safety. He won't let anyone near a job site unless they're wearing the right equipment."

My attention swivels back to Tanner, who doesn't look like he's budging. I don't have any real issues with the goggles, so I concede defeat and begrudgingly slip them over my eyes.

"Happy now?" I ask.

Tanner pushes off the wall, a satisfied grin on his face. "Don't you look nice," he says mockingly. "Construction just might suit you."

I hold back the urge to rip the goggles off and fling them at him. "Who knew you'd be such a hardass?" I mutter.

"You see enough guys slice off their fingertips being careless, and you learn a thing or two about safety," Tanner flippantly replies. I can't tell if he's exaggerating, and I don't really want to know, so I don't ask questions.

Tanner shows me and Jacob two methods for removing tile: scraping the grout from around the edges and then prying the piece off the floor or breaking it up by smashing it in the center. He gives us hammers and chisels and makes us demonstrate the different methods. Once he's satisfied with our tile-removing skills, he sets a small dustpan on the counter, reminding us to clean up tile shards as we work so we don't get splinters.

"Try not to injure yourselves," Tanner cautions as he leaves the bathroom. "I don't feel like driving either of you to the hospital tonight."

Once he's gone, Jacob and I exchange looks of mild annoyance.

"Has he always been so charming?" I ask.

"I think it's gotten worse with age," Jacob says. "Yesterday, he was complaining to me about some kids who tore up his tree lawn with their bikes. He's one busted hip away from becoming the Crazy Old Neighbor."

"These walls aren't very thick, you know," Tanner shouts from the other room.

"Don't eavesdrop if you don't want to hear it," Jacob replies.

"You should be working, not talking."

"We're capable of multitasking," I interject.

Tanner mutters something unintelligible in response, causing me and Jacob to share a quiet laugh.

"So, how do you want to do this?" I ask.

"I think the easiest way would be to split the room in half," Jacob says. "You take the front. I'll take the back."

After we establish parameters, we get moving. Grabbing my hammer off the counter, I crouch down and start on my first piece of tile. I use the back of the hammer to scrape the thin lines of grout from around the tile. It takes a few minutes, but once I remove most of the grout, it's easy to pry the tile off the ground. From there, I fall into a steady pattern, tossing discarded tiles in the small wastebasket in the corner of the bathroom.

"Tanner told me you two have basically known each other since birth," I say after a long stretch of silence.

Jacob glances up from the small blue tile he's hammering. "You could say that. Our moms have been best friends for ages. Growing up, I spent almost as much time at Tanner's place as I did my own."

"Is that how he roped you into all of this?" I ask, gesturing wildly around the bathroom. Jacob must be a good friend if he's willing to rip tile out of a stranger's bathroom just because Tanner asked him to. I love Kali and Mariah, but I'd be pissed if they asked me to do manual labor for someone I didn't know.

"Tanner's done a lot of work at my parents' place over the years," Jacob says. "I owe him. Besides, I was curious. It's not every day your friend tells you he volunteered to renovate a neighbor's house. I couldn't figure out if he was screwing with me or if he lost his mind."

"I tried to hire him first," I reply, not wanting Jacob to think I'm manipulating Tanner or exploiting him for his generosity.

"He told me the story," Jacob says. "I can see why he didn't make a great first impression. I would've negotiated for a free kitchen remodel, too."

I smile. "Tanner says he's doing this to protect the value of his property."

Jacob eyes me curiously. "And you believe that?"

"Honestly?" I chuck a piece of tile in the wastebasket. "I think he's doing it to get me out of the neighborhood faster." Tanner joked that one perk of helping me with the house was getting a new neighbor. We have a strange dynamic, but it wouldn't surprise me if his goal is to expedite my stay in Seaview.

"Tanner works a million hours a week," Jacob tells me. "He wouldn't be doing this unless he really wanted to."

"I think you're underestimating how badly he wants me gone."

"Delia," Jacob says. "Tanner's putting hours of work into this place for nothing. He liked your grandma, but he didn't like her *that* much."

Seventeen

Tanner

I hate that fucking shirt.

I've barely made any progress on the carpet in Aggie's bedroom, and it's all because of a ridiculous T-shirt. A T-shirt that once belonged to Delia's ex. Tightness spreads through my chest as I picture her wearing it, the baggy cotton tied at her waist. Seeing it once was bad enough. The second time, it struck me like a physical blow.

Why did she put it on again? Was it Delia's way of sending me a message? Telling me she's off-limits? Or did she throw on the first thing she could find after I asked her to help with the bathroom tile? Am I grossly overthinking things?

I try to shake off the uncertainty that clouds my thoughts. I'm not like this with women, jealous or possessive. I've never thought about their exes or wondered about the nonverbal signals they might be giving me. But something about the idea of Delia scraping tile in the other room dressed in some other guy's T-shirt has me seeing red.

I want to know everything. What's his name? How long were they together? When did they break up? Does Delia still have feelings for him? I pinch the bridge of my nose between my fingers, shoving the questions to the back of my mind. I have no right to ask them. I've only known Delia for a week. Who she dates is none of my goddamn business.

And yet you want it to be, a voice in the back of my head taunts. The voice is right, as much as I don't want to admit it. The length of time I've known Delia doesn't change the fact that I feel something. A pull. An attraction.

I don't like it.

I thought Delia was beautiful the moment I laid eyes on her. Did I also think she was a pain in the ass? Yes, but a beautiful one. And the time I've spent around her has only piqued my interest. She's smart, quick-witted. I like fighting with her, saying whatever outlandish words I can to make her jaw clench and her cheeks turn pink. She always has something to say. I've thought about a dozen different ways to shut her smart mouth up, and none of them involve talking.

It's hard for me to tell if this attraction is one-sided. There are moments when I'm certain she feels it, too. But then she shuts down, leaving me to wonder if I'm only imagining things. Seeing what I want to see. Either way, it doesn't matter. Nothing can come of it. Delia's leaving soon, and I get the sense that she doesn't do casual relationships.

Plus, there's the fact that I'm fixing up her grandmother's old house. Mixing work and sex would lead to complications. I need to tamp down whatever I'm feeling for Delia, but I can't do that when I'm in her house, thinking about her in that awful shirt. Realizing I won't be getting any work done tonight, I begin to pack up my tools. I didn't remove much carpet. I can come back tomorrow to finish the job, hopefully with a clearer head.

Grabbing my toolbox, I slip out of the bedroom and cross the hall to the tiny bathroom where Delia and Jacob are busy working. They're quietly talking when I reach the doorway. Peering inside, I see they've made decent work of the tile. They've been a lot more productive than me tonight.

I knock on the door to get their attention. Delia looks up with her wide brown eyes. A small dip appears between her brows. Understandably, she's confused. It's only been about a half hour, and the toolbox in my hand makes it clear I'm on my way out the door.

"I just remembered I've got to deal with some work stuff," I say. "I'm gonna have to finish the carpet another time."

Behind Delia, Jacob shoots me a baffled look. "What stuff, Tanner?" he asks.

I clench my fist at my side to keep myself from flipping him the finger. "I've gotta check on the oceanfront. I'm meeting with the client tomorrow afternoon to update her on our progress."

"Can't you check on the house tomorrow morning?" Jacob's tone is innocent, but his eyes are anything but. I send him a warning glare.

"I'll order a pizza," Delia says. "If you want to stay a bit longer. My treat." Normally, this would be the part where I tease her. *You offering to buy me dinner, darling?* But I'm not in the mood right now. Not when I haven't been able to stop thinking about her, and she's wearing some fucker's shirt.

"I'm not hungry," I lie.

Jacob shakes his head like I'm a complete dickhead. "You're blowing this," he mouths. He's not wrong, but it's for the best. At least that's what I tell myself.

Delia's face falls. "Oh, well, nevermind."

I shift my focus away from her disappointed expression, staring at the floor as Delia and Jacob finish up the tile pieces they're working on and then clean up. They hand me their tools and goggles, and the three of us head downstairs.

When we reach the foyer, Delia rushes forward to open the door. She looks uncomfortable as she says, "All right. Bye," and motions us toward the door. Jacob has enough sense to say goodbye and that it was nice seeing her again. I step onto the porch without saying a word. Seconds later, Delia shuts the door behind us with a resounding thud.

"What the hell was—"

"Not now," I say angrily. Jacob no doubt wants to give me an earful, but I can't deal with his criticism yet. Not when we're standing on Delia's porch.

Silently, we take the porch steps down to the driveway. Tools clank in the box at my side. With each step away from the house, the tightness in my chest eases, but it's replaced by a heavy feeling in my stomach.

Guilt.

I try to ignore it, but the feeling has a mind of its own, expanding until it occupies all my brain space. It's the same feeling I had after I called Delia a terrible granddaughter. And I know it's not going away until I give it what it wants. Right now, it's telling me I'm making a mistake. That I can't leave like this.

"Shit," I mutter, coming to an abrupt stop at the end of the drive.

Jacob pauses beside me. "What?" he asks. He seems confused, until he suddenly isn't. It's like he can read the direction of my thoughts. An amused grin appears on his face. "What is it, Tanner?" he asks, this time with taunt instead of curiosity.

"Go home."

"Why? What's going on?"

I shove the toolbox at his chest, forcing him to take it.

"Where are you going, Tanner?"

"Fuck off," I tell him as I head back up the driveway.

Eighteen

Delia

I'm humiliated.

Standing with my back pressed against the closed front door, I can't help but wonder if it's possible to die of embarrassment. Tanner said he had to leave, and I asked him to stay for pizza. What's wrong with me? Have I lost my ability to read a room? Tanner clearly wanted to get out of here, and I made things awkward. *I'm not hungry.* God, he couldn't have made his disinterest more obvious if he tried.

I let my conversation with Jacob get to my head. Tanner's friend thinks he likes me, but if tonight was any indicator, that assumption couldn't be further from the truth. Tanner wants nothing to do with me. He's here for one reason: to do a job. I need to remember that. No more impromptu beers or dinner invitations. Tanner's doing me a gigantic favor with the renovations, but that doesn't make us friends.

From now on, things between us will be strictly professional.

I'm still standing against the door when a knock rattles my back. I freeze. Wait several seconds to be certain I didn't imagine it. A second knock confirms someone is at the door. Panic lodges in my throat. It has to be Tanner or Jacob, right? I hope it's the latter. I don't think I can face Tanner again without getting struck by a fresh wave of mortification.

Schooling my features into the most casual expression I can muster, I turn around and open the door. To my disappointment, Tanner waits on the other side. What is he doing here? Can't he leave me to suffer in my humiliation in peace?

I lean my hip against the doorframe, refusing to look him in the eye. "Did you, uh, forget something?" I ask. I can't think of another reason he would come back so soon. Unless he wants to bask in the embarrassment he caused.

The next words out of his mouth hit me like an electric shock. "Let's get dinner."

The gears in my brain come to a grinding halt. Is this a joke? "You…want to get dinner. With me." Suspicion floods my thoughts. Five minutes ago, Tanner couldn't make it out the door fast enough. Now, he wants to eat together. It doesn't make sense.

"You said you weren't hungry," I remind him.

"I guess I found my appetite."

"Between here and the driveway?"

In lieu of answering my question, he asks one of his own. "You like seafood?"

Dazed, I manage to reply, "Um, yeah."

"There's a great place on Main Street," he says. "We could go there." He wants to go out? Together? But we can't go ten minutes without arguing. There's no chance of us lasting an entire meal.

"Think you can be ready in twenty minutes?" he asks.

I take a brief assessment of my work clothes. If I throw on something simple and skip a few steps in my makeup routine, I could probably be ready by then. Still, I need to figure out what's happening. "Tanner, I thought you had work stuff to take care of."

He sighs. "I was an ass before. I'm sorry." It's the second apology Tanner has given me in the short time we've known each other, and it sounds just as sincere as the first one. As brutish as I find him, I must admit I've never met a man so willing to accept when he's wrong.

"It's good to see you're starting to recognize your dickish behavior," I tell him.

Tanner rolls his eyes and checks the time on his phone. "I'll be back to pick you up in twenty minutes," he says. He heads down the porch steps, but then stops himself, turning back to look at me. He observes me like a puzzle he can't quite solve.

"You should change," he says. "This place is better-suited for one of your fancy tops."

I shake my head, baffled by his bluntness. "You always find something wrong with my clothes, don't you?"

"Only the ones that belong to your ex."

He's gone before I get a chance to respond.

***

Tanner's truck smells like pine needles. It's a good, clean scent. Breathing it in helps put my nerves at ease. I can't tell if it's coming from an air freshener or if Tanner has on some kind of cologne. Nevertheless, I inhale a large whiff, then curl my hands around the sides of the leather passenger seat.

My eyes bounce around the truck's dark interior. I expected his truck to be disorganized. I was wrong. Except for a few papers on the center console and a toolbox rattling on the floor in the back, it's empty. I wonder if Tanner keeps it like this all the time, or if he cleaned up after he invited me to dinner. The question joins the long list in my head of things I would ask him if I had the guts.

If someone told me this morning that a meteor was going to obliterate the planet, or Tanner was going to invite me to dinner, I would have cracked open a bottle of wine and waited for the meteor to finish me off. That's how certain I was that he wanted nothing to do with me. Clearly, I know nothing about what's going on in his head. I need to figure things out, pronto. Because I have no idea if I'm heading to a dinner between acquaintances or a first date.

Logic tells me this can't be a date. It didn't sound like it when Tanner pitched the idea. *You like seafood?* Those words don't suggest anything romantic. Then again, the way he ended the conversation said differently. When I asked Tanner why he always has a problem with my clothes, he said his issue was only with the ones that belong to my ex. If *that* doesn't scream romantic interest, I don't know what does. I wish I could ask him point-blank what's going on here, but I don't have the courage.

Trying to be discreet, I steal a glimpse of Tanner out of the corner of my eye. He's got both hands wrapped around the steering wheel, his eyes focused on the quiet road ahead. He's wearing a light-blue button down. The sleeves are rolled up to his elbows, putting his strong forearms on display. It took every ounce of my self-restraint to keep my jaw from dropping when he came to pick me up. He looks good. Really good. I have the strangest urge to run my hands along his forearms. I quickly shake it off.

No matter how good he looks, this can't be a date. Getting involved with Tanner would be a mistake. Half the time, I'm not sure I even like him. He's attractive, and he has his moments, but he can also be rude and dismissive. Tonight should be about reestablishing boundaries. Making sure Tanner knows that I'm not here to play games with him. He may see this as a date, but that's certainly not what I think.

A few minutes later, Tanner pulls into the parking lot of Saunders' Seafood and Grille. The restaurant glows like a beacon in the night as we climb out of the truck and make our way to the entrance. Tanner reaches the front door a few seconds before me. Instead of going inside, he opens the heavy wooden door and motions for me to go ahead.

"What are you doing?" I ask.

"What does it look like? I'm holding the door." Has the world shifted on its axis? Tanner doesn't strike me as a holds-the-door-for-you kind of guy.

"Why? Are you gonna slam it in my face or something?"

Tanner's jaw clenches. "Delia, just go through the damn door." There he is.

Folding my arms across my chest, I stare him down. "You know, snapping at me ruins the niceness of the gesture."

He sighs, but I can tell I've proven my point because he says in a much nicer tone, "Delia, will you please go through the damn door?"

Grinning triumphantly, I take a step forward. "That wasn't so hard, was it?"

Inside, the restaurant has pale blue walls and nautical decor. The air smells like melted butter. Tanner and I approach the hostess stand, where a pretty dark-haired girl not-so-subtly scrolls on her phone. She can't be older than twenty. At first, she seems annoyed to be interrupted. But then, she sees Tanner, and her face lights up.

"Welcome to Saunders' Grill," she says, eyeing Tanner like he's a four-course meal. "Are you dining in or picking up?"

"Dining in," Tanner replies. If he notices the hostess' interest, he doesn't show it. "I called ahead. Should be a reservation under the name Ryan."

She taps a fingernail on the tablet mounted to the hostess stand. "Two for Ryan," she says. "Got it right here." She snatches a couple menus off the stand and then motions for us to follow her through the restaurant, taking us through a back door that leads to a gorgeous outdoor patio lit up by fairy lights.

The hostess sets our menus on a small white-cloth table in a quiet section of the patio. The beach is visible in the distance, dark waves rippling on the horizon.

"Your server will be right with you," the hostess says as Tanner and I settle in chairs across from each other. "Is there anything else I can help you with?" Her focus is solely on Tanner. I could be bleeding profusely, and she would hardly pay me a glance.

"We're good," he says. "Thanks."

Nodding, the hostess puts her hand on the back of his chair. "Let me know if there's anything else you need," she says. She's not at all subtle. I might admire her brazenness under different circumstances, but I find it annoying right now. I'm hungry. I didn't come here to watch a college student flirt with Tanner.

"Thanks," he replies, grabbing a menu off the table.

As the hostess walks away, I can't help but let out an indignant laugh. "She's certainly enthusiastic," I mutter.

Tanner eyes me over the top of his menu. He says nothing.

"She was flirting with you," I add. "Obviously."

He shakes his head. "She's a kid."

"Isn't that what most guys want? Young women who will inflate their egos?"

"I prefer women over the legal drinking age," Tanner says. I'm tempted to ask what other traits he looks for in women, but I keep the impulse to myself. That line of questioning would teeter on the edge between casual conversation and flirting.

"Is that your only requirement?" I ask with faux innocence. "Or do they have to share your general sense of unpleasantness?"

"You looking for pointers?"

I scoff at the idea as I snatch a leather-covered menu off the table. My eyes go to the wine list. "Just wondering if I have anyone to set you up with. But I'm afraid I don't know any women with cloven hooves."

Tanner's eyes meet mine in challenge. "I like them with talons," he says.

Before I can respond, a freckle-faced server reaches our table. She greets us and sets a basket of soft rolls between us. She's friendly but distant, and she definitely isn't hitting on Tanner. I make a mental note to leave her a generous tip.

The server asks what we'd like to drink. I order a glass of chardonnay. I'm surprised when Tanner does the same. The shock must be visible on my face. After the server leaves, Tanner gives me an unimpressed look.

"What? You didn't think I could order anything besides cheap beer?"

"Can you blame me?" Tanner has been calling me snotty since we met, and he just ordered a glass of the second most expensive wine on the menu.

He rests his menu flat on the table. His expression turns serious for a moment. "It might do both of us some good if we stop making assumptions about each other." Is he…calling for a truce? That's more shocking than the wine order, but it's probably a good idea. We're going to be around each other a lot over the next couple of weeks.

"That seems reasonable," I admit, grabbing a roll out of the bread basket. I tear a chunk off the side and pop it into my mouth. The bread is soft and warm and practically melts on my tongue. I quickly rip off another piece.

"I went to college in Boston," Tanner says, piquing my interest. "Finlay University."

Given how much Tanner seems to detest the city, it's hard to imagine him going to school in a place like Boston. But we just agreed to stop making assumptions about each other, so I keep my disbelief to myself.

"I went to a small liberal arts college in Fitchburg," I reply. "But my younger sister goes to Finlay. She loves it."

"It's a great school. Nice campus. Lots to do."

"Did you consider staying in Boston after you graduated?"

"Not really. I knew I was gonna be in charge of Ryan & Son someday. I couldn't exactly learn the ropes if I was living two hours away. Besides, my family's here. This place is always gonna be home." I nod, understanding his point completely. A person will always have a connection to the place where they grew up.

"So, what do you like to do in Boston?" Tanner asks.

I consider my response in between mouthfuls of bread. "Run. Shop. Try new restaurants. My best friends and I get drinks together every Friday. We usually hit the same bar, but sometimes we mix things up. It's fun finding new places."

"You really love it there, then."

"It can be lonely," I confess, surprising myself. "I mean, it's a big city. You're never really alone. But one of my friends got married recently, and the other works as a yoga instructor in the evenings. We don't see each other as often as we used to."

Friday night drinks with Kali and Mariah are the highlight of my week, but I can't deny we've started seeing less of each other as we've gotten older. I don't see my sisters often either. Morgan's busy with school, and Izzy lives in New York City. Plus, I work from home. There are some days when the only time I leave the apartment is to go running. I try not to think about it a lot, but there are times when my life feels incredibly isolating. But I didn't mean to reveal something so raw to Tanner. I'm feeling uncertain and slightly embarrassed as I await his reaction.

"I work a lot," Tanner says. "Haven't had nearly as much free time as I used to before I became president. The long hours make it hard to have time for much of anything else." I recall Jacob saying something earlier about Tanner working long hours. I figured he kept busy as the owner of a small business, but it sounds like he works even more than I thought. I'm glad he brought it up. It makes me feel better about everything I revealed.

We spend the next few minutes talking about Boston. Tanner rattles off the names of several bars and restaurants he used to frequent when he was in college. None of them sound familiar, so I text Morgan to see if she recognizes them. It turns out Tanner's old favorite bar is also Morgan's favorite. She tells me to ask him if he's ever had a Party Like No Other. Tanner groans when I say the words, his face contorting in disgust. I ask what's in the drink, and he says tequila and bottomless regret.

The conversation flows smoothly. At some point, the server returns to give us our drinks and take our dinner orders. Tanner inquires about my favorite things in the city. I tell him about the farmers market I love in the summer. He says

Seaview has a small market every Saturday from May to September. Annabella and her husband started it a couple of years ago. Tanner says they make a homemade banana nut muffin specifically for the market, and that it's even better than the blueberry one at Ralph's. I don't believe him for a second, but I don't want to end our newly established truce over breakfast food.

Eventually, the server comes out with a large serving tray with Tanner's whitefish and my cod. Unrolling my silverware, I pick up my fork and knife and cut into my fish. It only takes one bite for me to see why Tanner chose this place. The fish is light and zesty and breaded to perfection.

Our words keep flowing as we eat. I'm relieved to discover that Tanner has enough decency to finish chewing his food before he talks. Austin used to drive me insane with his inability to swallow food before he started speaking.

"So," I say after a few minutes as I reach for my glass of wine. "Is your dad still involved with Ryan & Son or do you run everything yourself?"

A muscle ticks in Tanner's jaw. "My dad passed away three years ago," he says. "Had a heart attack on a job site. He was still running things at the time. I took over after he died."

A mix of sadness and astonishment fills my chest. It had to be horrible taking charge of his dad's company after his death. Losing a parent is hard enough. I couldn't imagine going to work every day knowing my father would no longer be alongside me. And the fact that it happened on a job site? I wonder if that's why Tanner's such a stickler about safety.

"I'm sorry," I tell him. "Were the two of you close?"

Tanner nods. "It's hard not to be when you're working together, but he was a great man. Fair and honest. He loved Ryan & Son."

"My dad died six years ago," I say. "Skin cancer. He was sick for a long time, and we knew it was coming, but that didn't make it any easier."

Tanner offers his sympathies. "Your dad was Aggie's son, right?" he asks.

I bob my head. "She couldn't be bothered to pick up a phone, even after he died."

His brows shoot up. "Aggie didn't contact you at all afterward?"

"Not once," I say. "I never really understood her issues with my dad, but I saw the kind of person she was after that."

Tanner looks down at his plate for a moment. "I really misjudged you, didn't I?" he says after almost a full minute of silence. There's a layer of earnestness in his voice that catches me off-guard. In a strange way, it makes me want to defend him.

"You couldn't have known," I reply. "To you, she was just the lonely old woman who lived next door. It would've said a lot worse about you if you hated her."

"Being old doesn't give you the right to be an asshole," Tanner mutters.

I can't help but laugh. "That's bold of you to say. Jacob was just telling me about the neighborhood kids you chased off your property."

"Jacob exaggerates."

"So I shouldn't expect to see a keep away sign in your yard anytime soon?"

He grins. "Nah. If I see them again, I'll just turn on the sprinklers."

Nineteen

Delia

By the time we finish dinner, it's almost nine o'clock. The server packs my leftovers in a to-go container, then tells me and Tanner to have a good night. I ask her about the bill, but she says Tanner already paid it. He must've done it when I went to the bathroom. I tell Tanner I wanted to treat him to dinner—after all, he's saving me thousands in renovation costs—and try to pay him back, but he refuses to take my money.

"Use that to get yourself a new T-shirt," he says.

On the drive home, Tanner puts on the radio, and a throaty blues singer croons over the truck's speakers. Thanks to the two glasses of wine I had with dinner, I'm feeling warm and relaxed.

A short drive later, we wind up in Grandma Aggie's driveway. Tanner puts the truck in park. I unbuckle my seatbelt, looking over at him. Shadows dance over his sharp features, the porch light illuminating half his face. In the dark cab, I let myself think about just how pretty he is. The perfect angle of his jaw. His strong, straight nose and sparkling green eyes. It feels like I'm looking at a man concocted by my wildest fantasies instead of real, breathing flesh.

I glance at the clock on the dashboard. "It's only nine," I say. "Saunders' is open till ten. You've still got time to swing back there and get that hostess' number."

Amusement flashes across Tanner's face. "You've had an awful lot to say about her tonight." I'll admit, I've probably gone overboard with the hostess jokes, but I can't help myself. The girl was beautiful, and Tanner hardly glanced at her. He said she was too young for him. I wonder what his type is. Does he prefer blondes? Tall women? I don't know anything about his dating preferences, and I'm suddenly curious.

"I just figured that would be your type," I tell him.

"I think we already established that I prefer women who aren't fresh out of high school."

"I meant the no-commitment type."

"No commitment?" He lifts a brow. "Are you slut-shaming me, Delia?"

I roll my eyes, earning a grin from Tanner. "Not at all. There's nothing wrong with casual dating. All I'm saying is that you don't seem like the kind of guy who's looking for anything serious."

"You love making assumptions about me, don't you?"

"Almost as much as you love making them about me. Are you denying it?"

Tanner shakes his head. "I've dated here and there," he says. "I'm not opposed to relationships. I just haven't found the right woman yet."

"That's, like, textbook no-commitment guy speak, Tanner."

"You asked for an answer," he points out. "I'm giving it to you straight. And since you're grilling me about relationships, does that mean I get to ask about the ex-boyfriend?" I suppose it's only fair that Tanner asks about my ex. If I'm going to pry into his relationships, then I can't be surprised when he does the same.

"What about him?" I ask, shifting my attention to the plastic takeout box in my lap.

"How long were you together?"

"About a year."

"When did you split up?"

"Three months ago." The next question goes unspoken, but I answer it anyway. "Austin's a commitment guy. I'm just not the person he wants to commit to."

"And are you…do you still have feelings for him?" I don't miss the uncertainty in Tanner's voice. It sounds as though he's unsure whether he really wants to know the answer. I try not to let myself think about why he would care.

I pick at the edge of my takeout box. "No, it wasn't like that with us. We dated for a while, but our relationship wasn't going to last forever. Proximity and convenience mattered more than anything else." Braving a glance at Tanner, I'm surprised to find him watching me with an intrigued look in his eye.

"Sounds like you're a no-commitment woman," he says.

I scoff. "Definitely not. I prefer relationships. They don't have to be passionate to be comfortable, you know."

"So you prefer relationships that have little to no meaning?"

I narrow my eyes. "Phrasing it like that makes me sound awful."

He raises his palms as if to absolve himself of guilt. "You said it, not me."

"It's just…" I let out a frustrated sigh, struggling to explain myself. "I don't want anything messy. Life's complicated enough without relationships. I don't need one giving me headaches."

"Spoken like a true commitment phobe."

Annoyance tugs at my chest. "Whatever. I don't expect you to get it." Tanner can poke fun all he wants, but I know my dating philosophy has merit. It's the safest way to keep myself from heartache. To keep my life according to plan.

"Oh, I get it," Tanner says matter-of-factly. "You like to control things. Put them in your neat little boxes so they only affect you when you want them to. I hate to burst your bubble, but life's messy, darling. You can't control relationships anymore than you can control the weather. Not any that are worth a damn."

How did he figure all of that out from only a few words? It's safe to say Tanner is more perceptive than I gave him credit for. Still, I don't want him to know just how accurate his assertion is.

"I'm glad to hear that you, a thirty-year-old single man, know everything there is to know about relationships."

"You wanna know what else I know?" Tanner asks. "That ex of yours was probably so clueless he didn't realize you were putting him in a box. And if he had any sense, he would've made himself comfortable instead of getting out."

He stares at me, and my heart drums like a marching band, the beat growing louder and more intense by the second. Every detail feels like it's in focus. The mossy swirl of Tanner's eyes. The quiet hum of the radio. The rippling energy that seems to pass between us. I must've shifted to face him at some point, because I'm looking directly at Tanner. His eyes drop to my lips for the briefest moment before flickering back to meet mine.

There's only one way this is headed, which is why I have to stop it.

I clear my throat, breaking eye contact with Tanner. "Thanks for dinner," I say in a voice much higher than normal. Wrapping my hand around the door handle, I pull the door open and step onto the driveway. "Bye."

Then I clumsily scramble up the porch, leaving my dignity behind.

Twenty

Tanner: Can I come by and finish the carpet tonight?

Delia: Not today. I have to pick up my sister from the airport this afternoon.

Tanner: What about 11:30? I can swing by on my lunch break.

Delia: I'm swamped with phone calls all morning. Sorry!

I send the last text to Tanner and then tuck my phone into the waistband of my leggings. Blowing him off might not be the most mature way to handle what almost happened in his truck the other night, but I'm not ready to face him yet.

I've successfully avoided Tanner for three days now, but it hasn't been easy. I nearly jump out of my skin every time I leave the house. I'm terrified of running into him. Yesterday morning, I was sipping coffee on the back porch when Tanner's back door slid open. I panicked. Shooting out of my chair, I spilled coffee all over myself in a mad dash to get inside. I think Tanner saw me, but I couldn't bring myself to turn back and check.

On a rational level, I know I can't avoid him forever. He's already texted a couple of times about coming over to tear out Grandma Aggie's bedroom carpet. If he's not already suspicious about why I'm brushing it off, he's going to be soon. At some point, I have to get over myself. The problem is, I don't see that happening soon. Getting over it would require me to come face-to-face with the horrifying fact that I am so deeply attracted to him.

Tanner frustrates me endlessly. He's blunt and judgmental, and he takes far too much pleasure in pissing me off. But he's also funny and generous and disgustingly hot. With that bone structure, I don't know how he hasn't been cast in a cologne ad already. It's probably because he'd ruin it with his attitude. I picture him on the set of a photoshoot, grumbling about the smell of the cologne or the ridiculousness of the advertisement concept. *Who in the hell would ride a horse shirtless in the middle of the desert?* I smile to myself before I realize what I'm doing, and then a wave of panic sets in.

I did *not* just have a laugh about Tanner being Tanner.

What is wrong with me?

Tanner reminds me of a magnet, pulling me to his surface. The attraction I feel for him is different from anything I've experienced with other guys. Stronger. More insistent. Even if I try to deny it, I know the pull is still there.

It's ridiculous. I've only known the guy for two weeks. Feelings don't develop that quickly. I dated Austin for a year, and I never felt an urgent pull toward him. Whatever weirdness has brought on my feelings for Tanner needs to be stopped. Nothing can happen between us.

I'm only going to be in Seaview for a short time, and Tanner technically works for me. Plus, I don't do flings. They're messy and spontaneous, two things I generally try to avoid. I certainly won't be having a fling with a guy like Tanner. Complicating our situation would bring a level of chaos to my life that I don't want or need.

My priority needs to be getting Grandma Aggie's place ready for the market. Fortunately, I'm driving to Boston in a few hours to pick up Izzy. Having my sister here should help distract me from whatever I'm feeling for Tanner.

I step inside Ralph's Diner a little after eight on Friday morning. Annabella greets me with a bright smile from behind the counter. She's wiping down the laminate surface with a rag. Her eyes light up behind the frames of her purple glasses, and she motions me toward her. I slide onto an empty stool at the counter.

"There's the woman of the hour," she says.

"Woman of the hour?" I repeat, feeling confused. I've stopped at the diner a few times this week for coffee and breakfast, but I don't think that merits such a distinction. "Is there something I missed? Because I just got back from a run on the beach. Unless there's an award for getting the most sand in your eye, I haven't done anything to earn that title."

"Room-temperature water should do the trick," she says. "Wash your eyes for fifteen to twenty seconds."

"Thanks. So, why exactly am I the woman of the hour?"

Annabella grabs the coffee pot off the counter and fills a mug. "Nancy Orson was just in here," she explains. "She told me she met Aggie's granddaughter. That she promised to give you a tour of the Seaview Historical Society."

Disbelief washes over me. "She said that?" I agreed to drop by the historical society to look at a few photos of Grandma Aggie, not tour the building. Either Nancy Orson likes to embellish or she has the world's worst memory.

Annabella nods. "Nancy talked about it for almost twenty minutes. She's very excited. She and Aggie were thick as thieves when they ran the historical society together." Shit. I never planned on following up with Grandma Aggie's friend. I only said yes to be polite. I never thought I would see the woman again. But if she's telling people she's going to show me around the historical society, then she definitely expects me to call her. Dodging her might not be as easy as I thought.

"Well, that's…great," I say squeakily.

Annabella chuckles as she tops off the coffee cup. "My advice? Get it over with as soon as possible. Nancy's a lovely woman, but she fixates." Wordlessly, Annabella slides the coffee in front of me. I stare at the column of steam rising from the top. I didn't realize she was fixing the cup for me. I haven't ordered yet. But after a couple of weeks of asking for the same items, it seems I've become a regular in Annabella's eyes.

"I'll be right back with your muffin," she says, waltzing over to the pastry case.

After breakfast, I head back to the house. I've got a busy morning ahead of me. I'm ready to knock out my work and then get Izzy from the airport. I'm excited to see her. We talk and text often, but we haven't been together since

Christmas. It'll be nice to catch up and have an extra set of hands helping at Grandma Aggie's.

As I pull into the driveway, I spot Tanner walking along the sidewalk a short distance from the house. He sees me park my car and then starts toward Grandma Aggie's. Panic stirs in my veins. It's too late to back out and pretend I didn't see him, isn't it? I'll have to be quick about getting inside.

Grabbing my purse off the passenger seat, I shove open the door and scurry toward the front porch. As I move, I scour my purse for my set of house keys, but I can't find them anywhere. What the hell? Now is not the time for my keys to disappear in the vastness of my purse.

"Delia," Tanner says, several feet behind me. I peek back at him, but I stare over his shoulder to avoid looking him in the eye. "Can we talk for a second?" His voice sends goosebumps running down my spine.

"Now's really not a good time," I tell him. I climb the porch steps, and Tanner follows closely behind. Where are my damn keys?

"You've avoided me for days, Delia. Don't you think that's long enough?"

"I haven't been avoiding you."

He leans a shoulder against one of the porch's support beams. "Then why did you bolt inside yesterday the second I opened my back door?"

"I didn't."

"I saw you spill coffee on yourself."

Heat rushes to my cheeks. Of course he saw that. Am I not entitled to one humiliating moment in peace? "Were you watching me?" I ask, irritated.

"Our yards face each other," he says. "I was looking out the window when you tried to make a break for it."

"That's not what—" I cut myself off mid-sentence, realizing there's no use in arguing with him. Tanner will find a way to contradict me, regardless of what I say. "You know what? You can think whatever you want. I don't care." I fold my arms over my midsection. "I don't have time for your mind games."

He laughs as though I just told the funniest joke in existence. "*My* mind games? I came here to have a real conversation. You're the one acting like a child. If anyone's playing mind games, it's you." He's not wrong. Avoiding him is childish. But it beats having this conversation.

"I seriously don't have time for this," I say in a clipped tone.

"You wanna quit playing mind games, Delia?" Tanner asks, a challenge in his voice. "Then admit you wanted to kiss me the other night." His bluntness sends my heart into overdrive.

My throat feels like sandpaper. I know Tanner is brutally honest, but I didn't expect him to come out and say something like *that*. "I—no. Of course not."

Smirking, Tanner pushes off the support beam and takes a step toward me. Something devious gleams in his eyes. "You sure about that?"

My breathing sputters as he closes the gap between us. He's close enough that I can smell his soap mixed with something strong and heady that I can't quite identify. It's impossible for me to see over his shoulder now. I'm stuck staring at his broad chest.

I know Tanner wants me to look him in the eye. His gaze barrels down on me like a missile. But I won't do it. Won't give him the satisfaction. Because if I look at him, he'll know I'm replaying the other night in my head. The stillness in the truck as we stared at each other, desire running like an electric current between us. Tanner will look at me, and it will confirm every suspicion swimming in his head.

"Positive," I say, my heart racing in my chest.

Gently, Tanner tilts my chin up using the pad of his thumb. Blood pounds in my ears as our eyes lock. "Ask me if I wanted to kiss you," he says. His thumb remains on my chin. I could push him away if I wanted to, but I can't think of any reason to. Logic has taken a backseat in my mind.

"Delia," he says. "Ask me if I wanted to kiss you."

I can't. Not when the answer is written on his face.

I shake my head.

Tanner releases his grip on my chin and then leans in closer, his lips hovering just above my ear. "It's because you don't have to ask, isn't it? I'm a grown man, Delia. I know what I want. You want to play games? That's fine. But don't think for a second that changes what's going on here." He takes up every bit of my personal space. His warm breath skates along my cheek, sending a delicious thrill through my body. His lips are so close to my ear that he would barely have to move to put them on it.

It would be so easy to let instinct take over. To push up to my tiptoes and wrap my arms around his neck and yank his lips to mine. Tanner seems like he would kiss hard, rough. I bet kissing him would be a lot like fighting with him. I imagine him pinning me against the side of the house with his mouth. My nipples harden beneath my tank top. Fire rolls through my veins.

I'm still teetering on the edge of sanity when I hear a car door slam, followed by footsteps and a voice that splashes over me like a glass of ice-cold water.

"Delia?"

Twenty-One

Delia

Izzy's mouth hangs open.

She stands in front of the house, a small duffel bag slung over her shoulder. Her baby blue eyes bounce like pinballs between me and Tanner. Recognition passes through them after a few seconds. Her shock morphs into amusement.

"Am I…interrupting something?" she asks, arching a dark brow.

Humiliation engulfs my body, hot and fast like a wildfire. I separate myself from Tanner, putting several feet between us. I can't bring myself to look at him, so I focus my attention on Izzy. "No, nothing," I say quickly. Too quickly.

Izzy and I have a wordless exchange.

Delia, oh my god.

Shut up.

But he's so—

Say anything to make this worse, and I will kill you in your sleep.

With the roll of her eyes, Izzy turns her curiosity toward Tanner. "You must be the contractor," she says, a smug sense of delight in her voice. She's never going to let me hear the end of this. "I've heard a lot about you."

"Nothing good, I imagine," Tanner says. I chance my first look at him, stunned by what I find. I expected Izzy's arrival to annoy him or make him uncomfortable, but he looks relaxed. Friendly, even. I didn't know Tanner had a friendly smile. All I get from him are scowls and sarcastic grins. The way he looks right now, you'd think he's president of the Seaview Welcoming Committee. "I'm Tanner. Are you Izzy or Morgan? Delia said her sister was coming, but she didn't say which one."

"I'm Izzy," she says. "Delia's favorite sister. At least I was until two minutes ago."

Until this moment, I never realized my sister had a death wish. I'm going to dismember her and bury her body in Grandma Aggie's backyard tonight.

Tanner reaches out to shake Izzy's hand. "It's nice to meet you," he says. "And I wouldn't worry too much about being in your sister's good graces. In my experience, her bark is a hell of a lot worse than her bite."

Izzy's smile stretches across her entire face. "Oh, I like you."

I find the fact that Tanner and Izzy get along deeply unsettling. I'll have to dissect this strange dynamic later. "Iz, what are you doing here?" I ask, confused. "I was supposed to pick you up. You said your flight wouldn't land till four."

"I decided to drive," she says, gesturing to the powder blue beetle in the driveway. "I haven't taken my car anywhere in ages. Seemed like a good time to put it to use."

"How was the drive?" Tanner asks. Although I can't see myself, I imagine I must resemble one of those cartoon characters with their eyes bulging out of their sockets. *How was the drive?* Is he serious? Since when did Tanner do small talk?

Izzy sighs, sounding exhausted. "Long." I notice dark blue circles beneath her eyes. She looks drained. "I forgot driving turns people into total savages. It's some serious *Lord of the Flies* type shit. People are ready to ram each other off the roads just to get somewhere a couple of minutes faster. Like, where are you going that's so important?" Usually, I warn people about Izzy's lack of a filter before they meet her. I didn't get a chance to do that for Tanner, but he seems to be taking her in stride.

"Half the drivers on the roads don't have enough common sense to be driving in the first place," he replies.

Izzy nods. "*Exactly.* Imagine how many fewer accidents would happen if you had to pass a common sense test to get your license? I'm not saying some mistakes won't happen. We're all human, right? Has Delia told you about the time she ran over our parents' mailbox?"

Tanner grins at me. "No, she hasn't mentioned that."

I glare at my sister. "Yeah, Iz. Funnily enough, I didn't feel the need to share that story with my contractor."

Izzy waves off my annoyance. "It wasn't a big deal. You were in high school. You were running late for class. You weren't paying attention, and you took down the mailbox when you backed out of the driveway. Honest mistake."

"It's hard to picture Delia running late for anything," Tanner says. "She really likes her schedules."

"You should've heard her after we found out about this place," Izzy says, pointing a thumb toward the house. "She had a plan for getting it up on the market before me or our other sister could get a word in."

Tanner chuckles. "That doesn't surprise me."

I've officially had enough of the two of them having fun at my expense. I need to break this up, pronto.

"Well, Izzy, I'm sure you're tired after that drive," I say. "We should head inside so I can show you where to put your stuff." Izzy's expression tells me she wasn't done embarrassing me in front of Tanner, but I don't give her a moment to argue. I dig through my purse again and miraculously locate the keys.

"It was good seeing you, Tanner," I say as I unlock the door.

"Hang on," he says. "I didn't tell you why I came over." Dread floods the pit of my stomach. If he brings up our almost kiss in front of Izzy, I might die. "My mom's having a cookout at her place tonight. Both of you are welcome to stop by."

"You're inviting us to your mom's house?" My voice sounds squeaky. I can't help it. Is Tanner seriously asking me to meet his mother?

"It's a big neighborhood thing," Tanner clarifies. My thoughts must be written on my face because he gives me a slight head shake. *Calm down, you weirdo. This isn't a marriage proposal.*

"I figured you would appreciate a home-cooked meal. Plus, Jacob will be there."

Izzy blinks. "Who's Jacob?"

"Tanner's friend," I say. "He's been helping with the renovations."

Izzy smiles at Tanner. "We'd love to come," she says. "Delia can't cook to save her life. It's probably been a while since she's eaten something that didn't come from the frozen food section of the grocery store."

I elbow her side, hoping I hit hard enough to leave a bruise.

Tanner nods. "I'll text Delia the address. It starts at six, but you can come anytime."

"We'll be there," Izzy says cheerfully.

Tanner heads down the porch steps, and Izzy climbs up them. I open the front door and grab Izzy by the arm, dragging her inside and slamming the door behind us.

"Oh my god, Delia!" she exclaims, practically giddy. "Why didn't you tell me you started sleeping with the hot contactor?"

"Because I'm not!"

"I know what I saw. That guy was about to push you up against the side of the house and have his way with you. It was like something out of those filthy romance books Morgan loves!"

"Nothing's happened, I swear," I say, ignoring the way Izzy's description makes my skin heat up. "We were just talking. I mean, there was a weird moment in the car after we had dinner the other night—"

"You had dinner together?" Izzy's eyes grow huge. "What else are you keeping from me? I need to text Morgan. She's not gonna believe this."

I groan in frustration. "Can you give me the third degree later? Please? I've got a shit ton to do this morning. If you want me to show you around before I start work, it has to be right now."

"Fine," Izzy relents. "But you're not getting out of a single one of my questions."

I take Izzy on a quick tour of the house, finishing in the guest room upstairs. We'll have to share the space since Grandma Aggie's bedroom is under construction. It'll be a tight fit, but we'll manage. Izzy jokes it will be just like our childhood vacations. She, Morgan, and I used to share a king bed when our family took trips to the beach in the summer. Izzy used to kick the hell out of me in her sleep. I hope she grew out of that habit.

Once Izzy gets settled, she decides to take a nap. I grab a quick shower and then fire up my laptop at the kitchen table so I can get some work done. I field a few calls from clients and then work on one of my ongoing projects for some time.

Around one, Izzy comes back downstairs, her hair matted from sleep. She pours herself a glass of water and sits at the opposite end of the kitchen table.

An expectant silence fills the air. Apparently, she's done waiting for an explanation about Tanner. I finish the email I'm writing, then shut my laptop. I give Izzy an abbreviated version of everything that's happened with Tanner. She listens with rapt attention. I watch as she traces a bright red fingernail around the rim of her water glass, her expression intrigued.

"So you're, like, really into him," she says. "Good for you, Del. You deserve a small town hottie."

"Have you not listened to any part of this story?" I ask, suddenly annoyed.

"What I heard was a story about two stubborn people who would rather argue than admit they have feelings for each other," Izzy replies. "But it sounds like Tanner's ready to fess up. So what's your deal? Why can't you admit you like him?"

"Because I don't," I say. "Can I admit from a purely objective standpoint that he's not bad to look at? Of course. But I'm not into him."

"But you're attracted to him."

I shrug nonchalantly. "So?"

"So what's the issue? If you're both attracted to each other, you should put yourselves out of your misery and bone already."

I scrunch my nose. "I already told you—I don't do hookups."

"But have you considered that this could be good for you?" Izzy asks. "You've got a really rigid sense of what a relationship looks like, Delia. Things aren't always so cut and dry. You like Tanner. He likes you. Let things happen for once instead of trying to plan them."

I stare at a groove in the table, saying nothing. Izzy's logic is the exact reason I don't want to get involved with Tanner. What I feel for him is strong and uncertain and out of control. It's like standing on my tiptoes on the ledge of a skyscraper. Thrilling and dangerous and one misstep from freefall. I like knowing what to expect in relationships. With Tanner, that would be impossible. I don't want to put myself in a position where I can get hurt.

"I have my reasons."

"Is this about your promotion? Because that will still be waiting for you, even if you do the hot contractor." I've hardly thought about my promotion since I got to Seaview, but admitting that would open another can of worms.

"Will you please quit pushing me about this? We have other things to worry about. Like, how are we gonna get out of this cookout?"

Izzy looks at me like I just killed a baby rabbit. "What do you mean? Of course we're going to the cookout. I've been living off energy drinks and stale bagels for months. A home-cooked meal sounds amazing."

"We won't know anyone there."

"Not true. Tanner said his friend will be there. You know him," she points out. "Is Jacob cute? Maybe I'll have a fling with a Seaview guy, too."

I ignore the latter comment. "I'm trying to distance myself from Tanner," I remind her. "Going to his mom's house is the exact opposite of that."

"But we already said yes."

"*You* said yes."

"Doesn't matter. We still gave him the impression we'd be there. Backing out now would only make things more awkward. Besides, if you're really not interested in him, you should have no problem attending a cookout at his mom's." The insinuation in Izzy's tone is clear as day. I've had enough of her interrogation. It's time for me to flip the questions onto her.

"I should be the one grilling you right now," I say. "You drove here, Izzy. What the hell? I was supposed to pick you up at the airport in a couple hours."

She brushes me off. "It was a last-minute decision."

"You didn't think to tell me about it?"

"Had I known you had a guy here, I would've given you a heads-up."

"I didn't have a guy here, and you're deflecting."

"I didn't see it as a big deal," Izzy says. "I haven't driven my car in forever, and plane tickets are expensive. And it saved you a four-hour round trip. Seemed like a win-win." Her tone sounds genuine, but I'm not totally convinced. Why would she wait till the day of her flight to make this decision? Why wouldn't she tell me about it before she left?

I want to press her about the issue, but unlike Izzy, I understand that forcing someone to talk about something isn't the most effective way to get them to open up. I remind myself to ask her about this again later.

"I'm sorry if I embarrassed you in front of Tanner," she says earnestly. "But I really want us to go to this cookout tonight. You've got to clear the air with him somehow. At least this way I can be there with you." She makes a decent argument. I won't be able to avoid Tanner forever. I need to find a way to be around him. Facing him at a crowded cookout seems a lot less nerve-wracking than doing it one-on-one.

"I'll go if you agree to do something for me," I tell her.

She nods. "Anything. You name it."

"I met an old friend of Grandma Aggie's the other day," I explain. "Her name's Nancy. She used to serve on the board of the Seaview Historical Society with Grandma Aggie. Anyway, she invited me to come by sometime to look at some old photos of Grandma Aggie. I want you to come with me."

"You *want* to do that?"

"No, but I sort of already said yes."

"Delia!"

"It sucks when someone agrees to something unpleasant on your behalf, doesn't it?"

"Okay, I deserve that," Izzy admits. "But seriously, Del, you're asking me to look at pictures of Grandma Aggie? Can't you dare me to eat a bug or jump in the ocean or something?"

"This is my condition." I'm not looking forward to touring the Seaview Historical Society, but I find a bit of satisfaction in knowing Izzy will be miserable, too.

"Fine. I'll do it." Izzy shakes her head as though she can't quite believe what she's agreeing to. "But that means we need to figure out what you're wearing to this cookout tonight." She glances at my tank top and leggings. "Because there's no way you're wearing that."

Twenty-Two

Tanner

"I invited someone tonight."

Mom abruptly stops shucking corn. Her eyes go round with surprise. "Please tell me it's not the Andrews kid again," she says, her face overcome with panic. "I know he works for you, honey, but this really isn't an appropriate place for anyone to be doing a keg stand. I *just* put new carpet in the living room."

"It's not Chris Andrews, Mom," I assure her. Last year, I made the mistake of inviting an employee to Mom's annual spring cookout. For some reason, the guy expected Mom's family-friendly party to be a full-blown rager. He showed up with a keg and half a dozen people I'd never met before. I vowed never to invite someone from work again.

"Her name's Delia," I explain, plucking strands of corn silk off the pale cob in my hand and dropping them in the nearby garbage can. We're outside on the back patio. Mom insists on shucking corn out here. Says it's too messy to do inside. "She's Aggie Forrest's granddaughter. I'm helping her with some renovation work." I don't like the smile that appears on Mom's face after I mention Delia's name. It's knowing. Too knowing.

"So it's true," Mom says mysteriously.

"What's true?"

"You're seeing someone. Jacob said he didn't think you were ready to introduce her to me yet. Apparently, he was wrong."

"When were you talking to Jacob?"

"I saw him the other night when I was having dinner with Brenda. I mentioned you seemed busy lately. He said it was probably because you're spending time with your new girlfriend." I grind my teeth. Fucking Jacob. He's a bigger gossip than any of the retired folks in town. I don't know what compelled him to spill my business to my mother, but I'll be kicking his traitorous ass later.

"Remind me to kill him later."

Mom swats my shoulder. "C'mon, Tanner. He was only making conversation. And it wouldn't have come as a surprise if you kept me updated on what's going on in your life. So, what's the story? When did you meet her? How long have you been going out?" She peppers me with questions, and it hits me that despite my threat on Jacob's life, I haven't actually contradicted the information.

"Mom, I'm not seeing anyone right now."

"Really? Because Jacob said you're not charging her a dime to fix up that house." Christ, is there anything Jacob *didn't* tell her? There's no way Mom knows about the way I treated Delia when we first met. Mom's a stickler about manners. She used to lecture me and my sister if we didn't say hello to guests who came into our home. If she knew the things I said to Delia, she'd be handing me my ass right now.

"If you're trying to convince me to cut ties with Jacob, you're doing a pretty good job of it," I tell her, tossing a corn husk in the garbage can.

"I'm only trying to make sense of the information I've been given," she says. "Which is minimal, since my son doesn't want to share the important parts of his life with his mother anymore." She heaves the world's most dramatic sigh.

"That's not what's happening here."

"Then what is happening, exactly?"

"I'm helping a woman with her house. That's all." It's not a total lie. Technically speaking, nothing has happened between Delia and me. We had dinner, and we almost kissed, and she avoided me for days. Then I confronted her, and we almost kissed, and her sister interrupted us. If Izzy had shown up only a few seconds later, she would've found us in a very compromising position. I was going to kiss the hell out of Delia, and I know she was going to kiss the hell out of me back.

It's true that I'm too busy for dating and relationships, but that hasn't stopped me from pursuing Delia. The days she ignored me after our first near kiss were excruciating. I wanted to see her. Find out what was going on inside her head. After today, it's clear she feels the same attraction I do, but she's pushing it away.

I don't know much about Delia, but it's obvious she likes control. Structure. Living life according to her plans. By that logic, I can see why she might be hesitant about giving in to this pull. We live very different lives, and she's not planning to be in Seaview for long. The circumstances don't make a solid foundation for a long-lasting relationship. But does she really want to ignore this? Pretend it isn't happening? I don't know what the future holds for us, but I'm still willing to test the waters.

I have to find some time tonight to talk to her. Alone. It won't be an easy task. I know she's going to have her guard up, but I have no issue working for her. If she needs me to prove that I'm worth taking a chance on, then so be it.

"You know, your dad and I met through work," Mom says, getting a wistful look in her eye. I've heard this story a million times, and she knows it, but I don't have the heart to tell her to stop. "He showed up on my parents' doorstep, saying he was hired to redo the kitchen. Turned out he wrote down the wrong address—he was supposed to be working at the neighbor's place. The next day, he showed up at my parents' again. When I opened the door, I asked him if he was all right in the head, and he said the only thing wrong was that he couldn't get me out of it. The rest is history."

"What are you getting at, Mom?" I ask.

She lays a hand on my arm. "I know you care about the company," she says. "And the reason you work so hard is that you want to make your dad proud. But I worry about you, honey. You never take time for yourself. It's okay to want things outside of work. Making time for dating doesn't mean you love your father any less."

She's right. Dad wouldn't be happy if he knew I was killing myself to keep the company going. There's no reason for me not to see where things lead with Delia.

The only problem?

I'm not the one who needs convincing.

Twenty-Three

Delia

Meeting the parents has always been a bad omen for me.

My first boyfriend, Jack, introduced me to his mom and dad on the night of our junior prom. Halfway through the dance, I caught him making out with the captain of the debate team in the janitor's closet. In college, my boyfriend, Steve, took me to lunch with his father, who broke the news that he and Steve's mom had separated. Steve dumped me a week later, claiming he needed to focus on family.

I was supposed to meet Austin's parents for the first time a few days before he ended things, but they canceled their trip to Boston at the last minute. Looking back on it, I wonder if they really decided not to visit, or if Austin realized he didn't want to bother with introductions when our relationship wasn't going anywhere.

Given my horrible track record with parents, it's no surprise I'm feeling anxious on the ride over to Tanner's mom's house. He and I are definitely *not* in a relationship, but we've nearly kissed twice. It wouldn't shock me if my bad luck strikes again.

Maybe I'll accidentally insult Tanner's mom or bump into a candle and set her house on fire. I wouldn't put either possibility past me. The best-case scenario would be not meeting Tanner's mom at all. Tanner said this was a big neighborhood cookout. Hopefully, his mom will be preoccupied with hosting duties, and she won't have time to introduce herself.

The GPS on Izzy's phone tells her to take a right, and she turns down a quiet street lined with brick houses and sidewalks covered in sidewalk chalk. Izzy parks along the curb outside a two-story home with a packed driveway.

She cuts the engine, grabbing a tube of red lipstick out of her purse on the center console. As she applies the color to her lips, I take stock of my appearance in the mirror on the passenger side. My hair is long and straight. My lips are shiny, thanks to the gloss I put on before we left. I'm wearing a yellow sundress with ruffled sleeves and a simple floral pattern. It's Izzy's. My wardrobe consists of black, white, and the occasional pink. I'm feeling a bit out of my element in pale yellow, but Izzy insisted the color looks great on me.

Smacking her lips, Izzy snaps the cap back on her lipstick. She turns to me. "You ready?" she asks, reaching for the door handle.

A wave of nerves slams into me. "Wait," I tell her, placing a hand on her arm. "We're only staying for an hour. We say hello. We eat. We leave. Got it?"

"Got it," she says. "Now, can we please go? I'm starving."

Letting go of Izzy's arm, I grab the bottle of wine I brought for Tanner's mom and climb out of the car. As we start toward the house, someone steps out of the driver's side door of a gray sedan parked near the end of the driveway. It's Jacob. He looks sharp in his wire-rimmed glasses and green polo. Seeing me, he waves.

"Hey, Delia," he says, slipping his car keys into the pocket of his jeans. "Tanner said you were coming tonight. I wasn't sure whether to believe him."

"I was kind of strong-armed into it," I reply.

"He can be pushy."

"Actually, it wasn't by Tanner." I toss a look at Izzy, who huffs with annoyance.

"Don't listen to her, Jacob," she says. "I'm paying for this tremendously."

Jacob's brow pinches. "I'm sorry. Have we met before?" he asks.

Izzy grins. "I'm afraid you haven't had the pleasure," she says. "I'm assuming you're Tanner's friend, Jacob. Unless there's another guy Delia failed to mention."

Realization floods Jacob's dark eyes. "You're Delia's sister."

Still grinning, Izzy gives him a patronizing pat on the shoulder. "They raise them sharp in Seaview, don't they?"

"Ignore her, Jacob," I interject. "She was dropped on her head as a baby."

His eyes dart between me and Izzy. "The two of you are certainly…different."

"You can admit you like me better than Delia," Izzy tells him. "You wouldn't be the first."
Rolling my eyes, I decide not to respond to her

dig. The three of us head up the driveway, with Jacob taking the lead.

When we get to the front stoop, Jacob opens the door and walks inside without knocking. Izzy and I trail behind him.

My first thought when I step inside is that the house looks like something out of an architectural magazine. It has vaulted ceilings and dark-wood floors and enormous windows that bring light into the space. A crystal chandelier throws rainbows across the foyer, and a grand staircase with a curved banister leads up to the second level. I suppose the advantage of your family owning a construction company is that your house is bound to be incredible.

Izzy bumps me with her elbow and motions to a framed photo on the wall. It's Tanner. I recognize his green eyes and light-brown hair. He looks about nine or ten. He's smiling at the camera, wearing a blue baseball uniform and a cap that says "Seaview" in script font.

"That's adorable, isn't it?" Izzy says. I ignore the comment, despite it being true. I don't need to see cute childhood pictures of Tanner. I'm trying to make myself like him less.

We follow the sounds of music and conversation into a sunlit kitchen that's brimming with activity. A large group crowds around a marble island covered in trays of sliced vegetables, stuffed mushrooms, and garlic knots. Four older women play cards at the kitchen table, their faces filled with concentration. A gaggle of young kids sit around the massive flatscreen in the living room, playing a video game.

I scan the crowded room for Tanner, but I don't
see him anywhere. Is he running late? Am I early?
It can't possibly be the latter. The party appears to
be in full swing. Plus, I made Izzy wait until six-
fifteen to leave so we would arrive fashionably
late.

"Found him," Izzy whispers in my ear. I follow
her eyes to the bay window in the living room,
where I see Tanner flipping burgers on the back
patio. My stomach does a somersault.

"Go talk to him," Izzy says.

Shaking my head, I say, "I'm not leaving you
alone in a house of strangers."

"You won't be," she replies. "My new friend
Jacob is gonna keep me company."

Jacob looks confused. "Uh, what?"

Izzy pays him no mind. "Go," she tells me.
"The hour doesn't start until you talk to Tanner.
I'll be watching."

Anticipation builds as I leave Izzy and Jacob,
setting my sights on the back door. I push open
the sliding glass and step onto a gorgeous stone
patio with wicker furniture and lush greenery.
Standing at the grill, Tanner glances back over his
shoulder. His eyes widen when he sees me. He
looks me up and down. His attention lingers on
my bare legs for one, two, three seconds more
than friendly. Goosebumps race down my spine.

"Delia," he says, his Adam's apple bobbing.
"You look—"

"You played baseball," I blurt, cringing at my
awkwardness. It's painfully obvious why I
interrupted Tanner, but I couldn't let him reach
the end of that sentence. "I, um, saw a picture of
you in your uniform."

He turns to face me fully. He's wearing a gray
T-shirt that shows off his impressive arms and a
loose-fitting pair of cargo shorts. "I played for
most of my childhood," he says. "Quit just after
my sophomore season."

"Why's that?" I ask.

"I started taking on more responsibility at the
company. It got difficult trying to balance
practices and games and workouts when I had to
be on job sites after school." I nod, slowly taking
the information in. This seems to be a recurring
theme with Tanner: work supersedes all other
priorities. Clearly, he loves his job. But I can't
help but think that a kid shouldn't have to give up
something fun for the sake of work. There's
plenty of time for that in adulthood. Kids should
enjoy being kids for as long as they can.

I tilt my head curiously. "Did you like
playing?"

Tanner grabs the spatula off the small table
beside the grill to flip the sizzling patties. "Loved
it. Well, the game. I wasn't too keen on the team
camaraderie stuff."

"You? The most approachable man ever? I'm
shocked."

He smirks. "I bet you were a ray of sunshine as
a teenager."

"As a matter of fact, I was. You're looking at a
two-time class president and the founder of the
Bromfield High School calligraphy club."

"So you've always been a nightmare with a
color-coded planner."

"One man's nightmare is another man's
dream."

"Sometimes, they're both."

My skin flushes, and I drop my eyes to the concrete beneath my sandals. "Listen," I say, pulling in a deep breath. "I wanted to talk to you about all the weirdness that's been going on between us the last few days."

He raises a brow. "By weirdness, do you mean you avoiding me?"

"Okay, fine. I was avoiding you. But I think both of us needed time and space to think logically about this situation." He says nothing, and I take his silence as my cue to continue. "I really believe it's best if we keep things professional from now on."

Tanner frowns. "When have things between us ever been professional?"

"Maybe they haven't been so far," I admit. "But moving forward, it's for the best."

"For who? You?"

"For both of us. I'm going back to Boston as soon as the house is finished, Tanner. There's no sense in complicating things, all right?"

"Things are already complicated, darling."

I want to scream. This conversation is going nowhere. "That's exactly why we shouldn't make them more complicated," I say with a frustrated sigh. "Look, after my last relationship ended, I sort of decided I was done with dating."

His eyes widen. "Done with dating? You mean permanently?"

"Yeah. Kind of."

"You said things weren't serious with that guy."

"They weren't." The more time passes, the more I've begun to question what I was doing with Austin. The guy wore socks to bed *and* refused to watch my favorite TV shows with me, claiming he couldn't be bothered with silly girl dramas. "But our breakup made things awkward. My friends became hellbent on getting me to hook up with every guy who came within a two-mile radius. So I figured I'd do us all a favor and just quit."

"Seems a little heavy-handed, don't you think?"

"Actually, it's been going well so far." Well, it was. Until Tanner came along. But he doesn't need to know that. "What I'm trying to tell you is that nothing can happen between us. I'm not dating anymore, but I'm not a casual sex person either. I don't have flings with random guys."

"Is that your way of asking to be my girlfriend, Delia?"

Embarrassment soars through me like a shot. "What? No. I'm—"

"You're the one who's fixated on labels," Tanner says. "I know you like to keep things in your little boxes, but denying this won't make it go away." He folds his arms against his chest. "Answer me honestly. Are you attracted to me?"

The heat in my skin kicks up another degree. I've never met a guy so blunt before. My instinct is to deny it or shy away from the question, but both of us know it would be bullshit. If I really want to be mature about this, then I owe Tanner honesty.

"Yes," I say in a small voice.

Nodding, Tanner takes a step toward me. "I don't know what this is," he says. "All I know is that I haven't been able to stop thinking about you since the moment you showed up here with your tight shorts and your pretty eyes and your bad attitude." He tucks a strand of hair behind my ear, letting his fingers card through it. My pulse is like a runaway train. "All I'm asking is that you give us a chance to figure this out."

My mind flashes back to the kitchen with Izzy this afternoon. *You like Tanner. He likes you. Let things happen for once instead of trying to plan them.* He's making the same point as my sister. I see their argument. Really, I do. But I don't know if I can let go like that. Jumping into the unknown without a plan or a parachute. What if I listen to my feelings and it winds up burning me in the end?

Twenty-Four

Delia

I'm so caught up in my thoughts that I barely register the slide of the back door. "Tanner, how are things going out here—oh, I'm sorry! I didn't realize you weren't alone."

I turn at the sound of a gentle voice and see a woman who appears to be in her late fifties. She has gray-brown hair and a pair of striking green eyes identical to the ones of the man beside me.

The woman smiles. "You must be Delia," she says. "I'm Ellen. Tanner's mom."

I smile back. "It's nice to meet you, Ellen. You have a beautiful home."

Her eyes light up at the compliment. "Thank you. It took a long time to get it that way. It certainly got easier to maintain after Tanner and his sister moved out."

Tanner shakes his head. "I'm gonna remember that the next time you call me crying because we don't have enough family dinners," he mutters.

"Oh, hush," Ellen tells him. "You know I love having you kids around the house. But you can't deny that it looks a lot nicer now than it did when you were growing up." She eyes the grill. "Do you think those burgers will be ready in the next few minutes? I'm putting together a salad, but I can hold off a little longer if you need more time."

"They're almost done," Tanner says. "I've just gotta add the cheese."

"Perfect." Ellen's attention whirls back to me. "I'd love to hear more about you, Delia. Come find me after dinner so we can chat some more, okay?"

"Do you need help setting up?" I ask.

"That's sweet of you, but I think I've got everything under control."

"Are you sure? I really don't mind." I wasn't looking for one-on-one time with Tanner's mom tonight, but it seems like a safer option than staying out here with Tanner and his hair-tucking fingers. I don't trust him. Or myself.

"I suppose I could use some help with the salad," Ellen says.

I grin. "I'm happy to help." Tanner's glare is like a spotlight. He knows I'm trying to escape our conversation, and I'm sure he won't let me get out of it that easily, but at least I've bought myself a few minutes away from him. Hopefully, it will be enough time for me to clear my head.

Without looking at Tanner, I follow Ellen back inside. When we get to the kitchen, I realize I'm still holding the bottle of wine I brought her.

I lift the wine in offering. "This is for you."

"How thoughtful," Ellen says as I hand the bottle over. "This sounds great, Delia. Thank you. I'm sure Tanner will be happy to have a good bottle of wine around here."

I let out a confused laugh. "I didn't know Tanner was into wine."

Ellen nods. "Loves it. Just like his dad. He always complains I don't buy the good stuff." Seriously? Tanner had the gall to call me a snob when he's a secret wine junkie? I want to call him out on his hypocrisy, but I don't think Ellen would take kindly to me telling her that her son is a fraud. So I keep my mouth shut as I help put together a simple garden salad. Ellen already has the ingredients laid out, so it's only a matter of chopping and dicing and throwing things in a giant wooden bowl.

"So," Ellen says as she dices a tomato, "Tanner tells me you're from Boston."

I nod. "Born and raised."

"Did he mention he went to college in Boston?"

"Finlay U, right? My sister goes there."

"The one who finagled her way into Gloria's poker game?" Ellen asks, motioning toward the kitchen table. Sure enough, Izzy has joined the group of old women playing cards. She studies her hand with an unreadable expression. "I've got to say, I'm impressed. Gloria doesn't let anyone join her poker games. Your sister must be quite persuasive."

"She's something," I say, tossing a handful of sliced onion into the salad. "But no. Our other sister. Morgan. She's the youngest."

"Three girls. I bet that was fun growing up," Ellen says. "I always wanted a sister. I got stuck with two brothers."

"It was fun. Mostly. Though there was a lot of fighting about clothes."

"It beats wrestling. My brothers went through a phase where all they wanted to do was pummel each other. There were a lot of broken bones in our house."

We make conversation while we work. Ellen's sweet and kind, and she asks thoughtful questions about my life and career. Tanner already told her I'm Aggie Forrest's granddaughter. Ellen says she didn't know my grandmother personally, and I'm relieved to hear that. Dealing with one of Grandma Aggie's old friends is enough.

With the salad and burgers ready, we set up serving dishes on the island, and Ellen lets her guests know it's time to eat. I fix myself a plate that includes a cheeseburger, salad, and mashed potatoes. I wind up at a table outside on the patio with Ellen, Jacob, Izzy, Jacob's mom, Brenda, and a forty-something woman named Alice, who lives in the neighborhood. Tanner joins us a few minutes into the meal, taking the empty space next to me.

Conversation flows steadily, led mostly by Izzy. My sister has a talent for charming strangers. Everyone at the table looks enthralled as she tells a ridiculous story about the time she used a motion-activated toy to catch her coworker taking things from her desk.

"Meg was my office nemesis," Izzy says, eyes gleaming with enthusiasm.

"Here we go," I mutter under my breath.

Izzy continues. "She and I never got along, but that didn't stop her from stealing candy from my desk. All. The. Time. It was getting to the point where I was having to restock my office stash on a weekly basis. I knew she was the one doing it because I saw the wrappers in her trash can, but she insisted it wasn't her. Sharing didn't bother me, but her lying drove me crazy. If you're gonna do something questionable, at least have the decency to own it."

"Like you with the decision to tell this story?" I ask.

She ignores my interruption again. "Anyway, I'm shopping online one night when I see an ad for a twelve-inch toy cactus that lights up and plays *Y.M.C.A.* by the Village People. It's twenty bucks, and it has a motion sensor. Obviously, I had to buy it. I set the cactus next to my candy dish one afternoon before using the bathroom at work. The next thing I know, music is blasting through the entire office. Meg never stole from me again."

"Couldn't you have stopped leaving candy on your desk?" Jacob asks.

Izzy appears outraged. "Where would be the fun in that, Jacob?"

"You ladies are a blast," Brenda says warmly. Her eyes brighten as if a lightbulb just went off in her head. "You should join us for our next Seaside Sip!"

"Seaside Sip?" I repeat, confused.

"It's Seaview's version of a kegger," Jacob says. "Except no men are invited."

"The women in town have an annual tradition on the last Saturday in May," Ellen explains. "We meet in the pavilion at the park for a big potluck. We call it Seaside Sip."

"It's mostly an excuse to get together for a few drinks," Brenda says. "Sometimes we'll have activities like painting or jewelry-making."

"We had a yoga instructor last year, but that was a disaster," Alice says, shuddering. "It turns out asking a group of one hundred tipsy women to balance on their heads isn't a good idea."

"I'm still intrigued about the whole men aren't allowed part," Izzy says.

"We had an incident a few years ago where a group of teenage boys tried to steal a keg," Ellen says. "After that, we decided it was just easier to rebrand Seaside Sip as a girls' night."

"Nolan Saunders and his band of goons ruined things for Seaview's male population," Jacob says.

"Smart men didn't want to be there in the first place," Tanner grumbles.

"You're not into drunken yoga?" I ask, feigning surprise.

"I'm not into seeing my *mother* do drunken yoga."

"I, for one, need to know everything about this event," Izzy says. "How do you score an invite?" I almost remind her that the last Friday in May is a month from now, and if things go accordingly, we won't be in town by then. But I don't feel like putting a damper on the conversation, so I keep the thought to myself.

We finish eating a while later. The night has been going well, but we've definitely stayed for more than an hour. After we clear our plates, I give Izzy a signal that it's time to wrap things up. We thank Ellen for her hospitality and delicious food, then say goodbye to the others. Tanner offers to walk us out.

"I'm gonna…get the car started," Izzy says, sprinting out the door. She's gone before I can ask her to hold up, leaving me alone in the foyer with

Tanner. We stand side-by-side in the small, empty room. My nerve endings feel like they're on fire.

I shoot Tanner an awkward smile, shifting on the balls of my feet.

"Sorry about Izzy," I tell him. "She can be a lot."

Tanner chuckles softly. "I like her," he says. "She keeps you on your toes." I'm relieved to hear that Izzy hasn't completely embarrassed me tonight, but that doesn't mean I'm not going to kill her later. She's done everything in her power to get me alone with this man, despite my insisting that that's the opposite of what I want.

"Tonight was fun," I say. "Thanks for inviting us."

Tanner nods. "I'll text you tomorrow to figure out a time for me to come by to deal with that carpet," he replies.

"Sounds good. Well, goodnight."

I wrap my hand around the door handle, but then he says, "Delia, wait."

I turn around, but I barely have a second to realize what's happening before Tanner's lips crash on mine. His mouth feels soft and warm. He moves gently against my lips, as if he's savoring the taste.

My eyes fall shut. Sparks dance behind the closed lids. Without thinking, I press my mouth against his, reciprocating the kiss. Tanner groans low in the back of his throat, and the sound sets my veins on fire. I run my palms up the planes of his chest. His hand goes around the back of my neck, fingers digging into my hair.

The pressure between us grows stronger, needier. I part my lips, and his tongue slips inside

my mouth and—*oh, god*, this is so good. It's
everything and nothing like I thought it would be.
Nothing exists outside of this moment. I have half
a mind to grab Tanner by the shirt collar and pull
him into an empty room. Which is why he catches
me off guard when he suddenly drags his mouth
away from mine.

He stares at me with a glazed look in his eyes.
His breathing is ragged. Mine is, too.

"You look phenomenal in that dress," he says.

Blood roars in my ears. "Um, thank you."

Smiling, he detaches himself from me.
"Goodnight, Delia."

Somehow, I manage to stumble to the car.

I'm in deep shit.

***

Tanner

I'm washing dishes a couple of hours after the
cookout when Mom comes up behind me. She
lays a hand on my shoulder. Her expression is sly,
knowing.

"I like her, Tanner," she says before heading to
the living room to clean up the empty glasses
scattered on the coffee table.

I stare at the running water for a solid minute.

I'm in deep shit.

198

Twenty-Five

Tanner

A knock at the door draws my attention away from the mountain of invoices piled on my desk. Looking up, I see Marvin standing in the doorway. He's got a blue Ryan & Son mug in his hand. Steam drifts from the top.

"Hey, Tanner," he says. "Got a second to talk?"

"Sure," I reply, motioning for him to step inside my office. It used to be a supply closet. Dad had it converted into an office after I started working at the company full time. It's a tight fit, but it serves its purpose. I don't spend much time in here, anyway.

Dad had a much bigger office with glass windows and a spectacular view of the beach. A few months after he died, Marvin offered to move my stuff into Dad's old space, but I couldn't bring myself to do it. The office sits empty now, a physical reminder of my father's absence both in my life and at the company.

Marvin hands me the mug. "Figured you could use this," he says as he settles in the chair across from my desk. "You've been here a long time today."

Offering him my thanks, I take a sip of coffee. My eyelids feel as heavy as bricks. It's a little after eight in the evening. I've been working since seven this morning. I usually cap my days at twelve hours, but the stack of invoices on my desk has gotten out of control. It looks like a mailroom in here. I need to make a dent in my paperwork or risk falling seriously behind.

"Busy is all. What's up, Marvin?" I ask.

"I wanted to give you an update on the oceanfront," he says. "Progress has been going well, but it looks like we're in for some storms over the next several days. We might have to adjust our timeline." Frustration slams into me. Marvin can't be held responsible for shitty weather. He and the rest of the crew have been working tirelessly to keep the project on schedule. But even a small hiccup like this one is something I don't have time for.

"Thanks for letting me know," I tell him. "I'll call the client in the morning."

Marvin nods. "These things happen all the time, Tanner. You can't beat yourself up over them. You're working hard. Everyone knows it." He pauses for a moment and then says, "but can I be honest with you for a minute?"

"I wouldn't want it any other way."

"You know I'm retiring after this job, right?"

I grimace. "I had a feeling."

"Between finding a replacement for me and everything else going on, you're gonna need some help around here," Marvin says. "I know you wanna do right by your dad, but you can't keep working like this, Tanner. It's not sustainable." He's right, and I know it. But unless Marvin can add an extra six hours to the day, I don't have time to hire anyone.

"I'm gonna hire somebody," I say. "Once everything's settled with the oceanfront, I'll start looking for help."

Marvin frowns. "There's always gonna be another project. You've got to make time to get done what needs to get done."

With those words, he stands up and leaves the office.

Alone, I run a hand over my face and sink back into my desk chair. My temples throb with exhaustion. My brain is fried. Losing Marvin is going to hurt, but I can't spend another second thinking about work tonight.

I spot my phone sitting in the corner of my desk. My fingers twitch with the urge to text Delia. I've barely seen her since we kissed. Work has been keeping me from her. But the thought of Delia Forrest's lips has me wanting to abandon my responsibilities.

The woman kisses like a fantasy. Soft and sweet and eager. I can still feel her tiny fingernails moving down my chest. Still taste the strawberry lip gloss on her mouth.

I've never needed a cold shower more in my life.

But I like Delia for more than just her looks. She's intelligent and thoughtful. She doesn't back down from a challenge, and she isn't afraid to argue about anything. I tease her about her obsession with planning, but Delia knows how to get shit done. In a matter of weeks, she's turned Aggie's junkyard of a house into something presentable. Someone with that kind of drive is truly impressive.

Then there are the little things about her. The way she bites her bottom lip when she's trying not to smile at something I've said. Her prissy blouses and her polished fingernails. The mole just below her collarbone that I've been dying to get my mouth on. When I'm around her, I get the urge to do whatever I can to capture her attention. Mess with her. Make her blush. Anything that gets those brown eyes focused on me.

I know she's freaked out by this attraction. I need to be careful so I don't scare her off. But she's been on my mind all day. I need to talk to her. So I pick up my phone and send her a text. I won't get anything else done when I'm thinking about her, anyway.

Twenty-Six

Delia

Izzy lets out a harsh laugh as she opens the cardboard box by her feet. "Well, what do you know," she says, pulling out a bulky gold lamp that looks like it came straight from the 80s. "Another lamp. Were the other seven not enough?"

"I don't think Grandma Aggie used any sort of logic when deciding what to keep," I say from behind a tall stack of boxes. My nose runs, thanks to all the dust swirling about. I wipe it with the back of my hand. "She just kept everything."

Izzy drops the lamp and then lays back on the floor, spread out like a starfish. "She really is trying to torture us, isn't she?"

With an eye roll, I grab a fluffy pillow out of the nearest box and toss it at my sister, hitting her in the stomach. "Complaining isn't gonna help anything."

"I'm not a suffer-in-silence kind of girl, Delia," Izzy says. "If I'm suffering, everyone should know about it." She knocks the pillow off her body. "God, who knew moving a bunch of boxes would be such a workout?"

While I don't share Izzy's flair for the dramatic, I must admit I'm feeling the effects of the constant movement. We've been in the attic for almost two hours, slowly making our way through boxes of Grandma Aggie's belongings. Having Izzy here has been a huge help, but we've still got a lot of work ahead of us.

"You can take a break, Iz," I say, wiping my dusty palms on my shorts. "I don't mind working by myself for a little while. I'm sure you've got work to catch up on." I know Izzy must be putting her work on the back burner. Balancing a full-time job on top of dealing with the house hasn't been easy for me. I imagine she's feeling the same.

"Maybe both of us should take a break," she says.

I glance around the cluttered attic. We've already gone through about half of the boxes. Giving up now feels like a missed opportunity. "I don't know. We're making such good progress. I think we could finish this tonight."

"That's funny. Because I don't see that happening at all."

"Let's at least do a few more boxes. Then we can call it a night."

I start to open a new box when my phone buzzes. Dread instantly pools in my stomach. It's probably Nina. Someone from the firm's human resources department emailed me this afternoon to schedule an interview for Nina's job. It isn't for a few weeks, but Nina has already been texting me about it. She even offered to do a practice interview with me.

Nina means well. She's excited for me. Which makes me feel even worse about my unease. Nina has no idea that the thought of taking her job makes me want to throw up.

When I pull my phone out of my back pocket, though, I'm greeted by a message from Tanner instead of Nina. He sent me a screenshot of what appears to be a conversation between him and his mom. She's asking him for email addresses for me and Izzy. She wants to send us invitations for next month's Seaside Sip.

Another notification pops up. *I hope you know what you've gotten yourself into.* The dread in my stomach is quickly replaced by nerves.

Tanner and I haven't spoken since he kissed me four nights ago. I was on a call with a client when he stopped by yesterday to tear out Grandma Aggie's carpet. Izzy let him inside. I gave him a half-wave from the kitchen table, but that has been the extent of our post-kiss interactions.

Amid the silence, my thoughts have run wild, and my brain has become a breeding ground for anxiety-provoking questions. What did Tanner think of the kiss? Was it as good for him as it was for me? Has it been stuck on his mind, too? Does he regret it? Does he want to do it again?

I've replayed our kiss at least a hundred times, committing every detail to memory. The softness of Tanner's mouth. The spark that ignited in me when he wrapped his hand around the back of my neck.

I knew I was attracted to Tanner. I expected that attraction to lead to physical chemistry. But I had no idea how good it would be. I've never felt so desperate and needy over a kiss. How would I feel if we'd taken things further? Would the intensity have fizzled out or grown stronger? Something tells me that kind of heat doesn't just disappear. I know I said I was done with men forever, but Tanner's talented tongue has me second-guessing that decision. Maybe I've been thinking too rashly.

I peek over my shoulder to make sure Izzy isn't paying attention to me. Once I see she's rummaging through a cardboard box, I type back a reply. *Tell her we'll bring shots.*

My phone rings. Tanner's name flashes across the screen. Oh my god. He's calling me. Anticipation swirls within me. I can't talk to Tanner with my sister in earshot. "On second thought," I announce, "now does seem like a good time for a break."

Izzy looks surprised, then confused, but I scurry out of the attic before she can ask questions.

Climbing downstairs, I sprint to the guest room on the second floor and lock the door behind me. I give myself a moment to catch my breath before I swipe to answer the call.

"Are you calling to share your mom's liquor preferences?" I ask. "I was thinking of making kamikaze shots, but I'm open to other suggestions."

"Careful what you wish for, darling," Tanner says tauntingly. "You're about to find yourself on the receiving end of a lot of Seaview email chains."

I sit on the edge of the bed, resting my palm flat on the comforter. "I saw some women playing poker the other night at your mom's place. Maybe they'll invite me to a card game."

"Gloria and her posse will take you for every cent you're worth."

"I'm not afraid of a challenge."

"So I've realized." I picture Tanner's smile. "What are you up to right now?"

"Not much," I tell him. "Izzy and I have been cleaning the attic for the last couple of hours. It's just as much of a disaster as you would expect it to be. What about you?"

"I'm leaving work."

"Now?" It's late. I can't believe he's still at the office.

"Long day." He says it like it's nothing. "Anyway, I've got muffins from Ralph's, if you're interested."

"I thought Ralph's closed at two." I was too busy to make my usual coffee and pastry run this morning. When I checked the hours online, the diner's website said it closed at two.

"I picked them up on my lunch break," he says. "Would've brought them over earlier, but things got busy." Tanner stopped at Ralph's to get me muffins? The idea of him going out of his way in the middle of the work day to do something for me gives me far too much pleasure. "Want to meet on your back porch in, say, ten minutes?"

Is this Tanner's way of apologizing for the kiss? Or is he hoping this meetup will turn into something more? I have no idea what's going on in his head, but saying yes seems like the easiest way to find out.

"Sounds good," I reply casually.

"And Delia?"

"Yeah?"

"I haven't forgotten about the other night," Tanner says. "I can still hear that little whimper you made."

With that, he hangs up, leaving me speechless. Is he serious? Did he just…?

Heat courses through my body like a live wire. I press my palms to my cheeks to help cool the flush. I can't let him rattle me like this.

There will be no kissing tonight.

***

I'm making out with Tanner.

It's his fault. We were innocently enjoying our muffins when he told me I had blueberry on the corner of my mouth and then offered to lick it off. Seconds later, I was in his lap.

We're sitting in a wicker chair on the back porch. Tanner's palms skirt up and down my thighs. He takes my bottom lip between his teeth, tugging slightly. Gasping, I rake my fingers through his soft hair. He smells like soap and something vaguely piney. I wonder what it is.

"Aftershave," he says against the side of my jaw.

My head feels like it's on a cloud. "Huh?"

His lips explore my neck. "That's what you smell. My aftershave."

"Oh." I didn't realize I said anything aloud. I blame Tanner's mouth.

He sucks the skin at the base of my neck, and my fingers dig deeper into his hair. I've only kissed him a couple of times, but it's safe to say he blows every other guy I've ever kissed out of the water. His mouth is soft but firm, commanding but adaptable. Tanner kisses like he's got nothing to prove—he's all skill and confidence.

I don't know what's happening. I'm a grown woman, kissing a guy I told myself I couldn't stand. If Delia of Two Weeks Ago could see me

208

now, she'd think I'd lost my mind. She might be right. It's illogical to let things progress with Tanner when I know nothing can come of them, but it's easy to cast my doubts aside when he's making my heart race like this.

I tug his mouth back to mine, meeting him in a frantic kiss. Explosions go off in my head with the push and pull of our lips. My legs rest on either side of Tanner's hips. I shift, finding him hard against the zipper of his jeans. The friction feels incredible. I rock slowly against him, relishing in the sensation.

There will be plenty of time for thinking and regret later.

Moments later, Tanner pulls his mouth off mine. "Darling," he says in a strained voice. He puts his hands on my hips, stilling their movements. "Any more of that, and I'll be done for it."

I feel light-headed. I blink several times as I gradually come back to myself, then I remember our surroundings. We're outside. It's dark, and the porch is secluded, but there's nothing stopping Izzy from walking out here and catching us. We need to take things somewhere else. I'm glad Tanner had the sense to stop us, because I certainly didn't.

"Izzy's home," I tell him. "Do you want to go to your place?"

Tanner shakes his head. "Not tonight." Shock and embarrassment wash over me at once. *Oh god.* I spent the last five minutes dry humping a guy who doesn't want to have sex with me. This feels like something out of a bad high school drama. I need to recover quickly. Make him think his rejection doesn't sting.

I unceremoniously climb off his lap, straightening out my rumpled clothes. "All right. Well, I should head inside. Izzy's probably wondering what's taking so long."

"Delia." Tanner reaches out and slips his fingers through mine. His palm is warm and calloused. He tugs me back into his lap. "I'd really like to take you to bed right now," he whispers. "Believe me. But I want to take you on a date first."

I study his face, surprised by the seriousness I find. That definitely isn't what I expected him to say. "A date?"

He raises our clasped palms, sliding his thumb along the back of mine. "I want to do things right," he says. "No skipping steps." The way he's talking sounds a lot like the start of a relationship, which confuses me.

"I thought we weren't putting labels on things," I remind him.

"No labels. Just dinner. I'll cook." His brow furrows slightly. "Your sister said something the other day about you not having anything decent to eat. I take it you don't like cooking."

"It's not that I dislike it," I say. "I just have a spectacular gift for burning everything."

"You are aware of these things called timers, right?"

I roll my eyes. "I use a meal delivery service at home."

"What a waste of money."

"It beats everything you eat being extra crispy."

He chuckles. "You like chicken?"

"Chicken's good."

"Then come over tomorrow night. I'll make dinner. You won't have to lift a finger. You can just have a glass of wine and look pretty. Afterward, I can show you my wood shop."

I shoot him a skeptical glance. "Is that a euphemism?"

"It can be."

I bite my lip to suppress a smile. As grumpy as he usually is, the bastard can be charming when he wants to be.

"Okay," I say. "I'll come over for dinner."

Tanner kisses me, and something heavy kicks in my chest. A warning, maybe. But I ignore it as I press my lips against his.

If I'm throwing my principles away, I might as well commit to it.

Twenty-Seven

Delia

"This place is…really nice," I observe as I shrug off my sweater in the simple but modern entryway to Tanner's house.

He raises a brow as he takes the sweater from me, hanging it on the nearby coat rack. "What exactly were you expecting?"

"I don't know." More chaos? Clutter? I should've known after seeing how neat Tanner's truck is that his house would be the same way. I guess I'm still having a hard time rectifying this version of Tanner—the one who opens doors and offers to cook me dinner—with my first impression of him. "Beer cans everywhere. Dirty laundry scattered about. The usual bachelor pad stuff."

"I don't think many people would take me seriously as the owner of a home construction company if my place looked like a frat house," he says, shutting the front door behind me. His eyes widen when he looks out the window. "You drove here?" I nod, glancing back at my car parked in the driveway. "You realize we share a property line, right?"

I roll my eyes, even though I know it must seem ridiculous. "I told Izzy I had a hair appointment. I couldn't leave my car, or else she'd know I was lying."

Tanner frowns. "You didn't want her to know you were coming here?"

"She asks too many questions."

Izzy called Morgan last night and gave her a dramatized (and wildly inaccurate) version of how she found Tanner and me when she arrived in Seaview. Afterward, Morgan called me for the real scoop. She had a lot of questions about Tanner. Now, both of my sisters are breathing down my neck about our relationship. I figured it was in my best interest not to mention tonight's date. I told Izzy I made an appointment at a salon thirty minutes away.

"A hair appointment. How much time does that give us? An hour?" he asks, sounding disappointed.

"A few, actually."

"How long does it take someone to do your hair?"

"It depends on what I'm getting done. If it's just a haircut, it might only take an hour. If I'm having highlights put in, it could be two or three."

Tanner looks horrified. "Jesus. It takes *that* much time?"

Feeling defensive, I run a hand over the back of my hair. "Well, yeah. It doesn't just look like this." I study the light-brown strands on top of Tanner's head. During our make-out session last night, I discovered they're just as soft as they look. Of course, Tanner wouldn't understand the time and effort that goes into hair maintenance. He probably gets his perfect, tousled look from a comb and cheap shampoo. "I could put you in touch with my stylist in Boston. I bet she'd love to do something with your hair."

From the look on his face, you'd think I asked him if he wanted me to rip out his teeth with a pair of pliers. "I'll pass."

We head through the foyer, following a short hallway that leads deeper inside the house. My heels click softly on the hardwood. We step inside a contemporary kitchen with stainless-steel appliances and a granite countertop lined with barstools. Something sizzles in a covered pan on the stovetop. A delicious blend of herbs and spices fills my lungs.

"It smells amazing in here," I say, taking a deep whiff.

"You gonna say everything in a surprised tone?"

"Not everything."

"You might give a guy a complex, darling."

"I'm sure you have enough ego to keep yourself afloat."

Chuckling, Tanner heads to the stovetop. He lifts the lid off the sizzling skillet and grabs a pair of tongs off the counter to flip whatever delicious-smelling food he's cooking. "I'm making lemon chicken and salad," he says. "Hopefully that's good enough for your sophisticated palette."

"Anything that doesn't require me to cook is sophisticated enough for me."

Over his shoulder, he shoots me a questioning look. "Wine?"

"Yes, please."

Tanner motions for me to take a seat at the countertop. As the chicken continues to fry, he snags a pair of wine glasses out of the cupboard and then grabs a bottle of white wine from the fridge. He removes the cork with a bottle opener. As I watch him, I think of the conversation I had the other night with his mom.

"Your mom told me something interesting about you the other night," I say vaguely as he fills a glass and hands it to me.

"Should I be worried?" he asks, pouring a glass for himself.

"Only if you're afraid of being exposed as a hypocrite. She said you're a big wine drinker. That you're even picky about the bottles she buys."

Seemingly unaffected, Tanner slips the bottle back inside the fridge. "How does that make me a hypocrite?"

"You've been calling me snobby for weeks, but you refuse to drink anything that comes out of a screw top. Do you not see the hypocrisy there?"

"Snobbiness has nothing to do with personal taste. It's about attitude."

"You think my attitude is snobby?" I narrow my eyes over the rim of my wine glass.

Tanner shrugs. "Sure." I open my mouth to argue with him, but then he says, "I also think you're smart and hardworking. That you dish out as well as you take and genuinely care about the people in your life. I like you, Delia. I wouldn't have asked you here tonight if I didn't."

His earnestness catches me by surprise. I've never had someone compliment me so openly. It warms my chest and leaves my head feeling light and airy. I knew Tanner was attracted to me. The whole kissing thing made that pretty clear. But his words go beyond attraction. He's complimenting me as a person. I want to show that I appreciate it, but I don't know how. Unlike Tanner, I'm not versed in this style of directness. I'm used to playing coy, keeping my true feelings at bay. It's not a switch I can suddenly turn off.

Tanner must understand this. He saunters over to the stovetop with a smug expression on his face and says, "you don't have to say anything. You made your feelings for me perfectly clear the other night when you were fishing for an invitation to my bed."

I hold my chin high, despite the blush I know must be staining my cheeks. "It's amazing how quickly feelings change, though, isn't it?" The sentiment applies to our situation in more ways than one. My feelings for Tanner have shifted a lot since we met. Two weeks ago, I never would've imagined myself drinking wine at his place, listening to him pay me compliments.

Half a glass later, Tanner finishes making dinner. He tells me to head over to the kitchen table while he plates the food. There's a vase with pale yellow flowers in the center of the table. Did he buy these for tonight? Tanner doesn't strike me as the kind of guy who keeps fresh flowers all the time.

When he brings our dinner to the table, he catches me eyeing the flowers. "Those are for you," he says. "They didn't have a lot of options at the grocery store."

"They're pretty," I say. "Between the flowers and the wine, I might actually start to think you have good taste."

Laughing, Tanner slides a plate in front of me. I nearly gasp when I see the perfectly golden chicken breast flecked with green herbs. The side salad looks amazing, too. Leafy lettuce with a generous portion of dressing and freshly grated parmesan cheese sprinkled over the top. My mouth waters.

"Okay. So you *really* know how to cook," I say, picking up my fork and knife to cut into the chicken.

Tanner sits in the chair across from me. "Jacob and I lived together for a couple of years after college," he says. "It was either learn to cook or survive off frozen pizzas."

I pop a bite of chicken into my mouth. It's warm, juicy, and flavorful. "When did you buy this place?"

"About three years ago," Tanner says. "It was a dump when I bought it. Looked a little like Aggie's place."

I scoff. "I don't believe for a second that it was as bad as Grandma Aggie's." A question pops into my mind. "Did you know how bad it was? Did she ever invite you inside?"

"The first time I went inside that house was the day I came over to give you an estimate. I had no idea it looked like that."

"It's strange. My mom told me Grandma Aggie loved that house. The reason she and my dad stopped speaking was because he wanted her to move in with my family, and she didn't want to leave Seaview. I know she was older, but it looked like her place had been piling up with junk for years. You would think someone who chose a house over her family would at least have the decency to take care of it." It's a thought that's been gnawing at me since I stepped inside

Grandma Aggie's house. Why would she let it fall apart?

"Maybe she realized picking the house was a mistake," Tanner suggests.

"You sound like my mom. She thinks stubbornness was the real issue between my dad and grandma. Neither of them could admit they wanted the fighting to end."

Tanner tilts his head curiously. "You don't agree?"

Shrugging, I cut another piece of chicken. "I don't know. I'm sure stubbornness had something to do with it. You don't hold a grudge for twenty years unless you're stubborn. But if Grandma Aggie really regretted her decision, don't you think she would've done something about it? Boston's only two hours from here. She could've visited if she wanted to."

"I don't know if it's that simple. Change can be hard, even when it means getting out of a tough situation. Sometimes the unknown is scarier than being unhappy."

"So, what? You think Grandma Aggie was too afraid to reach out?"

"Who knows? It wouldn't excuse the way she treated you and your sisters, but it might explain why she left you the house." Maybe Tanner's right, and Grandma Aggie couldn't overcome her fears to make amends with my family. Still, I don't think it's a good enough reason to justify her behavior. People have to change if they want to improve their lives. If Grandma Aggie was truly distraught over what happened with Dad, she would've found the courage to do something about it.

When we finish eating, Tanner whisks our empty plates over to the sink and then tops off our wine glasses. He asks if I want to check out his wood shop in the backyard. I say yes. Tanner's woodworking has been a mystery so far. He's shut down every time it's been mentioned. I'm excited to hear more details.

We head out to the porch and take the steps down to Tanner's yard, where a gray shed sits in the far back corner.

"Is this where you take your murder victims?" I ask.

He raises a brow. "A wood shop? Seems a little on the nose, don't you think?"

"Of course. I wouldn't want to mistake you for a run-of-the-mill serial killer."

Tanner grins and pulls a key out of his pocket. Outside, the shed looks small and unassuming, but that illusion shatters when he unlocks the door and guides me inside. He hits a light switch, revealing a work space with shiny wood floors and a large rectangular table in the center. Cabinets run along the perimeter, and various tools hang on a pegboard on the wall.

"Is it insulated in here?" I ask, noticing the temperature feels warmer inside.

Tanner nods. "I had it done last year. Couldn't do any work in the winter otherwise."

Wine glass in hand, I wander around the shop. A stack of wood planks rests on top of the cabinets, and a wireless speaker is suspended in the corner of the ceiling. By the work table sits a stool with a worn-looking leather seat.

"I take it you spend a lot of time out here," I say.

"Whenever I find the time."

"How did you get into this?" I know Tanner works in construction, but woodworking doesn't seem like the most common hobby for a thirty-year-old man.

Tanner stands at the head of the work table. "I thought it would be a good way to expand the business," he says. "We already build homes—why not make furniture? I taught myself by watching videos online."

"You taught yourself?" I learned how to embroider using YouTube videos, but that doesn't involve tools sharp enough to take off fingers.

"It wasn't so hard," Tanner replies. "Not with my construction background."

"So, did you teach your employees to build furniture or do you make everything yourself?"

"Actually, I decided not to sell anything. I like woodworking. It can be long and labor-intensive, but it's satisfying to make something that you can hold in your hand. I'd rather do it as a hobby than turn it into another work thing."

"I get that." Mariah and Kali love running as much as I do. They compete in races all over Boston, and they're constantly trying to get me to join them, but I have no interest in adding a competitive element to running. I like doing it for myself. No stakes or expectations. "It's nice to have something for yourself. Making it into work would probably take the enjoyment out of it. Anyway, what kind of stuff do you build?"

"Chairs, end tables, dressers—you name it," Tanner says. "Mom and her friends treat me like their personal furniture maker." He shakes his head as if he's annoyed by it, but the smile on his lips says otherwise. "I've got a couple of recent pieces over in the corner, if you want to check them out."

Intrigued, I take a few steps toward the far-left corner, where several wooden objects lay in a small circle, including a three-drawer chest with brass handles, a claw-foot end table, and a footstool stained a cherry-red color. Each piece is smooth and polished and evenly stained. They look like they belong in the showroom of a furniture store. I picture the chest of drawers as part of an elegant bedroom setup. Tanner could easily sell the items if he wanted to.

I run my fingers along the glossy surface of the end table and look over at him. "Now I can see why you hated my grandmother's dresser so much." I remember the look of displeasure on his face when I told him I didn't want to throw out Grandma Aggie's dresser. No wonder he seemed put off by the idea of keeping it. His handiwork is flawless.

"Hate is a strong word," he says.

"You offered to take it to the curb. You said it would be better as scrap."

"I wouldn't exactly call it a quality piece of craftsmanship."

I shift my attention back to Tanner's gorgeous woodworking projects, mesmerized by the quality and detail. I never would've thought the blunt, demanding man in front of me could create something so beautiful. But I suppose I misjudged him in a lot of the same ways he misjudged me.

"Your work is incredible," I say. "I can't imagine being able to do something like this."

"I could teach you," Tanner replies, his green eyes flashing down to my hands. "But I don't think those pretty fingernails would last very long." I glance at my outgrown French manicure. I need to find a nail salon in Seaview soon.

"I think I'd prefer to be an observer."

He places his half-empty wine glass on top of the nearby cabinets. "You probably wouldn't be a very good student, anyway." There's a taunt in his voice. He's trying to get me to react, and it's totally working.

"What makes you think that?" I was an excellent student in school. Hard working. Diligent. I took the best notes in class. My classmates always asked to borrow them when they missed a day. But I have a feeling Tanner's baseless assumption has nothing to do with my academic capabilities.

"You're not a very good listener," he says matter-of-factly.

"Untrue," I tell him. "I just don't like listening to you."

He folds his arms against his chest, putting his forearms on display. It takes every ounce of my self-restraint to stop myself from peeking down at them. I deserve a medal for my strength. Tanner has spectacular forearms.

"That would be a serious problem if we were working with high-power tools," he points out. "And you know how I feel about safety."

"I'm sure I could manage under the right circumstances."

Tanner inches toward me, closing the gap between us. He plucks the wine glass out of my hand and sets it on the cabinets. "What if I told you to be still for a moment?” He looks down at me, and my heartbeat soars. “Think you could manage that?” His voice is playful, teasing. It sends a delicious zing through my blood. Part of me wants to tell him no simply to prolong the tension.

Then Tanner kisses me.

Twenty-Eight

Delia

It's a slow, sweet kiss. His lips are warm and taste
like wine. He puts his hands on my hips, and I
wrap mine around the back of his neck. I close my
eyes, savoring the lightness of the moment. It
feels like watching a sunset on the beach. Like
slipping into a bath after a long run. Warm and
comfortable and perfect.

Then it changes.

Tanner parts my lips with his own, licking his
tongue inside my mouth. At the same time, his
thumbs rub circles around the dimples on my
lower back. I climb up to my tiptoes, tightening
my hold on his neck and pressing my body flush
against his. The kiss grows urgent, and our
mouths collide frantically.

In a swift move, Tanner lifts me off the ground,
holding me up by the backs of my thighs, and
places me up on the edge of the cabinets. He
lowers his mouth to my neck, leaving hot kisses
all over my skin. My head falls back on a sigh.
Tanner's hands grip my waist, my hips, before
sliding down to cup my ass.

I tangle my fingers in his hair as he continues
kissing my neck. My legs open slightly, and
Tanner takes that as his cue to slip one of his legs

between them. His hard thigh presses against my center. Pressure tightens in my core like a rubber band.

Tanner pulls back to look at me, breathing unsteadily. "Tell me what I can do, darling," he says, eyes brimming with heat. "Can I touch you? Taste you? I'll do whatever you want. Whatever you'll let me do. Let me get you off like I've been dying to for weeks."

My head spins. His words act like a drug, making me high. I've never had a guy say something so raw to me before. I can't think clearly enough to form sentences. The only thing I can do is close the gap between our mouths and hope it's enough to communicate the need growing inside of me.

Fortunately, it seems to work. Kissing me fiercely, Tanner slips his palms up the back of my silk blouse. His touch leaves a trail of fire on my skin. He finds the clasp on my bra and unclips it, the material going slack against my chest. Then he brings his hands around to my front, toying with the hem of my blouse.

"God, I love these little blouses," he says, undoing the buttons.

Somehow, I find my voice. "I thought you didn't like my clothes."

He shakes his head. "They've been driving me out of my mind, Delia. Do you have any idea how many times I've thought about tearing one of them off of you?"

"Then I hope you're prepared to shell out some serious cash," I say, half-teasing. "These blouses are expensive."

Finally, he finishes his work with the buttons. "I'll replace every single one." That confession shouldn't send my pulse into overdrive, but the materialistic side of my brain loves that Tanner would spend an ungodly amount on blouses just so he can get me out of my clothes faster. It's a powerful feeling, knowing I'm responsible for these desperate confessions. The fact that it's *Tanner* saying them makes it ten times better. He usually seems so collected and self-assured. Right now, he's ragged. Out of control.

Tanner lowers the blouse down my shoulders, leaving me in nothing but jeans and a lacy black bra that hangs loosely from my chest. Feeling bold, I slide off the bra and drop it on the floor. Tanner's eyes darken as they take in my exposed skin. He mumbles a string of curses, and then his mouth is on my neck again. His hands go to my chest. My breasts feel heavy in his calloused palms as he kneads the skin, my nipples tightening under his touch. He replaces his hands with his lips a moment later, pulling one nipple into his warm mouth. I gasp as he switches to the other.

"Tanner," I cry as the need builds inside me.

"I could listen to you beg all day, darling."

He drops a hand down the middle of my stomach, stopping when he reaches for the button of my jeans. He looks up at me expectantly, and I give him a small nod.

Popping the button, Tanner lowers the zipper and then tugs the jeans down my legs. He drops to his knees and lavishes me with his mouth and fingers. Stars dance behind my eyes. I nearly arch off the cabinets, but Tanner puts his other hand on my hip to keep me in place. After a moment, I find release.

Tanner stands and runs a thumb over the blush on my cheeks. "So fucking pretty," he says, sounding almost delirious. Desire comes alive in me once again. My heart feels like it might burst out of my chest.

I want him. Now.

As I grab the hem of Tanner's T-shirt, he puts a hand on my wrist to stop me.

"Don't tell me you don't put out on the first date," I say, somewhat joking. Sex or not, I'm fairly confident what we just did violated any sort of standard dating protocol.

Tanner laughs. "I don't have condoms out here."

He kisses my temple and helps me redress in a matter of seconds. Then we're rushing out of Tanner's workshop in a mess of clashing mouths and rumpled clothes. When we get back inside, Tanner lifts me up, wrapping my legs around his waist, and carries me upstairs. He opens a door to what I presume to be his bedroom, depositing me on a large bed.

I glance around the room for a moment. It's a simple, well-kept space with gray walls and basic furnishings. "You know, that end table you made would look great over—"

Tanner cuts me off with a bruising kiss. "Let's talk about your thoughts on the interior design later, yeah?"

I scramble to my elbows, and then his lips are on mine again. His knees rest on either side of my hips, pinning me to the bed. Tanner does away with my clothes as quickly as he put them on.

Then he sits up and sheds his own T-shirt. My eyes wander over the ridges of his stomach. He's all tan skin and lean muscles. Tanner shucks his jeans next. My heart hammers when I see the outline in his black briefs. He pulls his underwear down, then grabs a foil packet out of the nightstand and tears it open, slipping on a condom.

Tanner grips my hip and thrusts inside me. My back bows from the sudden intrusion, and tears prick the corners of my eyes. It's almost too much. With dark eyes, Tanner looks down at me, his features strained. "Christ, Delia. You feel so good. Just like I knew you would."

His words send a ripple of heat through me. Tanner gives me a second to adjust before he pulls back his hips and pushes inside me again. I wrap my legs around his waist as he moves faster, the pressure inside me becoming more urgent. His large body hovers over me. My hands find their way to his broad shoulders, gripping them for support. My eyelids attempt to shut, but Tanner won't allow it.

"Eyes on me, darling," he says in a commanding voice. I do as he says, keeping my eyes open and focused on him. A lock of brown hair has fallen over his forehead. His expression is ravenous as he drives me closer to the edge. White spots flood my vision, and I lose the ability to form thoughts. Tanner follows shortly after, and then he pulls my mouth to his in a sloppy kiss.

After he rolls off me, we lie there for a few minutes, silent and slick with sweat. As I stare at the darkened ceiling, one thought echoes in my mind.

I don't know how anything could top that.

***

Tanner

"I can hear you thinking, you know," I mumble over the top of Delia's strawberry-scented hair. "Sounds like the wheels in your head are turning a thousand miles a minute."

Delia lets out an uneasy laugh, her bare back brushing against my front. The movement causes my blood to stir, and I force myself to think about anything but Delia's soft skin. As much as I want to spend the rest of the night buried inside her, I know it would be a bad idea to start something right now. She's already freaking out.

Immediately following our mind-blowing sex, Delia grabbed the sheet and scrambled to the bathroom, mumbling something about needing to clean up. When she came back a few minutes later, her face was whiter than drywall. She hovered by the side of the bed, eyeing her clothes on the floor as if she planned on throwing them on and bolting out of here.

Her reaction didn't surprise me. Delia avoided me for days after we *almost* kissed in my truck. Of course she would panic after what I can confidently say was the best sex of my life. God, it was incredible. I knew it would be good, but I didn't expect it to blow every expectation I had out of the water. The details play on an endless loop in my brain. The noises she made. The way she dug those tiny fingernails into my back, no doubt leaving scratches. The thoughts alone are enough to set me on fire.

Get a grip, you asshole, I tell myself, shaking off the thoughts. I can fantasize about all the

229

things I still want to do with Delia Forrest later. Right now, my focus needs to be on keeping her here.

I pulled Delia back into bed before she could make any hasty decisions, tucking her body against mine. About twenty minutes have passed since then. She hasn't said a word.

I need to be careful about what I say or do next. Delia seemed serious the other night when she told me she had no intentions of getting into another relationship. Now that we've slept together, she's probably worried about what it means for us, but if she thinks I'm going to sit back and let her spiral, she's got another thing coming.

Delia turns her head, flashing her big brown eyes at me. "What am I thinking?" she asks in a groggy voice.

She looks beautiful like this, sleepy and rumpled. Her hair is a mess, thanks to the work of my hands, and a soft pink flush colors her cheeks and chest. It's a lot different from the prim and polished version of her that I'm used to seeing. I like it. Probably too much, if the hammering in my chest is any indication. I get the feeling Delia doesn't share this unguarded side of herself with many people. A possessive part of me loves that I'm one of them.

"That I shattered your expectations for all other men," I say, somewhat joking. That possessive side doesn't like the thought of Delia sleeping with anyone else.

She rolls her eyes. "You're certainly the most arrogant man I've ever been with." There's playfulness in her response, but there's an underlying sense of uncertainty, too.

I trace my thumb along the smooth crease of her hip. "What's really on your mind?"

She bites her bottom lip. "How complicated this makes things."

"What's the issue? You don't think you'll be able to control yourself around me now that you've seen me naked?"

"I think you're the one who needs to worry about that," she says, shifting her ass against me. I groan and flip on my back, fighting off the desire that courses through me. "I guess I'm just anxious. I wasn't expecting this."

"You mean getting me in bed wasn't part of your plan?"

"Definitely not."

I'm hesitant about my next words. I don't want to push her too much, but curiosity gets the best of me. "Can I ask you something?"

"Is it about taking care of your issue?" she asks, her eyes not-so-subtly trailing down my body. "Because I think you brought that on yourself." I pinch her side. She lets out a small yelp before turning to her side and folding her hands under the pillow.

"This need for planning and control…where did it come from?"

Delia's quiet. Her face is thoughtful, concentrated. As if she's weighing the question and debating whether to answer honestly. "My dad was diagnosed with skin cancer when I was in seventh grade," she says. "To call it a shock would be an understatement. Dad always seemed so happy and healthy. It didn't make sense for him to be sick. He spent a few months undergoing treatments and then eventually went into remission. But when the cancer came back a few years later, it was more aggressive. I've never felt more helpless than I did watching my dad get sicker, knowing there was nothing I could do about it.

"I did everything I could to help around the house, making school lunches for my sisters and washing dishes when the sink piled up. It was the one semblance of control I had. It gave me something to focus on. Made me realize how much I value order, structure. The ability to take charge of your own circumstances. It only got worse after Dad died. I was so sad. Planning and scheduling and organizing became the only thing I could control. So that's what I did."

I stare at her for a long moment, her confession hanging in the air. I sensed there was something more to her need for structure and planning, but I didn't think it had anything to do with her dad's passing. A lump builds in the back of my throat. The sadness in her voice is too much. I want to do something. To take the pain from her as if it's a tangible object. But I know from experience that it's not that simple. Nothing I say or do will erase the hurt. So instead of trying to fix things, I pull her body toward mine and press a kiss on her shoulder.

"I'm sorry you had to go through that," I say. "Thank you for telling me."

We lay there for a while, saying nothing. I'm not sure how much time passes, but eventually Delia worms her way out of my arms. "I should probably head home," she says, crawling toward the edge of the bed. "It's late. Izzy has to be wondering where I am." She snatches her bra and panties off the floor and starts to put them on.

A pang of disappointment hits me. I want her to stay the night, but Delia didn't tell her sister she was coming here, so she obviously wants to keep things under wraps. It annoys me that she doesn't want anyone to know about us. I don't care who finds out—if anything, I'd welcome it. I have zero interest in seeing any woman besides Delia. I hope she feels the same about seeing other guys, but I'm not going to push her on the issue tonight. Not when she's already opened up to me. That's a conversation for another time.

"I'll walk you out," I tell her, climbing out of bed.

We dress quickly and then head downstairs. In the foyer, I help Delia slip on her sweater and open the front door. We're about to step outside when I'm struck by a thought that has me coming to an immediate stop. Delia's face wrinkles with confusion.

"Hold on a second," I say, putting a hand on her shoulder.

Without further explanation, I turn and race up the stairs. Reentering the bedroom, I tear open the top drawer of my dresser and grab the first T-shirt I see. I jog back downstairs, where Delia waits with a puzzled expression. She eyes the balled-up fabric in my hand.

"What did you…?"

I thrust the shirt toward her. "Here." She takes it, visibly confused. "You can keep this. Wear it. Don't wear it. Just do me a favor and burn that douchebag's shirt, all right?"

She blinks slowly, looking at me as though I've lost my mind. I can't say that I blame her for it. But if making Delia question my sanity gets her asshole ex-boyfriend's shirt out of her wardrobe, then I'd consider it a success.

Her mouth twitches. "The shirt bothers you that much?"

There's no reason to deny it. "You have no idea."

We walk down the porch. When we reach Delia's car, I stop her and kiss her on the mouth, hard and fast. She looks dazed when I pull back.

"I'll call you tomorrow," I say, tucking a strand of hair behind her ear.

Delia nods. "Okay. Uh, goodnight."

Her flustered state sends pleasure through my blood. "Goodnight."

I stand in the drive, watching as she clumsily gets into her car and then drives away.

Twenty-Nine

Delia

I have dinner at Tanner's place again the following night.

It's a much more laid-back night than yesterday. Tanner didn't leave work until after seven, so we ordered takeout and ate on the couch in his living room. Afterward, he dragged me into his lap and kissed his way down my body, exploring every inch of me with his tongue. When I crept back to Grandma Aggie's house with flushed cheeks and rumpled hair a couple hours later, Izzy was sitting at the kitchen table. She greeted me with a raised brow. I told her I'd gone for a long walk, then I sprinted upstairs to take a shower.

Izzy definitely suspects something's going on between me and Tanner, but she hasn't forced me to talk about it, a fact I'm eternally grateful for. Not talking about it is the only thing keeping me from panicking over everything.

I like him. A lot. It goes against my better judgment to get involved with someone when I know it has to end, but I can't help myself. Being with Tanner is fun and easy. I'm not worrying about Grandma Aggie's house when I'm with him. I'm focused on our conversations. His mouth. Finding ways to match his playful teasing. It's hard for me to imagine what my experience in Seaview would've looked like had I not met him. He's filled up so much of it.

Now that we've given in to this attraction, there's no sense in stopping. What would be the point? I'm going to be in Seaview for a while longer, anyway. As long as I remind myself that things with Tanner can't progress beyond a few weeks, I'll be fine.

A few nights later, I decide to go for an evening run. I get back to Grandma Aggie's place about an hour later, feeling sweaty and exhausted. I tried the beachside trail Tanner recommended. He was right about the view—it's incredible. Plus, it's a concrete trail, so I got to enjoy the views without the challenge of running on sand.

Kicking off my sneakers by the front door, I head to the kitchen, where I use the fridge dispenser to fill a large glass of water. Music plays through my earbuds as I down the water in several gulps. I wipe my wet mouth with the back of my hand and then set the glass on the counter. My muscles feel sore in the best way.

I feel him before I see him. Tanner's warm breath skates down my neck as he presses his front to my back, trapping me against the counter. His piney aftershave hits my lungs, and goosebumps rise on my skin. I fish my phone out of the pocket of my running shorts, pausing the music and plucking the earbuds out of my ears.

"You know," Tanner whispers, his lips brushing against my ear, "if you were looking for a workout, you could've come to find me." His hands trail shamelessly over my hips. A thrill spikes inside me. I didn't expect the sneaking around aspect of this situation to be so enjoyable, but it's fun and exciting. It feels like I'm a teenager hanging out with the troubled guy my parents warned me to stay away from. I was never the rebellious type, but I can certainly see the appeal.

"Why?" I ask incredulously. "Are you offering to be my punching bag?" A quick glance over my shoulder reveals Tanner's full mouth, tipped up in a grin. A faint coat of stubble covers his square jaw. He must not have shaved this morning. The look suits him, but it makes me wonder how I smell his aftershave. Am I imagining it?

Tanner rubs a palm over the tight fabric of my shorts. "I'll be whatever you want as long as you're wearing these."

I let out a breathless laugh as his hand continues to roam. "You're less unpleasant when you're horny."

"I've been horny since I met you." I shake my head at him, ignoring the way his words make my pulse spike.

"I'm assuming Izzy let you in," I say. "Unless you were so desperate for some action that you actually committed a felony."

He chuckles. "I tried calling about an hour ago," he explains. "I had some time after work, so I figured I'd swing by to finish sanding Aggie's floor. I went to the front door when you didn't pick up. Izzy let me inside. She said you'd gone for a run, but that she was more than happy to let me do manual labor for her. Her words, not mine."

"Well, it's good to know this isn't a breaking-and-entering situation. It would be very inconvenient if I had to find a new contractor because my current one doesn't understand the concept of boundaries."

He brushes his mouth over the shell of my ear. "Another contractor wouldn't touch you like I do." Tanner's lips descend on my neck, covering the skin in kisses. My head buzzes like I've just had a few sips of wine, and my body sinks into his.

I try to talk some sense into both of us before I completely lose it.

"Izzy's here," I remind him.

"There are multiple rooms in this house, darling."

"What if she hears us?"

His tongue flicks across my neck. "I guess you'll just have to be quiet."

As I turn to press my lips to his, the sound of footsteps barreling down the staircase rattles through my ears. I barely have a second to push Tanner away before Izzy enters the kitchen. She's dressed in a pair of drawstring shorts and a gray camisole. Her curly hair sits in a messy knot at the top of her head. Her red lips tug into a smirk when she sees Tanner and me standing on opposite sides of the kitchen. She doesn't comment on the situation, even though I know my face must be bright pink.

Her eyes flash to me. "I'm ready whenever you are, Del," she says.

"Oh, yeah," I say as a memory dawns on me. "Give me fifteen minutes to shower, then I'll be ready to go."

Tanner looks between us curiously. "Where are you two headed?"

"Hell," Izzy grumbles in reply.

I roll my eyes. "We're going to the Seaview Historical Society to look at some old photos of Grandma Aggie," I explain. "I met a woman named Nancy Orson at the hardware store the other day. She said she was friends with Grandma Aggie and invited me to come by."

"And Delia foolishly agreed to," Izzy says with a huff.

"I didn't think she would actually hold me to it."

"That was your first mistake," Izzy says. "Don't you know what they say about making assumptions, Delia?"

Tanner smirks, as if this exchange amuses him. "I guess I should leave you to it then," he says. "Have fun with Nancy. I hear she's a talker."

Izzy groans loudly, and Tanner and I share a laugh. He's standing on the other side of the counter, staring at me. His fingers flex at his side. It feels like he wants to kiss me. Part of me wants to let him. A quick peck before he goes. But that would be romantic. Intimate. That isn't us. It can't be. So instead of giving into my impulses, I tell Tanner goodbye, then round the counter and head upstairs.

***

Nancy Orson likes to hear herself talk.

Her mouth hasn't stopped moving since Izzy and I arrived at the Seaview Historical Society a half hour ago. It's an old-fashioned storefront on Main Street, nestled between a taffy shop and a law office.

After I introduced Izzy as my younger sister, Nancy welcomed us inside and offered to show us around the quaint building. The wooden floorboards creak under our feet as we wander around the small space, which is filled with glass display cases containing vintage advertisements and license plates and brass compasses.

As we walk, Nancy rambles about the building's history. It was constructed in the late nineteenth century. About fifteen years ago, a big storm swept through town, collapsing part of the roof. Nancy and Grandma Aggie spearheaded a town-wide fundraiser to collect money for the repairs, bringing it back to its former glory.

"I didn't realize Grandma Aggie was so sentimental," Izzy says in a droll tone.

Her sarcasm goes over Nancy's head. The old woman gets a misty, faraway look in her eye. "She loved Seaview more than anything."

"She certainly had her priorities, didn't she?"

I pinch the back of my sister's arm when Nancy isn't looking.

After a few minutes, Nancy guides us toward a cluttered desk in the back of the room. She tells us to have a seat as she grabs a pile of weathered-looking photographs off the corner of the desk. Splitting the pile in half, she hands each of us a small stack.

"I found these when I was going through our archives," Nancy says. "Most of them are from historical society meetings and town events. There are a couple with your grandfather in them." I flip through a series of photos of Grandma Aggie beaming at the camera. Studying her features, I finally see the resemblance between us. We share the same thin brows, dark-brown hair, and puffy bottom lip.

In one photo, a forty-something Grandma Aggie stands with her arms around the neck of a tall man with a graying beard. It must be my grandfather. They look blissful, happy. I wonder if they were. I know nothing about my grandparents' marriage. They might be my relatives, but they're no different than any other seemingly happy couple I've ever seen. I share a look with Izzy. She must be thinking the same thing.

As I skim through the rest of the pictures, Nancy drops a large cardboard box on top of the desk. "This is everything Aggie left here after she…passed." Nancy winces as though she wishes there was a more delicate way to word it.

I peer inside the box. It's mostly filled with old notebooks and desk supplies. I fish around, pretending to be interested in its contents, and stumble upon a hardback leather scrapbook. Plucking the scrapbook out of the box, I see the front has an inscription in gold cursive letters. I quickly realize it's my initials.

"What's this?" I ask, turning the book to face Nancy.

The woman gives a sad smile. "Oh," she says quietly. "That's a little project Aggie asked me to work on for her." I flip to the first page, where I discover a collage of photos from the day I was born. In one shot, Mom cradles me in a hospital bed, Dad smiling beside her. A large banner that says "it's a girl!" hangs on the wall behind them. In another photo, I'm nestled in a car seat, sleeping peacefully. The third image shows

Grandma Aggie holding me in a swaddle of pink blankets.

I flip through the rest of the book, finding photos of me from various holiday gatherings and birthday parties over the years. The scrapbook ends when I'm six years old, which is the age I was when Dad and Grandma Aggie stopped speaking to each other.

I can't believe this. "My grandmother asked you to put this together?" I say, unable to hide the surprise in my voice. Why would she do that? What would possess a person to preserve memories of someone they purposefully removed from their life?

Nancy nods. "I'm sort of the town scrapbook expert. Aggie asked me to make one for each of you girls. I'm guessing she wanted to surprise you. I only ever got around to making yours, Delia." I try to meet Izzy's gaze, but she's still scanning her stack of photos, seemingly unaffected by the bombshell revelation. I can't tell if she doesn't care or if she doesn't want anyone to know she cares, but I don't blame her either way.

Grandma Aggie had years to reconcile with Dad. She had even more years to reconcile with me and Izzy and Morgan. She chose not to. A scrapbook doesn't change that. Nor does it erase the years of silence and hurt.

"You can keep this stuff," Nancy says, motioning toward the box. "I think Aggie would want you to have it."

I force a smile, despite the waves of confusion coursing through me. "Thank you."

Izzy and I leave the historical society an hour later, cradling Grandma Aggie's belongings in our arms. When we get back to the car, I toss my grandmother's stuff in the back and then hop into the driver's seat.

"Well, that was weird," I say, starting up the engine.

"Which part?" Izzy asks as she puts on her seatbelt. "Pretending to care about Seaview history or pretending to care about photos of Grandma Aggie?"

"The scrapbook, obviously," I clarify. "I mean, what was that? Why would Grandma Aggie have scrapbooks made for us?"

Izzy shrugs. "Maybe she wanted her friends to think she loved her grandchildren."

"Maybe. But those photos are, like, twenty years old. Why would she have kept them all this time?"

"I don't know, Delia," Izzy says. "But I wouldn't waste your time overanalyzing it. It's not like Grandma Aggie's here to answer your questions."

It's true. Grandma Aggie isn't here to explain her strange behavior.

The problem is, I don't think I'm capable of *not* overanalyzing it.

Thirty

Delia

Izzy and I finish cleaning the attic on Friday night.

It's a little after seven when we pack up the last box and lug it downstairs. Izzy looks giddy when we drop it in the kitchen. She declares that tonight calls for a celebration. To me, a celebration would mean putting on sweatpants and watching reality TV until my eyes glaze over, but Izzy has other ideas. She pulls up a list of local bars on her phone and finds a place called Seaview Tavern, which claims to have the best cocktails in town. I try to make the argument that having the best cocktails in a town with only three bars really isn't that much of an accomplishment, but my words fall on uninterested ears.

"I'm ordering an Uber now," Izzy says, her fingers flying over her phone screen. "Hurry up and get dressed!"

With no time to waste, I run upstairs and swap my tank top and leggings for a jean skirt and a black babydoll tee. I run a brush through my hair and swipe on a coat of lip gloss, then slip into a pair of wedges. They're probably a little dressy for a Seaview bar, but I don't care. You can take a girl out of the city, but you can't take away her love for good footwear.

As I grab my purse from the bedroom, it occurs to me that going out with Izzy means I won't be seeing Tanner tonight. I've spent every night at his place for the past week and a half. Some nights we've had dinner and watched movies. Others we've sat on his front porch and talked about our jobs, interests, and childhoods. It hasn't been long, but we've already fallen into a routine. A pleasant one. I wish I didn't have to break it. I have no idea how long Izzy plans on staying out, but her decision to order a car rather than drive to the bar tells me she intends on getting wasted. I should probably let Tanner know not to expect me tonight.

I send him a brief text. *Getting drinks with Izzy. Not sure what time I'll be back.* I try to ignore the disappointment that ripples through my body. I shouldn't get so attached to Tanner. Not when our relationship has an expiration date. Besides, I've been neglecting Izzy these past few days. She came to Seaview to make sure I wasn't lonely. I ought to be doing the same for her. Going out is a good idea for us.

I don't bother waiting for a response from Tanner before I stuff my phone into my purse. I head downstairs right as Izzy shouts that our Uber has arrived. We climb into the backseat of the car, making quiet conversation on the ten-minute ride to the bar. The driver drops us off in front of a lively red-brick building.

Music pumps through the outdoor speakers as patrons mingle on the small enclosed patio. Izzy and I follow a crowd inside, where we're met with a darkly lit interior crammed with people. Rather than stopping at the hostess stand, Izzy grabs my wrist and drags me over to the bar. We sit on what appear to be the only two empty stools at the bar. I don't know how my sister found them in the crowd, but she's nothing if not determined.

A young bartender with facial piercings and a patchy beard stops by to take our orders. Izzy opts for an espresso martini while I stay committed to my tried-but-true white wine.

Despite the bar's hecticness, it doesn't take long for our drinks to arrive. Izzy plucks the stir stick out of her glass and drops it on a cocktail napkin before bringing the drink to her lips. She leaves a smudge of red lipstick on the edge of the glass.

"Seaview might've won me over with this place," she says, observing the busy bar with eager eyes.

"Seriously? This place?" There's nothing wrong with Seaview Tavern, and we've only been here for a couple of minutes, but it seems like your run-of-the-mill small town bar. The space thrums with music and sweaty bodies, and it smells like beer and fried food. You could drive to any town in America on a Friday night and find a place exactly like it.

Izzy nods. "The drinks are good, and we didn't have to wait two hours for a seat. That's a win to me."

"It sounds like you're tired of the New York bar scene," I tell her.

She shrugs as though she's considering the possibility. "Could be. A bar opened just around the corner from my apartment that sells tequila shots infused with protein powder."

I wrinkle my nose, horrified by the combination. "That's disgusting."

"That's New York douchebag," she mutters.

We spend a few minutes talking about our least favorite drink trends. We agree experiential cocktails are the biggest waste of time—and money. They're nothing but watered-down mixed drinks that bars get away with upselling by putting dry ice in them. Once the initial excitement dies down, you're left with a thirty-five dollar hole in your pocket and a drink that can't even get you tipsy.

As the conversation continues, I find myself happy Izzy insisted on going out. I haven't had a proper girls' night since I left Boston. Plus, it gives Izzy and me a chance to catch up.

"So, how are things going with work?" I ask. "Is your boss still cool with you being remote?"

Izzy bobs her head in confirmation. "It's been nice not having to commute to the office every day. You have it made with this whole remote work thing, Delia."

I curl my fingers around the stem of my wine glass. "I like the flexibility. Work itself can feel isolating, but I'll usually go to a coffee shop if I need human interaction."

"It's something I'll have to consider when I look for my next job."

Her words surprise me. "Next job? You're thinking of leaving the design firm?" Izzy has worked for the same graphic design company since she graduated college two years ago. She never said anything about quitting. She's always been so passionate about her work, and she loves living in New York City.

"Eventually," Izzy admits. "I like the work, but there aren't many opportunities for growth for me."

"You've only been there for a couple of years, Iz," I remind her. "Getting a promotion takes time. You're a fantastic designer. I bet you'll be up for a promotion sooner than you think."

Izzy goes quiet for a minute, and I use the break in conversation to check my phone. Earlier, I sent a photo of my wine glass in my group chat with Mariah and Kali. I've got a few angry texts from my friends, who insisted I should've come back to the city for drinks. I also have a message from Tanner. *I can't stop staring at your legs.* I check the timestamp on the text—it's only a couple of minutes old.

Confused, I glance around the bar. After a moment of searching, I finally catch sight of him. He's sitting with Jacob at a high table near the back of the bar. Heat rushes to my cheeks when his eyes meet mine. He grins slyly. Biting my lip, I shake my head at him, my attention returning to my phone.

How did you know I was here? I write back.

There's only one decent bar in this town, darling.

"What's happening right now?" Izzy asks, brow furrowed. She must've noticed my sudden shift in focus.

"N-nothing," I stammer, quickly putting my phone away.

"Who were you looking at?"

"Oh, just Tanner. He's here with Jacob." I motion toward the back of the bar, feigning nonchalance.

Izzy's blue eyes go round like marbles. "Let's join them."

"What? No." We can't just waltz up to Tanner's table. He's here with his friend. What if he doesn't want me to come up to him? I don't want to seem desperate. "This is a girls' night, Izzy. We were just talking about your career."

"No offense, Delia, but I don't want to think about work right now." She grabs her martini off the bar. "C'mon. Let's go. I'm sure Tanner's dying to see you." With that last comment, she waggles her eyebrows, setting my cheeks on fire.

Before I can protest further, Izzy heads over to Tanner and Jacob's high top, leaving me no option but to follow behind. She shamelessly slides onto the stool beside Jacob, dropping her purse on the tabletop.

"Hello, gentlemen," she says in a ridiculously sultry voice. "We couldn't help but notice you from across the bar. Can I interest either of you in a drink?"

Amusement flashes over Tanner's and Jacob's faces.

"It's good seeing you, Izzy," Tanner says, chuckling at my sister's antics. "You too, Delia." My heart flutters at the sound of my name coming from his lips. He looks good tonight, though it's no surprise. The green in his eyes seems darker than usual. I wonder if it's the navy shirt he's wearing or the dark lighting in the bar that's affecting the color.

"I hope we're not interrupting anything," Izzy says, even though it's obviously untrue. No one would join another group's table without asking if they were worried about coming across as rude.

"We can leave if you're discussing Important Man Things. Sports and power tools and protein-infused tequila shots."

Jacob's brows go up at the last one. "Protein-infused *what*?"

"You're not interrupting anything," Tanner says. He offers me the vacant stool beside him, and I awkwardly sit down. It's a small table, so I can feel the heat radiating from his jean-clad thigh. I try not to think about the fact that I know what that thigh looks like bare and flexing as Tanner—*no*. I end that train of thought before it can continue. I can't have dirty thoughts about him right now. Not when I'm sitting in a crowded bar across from my sister.

Straightening my shoulders, I force myself to look across the table.

"So, you decided to check this place out," Jacob says, glancing over at Izzy.

She nudges him with her elbow. "Are you kidding?" she asks, her tone laced with sarcasm. "I had to see the place where Jacob Howell got to second base for the first time. It's practically a Seaview landmark, isn't it?"

I sputter into my drink. Did I hear her correctly? It sounded like she just said that Jacob felt up a girl in this trashy bar. I know Izzy likes making people uncomfortable, but the joke seems a bit much, especially for a near stranger. Jacob is probably wondering if she smoked something on the ride here.

"Izzy, what the hell?" I whisper-hiss. I don't want to spend the night wallowing in second-hand embarrassment because Izzy can't keep her mouth shut.

Surprise splashes over Tanner's features. "You told her that?" He shoots Jacob a look of pure bewilderment.

"It's *true*?" My eyes dart to Jacob, whose cheeks turn the color of strawberries. "Oh my god." I can't believe Izzy was being serious. How did she know something so personal about Jacob? She's only met him once.

"Jacob and I spent a lot of time together at the cookout the other night," Izzy says, looking all too smug. "We had to find something to talk about."

Tanner's eyes remain glued to his friend. "So you traded old hookup spots?"

"No," Jacob says, shaking his head. "That's not what happened."

"Jacob regaled me with the sordid tales of his youth," Izzy says.

"Sordid tales?" Tanner repeats, seeming unconvinced.

"They're not half as interesting as Izzy's stories," Jacob says.

Izzy's stories? I turn to my sister curiously, but she looks unflappable. "I'm an open book, Jacob," she says, tracing her finger around the rim of her martini. "You can tell them anything I told you."

"You see, I wouldn't do that," he replies, throwing her a challenging look. "Unlike you, I don't run my mouth." Jacob and Izzy share a look as if reminiscing over a private joke. What's so funny? I replay Jacob's words in my head. Realization strikes. Oh my god. Apparently, Jacob wasn't the only one who over-shared the other night.

"You told him about the Bobby Caldwell Incident?" I stare at Izzy in disbelief.

My sister had a bit of a wild streak back in high school. She was always getting into some kind of trouble. One night, she was making out with our neighbor, Bobby, in his family's hot tub. His parents were supposed to be out for the night, but they came home early, busting the two of them. Rather than stay and deal with the fallout, Izzy sprinted down the block in her soaking wet two-piece. She had to climb through my bedroom window to avoid getting caught by our parents.

Izzy gives me a dismissive shrug, but I don't buy her nonchalance. Nothing embarrasses her, but even she has admitted that her hot tub tryst with Bobby Caldwell wasn't her finest moment. Why would Izzy share that story with Jacob? What happened at that cookout?

"We talked about many things," she says vaguely.

"Were any of them dinner table appropriate?" I ask.

"It's not my fault Jacob has a dirty mind."

"I guess you bring out the best in me, Forrest."

Forrest? He calls Izzy by our last name?

"C'mon, Jacob," Izzy says, sliding off her stool. "I think we've traumatized Delia and Tanner enough."

"Where exactly are we going?" Jacob asks as he steps down from his own stool.

Izzy's eyes drift toward the empty billiards table on the other side of the bar. "I'm kicking your ass in a game of pool." She turns briefly to Tanner and me. "We'll be back in a few minutes. This won't take very long." Then, she and Jacob head toward the pool table, leaving me flabbergasted.

"Did you know about this?" I ask Tanner once they're out of earshot.

He shakes his head. "No idea."

I watch for a moment in fascination as Jacob empties a drawstring bag of pool balls onto the table. Izzy grabs two sticks off the rack on the wall, then passes one to Jacob. She says something that has him fighting off a smile, his eyes trained on her.

What's happening here? There's clearly something going on. Jacob's cute, but I'd be surprised if Izzy had a serious interest in him. Her type is usually of the douchebag artist variety. It couldn't be further from a khaki-wearing actuary.

"Izzy would eat him alive," I say.

"Oh, most definitely."

I observe the odd pair for another second before redirecting my attention to Tanner. "So, how was your day?" I ask. I don't know if it's the kind of question you're supposed to ask your temporary small-town hookup, but the words spill out, anyway.

Tanner curls a hand around his beer bottle. "Long," he says with a tired sigh. "I had to meet with the owner of the oceanfront property. Marvin thinks our work's gonna be pushed back a few weeks because of all the rain we've been getting. It's never fun telling someone the work they're paying a lot of money for isn't gonna be ready on time."

"Marvin?" I repeat. I rack my brain for previous mentions of the name, but come away with nothing.

"He works for Ryan & Son," Tanner explains. "Been with the company since my dad founded it. He's like an uncle to me."

"Is that weird?" I ask. "Being the boss of someone you consider an uncle?"

"It was at first," Tanner says. "But Marvin has never had an ego about it. He told me at the beginning that he wouldn't mind taking orders from me as long as I wouldn't mind if he told me when he thought they were crap. The only thing that matters to him is doing good work."

"I bet it's nice having that kind of relationship at work."

"Well, I won't have it for much longer. Marvin's retiring after we wrap up the oceanfront project." A frown tugs at the corners of his lips. He seems worried. I wonder if he already has a replacement lined up for Marvin. Is Tanner afraid his new employee won't be able to live up to their predecessor? Or is he concerned about working without Marvin?

Questions round my head, but I don't get a chance to ask them. Trading his frown for a smirk, Tanner hooks the toe of his boot under one of the support beams at the bottom of my stool and drags it toward his. I nearly yelp as my stool scrapes across the hardwood. I flatten my palms on the surface of the table for support.

"How's your day going?" Tanner asks, his hard thigh now flush with mine. Given that I can smell his aftershave and count the number of dark lashes framing his pretty eyes, it's safe to say we're sitting too close for a pair of acquaintances. I steal a glance at Jacob and Izzy, relieved to find them engrossed in their game of pool, before returning my focus to Tanner.

I narrow my eyes. "It was better before I was being manhandled."

His smile turns smug. "C'mon, darling," he says. "You and I both know what my manhandling looks like, and this isn't it." My face warms at his insinuation, so I elbow him in the ribs. His stomach is strong and muscular, so I doubt he even feels it.

"Keep it up, and you'll never get to manhandle me again," I warn him. I go to take a sip of my wine, finding the glass empty. Without prompting, Tanner slides his beer toward me. I bring the bottle to my lips and drink slowly, scrunching my nose at the taste of lukewarm beer.

"This is disgusting," I say, sliding the beer back to him.

"I know," he says. "But Jacob bought it. I wasn't gonna tell him that."

"Well, do you wanna dump it and get new drinks that don't taste like fermented dish water?" I ask, motioning toward the bar.

Tanner nods. "Fine by me."

He tosses his jacket on the table to make sure no one takes it, then we make the short walk over to the crowded bar. We work our way around the long counter. There aren't any available stools, but we manage to find an open spot.

I drum my fingers along the bar top as we wait for the bartender to take our order. We've only been standing for about two minutes when the guy sitting on the stool next to me gets up. As he comes down from his stool, he stumbles, bumping into me. The contact isn't enough to knock me down, but I stumble, and Tanner catches the upper part of my arm.

The guy turns to me. "Sorry," he says with a wince. He looks like he's in his mid-thirties and has an average build and dark-brown hair.

"It's fine," I assure him, expecting him to shuffle away. That might've been his initial plan, but as his eyes wander along my legs, it's clear he's not going anywhere.

"Maybe I can buy you a drink to make up for it," he says. "I'm Adam." He offers me his hand, and it takes every ounce of my restraint not to roll my eyes. Honestly, what's wrong with men? Does this guy actually believe that nearly bowling me over is going to get him laid?

Before I can turn him down, Tanner wraps an arm around my shoulder and shoots the guy a sardonic smile. "Bye, Adam."

The other guy mumbles something about not realizing I was with someone before skirting away from the bar area. Although he's no longer in sight, Tanner keeps his arm around my shoulder in what feels like a possessive gesture.

"What was that?" I ask, biting my lip to hide my smile. Was Tanner jealous? The thought thrills me, even though I know it shouldn't.

"That asshole was hitting on you," he replies matter-of-factly. So it *was* jealousy. Interesting. I'm not attracted to that other guy, but messing with Tanner could be fun.

"So?" I ask, pretending to be confused.

Tanner blinks. "You wanted him to hit on you?"

I shrug nonchalantly. "We never said we were exclusive," I say, though the idea of Tanner with another woman makes me want to scratch someone's eyes out. "Maybe I wanted that guy to buy me a drink."

"Well, it would've been the last thing he ever did."

I laugh. "Jealous?"

He shocks me when his eyes go intense and he says, "yes. Was the caveman act not enough for you?"

Butterflies take flight in my stomach. I try to play it off. "Rest assured," I tell him. "I have zero interest in that guy. I can only handle so much male ego in my life."

Chuckling, Tanner lowers his mouth to my ear. "Rest assured," he says, lips tickling my skin. "We might not have said we're exclusive, but I have zero interest in any other women. Just you."

I can't deny the way that makes my heart pick up speed.

Just you. I don't think I've ever liked the sound of two words more.

Thirty-One

Delia

"Don't look at me like that."

My lips twitch. "Like what?"

Tanner's eyes find me in the corner of the room. "Like you're thinking about what I did to you in the backseat of my truck last night." Heat pours into my cheeks, and I know from the smug look on his face that Tanner only brought up yesterday to make me blush.

We had dinner at Saunders' last night. As soon as we got back inside the truck, Tanner buried his face in my neck. *You have no idea how hard it is to keep my hands off you*, he whispered. *I'm obsessed with touching you*. I pounced on him after that. Luckily, Tanner happened to park in a very empty, very dark part of the parking lot.

I've never felt anything like this before. This desperate, intense need for another person. Sex has always been fine. Good. But it's never been tempting enough for me to hook up in the parking lot of a restaurant. Things with Tanner are out of control. It should terrify me, but I find it thrilling. Sleeping with him has been the most exhilarating experience of my life. I want it to keep going. To see what comes next.

"I wasn't thinking about that, actually," I tell him. "But now that you've mentioned it, there was this thing you did with your tongue that—"

He groans, cutting me off. His face is a mixture of desire and agony. "Stop. Talking."

He's standing on a stepladder in the middle of the guest room, installing a new ceiling fan. The room looks amazing. We painted the walls the same shade of gray-blue as Grandma Aggie's room, and Tanner finished staining the hard-wood floors a couple of days ago. "I'll never get this done if you can't keep your mouth shut."

I wrap my arms around my bare legs. "I figured you'd have more self-control than that."

"A smart man knows his limits, darling."

"Fine," I say, sinking back into the creaky wooden chair. "I'll stop talking." Tanner looks suspicious. I rarely agree with anything he says, and it usually takes several minutes of arguing for me to admit it. He's probably wondering what I'm up to.

After a few seconds of silence, Tanner still seems uncertain, but he goes back to installing the palm-sized metal bracket that will support the new ceiling fan.

I watch him for a while. He's dressed in his typical combination of a T-shirt, jeans, and a backwards ball cap, but there's something different about him when he works. He's calm, self-assured. Focused. The daring, playful part of me that's emerged over the past few weeks sees his concentration and wants nothing more than to break it.

Silently, I pull off my gray hoodie, leaving myself in nothing but a plain black sports bra and a tiny pair of athletic shorts. I drop the hoodie on the floor, and Tanner glances over at me. His eyes travel over the tight material covering my chest, then down to the strip of bare skin between my bra and the top of my shorts.

Desire swims in Tanner's eyes. He's got the metal bracket up against the ceiling with one hand and a screwdriver in the other, but he looks like he wants to throw his tools through the window and devour me.

"Are you trying to kill me?" he asks. The desperation in his voice makes my pulse speed up. His attention feels intoxicating. My veins buzz like I just drank an entire bottle of wine.

"No talking," I remind him.

Feeling devious, I stretch my legs on the ottoman in front of me. Tanner's knuckles are white around the screwdriver. My skin feels feverish, and the warmth I find in Tanner's expression makes the heat burn hotter.

He whispers "fucking hell," and then he's off the ladder, barreling over to me. He drops the screwdriver. It hits the ground with a clatter, and then Tanner is kneeling in front of me, yanking me to the edge of the chair and sealing his mouth over mine.

"I hope you didn't scratch the floor," I say breathlessly in between kisses. "My contractor just redid it."

He wraps an arm around my waist, pulling my body flush against his. "Your contractor will fix anything you damn well ask him to."

Twenty minutes later, we're lying in bed, Tanner's arm at my waist and lips at my temple. We're having a peaceful moment, until Tanner suddenly rolls away from me, muttering something under his breath about wanting to quit his job.

"Where are you going?" I ask, sitting up to watch him put his clothes back on. It's a crime against humanity, I quickly decide. Anyone with a body like Tanner's should be naked all the time.

He frowns as he zips up his jeans. "Work," he says. "I've got a meeting with a client later, then some stuff to take care of at the office." He snatches his shirt off the floor and slides it over his head. He gives me a sincere look.

"Oh, okay," I say, trying to conceal my disappointment over his hasty departure.

"But I'll call you later? I want you in my bed tonight." Warmth fills my body at the bluntness of his words. It's strange to think I used to find his directness off-putting—it's now one of my favorite things about him.

Tanner kisses me one last time before grabbing his tool box and heading out the door.

I don't linger in bed for long. Instead, I take a shower and throw the sheets in the wash. Izzy and I have been sleeping in Grandma Aggie's room the past few days as Tanner has been wrapping up work in the guest room, but that doesn't mean it's acceptable to leave my sex sheets.

After I move the sheets to the dryer, I spend the rest of the afternoon responding to work emails. It's a little after five when I shut down my laptop for the night. I change into sweatpants and an old T-shirt (not Austin's) before settling on the couch in the living room. I open my FaceTime app and press call on Mariah's name.

"She's alive!" my friend exclaims. She's sitting on the off-white couch in her living room, clutching a glass of red wine in one hand. I don't know how she isn't concerned about the possibility of her staining the pristine couch with her dark wine, but that's Mariah for you. She worries about the now, not the what if. "You have no idea how relieved I am to see your face, Del. I was beginning to wonder if this whole story about cleaning your grandma's house was made up by a kidnapper."

"She's not joking," Kali adds. She's sitting beside Mariah. Her dark hair is in a messy bun. "We were debating whether we needed to get the F.B.I. involved."

"Well, I'm happy to report that I'm coming to you by my own free will," I tell them. Then I pretend to look at something off-screen. "Sorry. The guy with the cue cards went to get a drink." Both of them laugh, and the familiar sound feels like a warm blanket draped over my shoulders. It's been too long since the three of us last talked. When Mariah texted me this morning to see if I was up for a virtual happy hour, I was more than happy to say yes.

"So, what's new?" I ask. "How's married life, Mariah? Still amazing?"

"So amazing," Mariah deadpans. "Jared and I geeked out over a new set of steak knives that arrived this morning. I think we've officially become a boring old married couple."

"There are worse things you could be," Kali says, nudging Mariah with her elbow. "Like single and desperate for some action."

"Amen to that." The response comes from Izzy, who breezes into the kitchen and shoots me a cheeky smile.

Mariah frowns. "Is there a connection issue on your end, Delia? Because I just heard words but didn't see your mouth move. Were you not kidding about the cue card guy?"

I turn my phone toward the kitchen. "That's just Izzy."

"Hi, Mariah. Hi, Kali," my sister shouts.

"Oh, hey, Izzy," Mariah says, blinking away her confusion. "Delia mentioned you were helping with the house. It must've slipped my mind."

"I haven't really done much," Izzy says. "Delia did most of the work before I even got here." On the surface, the words seem like a compliment, but there's an undercurrent of something else in Izzy's tone. It sounds like accusation.

Is she upset that I handled most of the cleaning? Why? No one wants to clean an old, dusty house. Then again, Izzy has seemed off lately. Ever since she showed up at the house, I've had the sense that something strange is going on with her. That feeling grew even stronger after the other night at the bar. She got weird when I asked her about work. And she didn't tell me she hit it off with Jacob. I haven't brought up the issues yet because I don't want to make things worse, but I don't know why she would keep secrets from me.

Izzy grabs her purse off the kitchen counter, throwing it over her shoulder. "Anyway, I'll get out of your hair," she says.

"Where are you going?" I ask.

"Shopping. I'll be back later."

"Okay." Now is not the time for Izzy and me to get into an argument. I'll have to talk to her later. "Have fun."

"Thanks. You too."

With a wave, Izzy heads out the door, leaving me with Kali and Mariah.

"So, how's everything going with your grandmother's place?" Kali asks.

"It's coming along," I reply. "Izzy's downplaying her involvement. She's been a big help. We hired a contractor to redo some of the outdated stuff. Everything looks great so far. It's coming along a lot faster than I expected."

Kali lifts a brow. "And how are you holding up? It must be tough being away from home for so long. I bet you're counting down the minutes until you can get back to the city."

I weigh my response carefully. When I first got to Seaview, I couldn't wait to go home, but now that things with Tanner have evolved, I'm not nearly as eager to get out of here. If anything, I'd prefer to stay for a while longer.

"It's not so bad," I say. "Aside from the mess, the house is in decent condition. And it's within walking distance of the beach. I get to watch the sunrise on the shore every morning when I go for my run. It's incredible. Honestly, it's been a nice break from the city."

Mariah looks stunned. "Seriously?"

"Yeah, Delia," Kali adds. "I never thought I'd hear you say you wanted a break from the city. Have you been body snatched?"

I roll my eyes at their dramatics. "It's not a big deal. I'm simply enjoying my time here."

The silence that follows could shatter eardrums.

"Oh my god," Mariah says in a tone of disbelief. "You met a guy."

Panic rolls through my insides. "What? No, I didn't."

"You most certainly did." She points a finger at the screen. "I can see it all over your face. You look guilty."

"Oh, would you look at that? The WiFi is acting weird. I think it's cutting out."

"Delia, do *not* hang up on us."

I remain silent for a moment as I try to decide how much I should share with them. Normally, I love talking about dating and relationships with my friends, but telling them about Tanner feels like a bad idea. I know my relationship with him won't last beyond my stay in Seaview. We live two hours apart. Tanner works ridiculous hours. Our lives are too different. But just because I know things won't last doesn't mean I want to talk about them.

Saying goodbye to Tanner is going to hurt. A lot. I don't want Kali and Mariah asking about him when I get back to Boston. Honestly, the only way I'll be able to get over him is by not thinking about him at all. So it's in my best interest to downplay our relationship. The less my friends know, the better.

"It's nothing," I say, purposefully shifting my eyes away from the screen.

"So you *did* meet someone!"

I sigh. "Yes, there's a guy. But it's not serious, and it's not like it could go anywhere." The words taste bitter on my lips, especially as I witness Kali's and Mariah's excitement.

"That's awesome, Delia," Mariah says encouragingly. "A rebound is exactly what you needed. Now you'll be ready for something serious when you get home."

Hearing Tanner be called a rebound feels like a huge disservice to our relationship. Comparing him to Austin is laughable. My ex-boyfriend falls short of Tanner in every way…except Austin lives in the same city as me.

I want to defend Tanner, but I can't do that without revealing too much, so I squash that instinct like a small bug. Then I paste a smile on my face and pretend as though this conversation isn't killing me.

Thirty-Two

Delia

By nine, Tanner still hasn't called.

I expected to hear from him after seven. That's usually when he gets off work. But the seven-and-eight-o'clock hours roll by without a call or text. At nine, I give up any hope I have of seeing him tonight. Disappointed, I trudge to the kitchen and make myself a pot of ramen, which I scarf down like a rabid animal. I'm starving. I was waiting to eat with Tanner, so I haven't had anything since lunch. After I polish off the ramen, I tear into a bag of pretzels. It's a weird combination, but I can't be bothered to cook right now.

I try not to let myself be affected by Tanner's no-show. So he didn't call. No big deal. He probably got busy at work and was too tired to do anything tonight. Or maybe he forgot. Either way, it shouldn't make a difference. I'm not the man's girlfriend. We're together, but we're not *together* together. He doesn't owe me an explanation.

Why doesn't my heart understand that?

Despite my best efforts, it stings to think that Tanner forgot about me or, worse, didn't feel like seeing me. I was looking forward to it. I've practically been counting down the minutes since he left this afternoon. Apparently, Tanner doesn't share the same level of enthusiasm about the idea of seeing me.

My stomach turns into a concrete brick. It sucks being an afterthought. I don't want to be more invested in this than Tanner. I want us to be on a level playing field. It's concerning that what I feel for him might be stronger than what he feels for me.

If I'm this disappointed about him not calling one time, what happens when he says he wants to see other people? Tanner said at the bar the other night that he's not interested in other women, but that could change. Who knows what he'll feel two, three weeks from now?

I freeze mid-thought. Three weeks from now. *Oh, god, what am I thinking?* I might not even be here in three weeks. How have I already gotten so attached?

On second thought, maybe it's a good thing Tanner didn't call. Separation will be good for me. I can't spend my nights waiting by the phone like a pathetic high schooler. I'm a grown woman. A sensible one. I can't lose my head over some guy just because he has pretty eyes and kisses like it's a professional sport. Tanner is a lot more than his looks or his skills with his tongue, but reducing him to those traits might be the only way I can shake some sense into myself.

I'm in the bathroom getting ready for bed when my phone rings on the counter. I finish tugging my silk sleep shirt over my head, then check the caller ID. It's Tanner. In a way, I'm not surprised. He's been my most frequent caller as of late. But the time at which he's calling shocks me. It's almost ten-thirty. Tanner can't be leaving work now. I wonder if he just realized he forgot to reach out to me after he got home. Maybe he's calling to apologize. That seems like the most likely option. I'm still feeling slighted, but I don't want him to know that. So I take a deep breath, pushing my frustration to the back of my mind.

Then, I answer the phone.

"Hi," I say in the most casual tone I can manage. I hope he pictures me lounging on the couch with a glass of wine. Totally unaffected by his silence.

"Hey, darling," he says in that low timbre of his. "Sorry it's so late. I'm leaving the office now. I should be there in about five minutes. I'll swing by your place first, okay? There's no sense in you walking over at this time of night."

I'm silent for several seconds as I process what he said. "You just left work?" Disbelief rings clear in my voice.

"My meeting this afternoon ran longer than expected," he explains. I hear his truck unlock, followed by the slam of a car door. "I had to stay back and deal with some invoices."

"For this long?" Tanner left my place at two-thirty in the afternoon. Almost eight hours ago. And I know he worked for a while this morning. He mentioned something earlier about stopping by his oceanfront project.

"It was a lot of invoices," he says. "Though I don't know why you're surprised. I told you I'd call when I got off, didn't I?"

"Well, yeah. But that was hours ago."

"So?"

"So, I don't know." I twist my hands uncomfortably, relieved that he can't see me. "It's late. I figured you forgot or something."

"Delia, what part of I want you in my bed tonight did you not understand?"

My heart roars like a freight train. I feel a mix of relief and ridiculousness. On one hand, I'm delighted Tanner didn't forget me. On the other hand, I'm embarrassed. I let myself get so worked up over nothing. Tanner's a decent guy. He's not playing games with me. I should've known he would keep his word.

"Think you'll be ready to go in a few minutes?"

"Yeah. I'll be waiting outside."

"See you soon."

I hang up and scurry downstairs, throwing an oversized sweater over my long sleep shirt. I notice Izzy watching TV in the living room. The bright TV screen shines on her face. She looks me up and down.

"I'm, um, going to sit on the porch for a while," I tell her as I slip on my shoes. "To enjoy the fresh air." It's a pathetic excuse. It's pitch-black and windy. Izzy appears to be amused by my obvious lie.

"Be safe," she says, a coy smile on her lips. Then her eyes go back to the TV.

Slightly mortified, I head out the front door. I only wait a couple of minutes before a familiar truck pulls up the driveway. Bolting down the porch steps, I throw open the passenger door and scramble inside.

"In a hurry?" Tanner asks teasingly. I'm about to give him a snarky response, but the words die on my tongue when I turn and face him.

Tanner looks exhausted. The dark circles beneath his eyes are bluish-purple, and his normally tan complexion is pale. His hair sticks up in the back, as if he's spent hours running his hands through it, and his clothes are rumpled. He looks…well, he looks like he just worked a fourteen-hour day.

I knew Tanner worked an ungodly number of hours. He's always rushing off to a meeting or job site. But I never noticed the effects of his excessive work schedule until now. It hits me like a cement truck.

"Delia?" Tanner says, giving me an odd look. I must have been silently staring for too long. "Are you all right?"

I swallow hard. "Fine," I say, holding my palms in front of the air vents. "Just cold."

He nods, though he doesn't seem particularly convinced. Then he puts the truck in reverse and backs out of the driveway.

I'm silent on the brief ride to Tanner's place. I can't stop stealing glances at his tired appearance. Does he always look like this? Have I never paid close enough attention? Given how much time we've spent together these past few weeks, it's hard for me to believe I didn't notice. Maybe I was so fixated on denying my attraction to him that I couldn't see what was right in front of me.

I have questions. So many. Is it normal for him to work so much? How many hours does he put in on a typical day? When was the last time he got a decent night's sleep? There's no doubt in my mind that running a small business takes a lot of hard work. But *this*? Leaving the office after ten? Looking like he's about to fall asleep at the wheel? I can't imagine most business owners live and work like this. It doesn't seem healthy or sustainable. There has to be balance somewhere.

I wonder how long Tanner has kept up this breakneck pace. He's been working for his family's company for years. Has he been running himself down all this time? If so, how much does he have left? You can only put yourself through so much before something breaks.

We arrive at Tanner's place. He parks his truck in the attached garage, then the two of us head inside. Tanner flips on a light in the kitchen. His exhaustion becomes even more apparent in the bright fluorescent light.

As I kick off my shoes by the door, I can't ignore the knots twisting in my stomach. Concern has spread through me like an infection, quick and all-consuming. It's not my place to say anything to Tanner about his work habits, but someone has to, don't they? If I don't do something, then who will?

After several moments of internal debate, I can't take it any longer. "Is it normal for you to work this late?" I ask, turning to him.

Tanner shrugs. "Sometimes." He shucks off his jacket, tossing it over the back of a chair at the kitchen table. He rests his hands on the back of the chair. *Sometimes.* What a vague and unhelpful answer. I hate when he's purposefully disagreeable. Still, I push forward with my line of questioning.

"Have you always worked like this? Or did it start when you took over the company?"

"Delia, I'm fine." He isn't looking at me, but I narrow my eyes at him anyway. No one who's actually fine would say it like that. All clipped and dismissive. For a guy who prides himself on transparency, he isn't being very transparent right now.

"That's not what I asked," I say, crossing my arms in a defiant stance. "It's not normal to work until ten-thirty at night, Tanner."

He closes his eyes, breathing out slowly. "I know."

"Then why are you being so evasive about it?"

Finally, he turns to face me. He steps forward, closing the gap between us. He places his palms on the outside of my upper arms, rubbing them up and down. I think it's supposed to be a gesture of reassurance, but I'm not sure who he's trying to reassure.

"I'm not trying to be evasive," he says. "I work a lot. I know that. But it's nothing I can't handle, Delia. Trust me. I'm used to it." He's clearly trying to appease me, but he still hasn't answered my question.

"How long have you been working like this?" I ask again.

"Since I became president." His jaw tightens, and he looks over my shoulder. I can tell those four words were a lot for him to admit. I don't want this to feel like an interrogation, but I'm not done asking questions.

I reach out to trace my thumb along the edge of his jaw, hoping the move will convey my sympathy. My touch seems to soothe him. Feeling emboldened, I wrap my fingers around Tanner's wrist and wordlessly lead him to the kitchen table.

Tanner settles on a chair. I take the one adjacent to him, maintaining my grip on his wrist. He's quiet. I wait patiently. I'll stay here for hours if that's what it takes for him to open up to me.

Eventually, he says, "It wasn't supposed to happen this soon. Me taking over Ryan & Son." He pauses for a moment, a dip forming between his brows. "Dad was perfectly healthy. He wanted to work another five, ten years. It was always the plan for me to take the reins, but he thought he had more time. There was a lot he didn't get to show me. The first six months after he died were the worst. I was floundering. Marvin helped as best as he could, but there was so much I didn't know. So much I was expected to understand already. I had to put in long days. It was the only way I could wrap my head around things."

"But you've been in charge for three years," I remind him. Late nights were probably inevitable when Tanner first stepped into his new role. I imagine it would be like that for anyone coming into a position of leadership. But after three years, shouldn't the dust have settled? Shouldn't Tanner be comfortable by now?

He nods. "I thought the long days would be temporary. But without Dad telling me what to do, I have no clue if I'm doing any of it right. He was a great boss, Delia. Hard-working. Fair. Compromising. Everyone loved him. I didn't want to be the disappointing, ineffective version of him. I figured the harder I worked, the less likely I was to fail."

"Did your dad work like this, too?"

"He worked a lot, sure. But I don't think it was ever this intense. Truthfully, I don't know how he managed everything on his own. I'm hanging on by a thread at times, and he was a lot better than me." Insecurity sounds strange coming from Tanner. It's like finding an imperfection in a painting in a world-class museum. He's always seemed so confident about his work. Then again, Tanner's self-assurance comes from his abilities with a toolbox, not his leadership skills. Maybe he has been doubting himself this entire time.

"Your dad had you, didn't he? I'm sure that made things easier." Obviously, I didn't know Tanner's father, but I know Tanner. He's smart and capable. He cares about his job, and he works incredibly hard. There's no doubt in my mind that he played an integral role in the success of Ryan & Son.

Tanner doesn't appear so convinced. "I don't know how much of a help I really was."

"Well, I do," I say earnestly, running the pad of my thumb along the inside of his wrist. "Tanner, you're the hardest-working person I've ever met. And you genuinely care about the quality of the work you do. You'd never be able to convince me you aren't a good leader." He looks like he wants to argue, so I press on. "Didn't you say that the oceanfront project is the largest in the company's history? That has to mean you're doing something right. Someone wouldn't put that kind of trust in you if they didn't think you were capable."

"They might if they knew my father and expect the same caliber of work from me."

Who is this uncertain man? It feels like I'm seeing a different side of Tanner. I wish I could make him see what I do. I trap his face between my hands, forcing him to look me directly in the eye.

"You don't have to be exactly like your father to be good at your job, Tanner. People have different leadership styles. Just because yours doesn't match your dad's doesn't mean you're doing anything wrong."

"My dad built this company on his own," he says. "It meant everything to him. I want to do right by him. Honor his legacy. Not screw things up because I'm not working hard enough." So that's what this all boils down to: fear. Tanner wants to impress his dad so badly that he's been working himself to the bone. What he doesn't seem to realize is that he'll never be able to receive the validation he's looking for.

"My dad used to love these little graham cracker cookies," I say, hands still cupping Tanner's face. "They were made by some obscure cookie manufacturer." Travelers? Trawell's? I could never remember the name. "Anytime someone in my family saw a pack of those cookies at a grocery store or in a vending machine, we bought them for Dad. A few weeks after he died, I found a pack at the convenience store near our house. I bought it without a second thought. It wasn't until I got home that I realized what I'd done. That I'd never have a chance to give those cookies to my dad."

Sadness shines in Tanner's green eyes. "Delia."

I shake my head, not wanting his sympathy right now. "The point is," I say, "you can't create new memories with someone after you lose them. You can reflect on the past. You can think about what they might've said or done, but you'll never know for certain. Honoring your dad by making sure his company stays alive is a great thing, Tanner. I'm sure he would be proud of you. But you're never going to get his praise or approval. Working a million hours a week won't change that. You have to find a way to be proud of yourself. To seek your own validation. Because if what you do now isn't good enough, then nothing ever will be."

He studies me for a moment. His expression is focused, thoughtful. I wonder what he makes of my words. I hope I didn't cross any unspoken boundaries, but I needed to tell him that. Coming to terms with grief means accepting that some things will never have resolutions.

Several seconds later, Tanner wraps an arm around my lower back, pulling me into his lap. My legs fall to either side of his thighs, my nightshirt bunching up around the waist. "I know my current situation isn't sustainable," he says. "But I've been doing this for years, Delia. I can't just abandon everything on my plate."

"Can you hire someone? An assistant or something?" Maybe Tanner's schedule wouldn't be so draining if he could hand some of his busy work off to someone else.

"I've been meaning to hire an office manager for a while," he says. "But that would require me to create a job posting, interview candidates, and deal with all the headaches and paperwork involved in the hiring process. It's more hassle than I have time for."

Frustration for Tanner rolls through me. He obviously needs more support. The fact that he's so busy he doesn't have time to hire someone speaks volumes. I wish there was something I could do for him. A way to fix this problem and tie it up with a neat little bow. But I can't. At least not tonight. It's late, and he looks exhausted. The best I can do right now is try to take his mind off things.

"Did you eat?" I ask.

He shakes his head. "I had a protein bar at the office. Figured I'd make a sandwich when I got back." The frustration within me quickly turns to sadness. I wonder how many nights he's come home after a ridiculously long day of work, only to make himself a crappy dinner, fall asleep, and wake up and do it again the next day.

Unceremoniously, I climb off his lap. "I'll do it." Tanner gives me a perplexed look. I can't tell if he's deliberately being dense or if my offering to make him food is so shocking that he doesn't realize I'm being serious.

"I'll make you a sandwich," I clarify. "Why don't you change clothes and put on the TV?"

His brow twitches. "Didn't you once tell me that you burn everything you touch?"

I roll my eyes, unimpressed by the jab. "You can't burn a sandwich," I say. "Whether I decide to spit in it is still up for debate."

Grinning, he slaps his palms against his thighs and rises out of his chair. He grabs me by the chin, dropping a quick kiss on my mouth. "Thank you," he says, his tone open and genuine. I shove him toward the staircase in response.

Then I head to the pantry to gather the ingredients to make dinner for my non-boyfriend.

Thirty-Three

Tanner

As we slide into a booth at Ralph's the next morning, Delia makes an announcement.

"I'm hiring a contractor," she says.

I stare at her for a moment. She's dressed comfortably in a T-shirt and athletic shorts, but her eyes look tired. Probably because I kept her up most of the night. Even though I was exhausted after my extensive work day, I had no trouble staying awake for Delia. My time with her is limited—I'll take all I can get.

It was a little after two o'clock in the morning when I walked her back to her place. Aggie's place. I bet she wouldn't be so tired if she stayed the night. She never does. I understand her reasons, but I'd love to wake up to find her soft legs threaded through mine and her quiet breaths filling my bedroom.

I'm so busy thinking about how I can convince Delia to spend the night that it takes a solid minute for her words to register. When they finally do, I shoot her a quizzical look. "What are you talking about?" I ask.

"I'm getting someone else to finish the work at Grandma Aggie's."

I raise a suggestive brow. "Are you not satisfied with the work I've been doing?" I'm hoping the comment will pull a smile out of her, but Delia doesn't seem amused. She tips her chin up defiantly.

"I mean it, Tanner," she says sternly. "I appreciate everything you've done for me, but you need to focus on your real work, not the work you took on out of guilt." She's serious about this. Shit. I can't believe I have to convince my girlfriend not to fire me. And, no, it's not lost on me that I called her my girlfriend. Delia might be reluctant to make things official, but she's not my friend, and she's more than a hookup.

"I didn't do it out of guilt," I insist, meaning every word. "You're underestimating how good your legs look in shorts." She still isn't smiling, but my obnoxiousness seems to thaw some of the tension surrounding the conversation.

"You're a pervert," she says, shaking her head in a way that tells me she loves what I'm saying even though she won't admit it.

"I'm just making an observation."

Sighing, Delia reaches for her purse. She pulls out a small piece of paper, unfolding it on the table. I glance down, surprised to see it's the contract we made all those weeks ago.

"What are you doing with that?" I ask.

Delia lifts the paper and tears it down the center. "Destroying it," she says, ripping the halves into fourths and then arranging them in a neat pile that she sets on the edge of the table. I'm not happy about this development, but I can't help but chuckle slightly at the organized stack of shredded paper. Arranging her mess. It's so Delia.

"You and I both know that isn't how contracts work, darling."

"It's not like this one was very official," she argues, folding her arms against her chest. "I mean, it wasn't even notarized. We can just forget about it, okay?"

I know what she's doing. I opened up to her last night. Talked about my struggles since taking over my dad's company. I've never told anyone about that stuff. It felt right, sharing it with Delia. But now, I can see she's feeling guilty. She doesn't want to add to my stress by having me continue with the renovations.

What she's forgetting is that I offered to fix up her grandmother's place. The decision was all mine. Plus, I like doing the work. It gives me an excuse to be around her. I don't really need one now that we're sleeping together, but it's nice to know I can pop over any time. I've sunk a lot of time into fixing up Aggie's place. I want Delia to be happy with the finished product. And I definitely don't want her paying some other asshole to do it.

"It was my idea to work on the house, Delia," I remind her. "I volunteered to do it. And in case you forgot about yesterday afternoon, it doesn't feel like work."

Her cheeks redden. God, I like making her blush. "I know. But ever since this started," she says, motioning between the two of us, "it's felt different. Like I'm using you or something. You've got enough going on. I don't want to be an unnecessary complication."

"Nothing that involves you is unnecessary." The words sound a lot stronger than I mean them to. I don't want to seem too intense. I know how I feel about Delia, but I don't think she's ready for that conversation. So I dial it back. "Honestly, Delia, I've been working on Aggie's house for weeks. I want to see it through. I'd feel the same way even if this hadn't happened." It's impossible. Us not happening. But I keep that thought to myself.

She bites her bottom lip, hesitant. "I don't know."

"Well, it's not entirely up to you," I say, reaching into my pocket to take out my wallet. I pull out my copy of the contract, holding it out to show her. I don't set it on the table, though. I don't trust that she won't try to tear it to pieces. "According to this contract, we both agreed that I would do all the work on Aggie's house."

Shock blankets Delia's face. "You still have it?"

"I told you I'd keep it somewhere safe, didn't I?"

"Um, yeah," she says, studying the paper in disbelief. "I just thought you'd throw it out." I almost did. Minutes after she gave it to me. I nearly chucked it in the recycle bin at the end of her driveway on the walk back to my place. Something stopped me. I don't know what, but I'm glad it did.

"I'm a man of my word."

Delia hesitates, then says, "promise me you won't try to do too much at once. I don't want to be a source of stress for you, Tanner. I know I told you I wanted to sell the house by summer, but that isn't a hard-and-fast deadline. I've got nowhere to be. There's no reason to rush. I don't care if that means the renovations take another six months."

"I promise," I tell her.

I'd be lying if I said there isn't a part of me that's tempted to drag out the work for another six months just so I can keep her here a while longer.

Thirty-Four

Delia

Per my insistence, Tanner scales back on the renovation work over the next two weeks. He already finished the work in the bedrooms and upstairs bathroom, but he still needs to replace the dated light fixtures in the kitchen and living room and repaint the dingy walls. We won't be ready to sell the house by the start of June, but I don't mind being behind schedule. I meant it when I told Tanner I don't care how long the renovations take. I don't want him to be stressed and frantically trying to get everything done.

Besides, Seaview isn't so bad. We have two functional bedrooms now. I've moved into Grandma Aggie's old room, while Izzy has taken the guest room as her own. Morgan's spring classes ended earlier this week, but I told her not to rush to get to town. Izzy and I have things handled right now. And if there's anyone who deserves to enjoy a little time off, it's Morgan. This semester was brutal for her. She should relax for a few weeks before she even thinks about making the trip down to Seaview.

After my morning run, I head to Ralph's Diner. Relief washes over Annabella's face as she spots me from behind the counter. I don't know why. It's the height of the morning rush. I know

284

Annabella likes me, but the diner currently resembles an airport terminal during the week of Thanksgiving. She shouldn't be happy to see any new customers.

"There you are," she says, slapping a palm on the counter. "You're later than usual. I wasn't sure if you were coming in. I almost gave your muffin away." She motions toward a white paper bag on the counter.

"Sorry. I overslept." A late night at Tanner's led to me missing my morning alarm. I'd probably still be in bed if it weren't for Izzy. She stormed into my room and told me to shut off the damn thing before she smashed it to pieces.

"Thanks for saving the muffin. I've been thinking about it all morning."

Annabella waves off my appreciation. "You want coffee, too?"

"Yes, please." There are no empty seats at the counter, so I stand as Annabella fixes me a to-go cup. "Busy morning, huh?" I say as I glance around the crowded diner. Customers cram around every table, their conversations buzzing like static in the air.

"Happens every year," Annabella says. "Tourists flock here as soon as the weather gets pretty. Wait till you see this place in mid-July."

I give an awkward laugh. "I'm not sure I'll get the chance." Even if it takes Tanner longer to finish fixing up the house, I doubt it will be later than early July by the time he wraps everything up.

"That's right. I got so used to seeing you that I forgot it's only temporary. How's everything going with the house?"

"Really well. The place is coming to life."

"You went with Ryan & Son, right? Aren't they fantastic?"

"They are." Heat erupts in my cheeks. Annabella doesn't know about my relationship with Tanner, so I know she isn't trying to insinuate anything, but that doesn't stop my brain from taking her words that way. I'm glad Tanner isn't here. He'd probably embarrass me by telling Annabella he's putting in long, laborious hours to keep me satisfied.

Annabella clips a lid on my coffee cup. "How much longer do you think you'll be in town?" she asks.

"I'm not sure. I still need to find a realtor."

"My niece is a realtor. She's pretty good. Helped me and Ralph find the place we're in now, and we love it. I could give you her number if you'd like, but don't feel obligated if you're not interested."

"That would be great, Annabella." Not having to find a realtor takes an item off my long to-do list. Annabella suggested hiring Tanner, so I know she has good judgment.

Reaching into the pocket of her apron, Annabella pulls out a notepad and pen. She rips off a sheet of paper and scribbles down a name and number before handing it to me. "Alicia's great. Be sure to tell her you got her name from me."

I pocket the slip of paper, then pick up my coffee. "Thanks. Well, I should probably get going. I've got lots of work to do."

Annabella shoots me a small smile as she slides the paper bag my way. "I'll miss seeing you when you go, Delia. And I won't sell nearly as many muffins."

***

Later that night, I'm lying in Tanner's bed, my head resting on his hard chest. My fingers trace patterns over the skin directly above his heart. Tanner wraps a large palm around my hip. I'm wearing nothing but his baggy T-shirt, which has ridden up to my midsection. The room is dark and quiet and smells like Tanner's delicious aftershave. We've been here for hours, making quiet conversation and staring at the ceiling.

I bury my face in the crook of his neck, breathing in deeply. "I love the smell of your aftershave," I whisper. The confession tumbles out of me without a second thought. I blame my sex-riddled brain for the lack of judgment. I'm grateful that the dark room hides my cheeks, which must be the color of fire hydrants.

Tanner's lips brush against my hairline. "I know." I pull back to examine his face. His expression is a mix of sleepiness and amusement. I've gotten to know many versions of Tanner over the past few weeks, and Sleepy Tanner might be my favorite. His hair is all rumpled and his hazy green eyes remind me of grass on a dewy morning.

"You know?" I repeat, slightly confused.

"You told me the night we made out on your porch, remember?" The memory of me mumbling something about his aftershave comes rushing back.

"Oh, right."

He fingers a strand of my hair. "It's not even my regular aftershave."

287

"Really?"

Tanner nods. "The grocery store was out of my normal stuff a few weeks ago," he explains. "I had to buy something different." He twirls a lock of my hair around his finger. "I decided to keep using the other stuff after I realized how much you liked it."

"Don't switch back," I tell him, settling against his neck again. "In fact, you should probably start stocking up on the good stuff. Does Seaview have a Costco?"

Tanner chuckles. "Nah. But I promise I won't change anything as long as you're here."

I should be touched. He's made this change for me. Because of me. But the only thing I'm thinking about is the last part of the sentence. *As long as you're here.* It hits me like a cool splash of water on a hot day. A shock to the senses. It brings me back to the conversation I had this morning at the diner with Annabella.

The truth is, I'm not ready to leave Seaview. To give up whatever this is with Tanner. The idea of going back to my empty apartment in Boston makes my skin crawl. Tanner and I haven't talked about the future, but I know this will be over the second I leave town.

We haven't defined our relationship. We're not going to put a label on things right when they get complicated. What would a long-distance relationship with us even look like? Me driving to Seaview every weekend? Tanner coming to Boston? We'd only be able to keep that up for so long before one of us would have to move. Tanner has his company—he can't leave Seaview. And I don't know if I'm ready to say goodbye to Boston.

I have friends there. Routines. Plus, I'd have nowhere to live in Seaview. Grandma Aggie's house belongs to me, Izzy, and Morgan.

My sisters are expecting big payouts from the sale of the house. I couldn't afford to buy them out for as much as we're hoping to sell for. And it would be way too soon for me to move in with Tanner. Assuming he'd even want me to stay. Who's to say he wants us to keep seeing each other? Maybe he's happy this thing has an expiration date.

This isn't forever. Which means both of us will have to let go. Move on. Be with other people. I know that, but it still makes my stomach twist.

What if Tanner meets another woman who likes the smell of his aftershave? Will he start using it for her? I want him to save it for me. But even if he does, it won't change the fact that there will be another woman in his life eventually. Another woman will lay in his bed and think about his sleepy eyes and be the center of his attention. And there's nothing I can do to stop it.

"Delia? Where'd you go?" Tanner asks, nudging my side gently. I don't know how he's so good at reading me, but he always seems to pick up on changes in my mood. I don't want to tell him I'm panicking about the hypothetical women he's going to be with after me, so I shove the worried thoughts to the back of my mind. I'll deal with them later.

"Nowhere," I reply. "I'm just thinking about the look on Morgan's face this afternoon when I FaceTimed her to show her the house. She couldn't believe how much it's changed since I sent her the first pictures."

"It looks pretty different, doesn't it?"

"That's an understatement." In a few weeks, Grandma Aggie's house has gone from practically uninhabitable to a pleasant place to live.

"Wait till I redo the porches," Tanner says. "The neighbors won't know what hit them."

"Porches?" I repeat. "As in plural?"

He grins. "Look at that. She's pretty, and she knows grammar."

I ignore his teasing words and focus on the facts. "You said you weren't redoing the back porch. That it would be pointless." I remember the conversation well. It was one of our first arguments.

"Don't tell me you've changed your mind," he says. "I already got the wood."

"Of course not." I love the back porch. It's one of my favorite parts of the house. I'd kill to see it returned to its former glory. But Tanner insisted that redoing it was meaningless. What could inspire such a drastic change of mind? My only thought is that he realized how quickly he was approaching the end of the renovations. Restoring the porch will buy us extra time. And if Tanner wants to prolong the inevitable, that's fine with me.

"Good," he says, sounding almost relieved. Did he think I'd say no? Does he not realize I'm dreading the end of this, too? "I mean, I'd hate to see that wood go to waste," he quickly adds. "Though I'm sure we'd find a way to repurpose it at work."

The mention of Ryan & Son reminds me of something important. "I have to grab something

from my purse," I tell him, sitting up abruptly.
"I'll be back in a second."

I climb out of bed and scramble downstairs to
the kitchen. The tile feels cold against my bare
feet. I reach inside the purse, pulling out the item
I'm looking for. Then I hurry back to Tanner's
room. He's sitting up against the headboard.
Shirtless. Normally, I would take a few seconds to
appreciate his muscular frame, but I'm too
anxious to enjoy it.

My heart picks up speed as Tanner's gaze
slides to my hands. "Whatcha got there, darling?"
he asks. Nerves shoot up my spine. I get the urge
to hide my hands behind my back, which is
ridiculous considering Tanner already saw them.

Nervously, I approach the side of the bed. I feel
like a student about to deliver a presentation in
front of the class. My throat is dry, and my palms
dampen with sweat. "I got this for you," I say.
"It's a day planner. The same one I use. I thought
it would be helpful for organizing your work
schedule. Writing my schedule always makes me
feel better when I'm stressed. Maybe it could do
the same for you. And I can help you set it up if
you want. We could plan so you actually have
time to hire an office manager."

I hold out the small, rectangular book. My skin
feels hot. It's like the temperature in the room
suddenly went up a thousand degrees.

This seemed like a good idea the other night. I
was having trouble sleeping after Tanner told me
the truth about his jam-packed work schedule. I
wanted to help him, so I ordered a copy of my
favorite day planner online. I thought Tanner
would benefit from having a place to organize his

schedule. Maybe a planner would help him figure out his priorities. Teach him to focus on what needs to get done instead of trying to do a million things at once.

Now that I'm standing in front of him, the gesture seems foolish. Tanner doesn't want me to solve his problems for him. And he probably doesn't want a planner. After all, he's always teasing me about my love for schedules. I've put him in such an awkward position. He's probably wondering how to turn down my offer without hurting my feelings.

"You don't have to take it if you don't want to," I add. "It's just an idea. A pointless one. In fact, I should put this back in my purse, and we can pretend it never happened."

Humiliated, I turn to head back downstairs, but Tanner grabs my wrist. He plucks the planner out of my hand and flips it open. He looks up at me, a half-smile on his face.

"You already started making a schedule," he says, studying my handwriting on the first page. As if this couldn't get more embarrassing. God, why did I do that?

"Not really," I say, shrugging. "I just filled in a couple of meetings I remembered you saying you had this week." I'm trying as best I can to downplay it. I don't want Tanner to think about how intimate this gift is.

He shuts the planner, setting it on his lap. "I love it," he says. I wait for the punchline. The smirk. Any indication that he's messing with me. Nothing comes.

"You do?"

"Of course." He moves the planner to the nightstand, then tugs me toward his lap. "If anyone's gonna figure out how to organize my shitshow schedule, it's the self-proclaimed queen of planners."

I roll my eyes. "I'm not the self-proclaimed queen of anything."

"Sure you are." His lips work their way down my neck. I'm not sure where he's planning to go with his response. Apparently, neither is he. Tanner trails off as he explores my skin with his mouth. I catch a glimpse of the planner on the nightstand before losing myself to his touch. I can't stay in his life forever, but maybe I can leave something behind.

Thirty-Five

Tanner

Most years, I stay as far from Seaside Sip as possible. It's nothing but a mass of drunk women looking for trouble. Several years ago, I made the mistake of agreeing to be the designated driver for my mom and a few of her friends. It was almost three o'clock in the morning by the time Mom called me to pick them up, and she and her friends insisted on stopping at Taco Bell on the way home. We sat at the drive-thru window for nearly half an hour as the poor night shift workers pulled together an enormous order of burritos. To make matters worse, Mom's friends killed the time with an impromptu karaoke session. Now, I can't hear *Jive Talkin'* without thinking of Cora Anderson's ungodly screech in the goddamn Taco Bell parking lot.

This year, instead of making plans to get out of dodge on Seaside Sip night, I offered to be Delia and Izzy's chauffeur. Delia said she wouldn't mind ordering an Uber, but I shot that idea down. There's no sense in her paying someone else to drive her when she has me. She might not agree with that phrasing, but it's the truth. The woman has me by the balls. Which is how I wind up pulling up to Beach Park a little after five and putting my truck in park.

I glance at Delia, who's sitting in the passenger seat. "Whatever you do, don't drink Annabella's punch," I warn her. "She brought it to a community picnic one year. That shit is lethal." In fact, it should be outlawed. I don't know what Annabella puts in it, but I've never been knocked on my ass so quickly.

From the backseat, Izzy leans over the center console. "Don't worry, Tanner," she says, giving me a not-so-reassuring pat on the shoulder. "I'll make sure she stays out of trouble." Yeah, right. I saw the way Izzy was slinging back tequila shots a few weeks ago at Seaview Tavern.

"You might be the trouble she needs to stay away from," I mutter.

Delia chuckles. "Thanks for the warning. And for driving us. I'll text you when we're ready to go. We're not planning to stay super late."

"Don't worry about it. I've got nowhere to be tonight. Stay as long as you want."

She nods, then unbuckles her seatbelt. She looks as though she wants to say more, but Izzy jumps out of the truck and throws open Delia's door, urging her out. "C'mon," Izzy says. "I want to be good and buzzed in the next fifteen minutes."

With an eye roll, Delia climbs out of her seat and follows her sister toward the park's entrance. She glances over her shoulder, locking eyes with me as she mouths "pray for me."

I watch until she disappears from my field of vision. It's strange to think I've only known Delia for a couple of months when she occupies so much of my attention. What would I be doing right now if I hadn't met her? Catching up on work? Sitting at a bar with Jacob? It's hard to imagine, but it won't be long until that thought becomes a reality.

Delia isn't staying forever. After I wrap up work on the porches, Aggie's old house will be ready for the market, and Delia will head back to Boston. I wonder if she's eager to get back to the city. She hasn't mentioned it in a while. Maybe she thinks that her leaving spells the end of our relationship, and she doesn't want to make things awkward. If that's the case, then she's got another thing coming for her. I'm going to make things awkward.

I'm waiting for the right time, but I'm going to tell Delia I want us to continue seeing each other, even after she goes home. I know we haven't defined our relationship, but I can't go back to living my life as though this never happened. It hit me the other night after she gave me a copy of her favorite planner. I can't let Delia go. I'm not capable of it. I'll regret it for the rest of my life if I don't try to make this work.

I'm all in with this woman. I'll do anything to keep her.

We could handle the distance. I tease her about the city, but I don't mind Boston. And I wouldn't mind driving up there if it meant seeing Delia. We could probably find a place to meet in the middle. A quiet hotel or bed-and-breakfast. Hell, it might be fun. Delia likes planning. She'd probably get a kick out of finding the perfect spot for us to meet.

Of course, these plans rely on Delia wanting the same thing as me. I need to talk to her and see where her head is at. Not tonight, though. I need Delia to be sober for this conversation.

I kill time in my wood shop while I wait to pick up Delia and Izzy. I haven't had much of a chance to get out here lately, and I've got plenty of planks to cut for Delia's new porches. It's close to midnight when my phone lights up with a message from her.

After I put away my tools, I text her that I'm on the way and then hit the road. When I get to the park, Delia and Izzy are huddled together in the parking lot. It looks like they're laughing. They glance up when I park in front of them.

Delia climbs into the passenger seat. "Hi," she says. She's all smiles and pink cheeks. She's so fucking cute that I have to dig my nails into the steering wheel to stop myself from reaching out and wrapping my arms around her.

Delia doesn't show the same kind of restraint. Leaning across the center console, she brings her warm mouth up against my ear and says, "thanks for coming to get us." She pulls back slightly, her face inches from mine. She smells like a minibar. "You have very nice eyelashes."

I chuckle quietly. I've never met Drunk Delia. Apparently, she's full of compliments.

"Did you have fun?" I ask.

"So much fun," Izzy interjects as she throws herself into the backseat. She flops around for a second before she finally gets herself upright. Her hair is a ball of frizzy curls. "You were wrong about Annabella's punch, Tanner. It's fantastic! I had two glasses, and I feel fine." Based on the way she practically shouts the last part, I'd say Izzy is just as hammered as Delia. That's good. If she weren't drunk, she would probably have something to say about how close Delia is to me right now.

I eye her in the rearview mirror. "I can see that."

Izzy huffs. "Your sarcasm is noted and unappreciated."

I slide my focus back to Delia. "What about you? How much trouble did you get into tonight, darling?"

She shakes her head. "I'm afraid I can't tell you that."

"Why not?"

"Seaside Sip is a very exclusive event. If you want to know what happens there, you need to score an invitation."

"I don't think that's gonna happen."

"That's too bad. Your mom knows how to party."

Christ. "Never utter those words to me again."

"Sorry."

"No, you're not."

Delia fumbles over her seatbelt for a few seconds before she gets it in place. As soon as I start driving, Izzy complains we need music. I offer to put on the radio, and she asks for the aux cord, which I refuse to give her.

"Why not?" she asks.

"Because it's a five-minute drive, and I'm not letting you blast whatever garbage you listen to in my truck."

"I have excellent music taste! Tell him, Delia."

"Sorry, Iz. Tanner's truck, his rules."

Izzy scoffs. "This is why I hate couples," she mutters under her breath. I don't think Delia hears her, because she doesn't react at all.

When we get to Aggie's place, I park the truck and help Delia and Izzy inside. Izzy thanks me for the ride, then says something about getting a snack before bed and heads toward the kitchen.

I turn to Delia, fists balled up in my pockets. "Well, I guess I should be—"

"Wait," she says, laying a hand on my forearm. "I need your help getting out of this. There's a zipper somewhere in the back." She briefly pats the back of her dress. I'm about to remind her that Izzy's in the other room, but she tugs me up the stairs before I can voice any objections. Not that I really have any.

I follow her across the landing and into Aggie's old bedroom. Delia mentioned she moved in here so she and Izzy could each have their own space, but I haven't been inside since I finished sealing the hardwood. Delia hits the light switch, illuminating the small but comfortable space. Her belongings are scattered across the top of the dresser I can't stand.

Delia pads toward the shoddy piece of furniture, toes off her heels, and grabs a T-shirt out of the top drawer. She comes back to me, shirt in hand, then turns around, giving me a view of her phenomenal backside. She moves her dark curtain of hair off her back, revealing a silver zipper.

"If you don't mind," she says, eyeing me over her shoulder.

Evil woman. Ignoring the desire that wells within me, I carefully pull down the zipper, which stops at the base of Delia's back. As soon as I'm finished, she slips her arms out of the sleeves, letting the dress hit the floor. She's wearing nothing but a pair of cotton panties. The sly grin that she gives tells me she knows exactly what she's doing, and while I'd love nothing more than to run my hands over her body, her sleepy eyes indicate she's ten minutes from passing out.

Delia turns to face me, giving me a full view of her smooth skin. Groaning, I take the shirt from her hand and slip it over her head, trying to cover her as quickly as possible.

"You really are trying to kill me," I mutter as I tug the shirt down.

She giggles, mischief lighting up her brown eyes. "Only a little."

I walk her toward the bed. I pull back the comforter, and she climbs in, but instead of crawling under the covers, she scrambles to her knees. Delia wraps her arms around my neck, burying her face against it. "Stay," she whispers.

"Delia." I run my fingers through her soft hair. I'm tempted to take her up on the invitation, but I've never spent the night with Delia. Certainly not at Aggie's. She made it clear she didn't want her sister knowing about our relationship. "I'm not sure that's a good idea."

"You can sneak out before Izzy wakes up," she says. "Please, stay." She pauses for an instant, then adds, "I missed you tonight." And, fuck, if I don't crack then and there.

I pull away for a second to turn off the light, then I head back over to the bed, where Delia has already settled in. I take off my shoes and slide in beside her, dragging her warm body against mine.

She twines our fingers against her hip and closes
her eyes.

I lay there for a while, thinking about how
much I want to keep doing this, and how badly it's
going to hurt if Delia doesn't feel the same.

Thirty-Six

Delia

Seaside Sip was a mistake. And I'm paying for it today.

My temples throb and my stomach churns as I make my way downstairs. Trudging into the kitchen, I stop in front of the coffee machine. I have to brace myself on the edge of the counter for a moment as nausea crashes over me, along with an overwhelming sense of regret. Why did I have to take that last shot? Why did I have to take any shots, for that matter? No single night of fun is worth the inevitable crash and burn of the next morning.

When the sickness finally subsides, I get the machine ready to brew a pot of coffee. It's not a particularly laborious task, but my tequila-soaked brain argues otherwise. Why are there so many buttons?

A knock at the back door steals my focus. I turn and see Tanner standing on the other side of the sliding glass, holding a drink carrier and a white paper bag. I move as quickly as my hungover body will allow to let him inside. His lips twitch in amusement as he gives me a once-over.

"I figured you could use this," he says, lifting the drink carrier, which holds two coffees, in offering. "The one on the left is yours. I got one for Izzy, but I wasn't sure how she takes her coffee. There's cream and sugar in the bag." I thank him, then lunge for the coffee. I almost groan as I inhale the sweet smell of fresh brew.

"Izzy's still sleeping," I say as Tanner sets the bag and the other coffee on the counter. "I think she'll be out for a while." No matter how bad I feel right now, I know it must pale compared to how Izzy's feeling. Last night is a blur, but I remember her having several cups of Annabella's punch. Tanner wasn't kidding when he called it lethal.

"She was in pretty rough shape last night," Tanner admits.

"I think she agreed to be on the planning committee for next year's Seaside Sip."

He chuckles. "You were in rough shape, too. For a moment, I thought I was gonna have to carry you from my truck." My face heats. I hope I didn't do anything to embarrass myself too spectacularly. I think I might have asked Tanner to stay the night. When I got up, I could smell his aftershave on the pillow next to me. And there was aspirin and a glass of water sitting on the nightstand. I was too drunk to put that out myself. Asking him to spend the night definitely violated the rules of not-dating, but we've probably violated those rules a hundred different ways by now.

Groaning, I declare, "I'm never drinking again."

"That's a shame. I like Drunk Delia. She told me I had nice eyelashes." *God, please let the hangover take me.* "I'm gonna work on the back porch for a while," he adds, motioning toward the backyard. "I'll leave you to suffer in peace."

After Tanner heads outside, I bring my coffee upstairs and hop in the shower. Washing away the grease and grime of last night makes me feel slightly better. Plus, the aspirin I took seems to be kicking in.

Fifteen minutes later, I step out of the shower, slip into a thick bathrobe, and towel-dry my hair. I can't be bothered to work a blow dryer right now. It's not like I'm planning to go anywhere today. No, today will be devoted to watching trashy TV shows and pumping myself with fluids.

I return to the kitchen to grab snacks before I start my reality TV marathon. I overestimate my ability to balance a bag of mini donuts, a box of cereal, and my coffee cup at the same time. The coffee slips out of my grasp as I walk across the kitchen. The cup hits the floor on its side, and the lid pops off, spilling coffee everywhere.

"Shit!" Dropping my snacks on the kitchen table, I scramble to get a roll of paper towels. Of course, in my moment of crisis, the roll on the counter is empty. *Dammit, Izzy.* I rush to the hall closet, throwing open the door. I'm scanning the shelves for paper towels when I notice a small, worn-looking shoebox on the bottom shelf. It's almost hidden by the blanket hanging over the edge of the shelf above it.

Without thinking, I reach for the shoebox. The lid is covered in creases and sags slightly in the center. I must have missed it when I cleaned out

the rest of the closet weeks ago. Or maybe
Grandma Aggie's junk has started respawning.

I tear off the lid, half-expecting an army of
spiders to come pouring out of the dusty
container. Instead, it's filled with keys and
documents. I pick up one key, which has a Post-It
taped to it. Garage spare. Another says backdoor
spare. The documents appear to be bank
statements and account numbers for different
utility companies. At the bottom of the box, I find
an envelope that says *For Delia, Izzy, and Morgan*
on the front in slanted letters.

It seems Grandma Aggie left me and my sisters
a goodbye note, after all. I stare at it for a moment
as shock courses through me. I'm tempted to
crumple it. Throw it in the trash and pretend I
never saw it. But, in the end, curiosity wins out.

With shaky fingers, I tear open the envelope
and unfold the handwritten letter tucked inside.

Girls,

*I saw you at your father's funeral today. The
three of you looked so grown up. I could hardly
believe it. The last time I saw you, Morgan was
wearing diapers, and Izzy was too small to ride a
bicycle, and Delia was missing one of her front
teeth. I'm sure it brings you no comfort to hear
this, but you've all turned into beautiful young
women.*

*I'm sorry about your father. We had our
differences, but I still loved him, and I know how
much he loved the three of you. You probably
don't want my condolences. I understand. If I*

were in your position, I wouldn't want them either. That's why I didn't go inside today. Why I haven't written or called. This isn't about me—it's about you.

I wish I could be there to support you through this difficult time. There are many things I wish I could do differently. Regret has a cruel way of finding you only after the damage you've inflicted has become too great to repair.

This house was my home for most of my life. My favorite memories were made within these walls. I hope you create some here, even if you're only here for a short time.

Aggie

Thirty-Seven

Tanner

The thing is, Delia Forrest doesn't have to say much to convince me to do unnecessary shit for her. In fact, she doesn't have to say anything at all. When I realized how close I was to completing the renovations at Aggie's place, I didn't hesitate before volunteering to build Delia two new porches. Anything seemed better than letting her walk out of my life, even prying rotten wood boards off a porch in the warm midmorning sun.

I wedge the pry bar in the space between two boards, then lift, pulling one up. The good news about the porch being old as dirt is that the boards come off with ease. The bad news is that the structure is completely unstable. I can't believe Delia has been sitting up here for weeks. It feels like it's ready to cave, even from the slightest pressure.

As I gradually work my way across the porch, I think about how I'm going to convince Delia we should keep seeing each other after she leaves town. She's careful with her feelings. If I approach this the wrong way, I might scare her off.

How do I show her what she means to me without freaking her out? How much is too much? We haven't known each other for very long, but you wouldn't know that based on the way I feel about her. Without a doubt, Delia is my future. How do I tell her that? I pride myself on being blunt, honest. But I'm not sure those qualities are going to help me. If Delia knew the depth of what I feel, she'd probably run for the hills.

It takes about an hour to finish taking off the base of the old porch. Satisfied with my work, I decide to take a break and go see Delia. I tell myself it's to give her an update on my progress, but the truth is, I've been itching to kiss her all morning.

I knock once on the sliding glass door before stepping inside the empty kitchen. I'm about to call out for Delia when a faint sniffling sound hits my ears. Is that her? I pause, listening closely. The next sniffle ends with a shaky exhale that definitely belongs to Delia.

Concern takes control of my brain. I follow the sniffling through the house, eventually finding Delia on the couch in the living room. She's sitting with her elbows on her thighs and her face buried in her hands, her delicate shoulders shaking with quiet sobs.

"Darling?" I say in a soft voice, not wanting to startle her. Delia looks up with puffy eyes and tear-stained cheeks. Her face is red, but not with the blush I love. It looks like she's been crying for a while. Something inside me breaks at the thought.

She wipes her eyes in a half-baked attempt to pull herself together. "Hey," she says, wringing her hands in her lap. She sniffles again. "Sorry. I-I just need a second."

Clearly, she needs a lot more than one second, but I don't even give her that. In an instant, I'm on the couch, pulling her into my lap. She doesn't fight me. Instead, she wraps an arm around my neck and places a palm on my chest, steadying herself.

I cradle her face in my hands. "What's going on?" I ask, skimming the pads of my thumbs over the tear tracks on her cheeks.

She swallows, averting her gaze. I don't want to force her to talk, but I need to know what's going on. She's scaring the life out of me. My muscles feel fuzzy, and there's a voice in my head screaming at me to do something. To fix this. I don't know what has her so worked up, but I'll do anything to make those tears go away.

"Delia, baby," I whisper, threading my fingers through the back of her hair. "Tell me what's going on. Please. You're scaring me."

Finally, her glassy brown eyes look at me. "She wrote us a letter."

"*Who* wrote you a letter?"

"Grandma Aggie. She wrote a letter for me, Izzy, and Morgan. I found it in the closet."

"What did it say?"

Delia motions to a sheet of notebook paper on the coffee table. "See for yourself."

Shifting her slightly in my lap, I snatch the note off the table. Sure enough, it's a letter from Delia's grandmother. I recognize Aggie's slanted handwriting from the thank-you cards she used to give me for mowing her lawn.

In the letter, Aggie admits to regretting the way she treated Delia and her sisters. It's a nice note, but it's barely half a page, and it doesn't actually contain the words "I'm sorry." It's not the heartfelt apology you'd expect from someone who was truly remorseful.

"It doesn't make sense," Delia says, working her bottom lip between her teeth. "Her regret. She said it was too late, but she had years to make things right. If she really regretted how she acted, then she should have done something. Not left us a note saying how regretful she was on her deathbed."

Anger for Delia and her sisters burns in my chest. They deserve better than a lackluster letter. I hate that they won't get it. It embarrasses me to know I once thought Delia didn't deserve Aggie. That she was selfish for ignoring her grandmother. If anything, Aggie didn't deserve Delia. Anyone who doesn't realize what a privilege it is to know and love this woman has no sense at all.

I hold her for a while as she cries quietly against my neck.

"I'm sorry," I tell her after some time. "You deserved a real apology from Aggie."

Delia sniffles. "That's the thing. I think she did mean it. In her own messed up way. Grandma Aggie didn't speak to my dad for the last fourteen years of his life, but I found a bunch of his old track trophies in her closet. And she asked her friend, Nancy, to make scrapbooks out of old pictures of me and my sisters shortly before she died. And she kept everything. The house, all the mess and clutter, I think it was Aggie's way of expressing her regret." I always had the sense

Aggie was lonely. Maybe she kept all that junk in her house to serve as a reminder of the relationships she carelessly threw away.

"I just…don't understand her," Delia continues. "She felt bad about the way she treated us, but she still ignored us. How can you feel bad about something if you aren't brave enough to try to make things right?"

"Would you have forgiven her if she'd come to you?" I ask.

"Honestly? I don't know. But I wish she'd given me the opportunity. How am I supposed to believe she was sorry when she didn't take accountability for anything? Then again, what's the point of being upset? I can't hold a grudge against my dead grandmother."

"There's nothing wrong with feeling what you're feeling," I say. "I can't tell you what was going on in Aggie's head. No one can. But I think people get complacent. They might not like the way things are going, but they get used to them, so they don't bother trying to change. I mean, look at me. Work has been killing me for ages. Until you and your planner came along, that is."

She breaks out a watery smile. "You haven't been using that planner."

"Hell yes I have. How else do you think I found the time to cut wood for your porches?"

Delia laughs, and I've never been more grateful to hear a sound. She wipes the tears from her eyes. "Thanks. And sorry for crying on you. I hate that I'm letting this get to me so much."

"No need to apologize. And you can't blame yourself for being affected. People are complicated, and Aggie was no exception."

"Complicated. Now there's a good way to describe her," Delia says. "It would be so much easier if she just sucked. Then I wouldn't have to feel mixed up about anything."

"Unfortunately, people don't always fit your expectations for them." When we first met, I thought Delia was a lot of things. Self-centered. Stubborn. Fiery. Some of those things were true, but I was wrong about her in other ways. Delia is thoughtful and generous. She works hard, and she cares deeply about the people in her life.

And as I look at her now, eyes red-rimmed and chin wobbly, it's clear to me that I'm completely in love with her.

Thirty-Eight

Delia

"So I backed over him with my car a second time, just for good measure. I wanted to make sure I really got him, you know?" Izzy's words register in my mind, slow and thick like honey. Wait, what? Did she just confess to vehicular homicide?

Blinking rapidly, I'm met with Izzy's icy glare. She's standing on the other side of the kitchen counter, making homemade guacamole. She's holding half of a lime in one hand and a juicer in the other. She looks like she wants to throw them at me.

She huffs. "Delia, I just spent ten minutes waxing poetic about killing a man in the parking lot of Ralph's Diner. You haven't listened to a single word I've said." She's right. Izzy could've gone into graphic detail, and I wouldn't have heard a thing. I've been too busy thinking about Grandma Aggie's letter.

"Sorry," I say.

Instead of acknowledging my apology, Izzy eyes the bottle by my elbow. "Can you pass me the salt?"

Immediately, I slide the bottle across the counter. Izzy sets down the juicer, tossing the lime in the trash. She grinds sea salt over the bowl of chunky-looking guac.

"Shouldn't you measure that?" I ask.

Izzy arches a brow. "Shouldn't you refrain from giving cooking advice?" Her tone is snippy, and I only have myself to blame. Obviously, she's annoyed by my distractedness. I wish there was a way I could turn my thoughts off.

I hid Grandma Aggie's letter in a drawer upstairs. Aside from Tanner, no one knows about it. I haven't decided whether I should tell my sisters. I know the letter belongs to Izzy and Morgan as much as it belongs to me, but would they really want to know? Reading it brought me nothing but worry and uncertainty.

Grandma Aggie came to our dad's funeral. She left us her beloved house in the hope that we would create new memories here. It seems impossible. Too outlandish to be true. If I hadn't read the letter myself, I'd think this was a misguided fantasy.

Grandma Aggie's regret doesn't erase the past. It doesn't change the fact that she let me and my sisters believe she didn't care about us. It does, however, muddy the picture of her in my head. Before the letter, I saw Grandma Aggie as nothing but cruel and vindictive. Knowing she wished she'd done things differently, that she died holding onto this regret, humanizes her.

She wasn't a cold-hearted woman who despised her family—she was a person with complex thoughts, feelings, and flaws. Even though I'm still mad at her, I can't deny that a part of me feels sad for her. She was never able to overcome her faults. It's hard to vilify someone once you understand them.

I clear my throat. "I'm just saying, there's a recipe for a reason." Ignoring me, Izzy finishes adding salt and then mixes the guac. When she's done, she reaches across the counter for the bag of tortilla chips, popping it open.

"Try it," she says, holding the bag toward me.

"You first." I'm not going to be her guinea pig just because she has a hankering for homemade guacamole.

Izzy plucks a chip from the bag and dips it into the guacamole. She shoves the chip in her mouth, crunching loudly. "Your turn," she says, not bothering to cover her mouth as she chews. I waste no time trying to correct her bad manners. Izzy knows how I feel about open-mouth chewing. She's doing it to mess with me.

I grab a chip, scoop some guac, and shove everything into my mouth. It's fantastic. *Dammit.* I was sort of hoping it would taste like a salt mine. I say nothing, but my facial expression must give away how much I enjoyed the guac, because Izzy looks smug as she goes for a second chip.

"So, what's got you so distracted?" she asks. "Aside from the usual?"

"Nothing," I reply, not wanting to delve into the whole Grandma Aggie's letter debacle.

"Is it the interview?"

"What interview?"

She gives me a funny look. "The one for your boss's job. That's in a few days, right?"

"Right. Yeah." I smack myself on the forehead. My interview for Nina's position is next week, but I haven't thought about it since I scheduled it.

What kind of person forgets about an interview for a huge promotion? "I guess I've been a little distracted."

"You don't have any reason to be nervous. I'm sure you'll kill it."

"Hopefully." Nerves crawl up my spine. I rack my brain for any way to change the subject. "What time is it?"

Izzy glances at her phone. "A quarter past five," she says. "Don't worry. You still have plenty of time to get ready to impress your boyfriend." We're having Tanner and Jacob over for dinner tonight. Tanner wrapped up work on the porches two nights ago, and we wanted to thank him for all the work he's done on the house.

"He's not my boyfriend," I say. "And you've got some nerve teasing me when I could say the same about you and Jacob. You two seemed pretty friendly at the bar." I've been meaning to ask Izzy about Jacob for weeks now. If it gets her off my back about Tanner, that's even better. "Why didn't you tell me you hit it off?"

Izzy rolls her eyes. "I'm charismatic, Delia," she says, licking the excess guac off her thumb. "I hit it off with everyone."

"Jacob is Tanner's best friend. It seems like it'd be worth mentioning."

"Why? Jacob's nice, but it's not like anything's happening between us. I'm not looking for anything serious. Besides, I just broke up with Dominic." I don't bother hiding my disapproving groan. Dominic's a douchebag. Izzy has been dating him on and off for the last several months. I've never had the misfortune of meeting him, but

I know he's flaky and pretentious and completely wrong for her.

"Hey," she says in a scolding tone. "If you don't want me judging your love life, then you can't say a word about mine."

I stuff more chips and guac into my mouth without responding.

I suppose we'll have to leave it at that.

Thirty-Nine

Delia

That night, I'm sitting at the picnic table on the newly renovated back porch, playing Jenga with Izzy and Jacob. The sun is setting, painting the sky a deep shade of orange, and the smells of fresh wood and grass mingle in the breeze.

I grab my virgin margarita off the table (Izzy and I are still recovering from Seaside Sip, so we've sworn off tequila for the foreseeable future) and take a look around me. Of everything Tanner has done for the house, his work on the back porch might be my favorite. He replaced the rotten wood with fresh sandy-brown planks and installed a new railing around the perimeter. I strung fairy lights around the railing and stuck a pair of potted plants by the door. It's simple yet tasteful.

Tanner and Jacob got here a little after six. Izzy poured drinks, and I broke out a few board games I found in the attic. During Scattergories, Izzy and Tanner wound up in a fierce debate over whether "Shark from Jaws" was an acceptable answer for the movie villains' category. My sister is as competitive as can be with board games. She argued that Tanner shouldn't get any points for the answer. *The shark's name is Bruce! Everyone knows that! Google it!*

Eventually, Tanner accepted defeat and offered to grill hot dogs and hamburgers. I was planning to grill myself, so I was eager to pass the responsibility on to him. The burgers would've tasted like hockey pucks if I made them.

After Scattergories, Jacob, Izzy, and I switched to Jenga. A few rounds in, and our block tower looks unsteady. Jacob tries to pull a block from the bottom of the stack, but the piece won't budge. Assessing the tower, he reaches for a different block closer to the top.

"Nope," Izzy objects, swatting his hand away. "You have to take the first piece you touch. That's the rule." She gives him a serious look—well, the most serious look a person can give someone when they're arguing over a game that involves a toddler's toy.

"*Now* you want to play by the rules? The only reason Delia lost the last round was because you blew on the tower while she was taking her piece," Jacob points out.

"That was a gust of wind."

"A gust of wind doesn't have margarita breath, Forrest."

Shamelessly, Izzy smacks the side of the tower. Blocks tumble across the picnic table. She looks Jacob square in the eye, her expression smug and satisfied. "Oops. You lose."

"What? How?"

"The tower fell during your turn; therefore, you lose." Jacob shakes his head in disbelief. "If you don't like the game, we can always play something else. How about poker?"

"So you can outwardly steal from me? I'll pass."

As Izzy cleans up the Jenga blocks, Jacob turns to me with a pleading look. "Please settle this for us, Delia."

I raise my palms, absolving myself of any responsibility. "I'm not getting involved."

Standing up from the picnic bench, I smooth out the back of my linen shorts. "Sorry, Jacob. Izzy can be sensitive about her margarita breath." Izzy shows me her middle finger, and I laugh to myself as I make my way to the grill, where Tanner stands with a metal spatula in hand. He sees me coming over and shuts the lid on the small grill.

"Who knew your sister could be so bloodthirsty?" he remarks, his eyes flitting between me and the picnic table, where Izzy and Jacob are still squabbling.

"You mean like the shark you didn't get any points for?"

"Who the hell knows the name of the shark from Jaws?"

"It's pretty common knowledge. The shark in *Finding Nemo* is named after him."

"I'll be sure to brush up on my fictional shark trivia before we play another game."

"That's probably for the best. Wouldn't want you to go down so easily again."

Amusement flashes on Tanner's face. "I didn't realize you were as bloodthirsty as Izzy."

"What can I say? It must be a family trait."

"Delia!" Izzy exclaims. I glance over my shoulder to find her holding up the margarita pitcher. "Will you split the rest of this with me?"

"No, thanks," I reply, showing her the still-full glass in my hand.

"But it's a celebration! And you've got the house *and* the promotion to celebrate!"

"That doesn't change the fact that my glass is full, Iz."

Finally, Izzy relents, setting the pitcher back on the table. I redirect my attention to Tanner, expecting him to be amused by my sister's antics. Confusion runs through me when I find him looking perplexed, a small crease sitting between his brows.

"Promotion?" he repeats.

"Oh, yeah." I laugh a little, but it sounds strained. I forgot that I hadn't mentioned it to him. "My boss is retiring in August. She recommended me as her replacement to our higher-ups. It's not official or anything, but she thinks I have a good chance of getting it." I hate the way my stomach clenches with those words. *Be happy, Delia*, I remind myself. *This is a good thing.*

Tanner smiles. "That's great, darling. Congratulations."

I almost admit the truth. Tanner told me about his problems at work—there's no reason for me not to do the same. Yet a cookout with my sister and his best friend probably isn't the best setting for that type of conversation. I'll be honest with him about this stuff later. It'll be much easier to confess the feelings I've been keeping to myself without other ears present.

"Thanks." I take a drink from my margarita. "Now, where were we?"

Tanner taps his chin. "I think we were discussing your family's tendency of turning simple board games into ruthless competitions."

"Oh, right. You should see us during the holidays. It's a total bloodbath."

He chuckles. "I bet."

A picture appears in my head. Tanner, sitting in the living room at Mom's house, shaking his head as he watches us play an intense game of Yahtzee. Mom would like him. She'd pepper him with questions about his business and his furniture making.

By the end of the night, she'd probably convince him to build her a new dining table. She's had the same one for ages, and the surface is all scratched up. I'd hide my face in embarrassment and tell Tanner he shouldn't feel obligated to do that. He'd just laugh and say it's no surprise that my mom loves him. *She'll probably like me better than you once I make her that table, darling.*

Warmth pulses through my body at the thought, but it disappears faster than a popped balloon when I realize what I've done. Why am I fantasizing about Tanner meeting my mom? That's never happening. Now that he's done renovating the house, it's time to put the place up for sale. I'll only be in town for a couple more weeks. At most. And when I go back to Boston, that will be the end of me and Tanner.

I warned myself at the beginning not to get attached, but here I am, picturing him at my family's holiday gatherings. Reality hits me like a tidal wave. I failed. Spectacularly. I'm as attached to Tanner as a person can get. Not just his mouth and his eyes, but his warmth and his teasing words and his kindness. I told myself not to fall, but I've fallen, anyway. Leaving him is going to feel like getting kicked in the chest.

"Delia?"

"Huh?" I blink slowly, as if coming out of a trance.

He eyes me strangely. "I said the burgers are almost done," he explains, gesturing to the grill. "Now's a good time if you want to start getting those sides ready."

"Oh, yeah. I'll get on that," I reply awkwardly, stumbling over my feet as I turn toward the back door. Tanner catches my arm before I face-plant on the porch.

"Are you okay?" he asks, concern etched in his brow.

My smile feels as brittle as plastic. "Perfectly fine."

I walk inside on wooden legs. Instead of heading to the fridge to grab the salad and mashed potatoes, I make a beeline for the stairs. Blood rushes through my ears. My hands feel cold and clammy.

I can't let this continue. Not when the end is just around the corner. It will only make things harder for both of us.

In my bedroom, I find my purse on the dresser. I fish around the bottom, and my fingers eventually land on a scrap of paper. I pull it out, unfolding it to read the name and number of Annabella's niece, the realtor.

Before I can talk myself out of it, I type the number into my phone and press call.

Three rings later, a woman picks up. "Hello, this is Alicia."

"Hi, Alicia. My name's Delia Forrest. I'm looking to sell my house."

Forty

Delia

Alicia comes to see the house the following afternoon. She's a bubbly woman in her late twenties with blue eyes and a sharp sense for residential real estate. As I walk her through Grandma Aggie's place, she talks excitedly, pointing out features she thinks will appeal to prospective buyers.

"This place is adorable," Alicia gushes, eyeing the back porch through the sliding glass door in the kitchen. "I know a great couple in the market for a starter home. I bet they'd love to tour this place."

"That's great," I say, injecting my tone with as much enthusiasm as I can muster. Which isn't much. "So, how long does this process take? I don't have any experience with this kind of stuff."

"It depends on how fast you want to move," she says. "I mean, I could get started on the paperwork today if you really wanted to." *Today? As in, today? I didn't realize you could list a home so quickly. I thought it would be a drawn-out process.*

I paste a smile on my face to mask my growing panic. "I share this place with my sisters. I should probably talk to them before making any decisions."

Alicia nods. "Of course. Take as much time as you need. You have my contact information. Call or text if you have questions or want to get the place listed. I have a feeling it'll sell fast."

I thank Alicia for her time, then walk her to the front door. Shutting the door behind her, I can't ignore the churning feeling in my stomach.

What's wrong with me? I should be elated that Alicia can get the house up for sale quickly. That's the objective, right? To sell and get out of here? My life is in Boston. My friends. My apartment. My beloved coffee shop and running spot. I've been away for so long. The knowledge that I can finally go home should excite me, not fill me with dread.

But leaving Seaview means no more runs on the beach or muffins from Ralph's Diner. It means no more Tanner. Sadness rips through me at the thought.

Things with Tanner are easy and light and exciting. I have more fun with him than I ever did with any of my exes. I've done everything I could to prolong what we have, but we're getting close to the end. As much as it saddens me, I know I have to go back to Boston. To the routines I've developed for myself over the years. My sisters and I agreed to sell Grandma Aggie's house, and that's exactly what we're going to do.

To distract myself from my impending departure from Seaview, I spend the rest of the day focusing on work. I'm sitting at the kitchen table several hours later, typing on my laptop, when a door slam echoes through the house, followed by Izzy's voice.

"Delia!" she shouts.

"In the kitchen!" I close my laptop right as Izzy enters the room. My jaw nearly comes unhinged when I catch sight of her.

"You got bangs." The words tumble out of me. I gape at my sister like a roadside attraction. Her wild curls are nowhere to be found. Her dark hair is pin straight, and wispy bangs fall over her forehead.

Izzy drags her fingers through her hair. "Um, yeah," she says. "I felt like I needed a change." I tell myself to stop staring, but it's impossible to tear my eyes away. It's a jarring sight. From a young age, Izzy always refused to use a hair straightener, and she hardly ever goes to the salon. I can't believe she made such a drastic change to her appearance—and without warning. Izzy told me she was going out to run some errands. I thought that meant shopping, not getting a dramatic haircut.

"I didn't know you were getting your hair cut."

She shrugs. "Neither did I. It was a spur-of-the-moment thing." Alarm bells sound in my head. A spur-of-the-moment thing is buying a trashy magazine at the grocery store checkout counter or stopping for an ice cream cone on the way home from work. Small, mindless indulgences with no real-world consequences. Impulsively getting bangs? That's a cry for help. It confirms the suspicion I've had for weeks. Something is definitely wrong with Izzy.

"Izzy, are you—"

"How did it go with the realtor?" she blurts, cutting me off mid-sentence.

"It went fine." Izzy stares at me with a blank expression. Is she just going to pretend she didn't stop me from asking if she's doing okay? "Alicia seems nice. She thinks we'll make a killing on this place."

"Did she say when we can get it on the market?"

"Any time. There's some paperwork involved, but we can put it up today if we want."

Izzy nods. "I bet you're thrilled." There's annoyance in her voice. *I bet you're thrilled.* That doesn't mean the same thing as "that's great" or "how exciting." It's purposefully singular. *You're* thrilled. Not us.

"I thought all of us would be thrilled," I say, hoping to ease the tension. "We've been trying to get the house ready for months."

"Have *we* really been getting the house ready for months? I've only been here for six weeks. Morgan hasn't been here at all." Okay, no subtlety there. Izzy's pissed. But where is this coming from? Doesn't she want to get back to her life in New York?

"Does it matter? We all had the same end goal, right? Besides, I don't think Morgan's too broken up about not seeing the house. She just finished a stressful semester. She deserves a vacation."

"Have you asked her if that's what she wants? Or are you making an assumption?"

Frustration bristles in my chest. "Izzy, what's your problem?"

"Nothing. I'm just pointing out that Morgan deserves a chance to see the place. It's her house, too."

"I know. The three of us talked about this. We agreed to sell."

"We agreed to sell *together*," Izzy clarifies. "You were only supposed to come to Seaview for a day, remember? You were gonna check out the place and go home. That day turned into a few days, which turned into weeks, which turned into you taking over the project entirely. Why do you think I came out here? I knew I wouldn't get a chance if I didn't."

"That's not fair, Izzy. I stayed here because I saw what a disaster it was. I couldn't leave that kind of mess behind."

"Why not? You're the one who said there was no rush. This was supposed to be about all three of us, Delia. You decided to do what you wanted without any regard for me or Morgan."

"I can't believe you're mad at me for fixing up the house," I say, shaking my head in disbelief. "Do you know how much work it was? How much time it took? I haven't been to my apartment in months, Izzy! I put my whole life on hold for this."

"But no one asked you to! Like always, you decided how you wanted to handle things, and you did them exactly that way. This entire project has been on your timetable. And now you're ready to get out of dodge, so it's time for us to pack up and sell."

I can't believe this. Does Izzy not recognize how much I've sacrificed to deal with Grandma Aggie's house? Does she think I wanted to spend hours upon hours cleaning a strange place by myself? I don't know what's going on with her, but I'm not going to sit here and listen to her tear into me like this. I'm not her punching bag.

I push out of my chair, the legs scraping loudly against the floor. "I'm not doing this," I tell her. "Come find me when you want to act like an adult."

As I leave the kitchen, Izzy says, "did something happen with Tanner? Is that why you're so hellbent on getting out of here?"

I turn to look at her. She's standing with her arms crossed over her middle, her hip pressed against the side of the counter.

"What are you talking about?" My mouth feels drier than sandpaper.

"C'mon, Delia. I'm not oblivious. I know you're sleeping with him." I don't see a reason to deny it. I figured she knew already. Tanner and I haven't exactly been discreet. Still, why is Izzy throwing it in my face?

"Tanner has nothing to do with this."

She lifts a brow. "Really? Because you've had no problem hanging around Seaview until now. So what gives? Did you two get into a fight? Did he do something to disrupt one of your plans?" Her voice brims with condescension.

My heart thuds loudly. Izzy's clearly hurting, and she wants to hurt me. I thought I could be mature and walk away, but the rage building inside wants me to hurt her back in any way I can. So I say the first cruel thing that comes to mind.

"You know what? You're right. It was easier dealing with this place by myself. Maybe the reason I wanted to do things on my own was because I knew you'd come here and make a mess of everything. The way you always do." I regret the words as soon as they leave my mouth.

There's a flash of hurt in Izzy's eyes, but it disappears quickly, swallowed up by anger.

"Do whatever you want with the house," she says. "I don't give a shit."

Then she storms out of the kitchen and up the stairs, slamming the door behind her.

Forty-One

Tanner

I grab the remote off the coffee table, hitting the pause button. I glance over at Delia, who's resting her head against my shoulder. "Let me make sure I've got this right," I say, motioning to the TV screen. "The redheaded woman. Tonya. She's engaged to the lawyer who's stealing from his family's law firm. Brett. But she's actually in love with Brett's best friend. The one who's hiding his heart condition from everyone."

I told Delia to put on whatever she felt like watching, and she picked some goofy soap opera. The acting is terrible, and the plot is hard to follow, but I'll admit I've become somewhat invested over the last couple of episodes. Plus, it seems to be making Delia happy. She's been off since she got here. I planned on taking her out for dinner tonight, but when I saw sadness on her face, I figured a quiet night of TV was a better option.

"That's correct," she says. "But don't forget about Kelly. She's the woman dating Dawson. She knows Brett's stealing from the law firm, and she's blackmailing him." I shake my head in disbelief. There are too many plotlines. It's like trying to untangle a giant knot of yarn. How does Delia keep up with this stuff?

"Is everyone on this show a horrible person?"

Delia shrugs. "I mean, kind of. But you can't help but root for them anyway. Couldn't you feel the tension between Tonya and Dawson in that scene by the pool?"

"You mean the guy and his best friend's fiancée?"

"Ugh. Forget it. Let's put on something else. You don't understand the complexities of *Twisted Hearts*." She lunges for the remote in my hand, but I pull it away before she can reach it. Delia winds up sprawled across my lap, her face inches from mine.

"We can't turn it off now. Brett just found Dawson's love letters to Tonya."

A cat-like grin stretches across her face. "So you *are* invested."

"Not invested. I'm simply paying attention."

She bites her bottom lip, looking totally amused. "You know, *Twisted Hearts* does a fan convention every year in Rhode Island. Maybe we can dress up as Dawson and Tonya and go next year." The words "fan convention" and "dress up" make my skin crawl, but that feeling fades with the words "next year." Delia probably isn't serious about this, but hearing her talk about the possibility of us doing something together *next year* has me feeling optimistic.

Maybe persuading her to give us a shot won't be as difficult as I thought.

It's the first glimmer of hope I've had since the cookout the other night. When Izzy mentioned Delia's promotion, it felt like a punch to the gut.

Don't get me wrong—I'm happy for Delia. But she never said a word to me about a promotion. I worried that meant she didn't see a reason to. Why bother keeping me in the loop if I'm not a permanent fixture in her life? I don't like not knowing what's going on with her. With Delia Forrest, I want to be fully informed. Always.

"I'm not dressing up as Dawson," I say. "Do you see how much product is in his hair?"

She looks back and forth between me and the guy on the screen. "You're right. You're more of a natural pretty boy."

I raise a brow, hooking my arm around her lower back. "Pretty boy?"

"Um, yes." She lays her palms flat on my chest. "Have you seen yourself? I hate to break it to you, but you're very pretty. It's almost disgusting."

In one swift motion, I flip us so Delia's back is pressed to the couch cushions, and I'm hovering over her. I lock her wrists above her head with one hand, pinning her to the couch with my hips.

"Careful what you say, darling," I whisper against her ear, loving the way goosebumps rise across her skin. "It might lead to something you can't handle."

Delia grins. "I don't dish out what I can't take."

I lower my mouth to hers.

Sometime later, I pull away from Delia to grab each of us a glass of water from the kitchen. When I return to the living room, Delia's sitting upright with a quilted blanket wrapped around her shoulders. She gnaws her bottom lip, seemingly lost in thought.

"Are you all right?" I ask, handing her a glass. "Seems like something's bothering you." She takes a sip, then sets her water on a coaster on the coffee table.

"I'm fine," she says. "It's just…Izzy and I had a fight today. It got ugly. I guess I'm still processing it." That explains why she's been quieter than usual. I wonder what happened, but I don't want to push if she doesn't feel like telling me.

Plopping myself beside her on the couch, I ask, "do you wanna talk about it?"

Slowly, Delia nods. "Izzy accused me of not letting her and Morgan be involved with Grandma Aggie's. When we found out about the house, we agreed that whatever we decided to do, we'd do it together. I was only supposed to come to town to scope out the place. But then I saw the mess and realized it would be a lot more work than I originally thought. I'm the one who pushed for us to sell, Tanner. It only seemed fair for me to take charge. I thought Izzy and Morgan felt the same way. You should've heard them on the phone the night we found out about the house. They were freaking out. I thought I was helping." The distress in her voice tugs at my chest.

"You *were* helping. Trust me. I saw what that house looked like before you did anything to it, darling. Your sisters should be relieved you stepped in."

"I'm not so sure. Izzy made it seem like she and Morgan felt excluded."

"Have you talked to Morgan about this?"

"Not yet."

"She might be able to give you some clarity. Maybe Izzy's upset, and she's bringing up Morgan to make it seem like a bigger deal than it is."

"Maybe."

"Any idea why Izzy picked a fight with you today?"

Delia frowns. "It happened right after we talked about my meeting with the realtor. Maybe she didn't realize how close we were to putting the house on the market."

"You met with a realtor?" I try to keep my voice even, but that's hard when it feels like the air is being sucked out of my chest.

"Yeah. Annabella's niece, Alicia. She gave me her number a few weeks ago."

"I didn't know you were meeting with a realtor."

She shrugs. "It was just an introductory meeting. That's all." She says it casually. Like she didn't just shatter every single one of my hopes and expectations. She met with a *realtor*, and she didn't tell me. What's next? Will she even have the decency to let me know when she sells the house? Will I wake up one morning with a text saying she's gone back to Boston?

Delia's a grown woman, and we've made no commitments to each other. She can do whatever she wants. But her not telling me about meeting with a realtor says a lot about her feelings on our relationship. You don't hide those kinds of details from someone if you want a future with them.

"Right," I say calmly. Scooping the empty popcorn bowl off the coffee table, I carry it to the kitchen and place it in the sink. I turn on the faucet, numbly listening to the sound of water hitting the bottom of the sink.

All this time, I've been working up the nerve to ask her to have a serious go at this, and she's been getting ready to leave. Did I misinterpret everything? I thought Delia and I were on the same page, but it seems we weren't even reading the same book.

She comes into the kitchen seconds later. "Are you mad at me now, too?" she asks, studying me with confused eyes.

"No," I reply, picking up the sponge to scrub the inside of the bowl. "I just thought you'd have the decency to tell me before you left town."

"It was one meeting, Tanner. That's it. And I *was* going to tell you about it."

"When? Before or after you sold the house?"

Delia sighs. "That's not fair. You've known this entire time that I wasn't planning on keeping the house. You can't blame me for meeting with a realtor." It's true. She's done nothing wrong. We agreed this was casual, temporary. It's not her fault I got other ideas. It's not fair to punish her when she didn't do anything to hurt me intentionally.

I shut off the faucet, wiping my wet hands on a nearby dish towel. "Sorry. Let's just forget it." My tone is short and abrupt, and I'm hoping that will be the end of it, but it only seems to make Delia more interested.

She frowns. "We can't just forget about it. You're pissed."

"Delia, it's fine."

"No, it's not. We have to talk about this."

"Why? It's not like it matters. You're not gonna be here much longer anyway." It's the wrong thing to say, and I know it, but I can't bring myself to take the words back. She's made it clear she intends to get out of Seaview. Go back to her regular life with her new promotion. All this fighting and apologizing won't change the inevitable: her leaving.

Shock appears on Delia's face, but it's quickly replaced by hardness. "You're right," she says, her bottom lip trembling. "It's not like this matters."

Shit. I can't handle her crying. "Darling, that's not what I—"

Delia shakes her head. "No, no. It's the truth." She sniffles, shifting on her feet. I try to meet her gaze, but she's looking everywhere but at me. "I'm tired. I think I'm gonna sleep at my place tonight." She lunges for her purse, which is sitting on the counter.

"Delia." I start toward her, but she holds up her palms, telling me to keep my distance.

"I've gotta go," she says, slinging her purse over her shoulder. "Lots of research to do on real estate." Turning on her heels, she scrambles to the front door. I listen for the inevitable click of the lock and slam of the door, wondering how things could've gone so wrong.

Forty-Two

Delia

I have to get out of Seaview. Tonight.

Tears blur my vision as I make the short walk back to Grandma Aggie's place. Tanner's words play like a recording in my head. *It's not like it matters. You're not gonna be here much longer, anyway.* I want to believe he didn't mean it. That he only said those things because he wanted to seem unaffected. But he sounded so cold. Dismissive. How could he say things like that if he didn't really mean them?

Emotion wells in my chest. I don't know what's happening in Tanner's mind, but I know one thing: I need to get back to Boston. I have a life outside of this town. A wonderful, structured life that doesn't involve arrogant green-eyed men. *This* is why I swore off dating after my breakup with Austin. I didn't want to be in pain. To give someone the ability to crush me with a few simple words.

If I had kept my senses, I would've nipped this thing with Tanner before it could take root. Now, I feel like a knife has been plunged through my heart. The best thing I can do is put distance between us. I've already spent too much time in Seaview. My feelings are affecting my ability to think logically. Getting out of here should bring me some clarity.

When I get back to Grandma Aggie's house, I immediately head upstairs. Light pools at the bottom of the closed guest room door. Izzy's home. I don't know if she's still mad or if she's cooled off since this afternoon, but I'm not sticking around to find out.

I enter my bedroom, grab my overnight bag off the dresser and begin shoving clothes inside. It doesn't fit everything, but I don't mind leaving some things behind if it means hitting the road sooner. Slinging the bag over my shoulder, I grab my car keys and head out the door.

It's late by the time I arrive in Boston. Hours of late-night driving have left me bleary-eyed and exhausted. I unlock the door to my apartment and dump my belongings in the entryway. Without bothering to turn on the lights, I drag my tired body to the living room and throw myself on the couch. Crushing my cheek to a pillow, I let my tears fall freely, and I cry until sleep finally takes over me.

***

I wake up the next morning feeling like I've been hit by a semi-truck.

Sleeping on the couch left a nasty crick in my neck. I massage the ache with my fingertips as I sit up slowly, wincing at the sunshine beaming from the nearby window. What time is it? Squinting, I reach for my phone, which rests on the edge of the coffee table.

It's almost eleven. I can't remember the last time I slept in so late. I ought to get up and do something productive. I have plenty to keep me busy, after all. There's no food in my apartment. And there's a dead ficus in my office that needs to be taken care of.

When I try to pull myself off the couch, however, my muscles refuse to cooperate. Instead, I grab the remote and put on a rerun of one of my favorite reality shows.

Hours pass. No matter how much trashy TV I watch, it doesn't erase the hollowness in my chest. Yesterday was a lot. I'm still upset about the fight I had with Izzy. I don't understand why she blew up at me or what's going on with her. But ultimately, I know the two of us will be okay. She's my sister. We fight all the time.

Tanner is a different story. Our conversation felt final. I might catch a glimpse of him when I head back to Seaview to finish dealing with the house, but I'll probably never see him again. Never hear his laugh or feel his touch or smell his aftershave. It's a hard truth to face, even though I knew it was coming.

I wish it hadn't ended so ugly. I can see why Tanner was upset about the realtor. Concealing the meeting from him probably made him think that I couldn't be bothered to include him in my plans. If only he had given me a chance to explain myself. I would've told him I only kept the meeting a secret because I didn't want to think about leaving him. Then again, it's not like that would've changed anything. Tanner and I were never going to last.

The ache in my chest deepens. I don't want that fight to be what I remember Tanner by. And I certainly don't want it to be what *he* remembers *me* by. These last few months have been the best of my life. I hate that they're ruined now. We've been playing pretend for too long. It was only a matter of time before reality caught up to us.

By late afternoon, I still haven't gotten up. I consider calling Kali and Mariah, but my friends are under the impression that Tanner is nothing more than a rebound. If they see me in this state, then I'll have to tell them the truth. I'm not up for that yet. So I decide to text Morgan. She's a rational person. Surely, she'll have some sense to offer.

Delia: Can you come over?

Morgan: To Seaview?

Delia: No, I'm in Boston.

Morgan: What? When did you get back?

Delia: Last night.

Morgan: Why didn't you tell me you were coming home?

Delia: I wasn't planning to. It's a long story.

Morgan: Is everything okay?

Delia: Yes and no. I could use someone to talk to.

Morgan: On my way.

I'm in the middle of another reality show rerun when I hear a soft knock at the door, followed by the slide of a lock. Morgan, thankfully, has a key to my place. I told her to let herself in when she got here.

"Delia?" she calls out.

"In here."

Footsteps patter across the hardwood, stopping by the side of the couch.

Lifting my head, I observe my youngest sister. She's dressed in a pair of slacks and a pale blue button-down. Her long brown hair hangs over her shoulder in a loose braid. She must've come directly from the diner where she waitresses part time.

Morgan's eyes widen as she takes in my appearance. I'm sure I look awful. I've been lying here for so long that crease marks are probably permanently etched into my cheek.

"Delia, what happened?" she asks.

"I got into a fight with Izzy. Then Tanner." My voice wobbles, and there's no way Morgan misses it. Slowly, I sit up, making space for her on the other side of the couch. She studies me like I'm a wounded animal.

"Why don't you start at the beginning?" she suggests.

So that's what I do. I start with the blowup with Izzy, then explain Tanner's reaction when he found out about my meeting with the realtor. Morgan, naturally, has questions about Tanner. The last she heard, we were barely civil with each other. I'm worried she's going to be upset about me keeping secrets, but Morgan assures me she understands.

"There's a lot of pressure that comes with telling people you're seeing someone," she says. "I get wanting to keep it to yourself for a while."

When I finish getting everything off my chest, Morgan leans over and wraps me in a big hug. I don't realize how badly I need it until her arms loop around my shoulders.

"It sounds like you've had a rough twenty-four hours," she says.

I laugh humorlessly, breathing in the scent of her vanilla perfume. "It must be some kind of record. How quickly I made everyone hate me."

Being the best at ruining relationships isn't a title I relish.

Morgan pulls back. "Don't put too much stock into anything Izzy said, okay? She's going through a lot right now. I'm sure she didn't mean it."

"What's going on with her, exactly?"

Morgan averts her eyes as she returns to her side of the couch. She saws her bottom lip between her teeth. "I promised I wouldn't say anything."

"About what?" Worry takes hold. "Morgan, what's going on with Izzy? You can't say something like that and then not give me any details." I'm not letting her out of this. I'll call Izzy myself and demand to know the truth if necessary.

"She got fired."

"What? When?"

"A few days after you left for Seaview."

"But…Izzy said she's been working remotely."

"She lied, Del." I don't want to believe it, but Izzy losing her job explains a lot. Her canceling her flight at the last minute and driving to Seaview. The comment she made at the bar about looking for her next job. The *bangs*. Oh my god. My sister has been having a full-blown crisis right in front of me, and I had no idea. What's wrong with me?

"I don't understand," I say. "Izzy's so talented. How could she get fired?"

"No idea," Morgan admits. "She says she's not ready to talk about it."

"Have you known all this time?" The guilty expression on her face reveals everything before

Morgan has a chance to. "Why would she tell you and not me?"

"Because she was embarrassed. You're about to be promoted, Delia. You can't blame her for not wanting to talk about her career imploding while yours is thriving."

"But I don't care about that." Izzy's my sister. I love her, and I want what's best for her. "I could've done something. Helped her apply for jobs. Figured out a budget. How is she doing financially? Does she have anything in savings?"

Morgan sighs. "Delia, have you considered maybe that's why she didn't tell you?"

"You think she kept it from me because she didn't want my help?"

"Not exactly. It's just…you have a tendency of doing what you think is best for other people without actually asking them what they want. Izzy's an adult. She doesn't need you to solve her problems for her." Huh. That sounds like a more delicately worded version of what Izzy shouted at me yesterday.

"Morgan, are you mad about how I've been handling things with the house?" I ask, hoping she'll deny it. The last thing I want is to be so insufferable that I can't see when I've been walking all over my sisters.

She sighs. "I know you're not doing anything to be malicious, Delia, but the three of us were supposed to decide what to do with the house as a group. You made a plan without asking for any input from Izzy or me. I mean, I haven't been there once, and you're already talking to a realtor."

"I…" The words fade from my tongue. I don't know what to say. Morgan has struck me with a particularly bitter dose of reality.

The way I've been treating my sisters isn't right. They feel unheard. They're keeping things from me to avoid having me try to fix their problems. I might have had good intentions, but intent doesn't matter if you're hurting the people who matter most to you.

"I'm sorry, Morgan," I finally say. "I wasn't trying to exclude you from the decision making. I thought it would be easier on everyone if I took over."

"It's okay," she says, sounding sincere. "But maybe in the future you should ask before you assume. Having a plan is great and all, but not if it's not what everyone wants."

I fall back on the couch, feeling suddenly exhausted. "I should talk to Izzy." This doesn't feel like a conversation that should happen over the phone. "I have my job interview this week, but I'll head back to Seaview after so we can have this conversation face-to-face."

Morgan smiles. "I think that's a good idea. So, what are you going to do about Tanner?"

"What do you mean?" Tanner made his feelings abundantly clear yesterday—he doesn't view me as a permanent part of his life.

"Look, I don't know the guy, but it sounds like you have pretty strong feelings for him," Morgan says. "If he feels the same way about you, then I can see why he might've been upset about you secretly meeting with a realtor."

"It was just a meeting, Morgan. It's not like I
sold the house. Besides, it was never gonna work
out between us, anyway."

"If that's how you feel, fine," she says. "But it
sounds like you're letting go of something good
because you're scared."

I can't face what it means if she's right, so I
don't. But that doesn't stop the gnawing feeling in
my stomach, instinct telling me I'm making a
mistake by letting Tanner go.

Forty-Three

Delia

My alarm rings at five-thirty Monday morning.

Rolling over in bed, I clumsily slap my phone in the darkness, then drag myself out of bed. Quickly dressing in workout clothes, I head to my favorite park for running. It's a dark and misty morning, so I pull up my hood before I begin my two-and-a-half-mile run. When I finish about forty-five minutes later, I walk to my regular coffee shop, where the barista greets me with a "hey, Delia. It's been a while." We make light conversation as she fixes my oat milk latte and spinach egg wrap.

Once my order is ready, I make the short trek back to my apartment. I hop in the shower, then get dressed and eat breakfast. Sitting at the kitchen table with my latte in hand, I have no choice but to acknowledge the empty feeling that *still* hasn't left my chest.

While I managed to get up this morning—a success in its own right—I feel as crappy as I did yesterday. Talking to Morgan helped me sort things out, but it didn't erase my feelings.

I thought getting back to my routine would improve the situation. My morning run, followed by a stop at the coffee shop, has served as a source of comfort and stability for me for years. It's the one thing that's always managed to get me going, even when I'm feeling sad or tired or lazy. Today, however, I feel no different than I did when I walked out the door. It seems it's going to take more than a breakfast wrap for me to get over Tanner.

The rest of the day is uneventful. For the first time in months, I work at the desk in my home office. The room smells like dust, and the puppy calendar on the wall still says April. I spend time cleaning in between work. Being back here feels like getting on a bike again after years of not riding, but I know things will improve once I get used to them. I've only been home for a couple of days. I need time to adjust.

That night, I text Mariah and Kali, letting them know I'm back in Boston. We decide to meet up at Bar Westbrook for an impromptu happy hour. Both of them pull me into massive hugs when I arrive at the bar.

Over a bottle of wine, Mariah and Kali fill me in on everything that's happened since I left the city. I nod and smile and pretend to be relieved about getting out of Seaview. When they badger me about the guy I was hooking up with, I tell them it was nothing and that we ended amicably.

I'm happy to see my friends. I missed our nights out. Kali's jokes and Mariah's laughter help me feel at ease for a few hours, but when I get back to my apartment later that night, the emptiness is waiting for me. I never realized how much time I spent alone. Am I always by myself? Are nights with Kali and Mariah the only time I socialize?

Give it time, Delia.

The week passes in an inconsequential blur. On Thursday afternoon, I have my interview with the marketing firm's human resources manager for Nina's position. Settling at my desk, I log on to my laptop and click the link to the Zoom interview. It buffers for a moment, then a woman with grayish-brown hair and long, penciled brows appears on screen.

"Hi, Delia."

"Hi, Ethel."

"It's nice to meet you. I think we've exchanged a few emails over the years, but it's great to put a face to the name."

"Likewise."

Ethel smiles politely. "Nina had a lot of good things to say about you, but we still like to do the formal interview process, even with our internal candidates."

"Of course. That makes sense."

"I appreciate you making time in your schedule," Ethel says. "Let's start with a simple question. Why are you interested in the position?"

It *is* a simple question. One I practiced a half-dozen times when I was prepping for this interview last night. Several canned responses sit on the tip of my tongue. *It's a great opportunity for me to grow in my career. I love working at this company. I'm ready to take the next step forward.* It's not rocket science, figuring out what Ethel wants in an answer.

The problem is, I don't want this job. And hearing the question asked aloud makes me realize how much I don't want it.

By textbook standards, it's a good thing. The position comes with a higher salary, more responsibilities, and a fancy new title. Yet none of those perks change the fact that my skin turns hot and itchy every time I think about accepting it. I'm applying for this job because it seems like the right thing to do, not because of genuine interest.

Isn't that wrong? Why am I forcing myself to do something that's going to make me miserable? It might make Nina happy and Mom proud, but I'm the one who's going to have to wake up every day and do it. I shouldn't be forcing myself into a horrible situation simply because it's what's expected of me.

Shouldn't I want what's best for myself?

Shouldn't the end goal be to create a life that makes me happy?

As I consider these thoughts, I can't help but think about Grandma Aggie's letter. She told me and my sisters she never reached out to us because it was too late, and she knew she could never make up for the way she treated us. She accepted the easy outcome. Did what was expected of her. And she died without family in her life.

In a different way, isn't that what I'm doing by accepting this job? Going with what I'm supposed to do instead of what I want because I'm too afraid to take a risk?

In an ideal world, I wouldn't be interviewing for this position. Then again, it's not being forced on me. I can turn it down. Choose a different path.

Instead of thinking about what I should do, I ask myself what I would want if I could have anything. The answer comes immediately.

Tanner.

I want his smiles and his thoughtfulness. I want morning runs on the beach and blueberry muffins from Ralph's Diner. I want quiet evenings on the back porch of Grandma Aggie's—no, *my* house. And I want to wake up in the morning with Tanner by my side. I want to lean on him, and I want him to lean on me. I want everything we've been doing these past few months to become permanent. Because I love him. And he deserves to know that.

***

The hardest part is telling Nina.

I call her shortly after the interview to let her know I'm withdrawing my name from consideration. I thank her for her mentorship and explain that I'm satisfied with my current position. When I finish speaking, I brace myself for disappointment. So it shocks me when she says she's happy for me and wishes me the best.

"The only thing that matters is how you feel, Delia," she says. "The rest is just background noise."

***

As planned, I drive back to Seaview that night to talk to Izzy. Her car is parked in the driveway, but the lights are off, and she's not in the kitchen or living room. Upstairs, I see light peeking out from beneath the guest room door.

With a deep breath, I knock.

"Iz," I say in a soft, hesitant voice. "It's me. Can I come in?" Nerves churn in the pit of my stomach. "Please, Izzy. I really want to talk to you. I'm sorry, okay? I don't want us to fight anymore."

352

Relief floods my veins as floorboards creak inside the bedroom. Then, Izzy opens the door. She's dressed in a ratty sweatshirt and leggings. Her eyes are red-rimmed, and her hair is in a messy knot at the top of her head.

"I'm sorry," I tell her again. "I didn't mean to trounce all over you and Morgan. We agreed to sell this place together. It wasn't fair of me to take over."

"I should be the one apologizing, Del," Izzy replies, shaking her head. "I was such a bitch for no reason. I know you weren't trying to exclude me and Morgan. And I appreciate everything you've done with the house. I guess I…" She pauses briefly, biting her bottom lip. "I guess I thought the house would give the three of us an excuse to spend time together. We don't see each other that often. I miss you. To me, you rushing to get everything done felt like you were saying you didn't care."

"I miss you, too," I say. "It probably didn't seem that way, but it's true. Being here with you has been the happiest I've felt in a really long time."

"I should've been honest with you," Izzy says. "I've been dealing with some stuff, and I wasn't in the mood to talk about my feelings."

"Morgan told me about your job. Do you want to talk about it?"

She shakes her head. "Not yet."

"Well, you know you can come to me when you're ready. I'm always here to listen."

"Thanks, Del. I appreciate it. I've just got a lot of shit to figure out."

"Take all the time you need. We've got this place. You can stay as long as you want."

"I doubt the house will be on the market for long."

"Funny you should mention that," I say. "I've been doing some thinking. How would you feel about me buying you out of your portion of the house?" Izzy's eyes widen, and I keep going. "I already talked to Morgan, and she's okay with it. I can't offer you as much as you'd make from selling the house, so if you're not interested—"

"You don't have to buy me out of anything," she says, interrupting me mid-sentence. "The house is yours. You did most of the work anyway. Besides, we wouldn't be here if you hadn't insisted on selling."

"Are you sure? Because I don't mind." Morgan also rejected my offer to pay her. Still, I don't want Izzy to feel as though I'm taking the house from her.

"I'm positive," she says. "As long as *you* don't mind having a roommate for a while."

Forty-Four

Delia

Convincing Morgan to spend the rest of the week in Seaview is easy. She drives down Friday morning, and Izzy and I take her on a tour of the house. In the afternoon, we pack a wicker basket with finger sandwiches and hit the beach for a picnic. The idea is better in theory than practice. It's windy, and sand gets everywhere, including our food. Two bites into my gritty turkey sandwich, I declare the picnic awash and suggest we order takeout.

We end up eating Chinese food on the living room couch. As we stuff our faces with egg rolls, we swap memories of Grandma Aggie. Morgan was only a baby the last time she was in Seaview, so she doesn't remember anything. Izzy has a few stories, though I don't know how many of them are true. I find it hard to believe my then-four-year-old sister had a run-in with a shark that no one in my family knows about.

"It was probably a wave," I tell her.

"Waves don't have heads," Izzy says. "Or eyes."

"Still," Morgan adds, "calling yourself the survivor of a shark attack seems like a stretch."

"It was right in front of me!" Izzy exclaims, sending a forkful of fried rice flying across the living room. "I was one second from being fish food. Grandma Aggie saw it, too."

"How convenient that the one person who could confirm or deny your story isn't around to do so," I mutter, earning a scowl from Izzy.

During a beat of silence, Morgan grows suddenly serious. "Do you think Grandma Aggie thought about us? Obviously, she had to. She left us the house. But do you think she did that because she had no one else to give it to? Or did she genuinely want us to have it?"

The question hangs in the air for a moment. It's as good a time as any for me to come clean. "There's something I've been meaning to show you," I say.

Setting my carton of rice on the table, I climb off the couch and sprint to my bedroom to retrieve Grandma Aggie's letter from my dresser. Izzy and Morgan study me with curious eyes when I return to the living room a moment later, holding the yellowed piece of paper.

"I found this the other day," I tell them. "It's from Grandma Aggie. She wrote it to explain why she gave us the house. I wasn't sure if either of you would want to read it. I can tell you what it says or give it to you—"

"I don't want to know anything," Izzy interjects. "I'm sure it's filled with nothing but excuses anyway." Her reaction doesn't surprise me. Of the three of us, Izzy has always had the harshest feelings about Grandma Aggie.

I turn my attention to Morgan, who stares at the letter for a moment. "I'd like to read it, I think," she says. "On my own time." I give her the letter. It feels good having it out of my hands, literally and metaphorically. Izzy and Morgan ought to make their own assessments of our grandmother. I can't be the one to do it for them.

As for me, I've reached a place of acceptance with Grandma Aggie. I don't agree with her decisions, but I understand she was flawed and scared and filled with regret. That doesn't make up for the hurt she caused, but it explains why she caused it. She was too afraid to take ownership of her own mistakes.

I'm not mad at her anymore. It's not important. Besides, I can't change anything about her choices. And, honestly, I don't know if I'd want to.

If Grandma Aggie hadn't exactly done what she did, who knows how things might've turned out? I'm glad I ended up in Seaview.

There's just one more person I need to make things right with.

Forty-Five

Tanner

My head hasn't stopped pounding for a week.

I can't sleep for more than a couple hours at a time. I can't shave either. No, I'm growing a beard in the middle of goddamn June because I can't smell my aftershave without thinking of Delia.

She's gone. When I went over to her place to apologize the morning after our fight, Izzy answered the door and told me Delia left town. I tried calling and texting, but she hasn't responded to my messages. She's finished with me, and I can't say I blame her.

I acted like a jackass after she brought up her meeting with a realtor. The thought of losing her terrified me, so I let my pride and insecurity do it for me. Instead of assuring her I wanted us to stay together, I made her think she didn't matter to me. I pushed her away, plain and simple. I only have myself to hold responsible.

With Delia gone, I've been throwing myself into work even more than usual. The office is the only place that isn't tainted by her absence. My house, my workshop, the running trail— everything else reminds me of her.

It's after nine tonight, and I'm still at Ryan & Son. I haven't left my desk in hours. You'd think putting so much work in would result in me being on top of things, but I've hardly accomplished anything. It's hard to concentrate when all I can think about are brown eyes and soft lips and beautiful laughter.

A knock at my office door jars me out of my thoughts. I assumed everyone had left by now. Confused, I look up to see Jacob standing outside. What's he doing here? He doesn't wait for me to open the door. Simply barges inside.

"I knew you'd be here," Jacobs says in an annoyed tone. "We were supposed to meet for drinks an hour ago, remember?" Shit. Jacob asked—no, demanded I come with him to Seaview Tavern tonight. He knows I've been struggling in Delia's absence. I think he wanted to cheer me up. I didn't expect a couple rounds of beers to help me get over Delia, but I didn't mean to ditch him. It was an honest mistake.

I scratch the back of my neck, which is sore from staring down at a desk all day. "Sorry. I've been busy. Time slipped away from me, I guess." I'm expecting him to nod, then tell me to pack up my stuff and meet him in the parking lot. So he surprises me when he crosses his arms and leans back against the door frame.

"So, this is how it's gonna be again, huh?" I knew Jacob didn't approve of my work habits, but he's never outright condemned them.

"I'm doing what I've gotta do, Jacob. It takes a lot to keep this place afloat."

"Bullshit. You haven't been working like this in weeks, and the company's been just fine." He's right. I've been scaling back my workload since Delia and I started spending more time together. I didn't want her feeling like she wasn't a priority, so I budgeted my time better, focusing on the important stuff and handing off tasks when necessary. Her planner helped, too. Now that she's gone, though, I don't see any reason for it.

"What happened with Delia?" Jacob asks.

"She left. The way she always planned to."

"So, that's it? You're never gonna see her again?"

"I doubt it." Delia will have to come back to town at some point to finish dealing with the house, but I don't think she'll want to talk to me. Had I known the other night would be the last time I'd see her, I would've handled things a lot differently.

Jacob frowns. "I don't understand. You two seemed solid last weekend."

"It was never gonna last. Both of us knew that."

"But that's not what you wanted, is it?"

"It doesn't matter what I wanted."

"You're miserable, Tanner. If Delia leaving makes you this unhappy, why not do something about it? Did you bother to ask if she wanted to keep seeing you?"

The throbbing in my temples intensifies. "Jacob, I'm not doing this." I spend enough time agonizing over my decision-making on my own. I don't need to add Jacob's opinion to the mix. "I've got a shit ton of work to do. If you're still up for drinks, that's fine. If not, I need to get back to work."

My friend shakes his head like a disappointed schoolteacher. "You can't bury yourself in work forever, Tanner," he says. "You're gonna have to deal with your issues at some point. Talk to her. We both know you're gonna regret it if you don't try."

With those words, Jacob heads out the door, leaving me to mull over my shitty choices.

I lean back in my creaky desk chair, covering my face with a palm. For weeks, I thought about how I was going to sell Delia on the idea of us staying together. I knew I had to be careful. Delia is protective of her feelings. Slow to open up. Yet, in a moment of frustration, I threw everything away. Right now, she's somewhere thinking I don't love her, when that couldn't be further from the truth.

Jacob's right. I'm going to spend the rest of my life bitter with regret if I don't at least try to make things work with Delia. How can I sit here claiming I want her when I haven't made an effort to get her back?

I'm being a coward. She deserves to know the truth, even if it doesn't change anything on her end.

Delia is nobody's afterthought. She improved my life simply by being in it. I can't let her walk away thinking our time together didn't mean anything to me.

What else is there to lose? She's not here, and I'm miserable. If there's even the slightest chance of her taking me back, I have to take it. Simple as that. And I'm not wasting another second.

Pushing out of my chair, I grab my keys, turn off the lights, and head out of the office.

I can only hope that it's not too late.

Forty-Six

Delia

It's almost ten by the time I get off the phone with Kali and Mariah. I called them to break the news about my moving to Seaview. It was a tough conversation. I love my friends, and I'm going to miss seeing them on a regular basis. Tears were shed, but they both said they were happy for me. Mariah is already planning a trip to Seaview, and Kali is spamming me with home decor ideas. I might not be able to come to weekly wine nights anymore, but I'm not losing my friends anytime soon, something I'm extremely grateful for.

I'm not tired. Unfortunately, Morgan and Izzy decided to turn in early tonight, leaving me to my own devices. After I fix myself a cup of tea, I slink out to the front porch. I sit in the wooden rocker, clutching the warm mug in both hands. Normally, I'd hang out in the backyard, but I don't want to risk Tanner seeing me.

He doesn't know I'm back yet. I'm still trying to figure out what I'm going to say to him. *I'm an asshole, and I'm terrified, and I love you* doesn't sound very eloquent in my head.

Not only do I need to figure out how I'm going to tell Tanner I'm in love with him, but I also have to prepare myself for the possibility of rejection.

I'm hopeful that he will reciprocate my feelings, but there's a chance I'll pour my heart out to him, only to learn he doesn't feel the same. I don't know how I'll recover. Which is why I have to be ready. I won't screw things up with ill-conceived words.

To distract myself from Tanner, I run through my to-do list in my head. First thing tomorrow, I'll call my landlord to let him know I'm moving out. Then I'll have to see about hiring movers to bring my stuff to Seaview. That'll take a few days, so I probably need to request some time off from work. Plus, I need to figure out how I want to arrange the house. Do I need a new dining table? Should I plant flowers in the front? Do I have to get rid of Grandma Aggie's furniture to make space for my own?

I also have to talk to Mom. I've been putting off that call for days. I love my mother dearly, but she's going to freak out when she hears I'm moving to *Seaview* of all places. She'll be at my door within hours. She's going to think I've been brainwashed or kidnapped or otherwise tricked into making this decision. Eventually, she'll come around, but this week has been overwhelming already. I'm not looking forward to adding in her brand of chaos.

I'm still debating how to approach the topic with Mom when a familiar truck suddenly appears. Bright headlights flash as the vehicle pulls up the driveway. My heartbeat picks up speed as the driver's side door swings open.

Tanner walks up the driveway, then the steps leading to the porch. Halfway up the stairs, he freezes, his eyes landing on me.

"Delia." That deep voice makes my stomach flutter, and my palms grow slick. I give myself a moment to pull it together before I look him in the eye.

Tanner looks awful. Well, awful by Tanner standards. The bags under his eyes have gotten darker and deeper since I last saw him. His clothes are rumpled, and his work boots are completely unlaced. As if he shoved his feet inside and couldn't be bothered to tie them. And there's a hint of a shadow on the underside of his jaw.

I hate seeing him like this, but in another way, it brings me a small sense of comfort. At least I'm not the only one who's been miserable since our fight.

Tanner's throat bobs as he assesses me from head to toe. I must look pathetic. I'm wearing an oversized hoodie and a pair of biker shorts. My hair is in a ponytail, since I haven't bothered to wash it in several days.

"I thought you left town," he says.

My mouth feels like sandpaper. I clear my throat before I reply. "I did. I came back."

"When did you…?"

"Yesterday. Morgan's here, too."

He nods. "That's…great." His tone doesn't match his words. He's not sad that I'm back, is he? That would make the whole declaring-my-love-for-him thing awkward.

He must be upset that I didn't tell him about coming back to Seaview. He only found out because he saw me sitting on the porch. Wait a second…if he didn't know I was back in town, then why is he here?

"I tried calling," Tanner says. "Texting. You didn't respond."

He did? The tiniest kernel of hope blooms in my chest. So he isn't disappointed to see me, after all. "I didn't get your messages. I blocked your number." I cringe at my own admission. In hindsight, blocking Tanner seems incredibly childish, but it felt necessary at the time. I was so hurt and angry after our fight. I wanted to scrub him from my life.

Tanner's eyes shine in the porch light. His expression is difficult to read. I'm worried my blocking his number might've given him the impression that I'm still mad at him. The air between us is stiff and uncomfortable. I hate it.

This is why I wanted to think things through before I saw him again. I needed a plan. If I had just had another day to sort myself out, I could've found a way to make it perfect. Now, I've got nothing to work with but my frantic thoughts and feelings.

Uncertainty grips my mind. How do I tell him I love him and miss him and wish I could take back the awfulness of the other night? God, I'm terrible at this. No more time for thinking. Or plans. I'm just going to say what's in my head. It will probably sound ridiculous, but Tanner knows me. All I need to do is make him understand what I'm *trying* to say. Hopefully, that will be enough.

"Tanner, I—"

"I'm sorry," he says, his features flooding with urgency. "The way I acted the other night…there's no excuse for it. I was selfish and scared, and I lashed out because I didn't want to admit how much it would ruin me to lose you.

Because that's what would happen, Delia. You came into my life and shook everything up for the better. I need your attitude and your planners and your smiles. I need you so I can shave my goddamn face again.

"I wasn't living before you came into my life. I was just getting by. You made me realize life's about more than work. You gave my life meaning. So you wanna stay in Boston? That's fine. We can make it work. I'll hire an office manager. Split my time between Seaview and the city. Whatever you need, darling. As long as this doesn't end. I can't lose you. Not when I love you so much."

He gives me an honest, desperate look. My heart feels like it's on the verge of exploding. Did he really just…? Are we…? Overwhelmed by emotion, I struggle to form coherent thoughts. I can't find my voice, so I respond with action instead of words.

Jumping out of my chair, I rush down the porch steps and throw myself into his arms. He catches me instantly, his piney scent invading my senses. I wrap my legs around his waist and bury my face in the side of his neck. Being close to him brings an immediate sense of rightness, like coming home after a long time away.

"I'm sorry, too," I whisper against his skin. My voice sounds watery. Am I crying? "I should've told you about my meeting with the realtor. I got scared."

Tanner lets out a shaky breath. "I was worried," he admits, "especially since you didn't tell me about the job. I thought it meant you didn't see a future with us."

I pull away from his neck to look him in the eye. "I didn't tell you about the job because I didn't want it. I only applied for it because my boss wanted me to. It's a good move for me career-wise, but it wouldn't make me happy. Which is why I turned it down."

"You did?"

I nod. "You helped me realize I don't always need to go along with a plan. Sometimes it's nice to take another direction and see where it leads."

Tanner laughs, swiping his thumb across my wet cheek. "You've given up on planning because of me, darling? I don't know whether to be flattered or concerned."

"Not given up. More like…become open to amendments."

"Amendments," he repeats, lips brushing against the shell of my ear. "Now, there's an idea. I have a few thoughts, if you're open to suggestions. Most of them involve you in various states of undress."

I elbow him in the ribs. "We're having a moment. Don't ruin it."

"We can have as many moments as you'd like," Tanner says. "We have all the time in the world. I'll put up a job posting for an office manager tomorrow. Once I hire someone to deal with the administrative stuff, my schedule will be a lot more flexible. I'll come to Boston whenever you'll have me." His mouth brushes against my temple, and it occurs to me that I haven't actually told him a lot of the stuff I meant to say.

"About that. I'm staying."

Tanner's eyes widen. "You are?"

"I talked to Izzy and Morgan. They're letting me keep the house. I'm moving here."

"You sure that's what you want?" He looks elated, but there's a sense of hesitancy in his voice. "I don't want you feeling like you have to move for me. If you want to be in Boston, I'll be in Boston. I'll follow you wherever you go." With those words, my heart melts. I know he means it. Which is why I finally muster the courage to say what's on my mind.

"I'm positive," I tell him. "I really love this place. The beach. The diner. You." My face gets warm, but I force myself to maintain eye contact. "I love you. I wish I could think of a more eloquent way to say that, but it's the truth." My confession feels sort of pathetic after Tanner's thoughtful words. I'm not very good at this. But at least it's out in the open now.

"Sounds perfect to me," Tanner says, kissing my face fervently. His mouth drifts from my forehead, to my cheek, to the corner of my lips. "Christ, I missed you."

Finally, his mouth lands on mine. The kiss is short but passionate and filled with promise of what's to come.

Epilogue

Tanner
Six months later

"Prepare to be impressed, boss man."

Most employers would be thrilled to hear those words coming from one of their employees, but most employers don't have Izzy Forrest working for them. My girlfriend's sister is unpredictable. One minute she's organizing a company karaoke night, and the next she's convincing our office supplier to give us a discount on desk chairs if we order in bulk. When she asks me to check out what she's done with the break room, I don't know what to expect.

As I follow her inside, I see the normally dull room is filled with color. Rainbow streamers dangle from the ceiling tiles, and a bunch of balloons the size of a small tree sits in front of the fridge. The long counter that usually houses the coffee maker is spread with pizza boxes, veggie trays, and assorted beer and soda. An enormous banner that says "Happy Retirement, Marvin!" in bold letters hangs on the back wall.

The setup is good. Too good. I told Izzy to make it nice, but I didn't give her a massive budget. How the hell did she pull this off?

"You did all of this with a hundred and fifty bucks?" My tone is dubious. Though it wouldn't be the end of the world if we splurged a little on Marvin's retirement party. He's done more than enough for me and the company over the years.

Izzy shrugs. "A lot of places in town offered to give me discounts when I told them I was buying stuff for Marvin's party," she says. "Besides, I didn't want to disappoint anyone. I can't have people thinking I only got here because the boss has a thing for my sister."

That's exactly why Izzy ended up becoming Ryan & Son's office manager. It was Delia's idea. I needed help, and Izzy needed a job. At first, I was skeptical. Izzy is…a lot. I wasn't sure how well our personalities would mesh, especially at work, but I knew it would make Delia happy, so I agreed to it anyway.

Five months later, I'm glad I did. Izzy's a hard worker. Although it can feel like working with an aggravating younger sibling sometimes, having Izzy around has helped a lot. I knew hiring an office manager would lighten my workload, but I never realized how much of a difference it would make. Most nights, I'm out of the office by six.

I'm still working hard, trying to do right by my father's company, but I've restored a much-needed balance to my life. I don't feel obligated to devote every waking minute to the company. Not when I have a certain brown-eyed woman to get home to every night.

Izzy checks her watch. "It's almost three. Delia should be here soon with the cake."

"You asked Delia to help with this?"

"I didn't ask—she offered. She wanted to congratulate Marvin." I introduced Delia and Marvin at one of Mom's cookouts several months back. I knew they'd like each other, but I never expected them to hit it off the way they did.

As it turns out, Marvin's hooked on the same trashy TV shows as Delia. They spent the entire cookout exchanging thoughts on some sort of betrayal that occurred in the latest episode of *Twisted Hearts*. Delia tried explaining it to me after, but it all sounded like nonsense. Still, I'm glad she and Marvin have something in common.

"You know, Delia coming in might be a good opportunity," Izzy says in an insinuating tone. I shoot her a confused look. I don't know what she's referring to, but Izzy is always up to something.

"Opportunity? For what?"

"For you to ask her to move in with you. I know you must be thinking about it." She eyes me purposefully. How does she know that? I haven't said anything to Delia. Yet.

"Just because you're Delia's sister doesn't mean I can't fire you."

Izzy grins. "She'll say yes, you know. There's no reason to be nervous."

"You have till the end of the day to pack up your stuff."

"Lighten up, boss man. I'm just trying to speed things up. For both of your sakes."

Both of us? "Has Delia said anything to you about this?" I ask.

I've been wanting to ask Delia to move in with me for months now. If it weren't for Aggie's house, I would've done it the minute she told me she was moving to Seaview. But the place is important to her. We put a lot of time into fixing it up. Delia deserved to reap the benefits of that hard work. So I held back on asking her to move in. Admittedly, it's been on my mind a lot recently. She spends most of her time at my place anyway. Why not bring the rest of her stuff over?

"Delia hasn't said a word," Izzy assures me. "And if it's me you're worried about, don't be. I'm sticking around for a while longer, even if Delia moves out." That *is* something I've been worrying about. I know how much Delia loves having Izzy around. I'd hate for my invitation to move in to result in Delia losing her sister. It's a relief to hear that's not the case.

"You should mind your business," I mutter in response. Relieved or not, I don't need Izzy voicing her opinions on my relationship.

"Not possible, I'm afraid."

A gentle knock at the door frame steals my attention from Izzy. Delia's here. She looks beautiful in her cream blouse and black slacks. Her hair hangs over one shoulder, and she's holding a large white cake box. "I hope I'm not interrupting," she says. "I'm assuming you want this in here."

I shuffle over to her, taking the cake box off her hands. "You're not interrupting a thing."

"Tanner was just trying to fire me," Izzy adds. "So your typical Friday afternoon stuff."

Delia arches a brow. "What did you do?"

"Nothing," Izzy says. "Thanks for bringing the cake, Del. I've got lots to do. I should really get a move on." Her eyes flash my way when she says the word "move," then she heads out the door. I

grit my teeth and remind myself I can't strangle
my girlfriend's sister if I want to convince my
girlfriend to move in with me.

"I'm guessing you let Izzy pick out the cake,"
Delia says.

"Yeah. Why?"

Unceremoniously, she flips back the lid of the
box, revealing a chocolate sheet cake with the
word "quitter" written in pale blue icing. "I know
my sister's handiwork when I see it." Fortunately,
Marvin has a good sense of humor. He'll
appreciate it.

"You know, if Izzy's being difficult, I can talk
to her," Delia says, chewing her bottom lip.
"You're not obligated to keep her on staff just
because she's my sister."

"Izzy's fine. I mean, she's a pain in the ass, but
she gets stuff done."

Delia looks like she wants to argue further, but
I'm not interested in talking about Izzy anymore.
Dropping the cake box on the nearest table, I wrap
my arms around her waist and tug her toward me.
Without preamble, I lower my mouth to hers. Her
lips are warm and taste like strawberry lip gloss. I
deepen the kiss, weaving a hand through the back
of her hair. A soft whimper escapes Delia as she
returns the kiss.

After several seconds, she pulls back. "We're
at your office," she says breathlessly.

"We were at my office the other night, too," I
remind her. Delia swung by last week to help me
move my things to Dad's old office. I decided it
was finally time for me to stop hiding in my tiny
storage closet office. I'm in charge of this
company. I need to do things my way. Working at

my dad's desk feels strange, but I can't live in his shadow forever.

Her cheeks turn pink. "That's different. It was late. No one was here. And we were in a room with a closed door."

"I can shut the door if that makes you feel better."

Rolling her eyes, she shoves me away. "Don't make me regret coming here."

I love our push and pull. Months later, it's still there. Riling up Delia is my favorite pastime. I never know if she's going to kiss me or threaten to cut off my balls.

"How are you feeling?" she asks, her tone growing suddenly serious. "I know it must be hard with Marvin leaving." To a degree, it is. I've been aware of Marvin's plans to retire for a while now, but it'll be strange when I come into work next week and he's not there.

Still, I'm happy for him. Originally, he planned on staying on until we wrapped up work on the oceanfront property. We still have a few months left on that place, but I told Marvin he should hang it up if he feels like he's ready. He was only staying on for me. As much as I appreciate the support, Marvin deserves to enjoy his retirement.

Besides, things are going well with the oceanfront. The client is pleased with the work we've done so far. In fact, Ryan & Son is already in talks to take on another rehab on the other side of town.

"I'm fine," I answer truthfully. "Not having Marvin here is gonna be an adjustment, but it's nothing we can't manage."

Delia smiles. "I'm proud of you," she says, playing with the buttons of my shirt. "You know that, right?" There's a slight shyness in her voice. Delia has gotten a lot better at saying what she feels, but it doesn't come easy to her. I know that. Which is why I feel compelled to respond with something of equal measure. Should I ask her now? In the break room? It doesn't seem very romantic. Delia deserves flowers and shit. Still, the words are on the tip of my tongue…

A boom of laughter echoes from somewhere in the office, disrupting the moment. Amusement flashes over Delia's face. "How much do you wanna bet that has to do with Izzy?" she asks. For a second, I'm annoyed by the interruption. But then, a sense of calmness washes over me, slow and gentle.

I match Delia's smile with one of my own. "Let's find out," I say. I slip my hand into hers, and we walk out of the break room.

We have all the time in the world.

***

Delia
Nine years later

"Liam, slow down!"
Panic sets in my veins as my four-year-old son races down the tall wooden staircase leading to the beach. He makes it to the bottom of the steps before he inevitably stumbles, crashing on the pale sand in a pile of tiny limbs.

"Are you all right?" I exclaim, rushing down the stairs after him as fast as I can. Which isn't very fast.

I'm twenty-eight weeks pregnant. My stomach is the size of a beach ball. My feet have swollen up a whole shoe size. Still, my symptoms aren't nearly as bad as they were when I was pregnant with the twins. By the third trimester, I was sleeping in the living room because I couldn't climb the stairs by myself. Tanner brought our mattress downstairs for those months so I wouldn't have to sleep alone.

Before I get to Liam's side, he jumps up like a shot.

"I'm fine, Mom!" he says, flashing me a toothy smile. He stands and dusts his sandy palms on his swim trunks.

I inspect him from head to toe, relieved not to find any cuts or scrapes. Liam is my wild child. He escaped from his playpen so many times as a baby that we had to buy an extra tall one. He dives headfirst into everything, which means I'm constantly worried about his physical well-being. Tanner tells me that I worry too much—he says he was just like Liam at that age. But seeing my kid hurt brings out a motherly instinct I never knew I had.

If I have gray hair before I turn forty, it's thanks to him.

Liam tugs on the hem of my terrycloth coverup. "Can we go in the water now?" he asks, trying unsuccessfully to pull me toward the ocean.

It's a perfect beach day. Seventy-six degrees. Sunny. A light breeze carries the scents of sunscreen and seaweed through the air.

Tanner and I take the kids to the beach as often as we can, especially in the summer. When we saw the forecast this morning, we decided we

couldn't let this gorgeous weather go to waste.
The boys start preschool in a few weeks, so we
don't have many days like these left.

"Not yet," I tell him. "We have to wait for Dad
and Noah."

"But they're taking *forever*."

"Then I guess I should tell Dad to leave your
sandcastle toys in the car." I turn as though I'm
about to head back up the stairs. Liam wraps his
arms around my leg to stop me.

"Nonono! I wanna make a sandcastle!"

I brush the light brown hair away from his
forehead. "Then you have to be patient."

Liam pouts. He's at that age where having to
wait any amount of time is unacceptable. When
Tanner and I told him I was pregnant, he was
outraged to learn that it would be months before
he could meet his new little brother or sister.

"You better not be causing trouble down there,
Liam!" Tanner shouts from the top of the stairs.
He's carrying our other son, Noah, along with a
folded lounge chair and two enormous beach
bags. I don't know how he's managing it all, but
my husband does so with ease.

"I'm not, Daddy!" Liam shouts back.

Tanner makes his way down the steps, wearing
dark sunglasses and navy blue board shorts. His
plain T-shirt shows off his tan skin and muscular
arms.

At thirty-nine, Tanner has laugh lines and a
few gray hairs, but I've honestly never been more
attracted to him. It could be the pregnancy
hormones, but I swear he gets better looking by
the day. He shoots me a cocky grin as he reaches
the bottom of the stairs and catches me checking

him out. My husband is aging like fine wine, and he knows it.

Tanner sets Noah on the ground. Immediately, Noah scrambles over to me. "Mommy, look what Daddy gave me!" he exclaims, showing me the toy dump truck in his hand. Noah and Liam are polar opposites. While Liam is always running after trouble, Noah is always running to show me things.

"That's great, Noah," I say, smiling at my kid's unbridled enthusiasm. Noah is pure sunshine. He's sweet enough to charm even the biggest of cynics.

Liam eyes his brother's toy with envy. "I want one!" he says.

"There's one for you too, bud," Tanner tells him. "It's in the bag. Let's find somewhere to set our stuff, and I'll give it to you."

Tanner's eyes meet mine, and I raise a brow. "More toys? Really?" I mouth. Our place is littered with enough of them already.

He shrugs. "They were on sale." Construction toys? Yeah right. I have no doubt Tanner went looking for these toys after Noah and Liam asked him about his job a few days ago. They were excited to hear about their dad's construction work. My marketing job? Not so much. Though in the boys' defense, power tools are more interesting than slide decks.

We find an open spot a few yards from the water. It's Wednesday, so despite the beautiful weather, the beach isn't very crowded. Tanner drops the beach bags on the sand and props up the striped lounge chair facing the ocean.

"Can I have my toy now?" Liam asks, staring up at Tanner with big brown eyes. It's amazing how short a kid's attention span is. Two minutes ago, Liam *had* to get into the water, but now that his brother has a new toy, it's the only thing he can focus on.

Tanner unzips one of the beach bags and pulls out a second toy dump truck. He hands it to Liam, who looks like he's just been gifted a lifetime supply of chocolate.

"Thank you!" he exclaims. "C'mon, Noah! I bet I can pick up more sand than you."

The boys run a short distance ahead before diving into the sand with their trucks.

"I give it ten minutes before one of them is crying," I say.

Tanner shakes his head, his eyes trained on Noah and Liam. "Imagine how it's gonna be when the third one gets here," he says.

"We're *not* having another boy." Well, I don't know that for sure. Tanner and I decided to leave the baby's sex a surprise.

I never understood why couples did that. Having more information about the baby means you can be better prepared, right? But after I found out I was pregnant, Tanner guessed it was going to be another boy. I think it's a girl. We've gone back and forth over this for the past few months. We've even roped our family into a little betting pool. We decided the best way to settle it was to wait for the baby to arrive.

Although I'm convinced the baby is a girl, I'll be happy either way. Liam and Noah have brought so much joy to my life. I can't wait to expand our family again.

"We'll see about that," Tanner says, resting his palm on the back of my neck. "I've gotta run back to the car to grab the umbrella. In the meantime, you can sit your pretty ass down and relax."

I roll my eyes. "I *am* relaxed." I've been having headaches recently. My doctor said it might be stress related and encouraged me to take it easy. Tanner has since made it his life's mission to help me destress. Every time I stand up to get a snack or clean up after the boys, he tells me to sit back down and that he'll do it for me. It might be annoying if he weren't being so considerate.

Tanner brushes his lips against my ear. "Humor me then." He motions toward the lounge chair, and I begrudgingly sit down. Kicking off my flip-flops, I bury my feet in the warm sand and tip my sunglasses over my eyes.

"See? I'm the very picture of relaxed."

Tanner smiles, then leans down to kiss the corner of my mouth. "I'll be right back," he says. "The yellow bag is for you."

Huh? He's walking away before I can ask questions, leaving me no choice but to look inside the beach bag. I grab the bag by the handle and drag it in front of me. Inside, I find a bottle of sparkling apple cider, chocolate chips and pretzels (my current cravings), and several furniture catalogs. I mentioned something to Tanner a few nights ago about us needing a new couch for the living room. It seems like he heard me.

My eyes drift back to the boys, who are busy playing in the sand. A warm feeling coasts through my body as I tear open the bag of chocolate chips and pop a handful into my mouth.

This is happiness.

Thank you

Thank you so much for reading *High Tide*!
Want more of Tanner and Delia? Follow this link
to receive a bonus scene.

https://dl.bookfunnel.com/v68a7qnoqa

The Seaview series will continue with Izzy and
Jacob's story.

About the Author

Paige Marie is an Ohio-based author who has been writing stories since she was nine years old. She loves romance novels, white wine, and long walks outdoors. *High Tide* is her debut novel. You can find her on Instagram @paigebwrites.

Content warning

This book contains sexual content, alcohol use, and discussions about the loss of a parent. The epilogue features pregnancy.